Praise for *A Woman of Bangko*

'Among the ten finest novels written
The Asian Wall Street Journal (Harry [illegible])

'Pulls no punches ... a book to remember'
The Age, Australia

'At times the lying, grasping, impenitent and wholly immoral Vilai becomes twenty times larger than life. She is the real thing ...'
The New York Times

'One night in Bangkok, so the song goes, makes a hard man humble. The city is, in fact, a combine harvester for the expat male heart. Jack Reynolds captures the ethos perfectly in this, the definitive account, written 50 years ago'
The Guardian, UK (Malcolm Pryce)

'Fascinating ... intensely readable'
Gore Vidal, author

'More than half a century ago, Jack Reynolds wrote the original Bangkok bargirl story, highlighting the dangers that can befall a man who loses his heart in the Land of Smiles. The story is as pertinent today as it was then and always will be so long as men continue to look for love in the wrong places'
Stephen Leather, author

'Jack Reynolds' 1950s *A Woman of Bangkok* (originally published *A Sort of Beauty* in 1956, republished under the new name shortly thereafter), a well-written and poignant story of a young Englishman's descent into the world of Thai brothels, remains the best novel yet published with this theme'
Joe Cummings, author

About the author

Jack Reynolds was born Emrys Reynolds Jones on 19 June 1913 in Hertfordshire in the south of England, the son of a non-conformist minister. Later at school in north London, he became known as Jack Jones, which is Cockney rhyming slang for a loner. His father wanted him to follow in his footsteps into the church but he rebelled and led a wandering life moving from job to job as a fish trimmer on a North Sea trawler, a sampler in a Lincolnshire sugar beet factory, a monumental mason and market gardener. To relieve the tedium of low paid jobs he was also a speedway racer, chancing his arm for one of the north London teams, and he wrote some fine poems, in 1937 aged only twenty four publishing a book of his own poetry. The parallels with Reginald Ernest Joyce, the anti-hero of his novel, are very apparent.

At the beginning of the Second World War Jack registered as a conscientious objector and was excused war service on condition he work on the land in food production or relief work with the Friends Ambulance Unit. Continuing as a market gardener, in March 1944 he joined the FAU, training as a medic, driver and mechanic and on 3rd September 1945, the day after the Japanese surrender, he sailed for China. There he spent almost six years with the FAU, distributing medical supplies over vast distances in appalling conditions. He survived a near fatal bout of typhus fever, plunged sixty feet into a ravine when his truck ran off the road and was captured and beaten by bandits. As the FAU's West China Director based in Chungking he led a team of western and Chinese workers, in 1950 opening a clinic to serve the local population. During this time he was constantly active as a writer, producing blog-like articles for the weekly FAU newsletter, a hoard of which has recently been unearthed in archives in London and Philadelphia. His experiences in China inspired his later book, *Daughters of an Ancient Race* published in 1974, a series of stories of the hard lives of the women he treated in his Chungking clinic.

Held under house arrest by the communists, he finally reached Hong Kong in June 1951 after a gruelling journey down the Yangtze river and by train. There he landed a job as a transport manager with UNICEF in Thailand and in August sailed for Bangkok. With no wish to return to England, he met and married a Catholic Thai much to his parents' dismay and raised a family of seven children.

Travelling widely throughout Thailand for UNICEF, Jack had time on his hands to write while in seedy hotels in dusty rural towns, and so his novel was born to immediate acclaim on both sides of the Atlantic. Nonetheless, despite his prodigious and versatile talent as a writer, he failed to produce another one. He put this down to his commitment to his large family, though, as he wrote to a friend, the manuscript of a second novel was lost when it slipped from his grasp while crossing a river in a small boat. It fell into the water and was eaten by a crocodile.

When his UNICEF contract came to an end in 1959, he took a further UN contract in Jordan, accompanied by his family until the political situation there became too dangerous. Leaving Jordan in 1967, he worked for the *Bangkok Post* and other journals as writer and editor, sandwiched between further unaccompanied postings with the UN in the Far East and Africa. He finally returned to journalism in Bangkok in the Seventies and was a favourite contributor of articles on a range of local topics with a strong popular following in Thailand. His principal resource was of course a rich fund of stories from a life time of extraordinary adventures in China and his years of arduous relief work in far-flung places.

Not long before his death, he told an interviewer that he was still working on the book that would be his masterpiece and he continued dreaming of literary acclaim to the end. On his death aged 71 in Bangkok on 2nd September 1984, the *Bangkok Post* published several warm tributes to 'Bangkok's grand old man of letters'. Writing was Jack's passion and he should be reassured that an author needs only one outstanding book to be remembered and celebrated, as this new edition now affirms.

A WOMAN OF BANGKOK

Jack Reynolds

monsoonbooks

This reprint edition published in 2011
by Monsoon Books Pte Ltd
71 Ayer Rajah Crescent #01-01
Mediapolis Phase Ø, Singapore 139951
www.monsoonbooks.com.sg

First published in 1956 as "A Sort of Beauty" by Secker & Warburg Ltd.

ISBN (paperback): 978-981-08-5430-0
ISBN (ebook): 978-981-4358-62-0

The publishers are grateful to the Estate of Jack Reynolds and
Random House UK (Secker & Warburg) for their assistance.

Cover design by Opalworks.

National Library Board, Singapore Cataloguing-in-Publication Data
Reynolds, Jack, 1913-1984.
A woman of Bangkok / Jack Reynolds. – Singapore : Monsoon Books, 2011.
p. cm.
ISBN : 978-981-08-5430-0 (pbk.)
1. Prostitutes – Thailand – Bangkok – Fiction. 2. Bangkok (Thailand) – History – 20th century – Fiction. I. Title.
PR6068
823.914 -- dc22 OCN748763542

Printed in Singapore
15 14 13 12 11 1 2 3 4 5 6 7 8 9

Part One

THE LAMB

The sunlight on the garden
Hardens and grows cold;
We cannot catch the minute
Within its nets of gold;
When all is told
We cannot ask for pardon.

Louis MacNeice

One

It is on the second Sunday in September that I am due to fly to Bangkok. The preceding day I spend with my parents. That entails going down to Malderbury by train. I feel sick with apprehension. I am afraid there are going to be tearful scenes, especially with my mother, and I am even more afraid that Andy and Sheila will show up and try to effect a last-minute reconciliation.

But as it turns out, these fears, like most of my fears, are groundless. My father is locked in his usual Saturday hell consuming ounces of tobacco over his sermons for the morrow. My mother is busy jam-making. No signs of Andy or his bride. After a few minutes I get out the lawn mower and lay absolutely regular strips of viridian and terre verte across the tennis court. For lunch there are home-grown tomatoes and Danish tinned ham and what talk there is deals casually with disaster amongst the parishioners, not with anything real.

After coffee I retire to my own room. All the poets are there from Chaucer and Langland to those two doubting Thomases of modern times, Edward and Dylan; but I can't settle to read anything; the salt hath lost his savour; symphonies sound like solos on the piccolo. I am glad when the gong booms for tea. It booms early, so that I can catch the 4.33 back to town. There is real butter, and some of my mother's famous bread, and the scum off the new jam, still hot. Again, all mention of my personal affairs is avoided. After emptying my fourth cup I look at my watch, say 'Well, I suppose,' get up rather clumsily off the straight-backed Chippendale chair, shake hands with my father, unable to look in his eyes, kiss my mother twice. To my annoyance I am nearly more emotional than they are. I am annoyed too because they aren't coming to the station to see me off. They are expecting some 'young people' they say to play tennis on the lawn I so kindly cut. Bitterly I recall how when

Andy first set forth for darkest Africa the whole family accompanied him to Liverpool and saw him safely aboard his ship ... But never mind.

I walk down the lane—perhaps for the last time: who knows what deadly tropical disease I may not soon contract?—and turn round under Mrs. Danforth's damson tree to wave goodbye. They are standing by the gate, my father, short and round and rubicund, clenching between his teeth the pipe which I am sure is more comfort to him than his religion, my mother, taller and more severe, automatically wiping her hands on her apron. I wave. They wave. I turn my back on them. Free at last. Or at any rate, adrift. I ought to walk more jauntily than I do, but my feelings are distressingly muddled: a lift in the heart but a lump in the throat, and in the bowels, a queasy debilitating fear.

Meeting the 'young people' is a godsend of an anticlimax. There's half a dozen of them packed into the Dennisons' new car. Some of them I don't recognize, for it is seven years since I last lived at home and during that time people seem to have been growing up much faster than I ever did. The only hand I really care to shake is young Dennison's own. He takes it from the wheel and stretches it out to me across the laps of two girls who are snuggled in the front seat with him. I grip it heartily, not because of any present affection for Denny (I scarcely know him any longer) but for the sake of auld lang syne. He must be doing pretty well at whatever it is he is doing: the silk scarf inside his open-neck shirt, the curly pipe in his mouth, the glossy new look of the whole ensemble, clearly proclaim success. And it seems to me (conscious as I am of a sports jacket baggy at the elbows and corduroys baggy at the knee) that those two girls in the front seat are adjuncts of his success, no less part and parcel of it than the car. I cannot help but feel that their waves are too set, their lips too red, their sweaters too tight and their shorts too short, for their own comfort or anybody else's: it is as if they have always considered themselves to be ugly ducklings and can't believe that they've suddenly turned into swans; they still feel it necessary to over-emphasize every potential charm, like fading courtesans. I blush under the upward scrutiny of their huge brilliant eyes and try to drag my hand from Denny's but he holds it captive, embarrassingly within the warm aura of their thighs. There is the usual flapping of tongues:

'Thought you'd gone, old boy.'

'No, not yet. Tomorrow's the day.'

'Tomorrow D-day, what? Flying, I suppose?'

'Yes. DC-6.'

'You'll find flying pretty boring.'

I stare at him cholerously. The cheek of the man! How dare he contrast before these girls, whose eyes have grown bigger and brighter as their coyly-revealed ears drink in this staccato men's talk, his own experience in the air (five minutes for ten bob in a Gypsy Moth at Clacton-on-sea, if that) with my own inexperience, which he insultingly assumes? And that huddle of limbs and racquets in the rear seat is equipped with ears too. I stammer lamely, 'Well, we'll see.'

'Where's he going?' asks the girl next to him, the one whose sweater is so tight in two places that you can see the white bulges of her brassiere through the expanded meshes of red wool.

'Yes, where *are* you going, Reg? Kenya, is it, where Andy—?'

'No. Thailand.' They all look blank. 'Siam, to give it its old name.'

'Ah, I knew it was somewhere that way.'

The sweater rubs his arm and he says, turning to her indulgently (though he is still holding my hand and our palms are getting objectionably moist), 'Si-am, honey. Haven't you ever heard of Si-am?'

Apparently she hasn't, but meanwhile the other girl, whose sweater is primrose-yellow, addresses me direct in a husky voice. 'Why on earth are you going there? And how long for?'

'My firm's sending me. For three years, I expect.'

Her eyes grow momentarily tremendous, then unfocus themselves from me, lose their brilliance and turn away. Three years ... Her hopes for the next month or so are centred nearer home. She looks at her wrist-watch.

Denny puts the car into gear. 'Well, mustn't keep you, old man. Wouldn't do for you to miss your train, I expect. Some little lady in Palmers Green waiting to say a last fond farewell, what? What?'

A chorus of so-longs, happy landings, cheerios, and a mock military salute from me. As the car draws away there is a commotion in the front seat and the head of one of the girls comes through the window.

Impossible to tell which one: they are lipsticked and powdered to such a pitch of similarity that only by their sweaters can they be told apart. 'Bring me back a sarong,' she squeals, 'you know, like Dorothy Lamour,' and she waves a slim arm at me. Mrs. Danforth's damsons intervene again and my last salute, an acknowledgement of that arm's, goes unobserved by mortal eye. To the eye of Heaven, if that happened to be trained on me at that moment, it must have looked a fatuous gesture. Young Reggie Joyce down there, saluting the arse-end of an Austin A-40 ...

As it happens, Denny guessed right. There *is* a little lady waiting for me. Not in Palmers Green—but to a man who thinks Thailand is in the same general direction as Kenya, the difference between one North London suburb and another must seem immaterial. Nor is she the sort of 'little lady' that Denny implied with that knowing upward twitch of one eyebrow. I have known her intimately for six years and never kissed her once. Nor wanted to.

She is sitting in the front room window with her hat already on. She is manicuring her nails to pass the time. When she sees me she throws down the orange stick and jumps up. I don't get a chance to use my key. She hurtles through the door, slamming it shut behind her. 'Good gracious, Mr. Joyce' (in all these years I have never been able to induce her to use my first name) 'I thought you never *was* coming. We'll have to queue, that's certain.'

I had wanted to go inside for a minute (those four cups of tea) but I decide to suppress myself for a while longer. For one who is fifty-seven years of age, and only about that number of inches high, and at a guess about twice that number of inches round, she can cover the ground at an astonishing speed. Her calves twinkle fawn-stockinged between this evening's particular flowery voluminousness and her run-over-at-heels but meticulously-polished shoes. Yet despite the energy she is expending, she has breath left for conversation.

'Did you see your Mum and Dad?'

'Yes.'

'How were they?'

'All right.'

'Weren't they—upset?'

'Why should they be?'

'Well, with you going away. For so long. To them foreign parts. I'm sure *I'm* upset.'

'Oh, you're just sentimental, Lena. We Joyces are a travelling family. We're used to our loved ones taking off for the antipodes.'

'Yes, but *you're* going to Siam.' Her next question is put almost warily. 'Did you see your brother?'

'No.'

'Nor his wife?'

'No.'

'Poor Mr. Joyce. But perhaps she'll be there tomorrow.'

I pretend to be astounded by the idea. 'Where d'you mean? At the airport? She certainly won't. And I damn well hope she isn't.' I hardly realize I am lying. Men are deceivers ever, especially of themselves. If she isn't there, it's going to be miserable. And if she is—

'There's our bus,' cries Lena, breaking into a fast trot.

The film is *Ivanhoe*. The book was required reading at school and like all Scott, a thorough bore. I queue with a bad grace. But blessed is the pessimist, for he shall receive occasional pleasant surprises. For two hours, swiftly past, tomorrow, the future, Sheila, this century, are all abolished. Sunlight sparkles on castle walls; Sordello cavalcades ride forest trails; the Saxon baron is courteous, after careful explanations to his Saxon guests, to Norman knight and even to wandering Jew; gauntlets are flung down, deadly insults hurled from lips pale with rage, trumpets raised to bray to the cloud-piled skies; the earth rumbles under the hooves of chargers in the joust; arrows fly as thick as grass from the mower's blades; bodies plunge off battlements into moats; swords clang on shields, which sound like dustbin lids. Ivanhoe is properly athletic and well-motivated but a silly ass over women.

A thousand plush seats have hiccups as two thousand buttocks ascend a few inches nearer heaven. If you reach the back aisle before the drum-roll you can carry on to the exit without convicting yourself of treason. If you are caught amongst the seats you must stand riveted amongst them, arms like pokers at your sides. Go-o-od save the Queen. All right, you can go now. The royal countenance is obliterated by sumptuous curtains and American jive steps sharp on the heels of Britain's most-played tune.

'How'd you like it, Lena?'

'Oh, it was all right. But I like Abbott and Costello better.'

We stand in a queue for the bus. We stand on the bus. There is one nice-looking girl, fair, self-contained, a little like Sheila. We alight: Lena walks on ahead while I queue again for fish and chips. When I reach the flat she has laid the table and put the kettle on for my cup of tea. She has taken her hat off and is carving bread in the terrifying female manner with the loaf pressed against her beflowered bust and the knife held as Lucretia holds hers in the Titian. A wisp of grey hair has come adrift from its clips and as she pauses to brush it out of her eyes I feel a pang of tenderness for her deeper than any I have felt for my mother all day long. The kettle lid starts rattling and I go out to the scullery to make the tea. Lena Braidman. To my parents she is merely the spinster sister of one of the sidesmen at Malderbury. To her neighbours in Pennywort Road, that queer old girl at 96, has a nice-looking young lodger, seems a bit too friendly with him too, goes to the pictures with him regular, rum goings on. To Denny, if he happened to see her, that old bag ...

'What time do you want to be called in the morning?' she asks.

'I'd better leave here about eight. I have to be at Kensington air-terminal at nine-ten.' I open a bottle of stout with my penknife. I fill the glass too rapidly and the froth rising with a slow but implacable ebullience passes the brim and slides down the outside to the cloth. 'Oh, blast ... Are you coming with me?'

'Of course.' She has unwrapped the fish; she screws the paper into a greasy ball and throws it into the coal-scuttle. 'I'm going to miss you, Mr. Joyce.'

I scrape a good helping of chips off the dish onto my plate. Got to say it somehow. 'I'm going to miss you, too, Lena. You've been like a—well, like a jolly good Aunt to me all these years.' She cascades the rest of the chips onto her own plate, takes the smaller piece of fish and hands me the other. Then she begins to saturate her plateful with vinegar. 'The bit I liked best was when Elizabeth Taylor was listening behind the curtain,' she says. 'I think Elizabeth Taylor's a lovely girl, don't you?'

'Not half,' I reply with relief. 'If ever I get knocked off a horse with a ten-foot bargepole, I hope Elizabeth Taylor's around to hand me the smelling salts.'

The washing-up done, I call 'Goodnight' to Lena and go to the back bedroom which has been mine ever since I came to London to seek my fortune. It looks bare tonight. The books, the portraits of sailing ships and speedway riders which used to adorn the walls, the two Negro carvings Andy gave me, the radio set I built myself, have all been removed to Malderbury. My remaining belongings are already packed in the two new suitcases standing by the wall: Only unpacked items: my pyjamas on the bed, the suit I'm going to wear tomorrow behind the door, my toilet articles on the dressing-table and washstand. I go through the drawers for a last quick check-up. Empty. Empty. Empty. An odd button, a few tintacks, the top of a broken fountainpen. The sheets of newspaper which were used as linings are all awry and yellowed. End of an epoch. I open the bottom drawer. Here virgins stow their hopes and dreams. What is a virgin bachelor without hopes likely to have put there?

I had expected it to be empty too but it isn't. There's an old exercise book. I recognize it with a shock. My novel. The one I started to write immediately after the Sheila episode. Begun in bitterness and ended in frustration. What in hell am I going to do with the thing now?

The title page is elaborately designed in Indian ink: '*Perfidy*, by Reginald Ernest Joyce.' On the next page there is a Note: 'This is a novel, and all the characters are fictitious. Any likeness ...' Etc. Etc. Blah blah blah. What barefaced lying. Who was I hoping to fool? The hero was Reginald Ernest Joyce. The heroine Sheila. The villain Andy. The perfidy Andy's and Sheila's.

I read the first few lines. 'Chapter One. Until I was twenty-seven I was like the Lady of Shalott. I lived in an ivory tower and never looked out of the window: I daren't. For my knowledge of the world beyond the panes I relied on my mirrors, books. Now anyone who has ever looked over his sweetheart's shoulder into her mirror as she powders her nose—'

God, what a shock I got that day!

'—and seen their two faces there, his own no less handsome and frank and open than usual, but hers suddenly strange, with unequal cheeks and lopsided smile, a travesty of her real face (though she appears to be satisfied with it herself, and even derives spiritual strength just from contemplating it), realizes that mirrors do not reflect facts; light travels in straight lines, as is demonstrated to you at school with pins and prisms, but the truth, as Einstein is said to have proved, is slightly bent; and it follows that some of the ideas I had formed in my private chamber were pretty queer. Yet for some of these misconceptions, wrong-headed though they were, I was prepared to lay down my life ...'

Plummy writing. Overripe Victorias. Every semi-colon is like a plum-stone in a plum-pie.

'... One of the strangest notions I had formed (at least it seems one of the strangest now: I left Shalott a year ago) was that there is no such thing as a Bad Woman.'

Etc. etc. etc. I get into bed and read the whole rigmarole. It was written in an unseemly rage, the rage of the jilted lover. It was written too soon after Sheila went off with Andy. In fact I started it while I was recovering from the effects of the barbital. It is the work of a shellshock case. The whole world appeared to me to have been knocked askew and ugly by that one blinding explosion. But it was not the world that was askew, it was the mind that observed it. I can see now how unjust I then was, pretending there was ugliness and bitterness only in days which I now recall again were often ecstatically happy. And so the novel is no novel. It does not re-create the idyll. It is just my outpouring of rage when the idyll broke to fragments in my hands, like a shattered vase. It is the yelping of a kicked dog.

I get out of bed and tear the book into little pieces.

As I finish the kitchen clock goes into the prolonged antepartum travail which can only end in the birth of a chime. One o'clock already. No, twins. Christ, two in the morning. And I have to be up at seven.

I dive under the bedclothes again. The brass knobs at the four points of the compass make their usual cackling protest. Six for a man. Seven for a woman. Eight for a fool. Tonight I'm going to get less than five. And I can usually do with nine. What does that make me, I wonder? A pervert? Or just a lazy sod?

If only one could banish one's anxieties. Will she be there?

Will she?

And if she isn't, what matter? Half the human beings in the world are female. The breed is produced by the busload. Billions of the bitches. And every one stamped in the same press. Rigged on the same jigs. That sounds slightly suggestive, but Thou knowest what I mean, O Lord.

I ought to try counting sheep. But being me I can only count women.

Those tarts in Denny's car. The one in red certainly had a pair of humdingers. Like coconuts. Soon to be brimming with milk. The one in yellow wasn't bad either. More restrained of course, but—but Addison makes his points no less tellingly than Carlyle. More tellingly, perhaps, in the long run ...

Oh, Sheila, Sheila, Sheila. Lying there moaning in the heather. My hand on your heart. My hand under your head. The odour of your hair and skin, as sweet as the heather. Your tense repeated cry: 'No, Reggie, no. Don't do anything we'll regret—please.'

I got up and walked stiffly twenty feet away. I leaned against a damned great boulder, staring over bracken that basked in the heat to the sweeping blue smear of the distant sea. I shouldn't have been so soft. In fact, I was a fool. I let her appeal to the Ivanhoe in me, the medieval Sahib.

The dream has a different me for hero.

Lena gives me a knock but there's no need. I've been uneasily awake for an hour. Now the crisis is definitely upon me. I throw aside the bedclothes and sit up. The sky outside the window is low and grey. Poor flying weather. Possibly dangerous. I turn, shamefacedly, onto my knees. I adopt the posture of the Moslem as he kneels to face Mecca, burying my head in the pillow. I am not a Moslem any more than I am a Christian; I am in fact non-religious, except when I am afraid, or when I want events to take a certain course. Then I pray. I always despise myself for praying: I should be more self-reliant. But here I am on my knees. Head down I feel more self-abased. Head down I feel I am adopting a more courteous attitude to the God one normally never thinks of, but who may be there ...

'O God I pray Thee, I mean You' (I despise these pulpit archaisms) 'make me strong to face the perplexities of this day. I've never flown before: but what's the point of telling You that, if You're omniscient? And if You aren't, it's no good praying to You anyway.' I sit up exasperated but on second thoughts burrow down again. 'And if Sheila comes to the airport today, give me strength to face her like a man. And if she doesn't come, still give me strength: I'll need it.' I pause for a moment. 'Bless—no, that's silly. Look after Mother and Dad, and Andy, too.' More often I've commended him to the devil of late, but I don't want to die, if the plane crashes, hating any mortal soul, least of all perhaps the elder brother I once worshipped. 'Look after poor old Lena and send her a new lodger as soon as You can; she's going to feel the pinch when I've gone, as of course You know.' Another pause. 'Bless Sheila. Protect her from all harm. Make her happy with Andy. If that is Your will, of course. Amen.'

Do I feel any better for—for throwing my burdens on the Lord, as my Father would put it? Frankly, no.

'Are you coming, Mr. Joyce?'

'Yes, Lena. Just going to shave.'

She is at the air-terminal before we are. As the taxi swerves in a half-circle across the street Lena cries, 'There she is, in the doorway.' My heart feels as if it has been plucked out of its ribcage and hurled full force against a brick wall. I look towards the great square porch but what with the taxi swinging round to a halt and the multitudes of skirts and trousers clotting into a frieze before eyeballs dazed with fear ... I busy myself opening the door and holding it while Lena alights, lifting my luggage from beside the driver to the pavement, fumbling for the fare in my pocket. I drop a two-bob bit and have to stoop and reach under the taxi, a typical gaucherie; it fills me with fury; it seems I never can act grown-up under Sheila's eyes.

'My word, aren't we smart this morning?' Her voice is unflinchingly clear and authentic at my shoulder as I rise. 'Riding around in taxis. And all these new bags too. Those on the pavement and those on the person. That suit really suits you, Reggie. You look more handsome than ever.'

My mouth opens and then it shuts, but no sound emerges. Cold and sharp and clear, like frost on a fallen leaf. Just as in the old days. But she's gabbling a little too much. The flippancy's forced. *She's* frightened too.

Lena says, 'You're looking wonderfully well yourself, Mrs. Joyce. That costume is really beautiful.'

'Thanks, guv,' says the taxi-driver. So I can't be preoccupied with him any more. I turn to face her.

'Don't you think her dress is lovely, Mr. Joyce?' Lena's face is bright with happiness because her high hopes have been justified; merely by coming here Sheila has indicated (Lena supposes) that she thinks more of me than I in my self-distrust thought possible.

I've got to say something. I still find it hard to focus my eyes on her. There are her face and that dress and her silk-stockinged legs and her blonde hair done up in a new way but I still can't see them clear because of the layers of memories, all those months of desire, all those months of defeat, my boyhood veneration for Andy turned to hatred, and that night—that night when willingly and in peace I died by my own hand—coming between her and me. 'It's all right,' I gulp at last. 'But it looks—baggy.' The word is the first that comes. I suppose it derives from her own pun on bags. It sounds dreadfully crude. I see her recoil. I add hastily, trying to make amends, 'I mean, it makes you look—fatter.'

Lena gives me a reproachful glare—something she has never done before in all the six years of our fellowship—and takes Sheila's arm with a sudden companionable gesture which says more plainly than words, Don't mind him, he's male and impossible.

Miserably I pick up the bags and follow them across the pavement, up the steps and into the shuffling, bustling vault of the terminal. Seen from the rear Sheila looks even less Sheila-like than from other angles. The scales of emotion have dropped from my eyes now she's got her back to me. The hair that used to fall over her shoulders in a Danae shower of gold is now pruned and attenuated in a fashionable horse-tail that makes her look like a pinhead with delicate ears. Her figure which used to be so lithe and Atlanta-like moves heavily now on earth-bound soles; the goddess has gone out of her; the Word is made flesh. Here is the lumpy oaken chest that Andy forced open and rifled of its treasures. She is now no more desirable than Lena, and a lot less pleasant company, I shouldn't wonder.

The first desk has on a sign over it the words 'Swissair, Zürich.' The clerk behind it is one of those scrubbed-looking, instantaneously polite people who always make me feel shabby and gruff. 'Good morning, sir. Where are you for?'

'Bangkok. Via Geneva.'

'Ah, yes, sir. You want desk nine—at the far end.'

Sheila wouldn't have looked at him, of course, far less stopped in hesitancy before him, looking waif-like and pathetic. She would have guessed in a flash that Swissair had two planes, one to Zürich, one to Geneva; her mind would not automatically have jumped to the conclusion, as mine, a pessimist's, did, that there had been a slip-up somewhere, that I was going to be posted to the wrong address and miss my connection and get into all sorts of complicated situations where the inadequacies of my French would be made only too plain.

She isn't taking any notice of me anyway, in fact she has her back to me. Lena is talking to her fast and low like an old intimate friend. The clannishness of these women! How many times have they met? About three times perhaps, on the occasions when Sheila consented to visit my lodgings for tea. Clearly they regard me as common property; I am owned in part by my ex-sweetheart, in part by my ex-landlady. Neither has in her heart that depth of feeling, overmastering, exclusive, destructive of peace and contentment, which I felt for one of them, which I still feel for her. In this climactic moment when I pass out of their lives for years, perhaps forever, they want to discuss her clothes. 'Don't you think her dress is lovely?' Dear Lord and Father of mankind. I have wasted my passion on her.

I am passed through the mill in a few minutes. 'Your ticket, sir? Thank you, sir ... How many pieces of baggage? Only two, sir? We'll just weigh them ... Fifty-two pounds ... Will you step on the scales yourself, sir? ...' Weighed like prime beef ... 'Thank you, sir. One hundred and seventy. Please pay five shillings over there. Yes, that's all, sir.' Another body disposed of. With an epitaph in pounds avoirdupois.

I pay my five shillings and wander back to the two women. They have stopped talking and standing as it almost seems shoulder to shoulder await my coming. Lena has a half-smile on her face but there is none on Sheila's. She looks utterly different. Can a change of hairstyle do all that? Her features seem heavier, fuller, more—cow-like. The word appals me. Before it was all sylphs, nymphs, dryads, goddesses—a Daphnis and

Chloe vocabulary. Her eyes have changed too: before like summer skies, blue and sparkling; now, 'quivering within the wave's intenser blue', something beyond my understanding.

I realize that the onus of speaking first lies with me but out of the multitude of things which could be said, what is not either likely to lead to embarrassment or else sound trivial? Yet silence is an embarrassment also. It happens that we all start to speak at the same moment but hearing Lena's voice too, Sheila and I both thankfully drop whatever it was we were embarked on: the floor is hers.

'Have you arranged everything, Mr. Joyce?'

'Yes, I—I think so.'

'What happens next?'

Anything could happen—that is the hell of it. 'The bus leaves in ten minutes.' I see a shadow flick across Sheila's face. 'That's not long,' I reassure her. 'Time to embrace. Or time to refrain from embracing.' I feel base the moment I have spoken.

She gives me a hurt look and then says in a low voice, 'Time to listen to one whole movement from the Oxford symphony, Reggie.' Our favourite records, once.

'Time for a cup of tea more like,' says Lena and her voice is the voice of Juliet's nurse croaking froggily, earthily, into the nightingale's duet.

Well, the nurse is a great comfort to the audience and no doubt she was to Juliet too and we move off towards the white clatter of crockery and the hiss of vast silver urns with the tension on our nerves relaxed a little. Somehow I have come between the two women and I am walking (I suddenly realize) as a man symbolically should, erect and tall between mother and wife. But to round the group off I should have a little girl, my daughter, riding on my shoulder or carried in my arms with her own wound round my neck. The whole conception is complete in a flash—my next poem—and the fact that Lena is not my mother or anyone's mother but one of Britain's two million surplus women, the fact that Sheila is not my wife but my brother's wife, carrying, not my seed, but if anyone's, Andy's in her—

The truth hits me like ball-and-mace on my unhelmeted brow. Of course, you fool, of course. That yellowish tinge under the make-up. That warmer, intenser luminosity in the once ice-brilliant eyes. The apparent bagginess of the costume

I stop and clutch her arm. Her face whips round and up at me, dread in her eyes.

'Reggie, Reggie, please—'

'Sheila, you're going to have a baby.'

'Well, what if I am?' There is anger, not dread, in her voice now. 'Let go of my arm, Reggie. You don't want to make a scene *here,* do you?'

O God in Heaven. 'Why did you have to come here this morning?' I cry. And ruin my dream, or what was left of it?

'Now, now, Mr. Joyce. I'm sure that really you're very glad that Mrs. Joyce has come to see you off. I'm sure I would be anyway if I was in your boots. She's feeling very poorly these days as you'd expect but all the same she's come all the way up from Bantingham to see you, bumping and bouncing around in that bus, and she hasn't even had a cup of tea this morning yet, and I'm sure you ought to be grateful to her, not—'

'I don't want him to be grateful,' says Sheila angrily. 'If only he could be just normal.' She turns to me and her cheekbones have reddened. 'But you seem to be more impossible than ever, damn you.'

'Sheila!' Surely she can't mean that. I was never impossible. I was, if anything, too gentle with her, too malleable in her hands, too much court sycophant, coming when beckoned, leaving on the word of command ...

'I've told you before what he was like,' she is saying to Lena. 'The most spineless goddamned lover. If I snapped his head off he'd slink away all sorrowful and apologetic like a puppy that's wetted the floor. Next day he'd be back again with some horrible poem about my right eyebrow or my left breast or something. How many poems did you write about me altogether, Reggie? Did you manage to cover all of me in the end? Do you still write poems about me?'

Laughing about me again. Just because of 'Upon her Navel.' Any mention of my poems always makes me feel red and resentful. I put my all into them; they are better than I am, by far; they are almost sacred writings. Sheila should be proud that she moved me to write some of my best but instead she is using them to jeer at me in front of Lena ...

'You seem to forget that I—I loved you, Sheila. I respected you.'

'So did Andy. But he never wrote a poem in his life. He did what a lover should do—he made love to me.'

My anger blazes up. 'And didn't I, too? Before he ever came back from Kenya? Before you'd ever met him? Don't forget our holiday in North Wales, Sheila. I haven't forgotten it; I never shall. I wanted you as badly as Andy ever did, I'm sure. And what did you say to me?' I imitate her female voice in the falsetto of my rage. '"No, Reggie, no. Don't do anything we'll regret—please." Is that the truth or not?'

'Of course it's the truth.' I start to speak again but she continues, 'So you walked away and after a bit you came back looking all noble like Sir Galahad and no doubt with a new poem in your head and you said "Come on, we'd better be getting back down to Aber."'

'What did you expect me to do—rape you?'

Lena gasps. 'Oh, Mr. Joyce—'

Sheila says, 'Why not?'

Lena gasps again. I almost gasp myself. 'Why not?' I repeat uncertainly.

'Yes, why not?' She is speaking without anger now, expressing thoughts which are not thrown up by the instant's emotion but which have been formulated in sessions of self-communion. 'It's a pity you don't understand women, Reggie. You read all that poetry nonsense and you think it's produced by the best and wisest men in the world but actually it's all written by frustrates—shades of Byron and Lovelace and Donne!—who don't know what they're talking about. You'd do better to read one good textbook on sex. No girl wants to lose her virginity—that's instinct—'

'Really, really, Mrs. Joyce,' cries Lena, looking nervously around to see if we are being overheard.

'—but how can a young girl know what's best for her? Maybe it would have done me good to be raped. Anyway you ought to have gone ahead, Reggie. I'd put myself in your power. But—you backed off.'

'You mean, if I'd gone ahead—'

'I don't mean anything. I don't know what I mean.'

'But when Andy came, he didn't—back off?'

'I don't want to talk about Andy. I want some coffee.'

We start to move towards the counter again but as we take the first steps the loudspeakers start to whirr and I know the moment has come. 'Attention, please, ladies and gentlemen. The nine-forty bus is about to leave for London airport. Will passengers with tickets marked number five …'

'Is your ticket number five?' Lena asks me.

I nod. I hold out my hand to her. She struggles to take her glove off and I take her cold fingers with their arthritic joints and clasp them cordially. Her eyes suddenly fill with tears and I am astonished, grateful, jubilant, moved. It would be discourteous to make any comment. I prolong the clasp and then reluctantly break it and turn to Sheila.

'Goodbye, Sheila.' I hold out my hand to her.

For a moment I'm afraid she isn't going to take it but then she does, holding her arm close to her body, not stretched out frankly like Lena's. She doesn't take off her glove and her fingers are limp in mine. I squeeze them. She doesn't look at me.

'I'm sorry if I upset you, Sheila.' I want to say—oh hell, I want to say something noble. Something self-abnegatory and forgiving like 'I hope you'll be very happy with Andy, I hope the baby will be beautiful.' But it is safer to stick to clichés. I say, 'All the best.' Then add, unable to resist the flourish, 'Now and forever.' I would like to kiss her. But I can't—not across that belly, with Andy's baby in it. I release her hand.

As I turn she touches my arm. 'Be careful, Reggie. Come back in one piece. And watch out for these nigger women. White ones are bad enough, but black—! And you're such a sucker where women are concerned.'

I want to tell her that the Siamese are not Negro, that I hate to hear her talk about 'niggers'—that is Andy's influence—that anyway I shall never look at another woman again. But the loudspeakers are repeating their message. 'Attention, please, ladies and gentlemen. The nine-forty bus …'

Lena is wiping her eyes with her handkerchief. I give that foolish salute of mine and join the throng of persons moving towards the door. A sucker where women are concerned! Once again I almost hate the bitch. But there's no time to refute the charge. And anyway what's the use? with Andy's brat—

My sight is so confused that I bump into someone heavily. 'Oh, I'm so sorry,' I say, but he keeps on muttering, being probably a bit upset himself about something or other …

Once when the track wasn't big enough to hold me I hit the safety fence hard and flew somersaulting up, and as I tucked my head in for the crump I saw the bike do a cartwheel too, right into my stomach. And then I was lying on my side with the bike on top of me and not a gramme of air left in my body, but only pain. The faces of the ambulance men gathered and swam above me but they were hardly real, only that incredible pain in the guts was real. It took five minutes to wear off, and only then did I begin to become conscious of my other bruises. Half an hour later, with the stupid valour of my youth, I rode again, and got, as I recall, a second place and a cheer. Not to mention a couple of quid.

Now it is much the same: only the hurt exists. Everything else is unreal. Humming out along the Great West Road in an odd sort of bus with a high poop and a loose prop-shaft. Being questioned by officials standing surrealistically behind small desks like overgrown schoolboys. Sprawling for hours, it seems, in a luxurious armchair amongst expensive-looking, wrought-up fellow passengers. Riding a matter of eighty yards in another bus to the plane. It is a Convair: I notice that. Soon it's my turn to ascend the wobbly stair. The two hostesses at the top bid me good morning with a bonhomie that must be spurious, for what can I mean to them, one passenger amongst forty, and all of us perfect strangers? A murrain on the bitches (whatever a murrain is).

The window seats are all taken. I find a place next to a plump dark windy man who plainly thinks his luck can't hold much longer. His jumpiness irritates me. He clings to his briefcase as a frenzied mother to her dying child. He can't do up his seat belt and goes into a panic. One air hostess leans across me and buckles him in like a mother securing her baby in his pram. Her bust comes too close to my cheek. I draw back in distaste, cross-eyed. God, how I loathe women.

Later the same girl asks me what I want to drink. I haven't the faintest idea what to answer so I say 'Water.' The nervous wreck, a little less worried now we're off the ground, chooses a Martini. Later, with his food, he has beer and Schnapps. With his coffee he has Dom. I have heard of them all before but never to my knowledge seen any of them but beer. And beer I have never tasted. I don't want any lunch and suddenly, up here amongst the clouds, bound for the glorious East, water seems a dull beverage. It is damned awkward anyway feeding off a tray on your lap.

I catch one glimpse of the Channel. It is transparently blue like the sky, but the wash has been unevenly applied in streaks and puddles as in a novice's watercolour. God can get away with his inexpertness, however, because His palette happens to be light itself. And can that narrow white band down there, like a bar of cloud, be really and truly the white cliffs of Dover? Or, at any rate, perfidious Albion? The nervous man suddenly jerks forward, blotting out the view. *Perfidy*, by Reginald E. Joyce. My pain rolls over me again and the rest of the world is washed out.

It is worst of all when I reach Geneva. I am the only passenger for the Bangkok plane. That is not due from Stockholm until four. Three hours to kill. 'You don't want to go downtown, of course,' the ground host says hopefully. I look at him in doubt. I answer 'No.' He directs me to the café. Somehow I manage to go wrong. I am stopped by a gendarme or a soldier, I don't know which. He has a gun and speaks fierce French. It is the first time anyone has addressed me in anything but English since I left school. I look and feel blank. The ground host perceives my predicament and bustles up, rescuing me from imminent arrest. I go on the right way moping. Why, oh why, must I always be taking wrong turnings? I seem to have a genius for doing so. This whole journey is probably down a sidetrack: I'm off the main road, heading straight for disaster ...

I sit for a time in the café but I am too shy to change any money and anyway I don't feel like eating and in the end I move to another table outside. It is a glorious afternoon. The sun is bright and almost unbearably hot. If it's like this in Switzerland, what's it going to be like in Siam? I feel butterflies in my stomach: I really am on my way to the Far East: the incredible is coming to pass.

Across the field mountains loom blearily through the heat-haze. Three light planes are giving joyrides to a holiday throng; they flutter along the runway like garish butterflies, sail up into the air, turn and dwindle into the blue. Somehow I never happen to see them land. All around me is laughter and talk in several languages. I ought to be lifted out of myself. Free at last. Rising like a soap bubble, detached from the clay-pipe, perfected, lighter than air, reflecting the multi-hued world. Adam awaking to his most wondrous dawn, a pain in his side but Eve there, naked, doing her hair. Stout Cortez up a gumtree. A young man in love, hearing the Oxford symphony for the first time ...

Suddenly I am transfixed by a shout from the public address system. ‘Attention, please, attention. Will Mr. Reginald Joyce please contact the TWA ground hostess immediately.’ I sit perspiring, and the public address system, anticipating this reaction on my part, reiterates its request. No doubt about it then. The possibility of the paths of two Reginald Joyces crossing at Geneva at three o’clock on one unespecial Sunday afternoon seems remote. I get up, feeling hundreds of eyes upon me.

She is like a Dresden shepherdess in up-to-date uniform. Her shining dark eyes look up at me amusedly. She is only returning the ticket and passport which the Swissair man took off me. There was absolutely nothing to fear. She says brightly ‘Have a good trip,’ and turns on ultra-smart heels. Of course it’s all make-believe. Professional sweetness, like the doctor telling you you’ll pull through when he knows damn well you’ve had it. The smile was applied like lipstick. But I let it fool me like lipstick too. My heart smiled back at her. And not purely from relief.

The DC-6 is a grand sight as she comes shouldering her way down through the hyaline levels of blue and streams silver along the runway with a last valedictory roar from her four engines. Coming up to us she is as majestic as a great ship, but less leisurely and patient; each nimble manœuvre is accompanied by a short bad-tempered roar. Her flock of passengers, straggling towards the café, look as undishevelled as if they had spent the afternoon in a comfortable lounge. Which is of course just what they have done, up there, all but three miles above the Earth.

I am given a window seat and I am glad. I look out on a vast stretch of wing and two engines. There is no hope for me today: to me they are the breasts of a technological angel. I am no longer merely anthropomorphic in my outlook; somebody must have made up a word that fits me: gynaemorphic, would that be it? Blameless though I am physically, more than a quarter of a century old, and not one notch on my pistol-butt yet, I belong to the cult of—Siva, is it?—I am the sort of savage who worships a goddess smothered in breasts, or a boulder with a hole bored through it, the work of some prehistoric Henry Moore. Somehow I have got to get all this prurience out of my system, it is laying waste my powers. I stare out of the window. The vast wing is shivering behind the fury of those twin tits. You can almost see the air being torn apart and hurled away by the glittering blades. The people watching, the buildings, the mountains beyond, are all dwarfed and abnormal, like objects in an impressionist painting, smaller, neater, brighter, more crowded than in life. Suddenly the canvas is snatched sideways: we've begun to move.

The next hour is magnificent. A few miles from the airfield we begin to circle up and up through layers of cloud. At first there are placid valleys below, valleys where doubtless dark blue gentians lurk, and cows wear bells, and skirts are starched, and men, not yet coerced by letter box and telephone, yodel to each other across the lush green meadows and the tumbled scree-falls. But soon the ragged underedges of clouds drag slowly by below us: something happens to the light, it becomes uncertain, as if there were a loose connection somewhere; one instant it is golden, turning the clouds to heaps of dazzling pearl, the next it is unaccountably dimmed; I feel apprehensive, and my fear is communicated to the machine, which gives a sudden shudder.

A few minutes later we emerge into sunlight of an ineffable brightness. The loudspeaker sounds again. 'We are now flying at eighteen thousand five hundred feet. From the port side of the plane you can obtain a good view of Mont Blanc, the highest mountain in Europe. The summit is about three miles away.' It is indeed a glorious sight. My first view of eternal snows. I feel a hand on my arm and look up in surprise. 'Excuse please.' The man in the next seat, who I think is Japanese, is standing up and leans across me. He holds to his heavy-lidded eye a camera no bigger than a matchbox. He gets Mont Blanc, two shots, then puts the camera away in the breast-pocket of his neat western-style suit. He smiles at me pleasantly.

'Would you like something to drink?' the hostess asks me.

'Yes. I'd like a—Martini.'

With my dinner I have beer and Schnapps. With my coffee Dom. Thanks to a nervous wreck who travelled from London to Geneva this morning I am able to order them with the aplomb of a man of the world. I'm sure the hostess doesn't realize she is serving one who until this moment was a strict teetotaller. And I feel I am acting like one of those soft-centred tough guys of the modern novels: they always get tight under emotional stress too.

That is to say, when they can't get their own way with some woman.

At Rome I have a ham roll and two glasses of wine. I like the ham roll.

We reach Cairo at two in the morning. The waiters are dark portly men who have been surprised by our arrival and have had no time to change out of their nightshirts. But they *have* remembered to put their fezzes on. They serve bacon and eggs, as if we were in an all-night café on the Great North Road. When I go to the Gents, a furtive little man follows me in, I presume to make sure I don't pocket the soap. As I stand at the trough he begins in a hesitant, utterly ineffectual way to brush me down. His expression when I jerk round is so scared, obsequious and pleading that it haunts me for hours. I've never seen anything like it on a human face before. Only on dogs. I feel I ought to have patted him on the shoulder and talked baby-talk to him to reassure him.

Dawn comes over the desert. Unable to sleep, I stare out of the window for hours. It is like flying over the surface of the moon, but that surface is hot, not cold, as scientists allege. The Indian Ocean when we reach it is an endless indigo lake on which tiny bobbles of cottonwool cloud float like white petals on a pond at home. This hop is interminable; my head buzzes from lack of sleep, my stomach is deranged by bacon and eggs in the small hours and I have begun to ache all over with weariness. Yet it would be a sin to shut one's eyes on such colour, indeed on any part of God's world which one hasn't seen before and may never see again, and I force my eyelids to remain open, sore though they are.

Slowly the telescoped hours drag by and it is teatime when we land at Karachi. The ground hostess there is something new in ground hostesses and the sight of her revives me somewhat. She is clad in white pyjamas and a crimson scarf which hangs in a loop in front, passes through epaulettes and streams backwards from her shoulders in two four-foot-long pennons. She has rich olive-blue hair and proud Indian curves to her features but she has none of that poise a gullible westerner credits all oriental women with, she seems in fact almost in an hysterical state and very officious, but her beauty exonerates her from anything and men do her bidding with alacrity.

Dumped in the café for the usual half-hour I call for beer. It is English and pretty well undrinkable. I begin to wonder whether I want to go in seriously for alcoholism.

Suddenly as I am pouring more of the stuff into my glass, the bottle is snatched from my hand. I look up startled. Above the white pyjamas and the lucky horseshoe of crimson scarf the Indian features are frowning imperiously.

'Why do you drink this beer? It is flat. Order the waiter bring you another bottle.' And she rushes away, the sash-ends floating behind her.

Meekly I do as I am told—(why didn't I realize?) The offending bottle is removed on a tray, exhibited to the manager, replaced. This time when I splash the beer into my glass there is a minor flood. I feel I ought to apologize to someone for making such a mess but the manager is involved in a violent quarrel with two of the waiters, I am all alone at my table, the other passengers are morosely engrossed in their orangeades and teas and the hostess has disappeared. I bury my nose in the froth and decide English beer is probably not so bad after all.

When we amble across the field to the plane again there she is at the foot of the ladder saying 'goodbye' to any of the passengers that will look at her. I approach her jauntily, feeling an old hand at this boarding of planes. Her smile seems extra warm for me.

'Are all the girls in India as pretty as you are?' my tongue says, and I stumble aghast to hear it act so fresh.

But instead of being offended by my tongue's rudeness she is amused. She laughs and says, 'I'm not Indian. I'm Burmese. I come from Rangoon.'

'I must make a note of that address—Rangoon, Burma,' I make my tongue say and this time the wit, if any, is my own, consciously invented. And to my amazement she seems to be pleased with this flippancy too and when I give her my silly salute, damn me if she doesn't make the same silly gesture back. I ascend the ladder like an angel in Jacob's dream. Is it just the drinks? Or am I already beginning to feel emancipated, free of the past and England, with all their crushing associations of Sheila, the ten commandments, the taste of barbital slowly chewed and washed down with pints of lemonade, the years and years of dismal drudgery in Islington, after the three mad years of broken bones and adulation on the speedways? It seems almost like treason to the image of Sheila to feel happy *already* ... I try to compose my thoughts in the accustomed vault but all the way to Rangoon they keep breaking out, arrogantly curling Indian (no, Burmese) features obliterating the clean-cut delicate English ones, an olive-blue cloud passing across the sunset gold ...

Rangoon, which we reach in the small hours, is a drab place, not at all what you would expect the cradle of such a houri to be. There are no buxom cushions, no hanging brocades, no shapely brass pots, no exotic perfumes, no Negro slave-girls (and why in blazes should there be?) naked to the waist, idly waving huge fans. There are only sleepy, irritable waiters, unpleasant coffee, a plain hostess in a white suit, and lost frogs flopping disconsolately across the restaurant floor ...

At seven on a sparkling morning we finally achieve Bangkok. The run-in is over a flat watery landscape. I am too apprehensive to notice anything about the airfield. Have I filled in all my forms correctly? Will I be met, or will I have to flounder around on my own, like a lost frog? Have I done the right thing? God, O God, is it going to turn out all right from the start? ... Then the world beginning to flow by with accelerated speed, and rising around us like a swelling wave; the plane beginning to wobble and bump a bit; the last throttling back of the engines until there is only a rushing nerve-taut sound; waiting for the bump; the bump; the bounce; then the softer bump and the rumbling race along the runway; that last furious roar in your ears; the slowing up; the clumsy turn; the gentle swaying tour back to the jumble of roofs and flags ... It has all happened before but then it was a game; this time it is final, when you go down the steps this time it will be into a new world, new dangers, a whole brand-new dangerous life ...

Two

One day about a week later I am captured by a ghoulish idea. That evening I sit down in room number seven of the South Wind hotel and begin to write on my best notepaper as follows:

September 20

My darling Sheila, I've been stricken with a ghoul's idea. Every week I'm going to write a letter to you. But of course I'm not going to post it. I'm going to bury it away in a file—what you might well call a Dead Letter File. And into these letters I'm going to put all that I would have put into them if you and I were still—well, as if we were still as close as we once were. I'm going to put my whole soul into them ... all that once before I tried to give you, the good and the bad: but you rejected it.

Well, I don't blame you for being so choosy. As a matter of fact I've just been rejected again, by three of my fellow countrymen, after only just one week in their company. To be more precise, Mr. Samjohn, Regional Managing Director of Broderick Peers, Mr. Drummond, accountant of ditto ditto (Bangkok office), and Mr. Frost, the last new recruit prior to myself, have gently eased me out of their abode, the House, where all European personnel of Broderick Peers are supposed to be put up, into a small hotel at the other end of town, where I am writing this. But let me tell the story from the beginning, so that you can understand what has happened and also (for you have enough brains for anything) *why* it has happened (you, dear heart, who actually are never going to hear one word about it).

I was met at Don Muang, the airfield, by two representatives of the firm, the above-mentioned Frost and a Siamese man called Mom Vimil. Actually it was the latter who contacted me first. He made a providential appearance just as I was getting into deep waters at the immigration desk, threw out the lifeline of a string of fluent Thai and pulled me, considerably shaken, to the shore. I have since been pretty constantly in the company of this Vimil, or Windmill to give him his nickname, and I consider him to be the nicest man I have yet met out here. He has been with the firm for more years than I have been on Earth and one of his jobs is to show the new boys like me the ropes. He is well-suited for his job, being a plump, pleasant, easy-going type who likes to make it seem that there aren't any ropes to learn, or that if there are, they aren't at all important. He never volunteers information but he will patiently answer endless questions, even those that must seem puerile to him. Therefore he is a much better educator than for instance Drummond who fired facts at my head for two solid hours one morning expecting them to stick, and who now, if I confess that one or two of them didn't, barks plaintively, 'But I told you that days ago' and then snaps, 'Better see Windmill or Frost about it. I haven't any time.'

But I'm still making a muddle of the story. A few minutes after Windmill had done his rescuing act, Frost appeared. He is a tall burly Englishman, as fair as I am and two years my junior, handsome I would say except for a pronounced cast in his left eye. His first remarks were characteristic.

'Sorry I missed the reception. I got a call. 'Ad to empty me 'od.'

As the first half of his remarks had been spoken in copybook English I realized that the cockney conclusion was supposed to be funny and dutifully laughed. 'What's the trouble? Stomach upset?'

'Don't know for sure. Too early to tell yet. I didn't turn in till four. Bit of a night out.' He winced and looked anxious. 'Blimey, it's flipping miles to the crapper. I hope they provide spare pants for the ones that don't make it.'

We went out to the car. It was a fairly ancient Riley. I noticed that it had recently been in combat. And that some humorist (I now know it was Frost) had painted a Purple Heart on the windscreen ('because it got scratched at the front').

Frost and I got into the front seat and Windmill and another man with a lot of gold teeth got into the back. This second man was Duen, the office driver, or that is what they call him, but actually he does very little driving; mostly he dozes in the rear while Frost drives.

I suppose I ought to describe that car ride, Sheila. You lap up local colour, I know. But I don't suppose I saw half the things that you with your bright eyes would have seen. I remember the asphalt road, and a humpbacked concrete bridge, and my first Siamese temple, my first paddy field full of brilliant green rice, my first wild egret, my first sarong, my first water buffalo with its enormous slate-grey barrel of a body plodding on inadequate legs and its patient, stupid antediluvian head borne down by the mighty sweep of fossilized horn, my first huge lotus-flowers, my first bare female breast and my first little Chinese boy flying a kite. Because I am I, the most enduring of these recollections is the breast but at the time, the most impressive was undoubtedly the temple, for the multi-coloured tiles of its steep and lofty roofs were glistening in the rays of the climbing sun and the yard around it, full of fantastic stone towers, was like a builders' yard where pre-fabricated steeples were being stored against the time when Hans Andersen's fairy tales will replace St. John's Revelation in the Bible.

Often we passed priests, shaven-headed, bare of foot, walking in single file. They were dressed in the most gorgeous saffron robes, like gaudy togas. They leave their temples to beg for their food at sun-up—they never eat after midday—and once I saw a line of them drawn up before a rickety wooden lean-to and a woman in a transparent white silk blouse and a red sarong placing handfuls of rice in their proffered bowls. It was a beautiful picture, full of peace and devotion; and the priests were fine-looking men, for so good is the shape of the Siamese skull that shaving its hair seems actually to increase its beauty, rather than to detract from it; you seldom see an ugly priest here.

Frost drove as if he were the Flying Dutchman off the Cape and that's why I didn't see more than I did. I hardly dared drag my eyes from the road. He asked me if I drove.

'I'm actually more of a motorcyclist.'

'You'd better drive here if you can. Never let a Thai drive you. They're too flipping reckless.'

As he said that he roared full-pelt over a crossroads just as a car coming from our right did the same thing. The other driver slammed on his brakes so fiercely he swerved into the gutter. Frost didn't even lift his foot from the accelerator pedal. As we snorted across the other's bows he continued calmly, 'It isn't driving skill you need in Bangkok. It's psychological insight. If you think you can scare the other bloke you've got the right of way. That was a typical instance just now. Some sixth sense told me that flipper would stop for me.'

'But which was on the major road, him or us?'

'They're *all* major roads. That's just the point. You never want to let the other bloke intimidate you. You've got just as much right to go first as he has.'

Somehow we reached Bankapi without qualifying for any more Purple Hearts. You know, my love (my late love), nor will you ever forget, that I could roar into the first bend as boldly as any man. But I confess I am daunted by Bangkok traffic. I reached the House trembling.

And the House and my reception there did little to restore my confidence. Perhaps inevitably, Sheila, after all those years in Lena's poky flat, there's only one big house that doesn't intimidate me, and that's Malderbury Vicarage, where I was born. All other large houses are associated in my mind with wealth and luxury; I can't help but regard them as anachronisms in these days of bedsitting rooms and kitchenettes—left-overs from an age of wrong values. Well, the House, Broderick Peers' home from home for their British exiles in Bangkok, is very big indeed, almost palatial. You go through large gates on to a gritty drive that is bordered on one side by a pond full of fish and blood-red lotus-flowers and on the other by a rather mangy lawn surrounded by exotic shrubs. The House itself is a pile of soaring over-balancing roofs, of spacious verandahs, gaping glassless windows, dazzling white walls, and trellises burdened with masses of purple flowers. Straight from England you are chilled by the absence of chimneys; clearly there ought to be stacks of them, but there isn't one. Behind, there's a long row of houses, almost like a street: these are the servants' quarters. You wouldn't be very much surprised to see a servant in livery emerge through the ever-open front door to receive you, but except at mealtimes, when Somchit puts on a white jacket, the whole tribe go around happily in singlet and shorts if male, and a blouse and sarong if female, and this informality enables me to accept their services with less sense of guilt than I would otherwise have felt.

The House is divided into two parts, one being occupied by Mr. Samjohn and his wife, and the other by Frost and Drummond. We went into this second part first. It appears that Mrs. Samjohn has gone upcountry to visit friends so for a few days the boss is eating with his assistants in their half of the palace. He and Drummond were halfway through their breakfast when we went in.

Since then I've sometimes wondered whether it wouldn't have been better if we'd earned another Purple Heart on the way to this place and so been delayed for a time. For it's always a nuisance when guests arrive in the middle of a meal and when that meal is breakfast ... What made it worse was the fact that Samjohn and Drummond are men who make a habit of getting out of the wrong side of the bed every morning and having to desist from bacon and eggs while they were introduced to me did nothing to dispel their normal morning misanthropy. I could see disappointment in Samjohn's eye and contempt in Drummond's. After breakfast when I went to my room and caught sight of myself in one of the innumerable mirrors I realized I was looking quite a wreck. The forty sleepless hours had left me crumpled and bleary, not at all the smart bright active cheerful sort that a traveller, commercial, is expected to be. But we shook hands as though we liked the looks of each other and Frost and I sat down at the places that had been laid for us.

Then the problem of Windmill cropped up. No place had been laid for him. Unfortunately he followed us in as if he was expecting sustenance. Somchit ran up with an extra chair and implored him to be seated; it was quite clear that the servant was making a great effort to atone for his masters' lack of courtesy. Mr. Samjohn after a short pause added his entreaties too: 'the boy can soon lay another place.' But Windmill, even more sensitive than I, had noted that significant pause before the gush of spurious heartiness. He hung back, coy and embarrassed, began backing away with repeated polite refusals, making it look as though the honour was more than he could accept, smiling and shaking his head—finally asked if he might borrow the car for a few minutes to go and attend to some private business. 'Well, if you're really adamant ...' Almost too promptly Mr. Samjohn signalled to Somchit not to bother to bring the cutlery he was assembling on the sideboard. Windmill went out, the car started up, Somchit left the room in search of fodder for Frost and me. I thought Windmill had been played a dirty trick. After all, he must have got up damned early to go to the airfield with Frost to meet me.

The breakfast was as good as any I've had in my life, not forgetting those we had at that farm at Aber, remember? It began with a slice of papaya, a new fruit for me, like a melon without pips, cherry-red, and having the consistency of Turkish delight; you squeeze lemon on it and eat it with a spoon; I didn't like it much, it was rather sickly, and also I'm scared of catching typhoid. But then came cereals, then bacon and eggs, then toast and butter and marmalade. The coffeepot seemed bottomless and the sunlight poured in on the silver knives and the lemon-coloured cups and plates, birds sang, flowers scented the air, and against the sky, coconut palms exploded like huge green mops—conclusive proof, romantic proof, that I had arrived in the tropics.

Unfortunately there were Messrs Samjohn and Drummond there and either of them by himself would have been sufficient to poison the atmosphere of Eden.

The first is a fierce little man with a hot red face, hot blue eyes and white hair. According to a legend which he made up himself he has lived on nothing but whisky, curry and cigars for the last thirty years (except for the four when he was interned by the Japs). The diet has had an effect on his figure, which is tubby, and his temper, which is vile. He is fond of saying that his bark is worse than his bite but that proverb is suspect when it is applied by a man to himself; ask the people he snaps and barks at if you want an unbiassed view. Everybody but Windmill seems to be scared of the blighter and I never feel comfortable in his presence myself.

Drummond is another misery. He is a tall thin hollow-chinned man who, dressed in the open-neck white shirt and light-coloured trousers which are the businessman's uniform here, looks like the village undertaker turning out for the village cricket team. This rather plebeian appearance makes his old school tie and officers'-mess affectations even more irritating than they would otherwise be, and moreover he makes a point of never being satisfied with anything either at home or at work.

He and Mr. S. finished eating before we did. Living up to his legend, Mr. S. lighted a cigar and said to me, 'We'll have to push off to the office. No need for you to come in today. You've got a lot of sleep to make up. Frost will show you round the house and we'll send the car for you in about an hour, eh, Frost?'

'Right-ho.'

'We're a bit pushed for room here, Joyce. Afraid your room isn't all that it might be. In fact we've been thinking—' But he didn't divulge their thoughts. He looked at the clock. 'Right, Drummond—'

Somchit said, 'Car not come yet.'

'What?'

'Mr. Vimil take car. Not have come back.'

It was a good job Windmill returned only a minute later. Mr. S. was on the point of bursting a blood vessel. But Windmill took a violent dressing-down very equably.

Afterward Frost led me upstairs. The room that wasn't all that it might be was at least three times as large as Lena's back bedroom. It was sumptuously furnished and had its own private bathroom and a verandah overlooking the pond. The bed was huge and snow-white and I fell into it without further delay.

It was three in the afternoon when I awoke. I found somebody had brought lunch and left it beside the bed. I wolfed it down, got up and had a shower. My cases had been brought into the room; I got out a shirt and shorts and put them on. Then, having examined the bookcases and found little but mysteries, I went out for a stroll. Just down the lane and back again. It was the hottest part of the day and nobody was out except myself, so I didn't see anything interesting.

When I came back I went upstairs to go to my room. To reach it I had to cross Drummond's. I barged in without thinking—it never occurred to me that he might be back from work—but there he was, just in the act of removing his trousers. His face went like the lotus-petals in the pond outside, not from outraged modesty, but with anger.

'Can't you bloody well knock?'

'I'm sorry.'

Since I was already in the room there was no point in withdrawing. I crossed to my own. I lay on my bed listening to the sounds of Drummond having a shower in his own bathroom. I felt very much of a stranger in the house.

I let ten minutes go by after hearing him leave his room before I ventured across it again. In a dim way I had been conscious of his grousing voice downstairs and as I went down the staircase I could hear what he was grousing about. Me. 'God almighty, I've been here ever since I was demobbed after the last show and I think I'm entitled to a bit of privacy and I'm damned if I'm going to put up with a young whipper-snapper straight from Blighty strolling through my bedroom at any hour of the day or night—'

'But if he knocks—' Frost's voice.

'That's just the trouble. The bugger doesn't knock.'

'I will in future. I didn't realize you were in your room.' They hadn't heard me coming down the stairs which are thickly carpeted and my interruption took them by surprise. Drummond jerked round and gave me a hard stare, then, without saying any more, walked out through the French window. He had a tennis racquet under his arm, and in a few minutes I heard the car start up.

Since then I've always knocked on his damned door even when I've known he's not in residence, just to keep myself in practice.

He didn't come back that evening and after dinner Frost and I succeeded in getting on to reasonably good terms with each other. Frost was still suffering from the night before, 'Or else,' he said 'I could have shown you round a bit.'

'What is there to see in Bangkok?'

'What are you interested in?'

'Well—I'm not quite sure. Historic buildings, I suppose and—and beauty spots.'

Frost's lips curled. 'I can show you a few *night* spots,' he said, 'but if it's culture you want you'll have to apply to old Windmill.'

'Oh, I'm interested in a gay life too.' As you know, Sheila, it's an axiom in our family that only very dissipated, reprehensible people go to nightclubs and places like that and I was lying. I suppose there must have been a lack of conviction in my voice because Frost laughed shortly.

'One of these nights I'll take you to the Bolero. Every man that comes to Bangkok has to go there once. It's part of one's education. Like going to see the Emerald Buddha. Which, by the way, I never *have* seen.'

'And what's this—Bolero?'

'Oh, a sort of nightclub. There's some very famous girls there. Especially two of them. Known round the world, from London to Tokyo, and from Sydney to the North Pole I shouldn't wonder. You'll soon hear people talking about them. They call them the Leopards—the White Leopard and the Black One. It's really something to see them at work.'

'Why, what do they do?'

'Oh—' He was going to be explicit, but decided against it.

'You'll see for yourself one of these days.'

I thought it would only betray a naive curiosity if I pushed the matter any further. After a third whisky and soda (which I didn't like very much) I got reminiscing about the speedway and I think Frost was impressed until I overdid it. We both went to bed early, before Drummond came back. It was a long time before I could get to sleep, partly because I'd slept so soundly during the day, but also because I was full of misgivings about my new life, and dreams of you, Sheila. One thing that puzzled me was why you had turned up at the air-terminal, and I was still sorting out about twenty possible motives when I dropped off.

The next few days were mostly taken up with getting to know my way around the office and Bangkok. I began my lessons in the Thai language with the young copy typist in the office, a half-Chinese, half-Thai youth named Somboon. He took the job on with a view to increasing his income and also his own knowledge of English, and without doubt he is going to learn my language from me much quicker than I learn his from him. He is a frightful dandy in his way—many Thai men seem to be—smells like a garden with his hair-oil, his lotions, his perfumes and his scented soaps. But he is smiling and pleasant, and when he invited me to go out with him the other night I gladly did so. He called for me in a *samlor*—that is, a tricycle taxi. In these vehicles you and your companion sit tightly wedged together in a seat shaped like an old-fashioned basket chair; your view ahead is obscured by the rear elevation of your driver who is most likely to be in a battered papier-mâché sola topee, a shirt flowing loose all round and patched pants; you will be fascinated by the play of muscles in his sinewy bare legs and by his traffic sense, which consists of ringing his bell wildly at any object animate or inanimate for half a mile ahead and utterly ignoring whatever may be overtaking him from behind. On this particular evening we wheezed down a long busy road between stagnant canals and magnificent overhanging trees and because there weren't many potholes we didn't do too many sudden and unsignalled swerves in front of speeding cars.

'Where do you want to go?' Somboon asked.

For a moment I thought of suggesting the Bolero, but then I told myself that that was to be Frost's outing, and moreover I didn't want to appear cheap (as I possibly might) in the eyes of this youth. So I said, 'Anywhere you like. You know this town. I don't.'

We went to a Chinese restaurant and then a movie and it was midnight when the *samlor* deposited me at the House again. Full of sweet-sour pork and rice and sharkfin soup, paying off the sweating *samlor*-man in Siamese notes under a blaze of tropical stars, I felt like a larger than life-size version of myself, the born traveller now, at home at the ends of the Earth. I walked into the lounge which was wide open to the night with all lights on and the ceiling fan swinging round and round. I decided I ought to have a drink before turning in. That surely was what a seasoned traveller, as much at home in Bangkok as anywhere else in the world, would do.

I was just examining the mass of bottles on the sideboard, trying to decide what to experiment with next, when the office car came up the drive and stopped under the porch. I heard Frost's voice and the slamming of car doors and after a moment or two he came in—with a woman.

'Hey, Joycey, you've got the right idea. Fix one for me. And Daisy too.'

He went to the radiogram and put on a few records. The girl flopped onto the sofa and after half a minute stretched out on it. I poured a whisky for Frost—I knew how much he liked by now—and took the glass and the soda water bottle to one of the armchairs. But he seemed to have forgotten about the drink as soon as the music began.

'Come on, Daisy, let's dance.'

'I too hot.'

'I know you're hot. That's why I brought you here. I'm hot myself.' He pulled his shirt off and threw it away. 'Take your shirt off, if you're hot, sweetheart.'

She tossed her head in my direction. 'Who he?'

'That's Joycey. Don't mind him. He's going to bed in a minute.'

'Why he no give me drink?'

'Yeah, why don't you give the lady a drink, Joycey old man? You're not much of a host.'

He went to the sideboard shouting 'What's it to be, Daisy old girl? Beer? Gin? Whisky? Methylated spirits? Arsenic? What?'

'I want gimlet.'

'You would want something like that.' He began to busy himself while I, to whom until this moment a gimlet was nothing but a carpenter's tool, tried to see what he was doing from the arm of a chair.

The girl—if you could call her that—was looking at me interestedly. She was very well-built, not to say plump, with a great mass of black hair, brilliant dark eyes and a double chin. Her backless evening gown, white and to my untutored eyes, expensive-looking, threw into relief the tawny splendour of her skin. She seemed very free and easy in her ways, I mean lying full-length like that before she'd even been introduced to me. She said now, fixing me with her shining eyes, 'You want dance?'

I flicked my eyes nervously towards her and away again. 'No'.

'Please give me cigarette.'

'I'm sorry. I haven't any. I don't smoke.'

She laughed. 'Not dance. Not smoke. What you d'ink? I sink only ollange clush, maybe.'

'I drink a little.'

'A very little, I sink.' She suddenly sat up and to my amazement began undoing the zip at the back of her dress. It stuck and without any hesitation she came across to me and presented her back to me, saying, 'Please help.' I got up awkwardly. I think you could guess my feelings, Sheila. It was the first time I'd ever been asked to act as a lady's maid. You yourself were always competent enough to manage your own clothes.

I think she sensed my unease because before I'd accomplished anything she wrenched herself away from me, calling to Frost: 'What is matter with your friend? Why he not enjoy he-self? Why he 'fray'?'

Coming back with her drink Frost said, 'He's a good boy. That's a type you never met before, darling, and I'm damn sure I could never explain it to you.'

She said, stepping out of her dress, 'He very han-sum. I sink many girl must like very much.'

A scowl appeared on Frost's face. She took the drink from him and sat down on the sofa and sipped it and put it on the floor and then got up and began laying her dress smoothly over the back of a chair. With as much care as if it was going to be there for quite some time. She was clad only in a bra and panties and a bracelet or two and white high-heeled shoes and I'd never seen anything like it before except in movies and magazines. She stooped to remove her shoes and then she took another sip at her glass and then suddenly she turned to Frost with her arms up. 'OK, darling, we dance?'

'I think I'll say goodnight,' I said, but the gramophone was making too much racket; they didn't hear me.

I edged across the room to the stairs. As I ascended like an angel up Jacob's ladder I couldn't help a backward glance at the naughty Earth. The two were doing a waltz, I suppose it was, with long slow strides involving a dip and a swirl; each stride was longer and more tottery than the last and when they collided with the table on which I had stood Frost's drink, there was no help for them, they and the table and the drinks all went over together behind the sofa. I couldn't see them but I heard the bump of their contact with the floor and then their laughter, continuous helpless laughter as if something very funny had happened.

I rushed upstairs and I was so agitated I forgot all about knocking on Drummond's door.

'God damn and blast you—'

He was sitting on his bed stark naked. On the stool in front of his dressing-table was a Siamese girl in a sarong. I just saw that she was doing her hair as I ran between them to my own room. For some reason I bolted my door. I could hear Drummond cursing for what seemed hours. Later they were downstairs and I could hear him complaining to Frost again. I got out Spengler's *Decline of the West*, which I had found in Mr. Samjohn's half of the house the night he invited me round there, but I couldn't concentrate on it. I was too upset by the rawness of life in the East.

Next morning the atmosphere was wintry round the breakfast table and yesterday afternoon Mr. Samjohn called me into his office and said that while they were so pushed for room at the House it would be better for me to put up at a hotel. Windmill knew just the place in the Chinese quarter of Bhalangpoo, not too expensive but very comfortable, and the office car would pick me up every morning at eight fifteen.

So here I am, Sheila, and such have been the outstanding incidents of my first week in Bangkok ...

October 17

Sheila, my lost darling, I promised you a weekly letter but I've only written one in a whole month and this second one I'm writing now is going to be very short because tomorrow I am going upcountry on my first field trip and I want to finish it before I leave. And in a few minutes Somboon will be here to take me out to a farewell party for just him and me. This time I am definitely going to go with him to the Bolero, for Frost will never take me there now. Frost dislikes me. Samjohn dislikes me. Drummond dislikes me. They all dislike me for the very good reason that they have me on their consciences; they know they had no right to evict me from the House. That is the real root of their dislike but there are side-roots too. There are the facts that I am not too bright at my work and that I lead a blameless life except for my two or three bottles of beer a day, that I am friends with Somboon who in their opinion is a very minor character and that the awkwardness which comes so often into my manner when I try to fraternize with my fellows gives them the impression that I am priggish and contemptuous of them.

Only one person thinks highly of me—Mrs. Samjohn, and she's a repulsive old frump. But she thinks I am handsome and lonely and intellectual and she has invited me five times to the House for dinner and included me in a party that went to the seaside at San Soek one Sunday. The other members of the party were Mr. Samjohn and a fat White Russian couple and it was a tight fit in the Riley. The sea was so full of jellyfish that bathing was out of the question so most of the time we just sat under the coconut palms which fringe the shore, drinking coconut milk with whisky in it and slapping at ants. But the sea and the sky were beautiful and so were the sands and the people and children sprawling and lazily playing on them, and I enjoyed the day. I hope tomorrow's trip is equally pleasant. It had better be, because it is going to last for six weeks.

I'm sorry to be so brief, Sheila. Although I don't write often it's not because I don't think of you. As a matter of fact during this last month in Bangkok you have been in my mind more constantly than you have ever been before, even when we were closest to each other. For it seems we take ourselves with us wherever we go; if we are obsessed in London, we shall not shake off our obsession merely by removing ourselves to Bangkok. But I'm still looking forward to tomorrow.

Here's Somboon. All my love. Your ever-dog-like

Reggie

Three

There are five of us around the table. And I'm not by any means the least boisterous of the gang.

I'm still uncertain how it's all come about. I was supposed to get up frightfully early this morning to catch the Korat train. But I had one bottle of beer too many at the Bolero last night and I was still snoring when Windmill arrived. Luckily he was in plenty of time. I washed and dressed and Duen drove though the morning streets and we still had twenty minutes to wait before the train pulled out. As soon as we were out of the station Windmill said, 'You want beer?'—'What, at this time of the morning?'—'Why not?'—'OK then.' And since then it has been beer beer all day long. Bottle after bottle on the train. Bottles at the hotel as soon as we arrived. Bottles at the club to which we repaired as soon as we had bathed and changed. And in a second they'll be ordering more, I suppose, in this chophouse.

I gaze blearily around the table. There is a ringing in my ears that is so loud it makes my companions' words hard to catch, though they're all shouting, you can tell that from the bulge of veins and muscles in their throats and the way the sweat is standing on their brows. A wedge of ache has been driven downwards between my eyes splaying them outwards, I no longer see my friends as an old master would have painted them, they are like his studies for a masterwork, a dozen slapped-in outlines, one of which is right, but it's hard to tell which is that one. But they're all good chaps, good chaps, an' I'm blurry lucky—

Who the hell are they all, anyway?

First on my left is Windmill. Good old Windmill. Of all the people I have met in Thailand he is still the one I like the best. Yet even him I can't wholeheartedly esteem. He has oriental characteristics which are disconcerting to a westerner. For instance he is never anything but *polite* with me, but he is *cordial* with his own race. While his mouth smiles over anything I say, his eyes don't find me half such amusing company; the teeth flash but the irises fail to light up. He is still sizing me up and, I know, finding me wanting. And then he's such a damned dandy; his case is as full as mine of lotions and perfumes, but whereas mine are samples his are for his own use, and in his hotel room a few minutes ago I caught him actually powdering his nose. 'Not want it shine,' he said. What real man knows enough about his own nose to know—? It took him as long to do his hair, alternately combing it and smoothing it with a podgy hand, as it used to take Sheila with all her golden mane. The ineffable sissy! But he is a friendly bloke and helpful and not easily upset by my western crudities of conduct. And this is all the more remarkable when you remember that he is a Mom, a prince of the fourth rank and it must seem to him that there is little compulsion for him to be courteous to a man like me, who have only plebeian blood in my veins, and a very uncertain claim to the title of Mister ...

Next to him is a man with the promising name of Prosit. He is our agent in Korat and one of the objects of our visit is to make him get on his toes. He is a slight and boyish person with an extraordinary mouth, like a harmonica; when seen in profile, it protrudes beyond the end of his nose, which is not such an uncommon phenomenon, but seen head on it protrudes beyond his hollow cheeks, which seem to cave in behind it; at certain angles it almost blots out his ears. His eyes are deepset, huge, and anxious, and his skin is very dark; Windmill told me he is Thai all right, but from the deep South, close to the Malayan border; and his appearance is proof that more things are smuggled across borders than officials search for in the labelled bags ...

At the far end of the table facing me is an American. The introduction was ill-managed and he appears to have caught only my Christian name while I have caught only his surname which is Boswell. He is nothing to do with Broderick Peers. He is in fact doing something he seems to be a bit vague about with a branch of the United Nations of which I have never heard before. He has been in Thailand for about six months. He was invited to join the party because he is occupying the room next to mine at the hotel and because Prosit seems to think that two white men meeting by accident in a Far Eastern city will automatically deem each other's company indispensible. But I haven't made my mind up about him yet. He has pale blue prominent eyes with drooping lids; with his high-bridged nose and receding chin they give him the look of a tired chicken; he seems very pale compared with the others, and his Hawaiian shirt is like a flowerbed; but he speaks slowly and clearly and his jokes are simple ones which call forth ready laughter from all—even from those whose grasp of American is so uncertain that they tend to be preternaturally solemn when using it.

They are all roaring now at one of his quips but I missed it.

And on my right, facing Windmill and Prosit, is Boswell's right-hand man. I'll swear he was introduced to me as Dr. Custard-tart. He's older than the rest of us, with thick grey hair and oversized spectacles; with his sloping forehead and leathery skin he resembles a tortoise, and his head seems always to be on the point of sinking into his collar, as into a shell. His English is not too deft, but his eyes are light-coloured and shrewd, and his lips make a single straight line denoting authority, like the firm dash under a dictator's signature. I think he could be relied on in an emergency, which is something that can't be said for either Windmill or Prosit; they clearly take the line of least resistance always and everywhere, no matter where it leads ...

At the head of the table is myself. I've achieved this exalted position not because I am important but because I am the latest foreigner to arrive in town and tonight they must do me honour. Tomorrow I shall find my true level, somewhere below the United Nations if not below the salt, but tonight it is to me that Windmill turns first, saying, 'What d'you want to eat, Mr. Joyce? You want ecks? All Europeans like ecks, I think. Some Europeans in Thailand eat nothing only ecks.'

I reply, 'If I am to eat eggs let them be the hundred-year-old variety, for young fresh eggs—' But at this point my grandiloquence peters out and I realize that for the first time in my life I am tipsy. I blink hard several times as if it were my eyes, not my brain, that's fuddled. 'You know what I mean? Windmill, you know—what—?'

He knows but he's incredulous. 'You mean those ecks, black like jelly? In Thai we call *khai yu ma*. That means eggs like horse urine.'

'It is a napt—an—apt description,' I rejoin, 'and the more my eggs taste like horse urine the better I like them.'

'You're depraved,' Boswell shouts. 'Eat your horse piss if you want, but give me a good rare-done beef steak.'

'I think they not have biff steak,' says Windmill. 'But ecks like horse urine, yes, you can get everywhere in Siam. I order. What else you want?'

Several suggestions are made, and the one-eyed youth who, clad in nothing but a pair of torn shorts, performs the functions of head waiter in this establishment, goes howling to the kitchen, each undulating yelp a dish. Then Prosit, bracing himself like a man about to leap from the fourth storey of a burning building, leans towards me and says,

'Mr. Joy, how long time you stay in Thailand?'

There are two possible answers—one month, if he wishes the question to be interpreted in the past tense, three years if the future is intended. I plump for the first and his mouth is like an estuary widening to the sea, his laughter is cackling and infectious.

'So short time, yet already you like eat horse urine,' he says delightedly. Then the laugh vanishes and the eyes become troubled again. 'Ecks,' he explodes suddenly; I realize he has been reviewing his sentence and found it incomplete.

But by then the damage has been done and Boswell is shouting, 'Yes, and you ought to see him gobble up rats' livers, he eats them with pickled walnuts for breakfast' and more of the same until Windmill asks,

'Where you have *khai yu ma* before, Mr. Joyce?'

'In Bangkok. I've had 'em twice when I've been out with Somboon.'

'Who?' And then his eyes harden as he realizes who I mean. He doesn't approve of my friendship with Somboon any more than Mr. Samjohn does.

'Can you use the chopstick?' asks old Custard-tart and when I nod 'Mr. Bosswill can not.'

Boswell is hunting for an excuse but I save his face by saying, 'P'r'aps he can't use chopsticks but he's an American which means he can cut up beef steak with just a fork—and that's something no other nation on Earth can do.' I proceed, quoting Somboon, 'Personally I deprecate the Thai custom of imbibing rice off a plate with fork and spoon. That's the way to eat apple pie. Rice should come in a bowl and be sucked up off two sticks—' I give a demonstration of a Chinese human suction pump in action, but nobody has been listening to me.

Then One-Eye returns with a bottle of mekong in one hand, and three bottles of soda clutched to his bosom by his forearm, and five tumblers threaded on the five digits of his other hand. With a warning shout he slaps all this on the table. From the rags around his middle he produces a bottle-opener and with three flicks sends the caps of the soda water bottles spinning to the floor; they foam over and he sloshes the froth on the floor too. Meanwhile Windmill has folded one soft hand lovingly around the neck of the mekong bottle, inspected it carefully, up-ended it once, turned it sideways, and given it an expert smack on its bottom. Thus the cork is sufficiently loosened for him to be able to pull it out the rest of the way with his teeth. Soon each of us has a tumbler of golden liquid before him. '*Yu ma*' I say privately to Windmill, but they all hear this time and suddenly it dawns on them that the new boy has cracked a joke in Thai, and Groucho Marx couldn't get a more gratifying reaction.

'What did he say?' Boswell asks plaintively, jealous as the waves of laughter buffet to and fro.

'He say mekong like horse urine,' says Custard-tart, taking off his glasses to wipe his eyes. 'Mr. Joy, you spick Siamese a little?'

'*Phud Thai nit noi*'—I speak a little—I admit, and that, modest claim though it be, is sheer conceit, for about all I can actually say so far is Good day, Go right, Go left, Go ahead, Stop, and How much?—but the latter isn't any use to me as I haven't learnt the numerals. However I have now added Horse-piss to my vocabulary—always a useful term to know in any language.

At the other end of the table, Boswell, nettled by my linguistic brilliance, is trying to gain credit for having lived six months in the country without picking up a single word of the vernacular. 'Except Thank you, of course, and Tricycle, and—what's that expression you use every two minutes—'

'Express what?'

'The one you use when you want to say Never mind, That'll do, To hell with it anyway, Mañana-man—'

'*Mai pen arai?*' I ask.

Boswell gives me a hard look, as much as to say, You've been studying, that's not fair. But then the arrival of the first dish, my eggs, changes the subject. The chopsticks are plastic, not bamboo, and picking up a segment of egg is difficult, for the convex side—the 'white', now amber-coloured—is smooth and tough and slippery, while the yolk is a soft black yielding odoriferous mess. All eyes are fixed on me. My prestige can be raised in this hour. Dexterously I steer a piece into the clear, nip it exactly amidships, turn it over, so that the gluey black yolk adheres to the lower chopstick whilst the other chopstick rests lightly on the amber cheek to prevent side-slip, and sweep it in a gesture in which there is some nobility of style to my lips—and by Heaven it is delicious and I champ it in ecstasy, the saliva pouring in over my teeth to get itself mixed in the gobbet like the tide flowing into a bay through the piers of a breakwater. Boswell gazes at me with the expression with which he would watch a python engorging a live goat and then with a shudder, refuses to contaminate his lips with 'such crap.' I bungle my second piece but my reputation is made and anyway I am more successful with the third. Boswell balks again at dish number two, a sort of cold fat pork called, they tell me, *mu pa roo*. The third dish, geese-feet in asparagus stew, seems to infuriate him. 'Haven't they anything canned?' he cries. 'Something sahlid you can eat with a knife and fahk?' Agitation turns all his oh's to ah's. But they have nothing canned in the place so finally he agrees to venture on an omelette. When it comes it is stuffed with meat and onions. He removes every vestige of meat and toys with the rest, enquiring what sort of oil it was cooked in. 'Thank your God it isn't t'ung-oil,' I say, remembering some more Somboonana.

'And what in hell is t'ung-oil?'

'It's the oil in the lamps of China. It's also the oil in a good lot of American paints. Sometimes it's used for cooking in China when they run out of pork fat. It has a powerful action on the guts, I believe. Something like cholera.'

'Sounds even worse than horse piss,' he comments, and I perceive that I am annoying him, first by eating everything they put in front of me, then by talking more Thai than he does, finally by handing out unsolicited information.

But by this time the Thai and I have finished the hors-d'oeuvres and are ready to begin serious eating. Another solemn discussion takes place. *Dum-yam-pla* appears to be a must. I haven't any idea what *dum-*

yam-pla is and await its appearance with interest. They ask me what I propose. I prefer to leave it to them. Windmill suggests stewed ox-tongue and Custard-tart, prawns. Prosit is all for salt fish. One-eye goes off howling again.

'Where you go when we finish eat?' Windmill asks me, slopping more mekong into my glass. He has never looked more affable.

'Whither thou goest I will go,' I reply. 'Is there any place you can go to in this town?'

'I think maybe we take a long walk,' he says, and there seems to be something meaningful in his tone, and of course it's unheard-of for Windmill to go on foot anywhere.

'Does Mr. Joy want to take walk?' Custard-tart interrupts, and suddenly he squeezes my hand and says, 'I think Mr. Joy is very nice man to know. Talk a little Thai. Eat like Thai man. Like to take walk like Thai man too.'

I still don't get the point and say lamely, 'Well, it's too early to go back to the hotel yet. Better to go for a walk if there's nothing else to do.'

'Yes, yes, much better, I think so too,' cries Custard-tart and he laughs immoderately. D. H. Lawrence once heard a tortoise scream and got so worked up he wrote a poem about it. I've just heard one laugh and it's the dirtiest laugh I've heard for years.

Boswell is looking at me sardonically and he says, 'You may know a bit about the lingo but it's clear you're still only a greenhorn in Thailand. "Take a walk" means something extra special when your host invites you and the rest of the company is all male. What it really means is, "You wanna go to a brothel?" You've just said you do.'

I'm so amazed that only the Malderbury dialect can express my condition: I'm 'properly gobsmacked.' I'd been thinking I was holding my own in this male company. I'm drinking as fast as they are. With two well-chosen words I created the biggest laugh of the evening—and in a foreign language, too. But there is more to being a man than being a good fellow. Going to a brothel is something I have never contemplated doing, even in my loneliest dreams. (In fact I don't think there *are* any brothels in England—I've never heard of any anyway.) And the thought that I have just said that I would like to go to one—tonight, in a few minutes—causes a queer agitation in me, a physical agitation. And an idea swirls round in my brain, making it spin faster than the beer and mekong do. Of course. Of course. That's what I ought to have done years ago. Instead of trying to break my dam-fool neck on the speedways. Instead of writing all those sexy poems—'Upon her Navel'—'O like a bow is the bony spire of her spine'—and all the rest of them. Instead of gobbling a whole bottle-full of barbital tablets; instead of drinking too much beer and mekong, which just makes you feel dizzy in the head and insecure lower down ...

I feel I want to be sick. As I did that morning back home when I opened my mother's letter, 'Dear Reggie, I have some news for you about Andy and Sheila Bowers which I fear will give you an unpleasant surprise ...' But don't think about that. As I did that night when Lanky Spence fell right in front of me, and I rode into him, and saw his face scream as my front wheel hit him. All the props on which you build up your confidence knocked from underneath you. Yourself not the injured, but the culprit, right from the start. And the crowd booing, booing, till your heart breaks ...

'Try the *dum-yam-pla,* Mr. Joy. See if you like.'

It is a fish soup so hot that it takes the skin off my uvula and brings the tears to my eyes and no matter how carefully I swallow it some of it always seems to go down the wrong way. But I keep on spooning it up to seem willing. And the tongue is delicious, and the salt fish superb—so rotten it just melts in your mouth, and if you were stuffed to the gills you could still down another bowlful of rice taking it along with such a delectable condiment. When I have finished, I have just that degree of discomfort in the midriff which tells me I have truly appreciated the food.

I lean back to take stock of my surroundings. There's no doubt it's a pretty scruffy shop. On the uneven floor wobbly tables and chairs are crowded together. Two walls are covered by glass-fronted cupboards full of bottles of beer. The third is covered by advertisements mostly exhibiting blondes more or less nude, and half a dozen actual nudes in which the palm for artistry goes to the model rather than to the photographer. There is no fourth wall. On that side the fight of the hurricane lamps spills into the street, turning the passing tricycles with their glinting spokes and festoons of coloured lights into fairy chariots, making every girl who stalks softly by, majestic in her bright-coloured sarong, straight-backed and slim of form, at least as beautiful as a fairy-tale princess.

Behind, the velvety blackness of the tropical night is sparkling with stars: a perfect backdrop. Somewhere not too far away a *ramwong* is going on: the metallic percussive music falls through the air in long drooping silvered speedy lines, like the bent stalks of a fountain dropping into a floodlit pool. There is terrific sexual excitement in such music, I sensed it the very day I landed in Bangkok. It is quite different from any other music—fierce and impatient yet at the same time relaxed and happy—the music of a people who die young but without regrets, worn out by the unbearable pleasantness of life, its alternating delights of desire and satiation ...

There is the usual palaver about paying the bill, everybody pulling out his wad (but some more slowly than others, and my own wallet always gets jammed in my pocket in the most exasperating fashion), and Boswell as an American makes the inevitable query, 'Let's see, how does this split up?' which wipes out all Point Four munificence in a few syllables, and convinces the Far East that the Americans are a nasty mean race. Anyway it is up to Prosit to pay and we all know it except possibly Boswell: Prosit is host and if anyone else pays, he will lose face; our offers are only show, proofs that we are solvent; by retracting them, with bitter smiles, we acknowledge our social master. Later each in his turn will get an opportunity to make the supreme gesture—to pay for all of us—and that will be a memorable moment in his life, remembered by all present, in case he tries to evade another moment of glory when his turn next comes around again.

We debouch into the street. All Siamese bronchial tubes are emptied into the gutter. The westerners exchange tritenesses about the night. How cool after Bangkok. What stars. And look, there's the moon. First quarter. No, third. Hell, I don't know. Who looks at the moon anyway, nowadays? With MSA generators humming round the globe?

'First we go to see *ramwong,*' Windmill says.

'Why don't we go in my jeep?' Boswell asks.

'I think not good. Better to walk. Then we can go *everywhere.*'

'Hell, don't tell me you guys are getting self-conscious about driving up to the old red lamp in a UN jeep,' Boswell jeers. To me he adds,

'When the Thai start to get shy about seeing floozies it'll be time for us westerners to go home—But that'll never happen,' he goes on cheerfully. 'The whole economy of this country is founded on rice and prostitution. It's the floozies that keep the bloody police in pocket money.'

'The old League of Nations did a lot to clean up the white slave traffic in different parts of the world,' I answer, being informative again, and wishing they'd got round to Korat.

'Is that so? Well I hope the UN has more sense.'

Custard-tart, his official mentor, says, 'You know, Mis' Bosswill, tonight our jeep is red jeep. It is not good to go for a walk in red jeep. Police jeep is red. We not want frighten all the ladies.' To me he continues: 'It is same when we go to country. Go in grey jeep, everyone come, very happy have injeckshun. Go red jeep, everyone run away into jungle. Police always much trouble. Always want money.' He turns to make the same observations to Windmill, speaking volubly in Thai: I hear the words *'rod deng mai di, mai ao-la'*—the red jeep is no good, not wanted—and the word *'tumluat'*—police—used several times.

'Christ, I could do with a leak,' says Boswell.

'Same here.'

We go to the side of the road and let go. It's the first time I've ever been guilty of indecent exposure in a city street. There is a grass verge and a hedge and the jet-black glint of water and over us the palm leaves chafing dryly, black against the now dove-grey, star-dotted sky. The fight of shop windows falls on our backs, women in wooden sandals go clacking by, but there's absolutely no likelihood of our being fined five bob, as there would be a mere ten thousand miles to the west, in dear old England.

'Jesus, what a relief,' I sigh, and this is another innovation: the first time in my life I have used that name as an expletive.

It's the first time I've seen the local Saturday-night hop. It's alfresco, of course. There's a core of blaze and racket, and round it a ring of men and boys all stilled and intent on the mystery. Without straining I can see over their heads. It's hard to understand what holds them so spellbound. In the centre of the ring a man is singing into an amplifier. He has been singing, or rather yelling, indefatigably ever since we reached Korat, and he seems all set to continue his performance till morning. Behind his voice the xylophones and cymbals rattle out their long rapid cadences and the amplifier bawls them, hideously distorted, to all points of the compass. There is a bench loaded with girls; they are garishly dressed, some in western dance frocks, some in local style; they are heavily made-up and look unspeakably bored. A few others are going round the ring with young local men. The pace is a fast slinky trot with wonderful twistings of arms and hands, like the smoke curling up from a fag-end in a draught. At two-minute intervals a whistle blows; singer and orchestra stop short in mid-phrase; there is a shuffle of feet as males clear off the floor, females return to their bench; in twenty seconds the whistle blows again, the music clatters off to a new rhythm, a new troop of males comes on, bows briefly to its choice on the form, hands it a ticket and follows it into the ring. The spectators stand agog, as if the show were wondrous.

'Why in hell do the Thai get such a kick out of this?' Boswell wonders. 'After all it's only just walking round in circles.'

There speaks a representative of the race which produced the jitter-bug. Because the dancers never touch, because they do no fancy steps but just keep sliding forward in concentric circles, girls on the outside, partners a little to the rear, because the girls' faces are as immobile as the painted waxen faces of dolls, because the dance consists mainly in those extempore posturings of arm and hand, it is a waste of time and fifty satang, stupid and pointless. He cannot read the erotic significance of the gestures (neither can I but I divine that it is there), cannot hear the edge of excitement in the music, isn't subtle enough to realize that promise has a flavour as rich as fulfilment's, that the easy embraces of the western dancehall spoil the palate for meatier fare, that this dance has something—he'd laugh like hell if I spoke the word—*holy* about it, the reverence of man for withdrawn mysterious exciting woman—a reverence felt even here, in a country where both sexes pretend to believe in the inferiority of one of them. 'Hey, Windmill,' he calls, grabbing my fat fellow traveller by the arm, 'Let's get the hell out of here. Take a walk.' The mekong seems to be working in him too.

'You not want dance *ramwong*?'

'Hell no. 'Nother sort of dance. Less go.'

'Less go, less go,' they all chorus.

So from the *ramwong* we cross a spacious square where the ancient main gate of the city stands up in white-washed magnificence under the moon. In a circle behind it stands a statue of Seratnari, Korat's Joan of Arc, a heroine who led the Thai against the Laos, or the Laos against the Mons, or the Mons against the Cambodians, I'm not sure which (Windmill's history notes are pretty garbled to my ears) but anyway she routed them whoever they were: there is a garland of faded flowers around her bronze neck and jeeps and *samlors* circle her in a clockwise direction. Scattered about are stalls, knee-high, tended mostly by women; the glare of carbide lamps falls seductively on their wares and not less seductively on themselves. This is the sort of setting in which I am accustomed to take my pleasure of the opposite sex, and fain would I stay here, feasting my eyes on so much colour and movement: 'Women and fruit,' I begin saying, mainly to Boswell, 'that's two of the elements in the world of Matisse: the third is sunlight, but that's cruel; this night is kinder to one's illus—'

'Hey, Mr. Bosswill, where you go? Why you walk so fast?' they are all shouting, and laughing and stumbling with the rest, I follow him, though my heart is in my mouth and my guts are working as they used to do before a big match.

'You know, I never touched beer until I was twenty-four years old,' I find myself saying. 'Then one night I came home from the dirt-track—this was after I'd packed up riding; I'd just gone to spectate—and accidentally at supper I knocked over my cup of tea twice running and my old man said 'you've been drinking' and he and my mother gave me such a bloody jawing, though I was stone-sober ... The very next night I went into a pub and got myself half a pint; I couldn't see any sense in being called a drunk if I wasn't one. That's the first time alcohol passed my lips.' (This is an incident from *Perfidy*: I don't want him to know that I first broke the pledge only one month ago.) 'Since then I've shipped enough to sink the *Queen Elizabeth*. I'm just wondering if it's going to be the same tonight.'

'Whadya mean?' he asks, not very interestedly.

But I can't bring myself to admit that I've never been to a whore-house before, and am fearful that if I take the plunge tonight I shall be going for the rest of my life. It is important to have men respect you. They never will if you claim to be chaste. Just assume you're a liar.

We enter a broad street flanked by shops. 'This is it,' says Boswell. 'I been here before.'

My bowels re-echo, this is it. I have a moment of panic. I want to cut and run for the hotel. A hundred nonconformist ancestors lying straight and austere in the churchyards of East Anglia turn in their narrow graves. I hear the clatter of old bones and prejudices and I am scared. 'Joyce is in a brothel and ten thousand miles away.' But out of every gallon of my blood only one pint does not derive from those graves. It's not miles which count, it's the years. When I was young and malleable, straight from the furnace as you might say, I was clutched in the pincers of tradition and laid on the anvil of life; I was shaped by cruel repeated hammer blows and every blow a pulpit fulmination ... Hey, where's Bozzy? Wouldst that thou wert thy famed namesake, chum; then couldst thou jot down this my dictum, and work it up tomorrow morning and put it into a book, *R. E. Joyce, His Life, Works and Women*, and I would be famous forever ...

Christ, it's a rotten feeling when your head does a lurch to one side and the liquid brains slop to and fro ...

Suddenly Custard-tart, who has been getting more and more excited since we left the *ramwong*, plunges to the left shouting 'Follow me, Mr. Joy. Come on, Mr. Bosswill, this way. Let us take a walk in here.' And he dives into a sort of tunnel, a square of black between dim-lighted shops. I stumble over rubble and potholes as we follow. The gateway to Hell? But that's supposed to be easy, smooth. Maybe I'm heading for Heaven. I know that road's all potholes, dug by the Devil. My old man's a parson and he told me. Worthy father of a silly fool. Believes everything he says. Says only what he believes. What would he say if he caught me now, half-seas over and hell-bent for Jezebel?

'Where'er she be—That not impossible Shee—Who shall command my heart and me—'

'What?' says Boswell. 'God, what a hole this is.'

'Where'er she lie—Lockt up from mortal eye—In the shady Leaves of Destiny—'

'You're drunk,' he says. 'Jesus, listen to that.'

I've already heard the sound and it has made my blood run cold.

'Strewth, what are they doing to her?' I cry, and almost reveal my innocence. But even as Boswell's eyebrows shoot up I retrieve my honour with a cynicism: 'Sounds as if she's having a baby.'

Windmill has heard the long-drawn moaning too and he laughs his cheerful laugh and cracks some joke in Thai. Then he says carefully in English, 'I think that woman earn her twenty tics the hard way.'

'One of the twenty-four hard ways,' I say and Boswell bursts out laughing and claps me on the shoulder. But all my viciousness is in the mind and that moaning, like a cat's before the explosion in spits and yowlings and flying fur, has made me want to spew. God knows it was bad enough at the Bolero last night, watching the girls vying for the men and the men for the girls and finally just after midnight the exodus in pairs, the girl I liked the look of best ... God, what a monster she had picked, and she practically had to hold him up, he was so tight ...

Suddenly I am sick of Thailand where Sex stalks naked and men and women hurt themselves and each other so much in worship of him. It is more decent to hurt yourself in solitude, shut in with yourself and the horror; self-flagellation is fit only for the cell ... But I am with this gang now; nor do I altogether want to escape.

It's a curious street. At first I can't make out what it is that's so queer about it. Then I suddenly realize. There are no lights. On both sides there are the continuous walls of houses but there are no windows. What pale radiance there is comes from the moon. And there is no loud talking or laughter. There are men everywhere but they only whisper to each other, conspiratorially. There is an atmosphere of furtive suppressed excitement. Footsteps make no sound in the powdery dust. We might all be creeping about. Most of the men are dressed in white; they glide silently by, like spectres. Here and there a white form, dim, motionless, intent, stands with its eye glued to a knot-hole in the wall. Light coming through the hole makes a pale splotch on the face, like luminous paint ... Once again, as at the *ramwong*, I get that feeling of being in a cathedral; sordid though this street is, the religious spirit of man is flowering in it, though in its crudest, most impure, most debased form ...

Custard-tart has stopped by a denser patch of black in the black walls.

'Do we go in here?' Boswell asks him.

'Of course. Go everywhere. See everything. Many young girl in here, very beauty-full, you must see them, maybe play game with them.' He catches sight of me and says, 'Mr. Joy, have you been to see Thai prostitute before?'

'No.'

'You must come often. Have you wife in Bangkok?'

'I have no wife anywhere.'

'No wife? You are very lucky. How old are you?'

That's usually the first or second question you're asked in Thailand and the fact that he hasn't put it to me before tonight shows how animated our proceedings have been. Then the door opens and I don't have to tell him even now. There's more important business afoot. (Or in bed.) Years seem to have slipped from Custard-tart's shoulders. He skips through like a boy. I follow like an old man, last of our group.

It is a ghastly place. Earth floor. Wooden walls on three sides, black with dirt and covered with cobwebs. There are a few photographs of past and present favourites of the establishment and a few pin-ups. The latter, cut from film magazines and pasted up years ago, are torn and peeling off; the old-fashioned hairdo's make the leers look obscene; I perceive that beauty has to be up-to-date to be seductive. A rickety staircase, little more than a ladder, goes up steeply into blackness. The fourth wall is a corrugated iron partition with a gap in it. Over the gap hangs untidily a dirty cretonne curtain. Benches are placed against the walls. There is no other furniture. And the place is deserted. One forty-watt bulb, encrusted with fly-droppings and hung high up, reveals this much to us.

'Where everyone go?' Windmill asks fretfully.

'All busy, I expect,' says Boswell.

'Let's go,' I urge. 'No good wasting time here.' Such a den cannot possibly house—that not impossible—

Then the cretonne is agitated and Custard-tart's face, which I hadn't missed, comes through, less like a tortoise's now than a leprechaun's. His forehead is shining with sweat, his huge glasses are glazed twin pools, his straight line of a mouth has split into two, revealing teeth which stay clenched even when he laughs. 'Come on,' he cries. 'Very speshull lady in here.'

The feel of that curtain which I have to get hold of revolts me. We pass down a damp passage between corrugated iron walls to a source of light. And damn—it is Sunday night. Out of the shadows I hear my old man's voice. 'Let us now sing hymn one hundred and seventy-two. "Lead, kindly light, amidst the encircling gloom." And mayst Thou not lead Thy children up the garden path, for Thy Son's sake. One. Seven. Two.' Then the organ sketching the first two lines, slowing up on the second, and the congregation rustling to its feet on the penultimate syllable, and then—

It is a smaller room than the first, and seems brighter-lit, and it contains a table and chairs, and a glass of dilapidated flowers, and its own staircase, and one girl. I hardly dare look at her. Very speshull lady? I can think of other terms that would fit better. Drab. Slattern. Trollop. Good old words. Fit her like a bra. Judging by their expressions Windmill, Prosit and Boswell agree with my view.

All the same I resent the candour with which they allow their faces to express their distaste. God knows I feel the same as they do, but I can put myself in her place, and I get hot on her behalf. They are sneering at her as they would at a piece of inferior cloth a salesman was trying to palm off on them. There is chivalry in me yet—Ivanhoe was never downright discourteous even to Jewish wenches—and I am angry with them.

Rebecca is indifferent. Her face is a mask. A pale, moon-shaped mask, puffy about the eyes and jaw-line. But those eyes are alive enough, dark and intense under the accanthic folds, with short, sticky lashes: the eyes, I suddenly perceive, of those little patient ponies of the East which have been beaten and starved all their lives and expect nothing but thrashings and starvation forever, being unable to conceive of death. Her arms are brown, the upper arm fat, with a slack curve of muscle abaft the bone; the forearm slimmer, ending in beautiful hands, as good as Sheila's. Windmill says something to her and suddenly she laughs, the red daub of mouth divides into two with teeth between. Four or five are gold, and one is missing altogether. She talks to him huskily.

I gather that all the other girls are engaged. She doesn't seem to expect any of us to want *her*. She makes no attempt to seduce us. She seems dead from the mouth down.

'Mr. Joy, you want?' Custard-tart shouts to me.

I don't by any means, but I hate to hurt her feelings.

'Of course he doesn't,' Boswell says. 'Rejoice is an artist, a poet. He's like the rest of us, he wants to get the hell out of here. Come on, less go.'

'Less go, less go,' they all shout, and we all troop out. I can't help looking back. She is lighting a cigarette that Windmill gave her, and she stares straight back at me with sombre unblinking eyes. I am sorry to be leaving. She is about as attractive as a lavatory seat. But she would do. I feel the first tingling of interest in our expedition. Can it be that amidst all this filth and unloveliness—

'Till that ripe birth—Of studied Fate stand forth—and teach her dear steps to our Earth—

'Till that divine—Idea take a shrine—Of crystal flesh wherein to shine—'

'What in God's name are you muttering about?' Boswell ejaculates.

Not for the world would I tell him. And anyway his attention is instantly diverted. For the first room we entered is no longer empty. On a bench against one wall sit two girls. On the bench against the opposite wall sit three young men. The latter are looking at the former. The former don't seem to be looking at anything in particular. They sit awkwardly with their legs to one side, supporting the weight of their bodies on one arm. The Thai as I have already noticed are a remarkably supple race, and their supporting arms are not straight but kink inwards at the elbow, as a westerner would say, the wrong way. One is dressed in a yellow blouse and a sarong like a navvy's handkerchief, red with white spots; her brow is of the kind called beetling, and overshadows her other features—the great deepset brown eyes, the small tilted nose—except for protruding lips, which are peony-red and startling; she is maybe seventeen years old. The other is more seasoned, with dangling hanks of hair and a dangling lower jaw—the adenoidal type. *Her* blouse is green with red, white and black flowerets on it; her sarong is black. Her toes, bare in wooden sandals, are the scarred spatulate toes of one who seldom wears shoes.

'Humph, dishtinct improvement,' says Boswell, and drops down on an empty bench.

'You like? You want?' cried Custard-tart instantly. He has all the instincts of a pander. He approaches the younger of the two girls and tries to catch hold of her hand. He says a few words to her in Thai but she doesn't reply, only gives him one surly glance and turns away again.

'I think she very good,' he tells Boswell. 'Her breasts very hard. You come and feel.'

'Hard as goddam rocks, I expect,' says Boswell dismally, but to my dismay he heaves himself off his bench and drops between the two girls. Ostentatiously they wriggle away from him. He puts his arm around the younger one and grabs a handful of flesh. For five seconds there is no reflex. Then she tries to shake herself free. The belatedness of the movement amounts to an invitation and its nature must be gratifying to Boswell's arm. He laughs and she makes an offended exclamation and strikes out at his chest. It is an ineffectual female slap that titillates rather than intimidates and he laughs again. Then she smiles, unwillingly, it seems, turning her head so he can't see. If it wasn't that her mouth is so plastered with paint it would be an attractive smile. It creates a deep dimple in one cheek.

Custard-tart is in ecstasy. He speaks to the girl urgently and she replies dubiously and he urges her again and suddenly she twists into Boswell's lap and puts her arms around his neck and presses herself against his Hawaiian flowerbed, giggling. His face appears beaming over her shoulder and his eyes are screwed up but Custard-tart shrieks (like Lawrence's tortoise) 'Her breasts, Mis' Bosswill, they good not good? Very hard, I think' and Boswell opens his eyes and says, 'Not hard at all, but getting harder. No toomers.' The pronunciation is so American I almost miss the word. 'Plenty of dimpling, I think, but non-carcinomatous, not pathological at all. Hey, Rejoice,' he shouts, catching sight of me, 'what you looking so effing miserable for? Horse piss making you feel sick?'

'Just bored,' I say feebly.

'What, in a brothel?' he yells. 'It isn't our sex that gets bored in brothels. Take a seat, pal. Make yourself at home.' The girl on his knee objects to his attention wandering from her and with a petulant shimmy brings it back to herself. His hand, very white and long-fingered, lingers down her spine. Shamefacedly I slink to the only unoccupied bench. The three young Thai men on the neighbouring form—they are only young country boys in shirts and shorts with check scarves tied round their waists, but one of them has a battered Homburg too—watch me and grin. They are more sophisticated than the rich westerner. I flush.

'Mr. Joy. You want this other lady? Very beauty-full.' Custard-tart at work.

Front her, accost her, board her, woo her, sir knight. The raddled hag.

'She has hollow cheeks and a hollow chest,' I say, struggling to sound tough and at my ease. 'No, thanks.'

'What is wrong?' Windmill joins in the arraignment. 'Why you sit alone? You must enjoy yourself. Make like at home. Anything you want to do, these girls must let you.' He tries to get the disengaged one to cross to me.

I look at her. She looks at me. The divine spark is not kindled. Undoubtedly she would let me do anything as Windmill said but there's nothing I desire to do. Except clear out. When can I decently do that?

'My chace hath another hart in view,' I say. Christ, why am I getting so depressed? The mekong?

But it isn't that and I know it. It is those austere white bones ten feet below the blowing nettles paled by the fenland moon. It is the voice of my old man, 'You will find my text this evening in the Gospel according to Saint someone or other, chapter this or that, verses so and so.' It is knowing that I am not an ordinary sinful man, the type who commits this sort of enormity in a light-hearted manner and forgets it tomorrow. It is memories of Sheila. Syphilophobia. And my ingrained timidity ...

'I just want to look around,' I say. 'But I don't fancy anything here.' I try to sound like a fish-buyer looking at boxes of haddock. 'Isn't there some other joint we can go to?'

Windmill, Prosit and Custard-tart are eager to try elsewhere. But Boswell has his nose in that girl's hair and his hands inside her blouse, one behind and one in front. He is making a lot of noise. The three young Thai boys, obviously unused to seeing a westerner unbend, are deriving entertainment from his performance. The girl suddenly grabs his hands and jumps up from his lap. She holds his hands in both of hers and tries to pull him to his feet.

'Bai,' she commands, jerking her head over her shoulder. *'Bai.'*

'She want you to go to bed with her,' says Custard-tart. 'You want?'

'Why not?' says Boswell. 'What are you guys going to do?'

'If you want her, we wait for you here, while you finish your game.' He talks to the girl who answers briskly and then returns to tugging

Boswell's arms. 'She say she want thirty tic.'

'Thir-tee tics!' Boswell exclaims. 'Jesus, she must have a pretty exclusive brand of spirochetes, if she wants all that for them. That's nearly two dollars.'

Custard-tart addresses the girl again and she pulls even harder at Boswell's arms. She is really rather pretty, if she wasn't so daubed up, and when she stops tugging momentarily to tuck her blouse into her belt of brass links there is grace in the movement and her form has neat girlish curves under the gaudy cloth. She says something more and grabs Boswell again. *'Bai, bai, bai,'* she orders him peremptorily.

'OK, she say twenty tic,' Custard-tart interprets. 'I fix it.'

I'd give her thirty—maybe more—I'd give her anything she asked for, I catch myself thinking to myself, but Boswell seems to be still hesitating and losing patience. The girl stamps her foot and re-seats herself on his knees. Why are you holding out on me, her expression seems to say, when you are demonstrably so ready to pay up? What occidental oddity of behaviour is this? She puts her arm round his neck and nestles her cheek against his. I desire her myself now, well, slightly. If Boswell renounces his claims ...

But at this point, fate intervenes and what was up till now merely a sordid night out becomes a red letter night, one of those dates in your diary which in future years you will read with special pleasure or skip with a feeling of pain, it is far too early yet to tell how it will all look to the memory, the one thing you certainly know is there'll never be a forgetting, tonight will be sewn into the consciousness of Reginald Ernest Joyce, it is giving a new twist to his character.

For the girl coming down the rickety staircase now from the regions of gloom above is not one of those multitudes of girls—'inopportunely desired on boats and trains' as Louis MacNeice says—whom you have noted swinging along roads with that swift hip-dipping gait of the woman under a laden shoulder-pole, or riding in *samlors* with their noses up, or stooping in pools to wash the family water buffalo, or pulling their skirts down as they pass you on bikes, or bringing files at your behest, or lifting their blouses to feed other men's heirs: no, this is one of the 'very speshull ladies' whom Custard-tart mistakenly sought for in the inner room, a lady like Sheila, your love for whom has held you in thrall these four long years, or Annette, or Dilys, who seemed to the youth you were then—that very speshull youth, these ten years dead—La Belle Dame Sans Merci, Helen, Beatrice, Dulcinea, yes, Moll Flanders too: Woman, to put it in one fruity word, with all the solace for man that word implies to the hapless bachelor: Woman personified in one woman's form ...

I know it when only her sandalled feet and firm brown ankles have descended out of the dark; it's a premonition, as if Venus were descending feet-first out of a thundercloud, to me, some especially handsome mortal, marked for an early translation to her sphere. The long slim sarong, surrounding her in an orange shell on which spiky diamonds of gold strike subdued cabbalistic spirals, confirms the impression. Oh, how can I know that the parts concealed within this flattering vest are very speshull ones, parts that I have been seeking ever since Sheila's (promised only) were snatched away, parts that could transport a man from earth to inexpressible heavens? The belt of glinting copper links is the zone of Venus and above it her fine solid form is encased in a dead white slip that fits like a glove and contrasts with the rich brown skin. Thin shoulder straps cut direct paths over the broad well-modelled expanses of chest and back and from between them her neck rears up as proud as a swan's but not too long. I catch a glimpse of a wide-cheekboned face with narrowed dark slanting secret eyes and a sensually-bowed upper lip and swift-rounding chin; then a great cloud of shining black hair comes between it and me. She reaches ground-level and clucks in her sandals past the curtain and into the passage beyond. All my soul walks after her, yearning.

The girl with the hollow cheeks and the hollow chest gets up and sits on my knees. She laughs as she does so and that makes her start to cough. She sits bent up in my lap with one arm round my neck, trying to control her coughing. It is inevitable that I should put one arm round her steadyingly, I think comfortingly, too. I can feel the bones of her thighs at right angles to the bones in mine and her ribs moving under the thin flowered stuff.

'You like?' Custard-tart screams delightedly. 'That is good. This girl play very good game. I know. I play with her myself many time.' And he speaks encouragingly to the Corpse which stifles its coughing and suddenly gives me a wet noisy kiss on the cheek.

Boswell is looking at me and I say over her perfumed lank hair, 'Just because I like to eat horse piss they think I like to lie with cadavers too.' Thoughtfully I have chosen the transatlantic word. 'But there's more chance of catching phthisis than syph from this one.' My drugged tongue has a real job with that last sentence.

'I'd say there was equal danger of both,' Boswell says. 'Are you going to—?'

'No. I've only seen one good dame in this place.'

'Mine?'

'No. No. She'd do in an emergency, of course. But I mean the one that just went through.'

'Oh? I didn't see any.'

'I think she's coming back now.' For my ears have already learned to recognize the sound of her sandals. Sure enough she re-appears at the curtain and crosses to the ladder. She doesn't look at us after a cursory glance. In her hand she carries a pail with a bottle in it. She begins rather leadenly to ascend.

'Her!' Boswell exclaims.

So I've done it again. Seen beauty where others cannot. He thinks I have odd tastes in women as well as in eggs.

'You can't have that one now,' he says. 'When they have their blouses off it means they're engaged.'

There is the sound of a door being dragged to upstairs. The Corpse grabs my hand and makes me take hold of her breast. It is meagre and limp, with a stub-shaped nipple that feels like a cherry-stone. The Corpse gives a groan and shudder and throws both arms round my neck. As her mouth brushes by mine I am enveloped in a cloud of garlic. I part her arms and get up. I am too fastidious.

'Going?' Boswell asks.

'Yeah. But don't you bother.' He has made a move as if to dump his own load. 'You go ahead and have a good time. I guess I'm tired. Train journeys always wear me out.' That's a lie but it will do. 'I had to be up at five this morning, you know.'

With extreme American ceremony he has to rise and shake hands. It looks as if I'm breaking up the party. Custard-tart will never admire me again. Windmill looks glum. The two girls examine me sideways with hostile eyes, muttering to each other. Prosit is deputed to accompany me to the hotel.

What a fuss about nothing. I feel them all draw a breath of relief as I leave. That goddamned Puritan son of a bitch.

Outside the moon has gone higher and smaller and the ghosts in the alley are few. In a quiet corner is a *samlor* with two men and a girl in it. Her face, laid back on the back of the seat, is white as chalk. The rest is shades of blackness. They make no sound.

'Mr. Joy,' Prosit begins,—his conversational powers are strictly limited—'have you go to India?'

Well, I landed in Karachi for forty minutes. There was a ground hostess there, I remember. I reply in the affirmative.

He braces himself for his set-piece. 'Mr. Joy, how long time you stay in India?'

Oh Sheila, Sheila, Sheila. Oh Venus already engaged. Oh girl with lovely depraved Mongoloid face leading that drunken sot out of the Bolero last night, self-sold to him till this morning for one hundred tics ...

'The next time I come here.' I say, ignoring Prosit's question, 'I want to be jusht a little bit more drunk.'

Back at the hotel I strip off quickly and climb in naked under the mosquito-net. It is a huge bed. I can lie in it at any angle without overhanging the edges. There would be room in it not only for my bronze Venus and me, but for Custard-tart and the Corpse, and Boswell and his sweetheart too; and at a pinch for Prosit or Windmill and whatever they will pick up. It is so damn big, it is lonely. I toss and turn, distressed by the heat, by the rich foods and sickly spirits in my guts, by my quite incommensurable folly, by my frustration, by everything; and finally I get up and tramp the room, feeling gaunt and naked and upset like Rodin's St. John ...

Boswell will have finished by now. She will have arisen from his side. He will stretch and yawn and contentedly, lazily, start putting on his shoes again. No doubt about his virility; he has proved it once again to his own satisfaction and one witness's. Now his only desire is to get back to this hotel, to the room next door to mine, and sleep. I hope the mean bastard gave her thirty tics. Ten bob. Surely to Heaven she's worth that. Any woman that will let a perfect stranger ... And he's an expert with some UN organization, presumably rolling in the stuff ...

My mouth is as dry as the ashes under Lena's kitchen grate. On a modernistic teak table there is, in a padded wicker basket with a padded wicker lid, a brass teapot which is hot to the touch. I turn one dainty cup right way up in its dainty saucer and fill it. The tea is warm but stale. Horse piss. There's also a large glass flagon containing water. I try that. It's lukewarm but I must have something. I swallow several cups.

If only I were like other men. Like Boswell and the rest of tonight's grisly crew. Like those Siamese yokels sitting dumb and watchful on that form ...

In fact I am the antithesis of the Pharisee. I do not thank God that I am not as other men are. I am ready to curse Him because He has made me different. Oh I know this is only the other face of spiritual pride, just as prudery is the obverse face of lust. But I'm not bothered about right or wrong tonight. I am staring straight at Reginald Ernest Joyce and seeing him stripped. I see that the said Reginald Ernest would cheerfully change places with Prosit—yes, gladly accept that skimpy form, that enormous *bouche*—if, with them, he could take on too Prosit's easy manner in society, Prosit's uncomplicated delight in the company of those—whores, I suppose one must call them ...

Once, I believed there was no such thing as a bad woman. I called that phrase a contradiction in terms. In the novel it took six months to write and three minutes to tear up I called it that. But do I believe it now? Can Sheila be forgiven? Were all those girls at the Bolero last night victims of circumstance? The one I liked—the Mongol, let's call her that—if she didn't like the job, if it was just the only job she could do, she seemed to be putting an excellent face on it. I watched her for a long time as she sat first at a table alone, smoking quietly, casting her narrow dark eyes thoughtfully around the place. Once they dwelt on me, but only for a brief indifferent moment, then they moved on. When all those Yanks blundered in with their shirts flowing and disposed their endless limbs in a cluster of wicker armchairs she still went on smoking quietly, but she had them under survey, and after a time she got up and walked casually past them. She had taken off her little gold jacket and was in a gold evening dress which left her chest and shoulders bare and magnificent. She walked by them twice and when she returned to her table one of them went up to her and asked her to dance. Soon she was dancing with them all in turn and in the intervals sitting at their table, drinking a long green drink and smoking a lot. Then that drunk came in and somehow before long she was at *his* table, talking earnestly to him and plying him with whiskies. Two or three of the Yanks who had danced with her the most got huffy about it but in the end it was the drunk she took out. She had to put her arm round his waist to steady him, and she didn't seem any too sober herself ...

Why do I keep thinking about that cow?

And these girls tonight. What is the history behind a mere child such as Boswell is still possibly fondling? Or a truly beautiful woman like the Venus—why does she have to go up a stepladder to her tryst armed with a bucket like a charwoman? And then come down and sit in that filthy ante-room until some other Reginald Ernest, not quite so inhibited, not quite so preoccupied with morals, his own and other people's, sees in her the possibility of a moment's satisfaction, and springs the required twenty tics?

Oh God, tonight is going to be worse than even normal nights.

I get in under the mosquito-net again but sleep is impossible. I don't want to read. I have no barbital. I get out of bed again, almost tearing the net down in my fury, and walk up and down, up and down. The room isn't big enough to contain my restlessness. The night isn't big enough to swamp my despair. I want to do something violent, but what? What can I do?

'You could go back there again.'

I stop in the midst of a pace, aghast. The idea has sprung into my brain from God knows where and it leaves me trembling. I lick my lips and drop into a chair.

Go out of the hotel. Turn right. Right again at the first turning. Then the first on the left. Then, just past the cinema with its glare, the black tunnel on the left again. I think I could find the same door.

I sit stock-still, stupefied by the temerity of my thoughts.

If I go now—but I can't do that. I might meet Boswell and the gang. They'd think I was daft. (I am.) I would have to wait till they were safely stowed away.

I am shaking with sexual excitement. Shall I do it? If I do, I will prove myself a man. If I don't, then still, all tonight and tomorrow and forever perhaps, the same phobias, the same sense of inadequency, the same debilitating knowledge of one's never-ending adolescence ...

Mechanically I start putting on my clothes. I am amazed at myself. Can I really be going to do this thing? Am I going to be such a bloody imbecile? Stay safe in your hotel, Reginald Ernest boy; be a good lad, worthy of your beloved Sheila ...

Already I can hear Boswell and Windmill returning. They come stumbling up the steps, talking noisily. Boswell's shoes thump to the door next to mine, and I hear him cursing as he searches for his key. Then the sound of it in the lock.

'Well, goo'ni', Windmill. You're a good kid.'

'Goo'ni', Mr. Bosswill, Goo'ni'.'

He pads away to his own room and Boswell enters his. He is humming that song, 'I wonder—who's—kissing her—no-oo-ow ...' He drops his shoes with two loud bangs and goes to the bathroom. I hear him dipping up water from the jar and sloshing it around.

Now is the time or never. I am trembling like a leaf. It takes cunning to open the door soundlessly, it is trickier still to lock it without making a noise. But I succeed, and slip the key into my pocket, and cross to the stairs. Sitting on the top one, I put on my sandals. When they are on I sit for a further moment, sweating. I could still go back to my room. It would look silly, but to no one but God and me. And perhaps I could get the Mongol when I return to Bangkok ... But that would mean six more weeks of being baffled and incomplete. No, no. Tonight I'm just drunk enough to carry this business through, get it over once and for all ...

I hear Boswell return to his room and his voice shouts across the partition which divides it from mine. 'Hey, Rejoice, you asleep already? You missed a rattling good time tonight, pal. And when I say rattling—'

I go down the stair, across the quadrangle, through the gate of the hotel, and turn right. A dog lying in the dust raises his head sleepily, then snuggles his nose back on his hind legs. Nobody else even seems to see me. And across the square the *ramwong* is still clattering away, the amplified voice of all Nature's fiercest obsession ...

Four

Thus it comes about that the Reginald Ernest Joyce who returns to Bangkok is a different person altogether from the Reginald Ernest Joyce who left that city six weeks earlier.

It isn't merely that I have been into comparatively unknown places and seen sights I never expected to see except by grace of other men's cameras. The real reason for the renascence of my spirits is that for the first time since my speedway days I feel I am a success. I am a success at my job. I have been a success with the Thai and Chinese merchants with whom it is my job to be successful. And—this is the point that is most important for my ego—I have been a success with the girls. My pistol-butt is no longer un-notched; my belt is hung with scalps.

Seated in the first class coach I find myself wondering how things would have worked out if I hadn't drunk mekong on top of beer that night and so got up enough courage to cross the windy Rubicon from virginity to manhood. I suppose I would have gone round Northeast Thailand as previously I had gone round Britain and Bangkok imagining that I was deriving enormous pleasure from the things that an intelligent westerner is supposed to derive pleasure from—cloudscapes and views and the western books in my suitcase—deluding myself that these pleasures were all I needed from life, that savouring them I actually knew a greater contentment than the run of men around me who seek their joys on grosser levels. I suppose I would have taken photographs of temples (fairy-tale architecture), houses on stilts (reality), boats on rivers (such groupings and atmosphere), the different types of oxcarts (native ingenuity), weaving (they are not without a sense of beauty), the different methods of pounding rice (quaint of course, even a little laughable, but the educated person doesn't laugh at the backward). And back in Bangkok I would have developed my photographs and received everyone's congratulations and known in my heart of hearts that I had missed something, as I've been missing something all down the line wherever I've gone ...

But as it is, I have hardly taken a snap, hardly read a book, and not missed my symphonies one whit. For the first time I have been able to take a direct sensual pleasure in the world instead of getting my ideas of such delight second-hand through the works of writers and artists. I've been living in the moment as I was never able to do before except during the seventy frantic seconds of a speedway race when to let your concentration relax at all was to court disaster. Then it was largely fear that enabled me to live fully one minute at a time, six times a night, two or three nights a week. Now, curiously, it's the opposite, the conquest of fear, that is enabling me to enjoy twenty-four hours a day.

Curiously, too, I am beginning to feel less alien in Thailand than I used to feel in Islington. I am actually beginning to feel at home in this country which is more like a lake with islands than like land with lakes. I never saw so many different sorts of birds in my life. I never saw so many happy people in boats. They sit in the sterns of their boats, facing forwards, paddling with long lazy strokes; the women wear enormous straw hats perched high on their heads like upturned ornamental flower-baskets. The light is so intense you can count the leaves on a tree a hundred yards away. The stations are infrequent but kaleidoscopic with crude colour; their names are set forth in the Thai script which looks very much like the Hebrew in my father's study at home, and also in English. Ban-phagi, Ban-pa-in, Klong Rang Sit, Ayudhya ... The last is the ancient capital of the country. A few ruined pagodas soar above the tree-tops, themselves covered with bushes ... Don Muang is a sea of corrugated iron glittering in the sun; incredible that here I landed only last September—a lifetime ago—scared and forlorn ... Bangsue, and the first ragged edges of the city ...

Windmill wakes up and begins to prepare for disembarkation. Characteristically, his first act is to comb his hair. But there's still a few minutes left before life need begin again.

Suddenly I recall one hour in the remote district of Pyakaphoom. It was perhaps the most perfect hour I have known, except for some few dead ones passed with Sheila in a previous incarnation. We had finished our business and eaten and drunk too much and Windmill and the rest had disappeared for their siestas. I went out into the blinding heat of the afternoon, down the street of baked mud, into a lane of deep sand twisting through the jungle. There was no one about; even the birds had fallen silent, too hot to sing. I turned down a path through a thin scatter of trees and soon found myself on a sort of heath raised above the surrounding forest. Shade was hard to find but after a while I came on a patch under a silver-barked tree soaring upwards out of the clumps of bushes that dotted the heath. I sat down. How would I have spent the ensuing minutes a month before? In lugubrious yearnings over Sheila or in painful mental woodwork shaping another poem, another coffin to engulf the remains of my love. How did I spend them now? Using my eyes to see, my ears to hear, my nose to smell. There were fifteen different sorts of leaves within a few feet of me. There were six different sorts of flowers and the most beautiful were some that were already dead, their withered petals folded like classical draperies. There were twigs and stems of many patterns and a dozen sorts of insects flying and crawling around and upon them. There was a sky you could hardly look at, it was so bright. And there was solitude, and this wonderful new ability to be happy even when idle. Here was a sort of Eden, and I a sort of Adam in it: a man just born adult and fully alive to Eden's beauty. My perceptive powers had been awakened: the poet, the philosopher, had become an empiricist, and found delight at last ...

'You'd better put your shoes on,' says Windmill. 'That's Petchburi road crossing. In five more minutes we there.'

Walking up the platform at Hualalomphong Station I am conscious of a new swagger in my gait. For the first time in my life I don't feel apologetic to the porter. Heretofore I have always suspected in him a person superior to myself but forced by unkind circumstances to act as my minion. Now I ask myself, 'Has *he* had seventeen different women in six weeks, and one of them half a dozen times?'

The office car has come to meet us. Duen looks like an old friend. I return his golden smile with one that is only ivory but probably more sincere than his is. I say to Windmill 'How are we going to arrange this? Shall we go to your place first, or mine?'

Duen says, 'First to office. Mr. Samjohn want to see you.'

My spirits droop, for whatever my new attitude to porters I still don't feel equal to the boss and I was hoping this interview could have been put off till the morning. It is four-ten now; the office shuts at four-thirty; 'Don't you think it's absurd—?' I begin.

But Windmill laughs, and now his eyes laugh with his lips, for we are good friends. 'Never mind,' he says. 'I think Mr. Samjohn not want eat you. I think he must be very pleased with you after this trip. Me too,' he adds with satisfaction.

Our reception in the outer office is certainly more heart-warming than anything I had expected. Somboon leaps up with a glad cry and seizes my hand. The three pretty girls, all identically clad in transparent white blouses and short blue skirts, smile their identical lipsticked smiles. Frost bawls, 'Hey, where you been, you two? Get lost in a teak forest?' And even Drummond allows an aborted grin to pass across his hollow-cheeked face before he burrows back into his ledgers again. Windmill, puffed by the stairs, falls into a chair in exaggerated distress and one of the girls flies for iced water for him. Somboon continues to fuss round me like a delighted pup, asking all the inevitable Siamese questions: 'Was it very hot? Are the girls pretty in Korat? Where are the girls prettiest, in the Northeast or Bangkok? Have you A Friend in the Northeast?' Given that intonation the phrase means a girl, amateur or professional, with whom one sleeps. I think of Venus and nod. 'You must tell me about her,' he coos. 'Tonight you eat with me? My dear, dear friend?'

I shake my head indecisively—I am afraid of an invitation from Mrs. Samjohn. Then a bell rings, and I know what it means. One of the girls darts to the swing doors and returns quickly to say with a smile, 'Mr. Joy, Mr. Samjohn want to see you.'

'Now?'

'Now, yes.'

'Don't be fright-end,' Windmill calls after me.

But I am. Mr. Samjohn is rumpling his shiny pink brow over a chaos of papers. The ceiling fan, wheezing round and round above him, ruffles what is left of his hair and the corners of a hundred different sheets of paper on the desk. For some reason (I have noted this before) he never seems able to get a clean shave on the left side of his jowl; there are the usual white specks on the choleric skin, like grains of face powder. He looks furious, as usual. But to my amazement when he eventually looks up his face breaks into a grin and he says 'Ah, Joyce, glad to see you back again. Sit down. You're looking very fit. Must say the reports on your trip sound very healthy too. Cigar? No, you don't smoke. Wish I didn't. How about a beer instead?' He thumps his bell and when one of the three pretty heads is thrust through the swing doors, barks, 'Beer for Mr. Joyce. Small one.' He lights a new cigar for himself and finding a brimming ash-tray after search under the papers, crushes out his match in it. Through a thick haze he says, 'Beer, now. That was the one line you didn't do so well in. Why was that?'

'They don't seem to be partial to English brews. They prefer Danish or German.'

The two white tufts of eyebrow draw together ominously. 'What d'you mean, Joyce? English beer is the best in the world. You've got to push it, man. *Make* the blighters like it. You understand?'

'Yes, sir.'

'Too much continental beer is no good for anyone. Almost as bad as too much American beer. The Siamese need building up. They want something with plenty of good Kent hops in it. Something that will put weight on them, the poor little sods.' A bell rings in the outer office. 'What's that? Knocking-off time? Great Scott, how tempus fugits.' He shuffles the top layer of letters and then bangs his own bell again. Almost before the head automatically appears he shouts 'Cancel that beer, Mary.' (He calls all three girls Mary with an occasional inconsequential switch to Betty). 'Mr. Joyce won't have time to drink it now.'

'But—' the girl begins, and I observe that she has an opened bottle in her hand.

Mr. Samjohn sees the bottle too but perhaps he doesn't notice that the cap's off. 'Put it back in the fridge,' he orders.

'But—'

'And tell Mr. Windmill to come in here immediately.'

The head gives me a small commiseratory grin and withdraws. I judge I am redundant like the beer and rise.

'Oh, Joyce, one other thing before you go. Where are you planning to stay this time while you're in Bangkok?'

'Same place as last time.'

'That hotel?' He is actually looking a little uncomfortable. 'No need to go there really, you know. Plenty of room at the House.'

I resist the temptation to snap, 'Why, who's moved out?' No sense in starting ructions. 'Actually I like being at the hotel. It's not so much more expensive than being at the House. And anyway I'm only due to be in town for a few days—'

'Right, then off to Chiengmai with you.' He sounds relieved. 'Well, glad you're comfortable. Feel free to come to the House at any time. After all, you're one of us.—Ah, Windmill,' (as my stout guide parts the swing doors) 'glad to see you. Sit down. Have a cigar. Oh, don't be bashful, man. You've had a wonderful trip. More solid orders than you've ever booked in a single trip before, eh?—See you tomorrow, Joyce.—To what do you ascribe your success, Windmill, old man?'

Dearly would I like to hear the reply but Windmill maintains a discreet silence until the swing doors flop past each other behind me.

Back in the outer office I catch Mary, whose real name is Verchai, putting the beer back in the refrigerator as ordered. I shout, 'Hey, what are you doing?' in a scandalized voice and leap towards her. It is the first time I have raised a laugh in the office by intention; heretofore what laughs I have inspired have all been behind my back, provoked by my blunders and awkwardness. The new friendly note sounds sweet. I seize the bottle and drain it in three gulps.

Frost cries, 'Blimey, that's the first time I ever saw anyone actually drink one of the beers we sell. Better call an ambulance, Verchai, just in case.' He takes the bottle from me and holds it upside down so that all can see that it's too empty to drip even. 'Joyce, we owe you an apology. I mean Drummer and me. We completely misjudged you. I mean, when you first came, you *did* seem a bit of a pansy, damn it. You didn't smoke. You puked over your Scotch. And that night I had Daisy in—holy Christopher, you were like Mrs. Grundy herself, only worse. But, judging from what old Windmill's just been telling us, you've merely been biding your light under a bushel. Hell, don't look so windy, chum; he hasn't said anything bad about you; just made us envious of your powers, that's all.—Hey, Drummer, how many poor unfortunate women did *you* lay your first trip upcountry?'

'Too many.'

'My own tally was ten—no, eleven: for some reason I always forget one little Annamese in Mukdahan. She spoke French too. Now come on, Joycey, let's have the vital statistics. How many women have *you* really, honestly, truly, slept with, this last six weeks?'

Do they really want me to tell? 'I've lost count,' I lie defensively, and instantly they are all laughing again as if I had cracked a good joke. Verchai and the other girls are laughing along with the men and I would swear there is admiration in their sidelong glances, tinged with only the slightest hint of reproach ...

By a stroke of luck I get the same room I had before and that increases my sense of homecoming. I have a shower, my first for six weeks, and throw myself on the bed to savour my contentment. The electric fan, turning from side to side with perfervid attention to duty, sweeps me with a cool beam of air. On a chair within easy reach are a bottle—good German beer this time, ice-cold—a glass, and a plate of horse urine eggs garnished with sliced raw ginger. It's hardly the sort of tea my mother provides at Malderbury vicarage, but scones and strawberry jam are the other side of the world, and these are the items that I happened to fancy this afternoon, here in the Far Far East.

God, it's great to be back home again.

Not that the room has anything especially attractive about it. The bed, like most hotel beds in Thailand, is square and rather hard. There are, as always, two pillows (for nobody is ever expected to sleep alone in this amorous country, especially in a hotel), and two blankets, one each, neatly folded at the foot. No other covering unless you count the mosquito-net. There is one large window which opens onto a mango-tree; it is just a square hole in the wall, with bars and a flimsy curtain across the lower half; if it rains, you have to pull the shutters to and stew. You don't have to stew long, for the storms are so furious they quickly wear themselves out, and when they're over for a time it's almost too cool. The walls are pale green and bare, the teak floor bare, the furniture minimal—one table, three chairs, and a chest of drawers. The only touch of opulence is in the spittoon which is of brass and as big as a young milkchurn. In fact nothing is provided which is not absolutely essential to the physical well-being of a never-ending series of casual occupants arriving mainly in pairs. But light and space and air have crept in too, and the place is clean, so the spirit soars.

At home there was the oilcloth in the hall, cold and hard to chubby bare knees. The thick prickly pile of the carpet under the dining-room table. The coal-cellar which stank of cats and gas leaking from the meter; a terrifying place, really, from which one was always glad to emerge alive. In the attic the toy train whizzed punily, disproportionately fast, between the stacks of old newspapers, which were mountains, and there was a window, high, small, covered with cobwebs, from which one could obtain an airman's view of the neighbours' gardens. The study was the sacred grove which one entered only by special invitation; it smelled of musty tomes and stale tobacco; one had to sit quiet on the floor looking at the steel engravings in a huge old Bible. Even Isaiah or was it Elijah being fed by ravens in the wilderness and Job smitten with boils had the frame and musculature of Samson or Joe Louis, but all the women subsequent to Eve, the Delilahs and Jaels no less than the Ruths and Virgin Marys, were monotonously anaemic, with worried expressions and voluminous clothes like nuns'. As for Eve, she was being tempted behind a frustrating twig in Plate One, and expelled from the Garden with her hand over the part which most aroused one's curiosity in Plate Two. Then there was the pantry, full of the pale smells of cold food, and the kitchen, from which one was forever being shoo'd, either into the hall, if it was wet, or the garden, if it was fine. Six bedrooms, six worlds, all but your own an adventure to enter.

Sure enough environment shapes you, but environment is more than the interiors of a few rooms. Environment was the copper fender round the hearth-stoned hearth and the giant scuttle which emitted, when its iron handle dropped on its iron black cheek, a bass note if full and a tenor note if empty, but it was also the *Children's Encyclopedia,* in which eight battered volumes you browsed by the hour. Environment was the tools in the toolshed, the hanging rakes and spades and forks and hoes, the scythe you were forbidden to touch with its Ivanhoe blade tied up in an old sack, the lawn mower smelling deliciously of oil and grass; but it was also aniseed balls at twenty for a ha'penny, and putting three of your six weekly pennies into the red velvet bag on the end of the comic pole, and having your hair cut by Mr. Styles, who had only one eye, and was Scoutmaster, and that was why you couldn't be a scout. Environment was a million things—the speckled Ancona cock who once nipped your finger surprisingly hard when you were simply admiring him and had no intention at all (on that particular occasion) of depriving him of one of his tail-feathers, the kittens foolishly trying to climb the hollyhocks at the back of the herbaceous border, the snails amongst the mint which grew around the scullery drain; but it was also the wraiths, your parents, your brother, Ellen the maid and Tripp the gardener, who were so much filmier, so much less real, than furniture and worms and places. I suppose I was rather inhuman; perhaps all children are; but that's how the past looks ...

Denny was the only human being who seemed real. Andy was too much older than I—six years—and most of the time away at school. It was later when my hero-worship began, when I became a first-former in the school of which he was School Captain. He was captain too of both the soccer and cricket teams, the idol of all the small fry, a paragon I could never measure up to, but against whom I was always being measured ...

Jesus, what hell it was being Andy's brother at school. 'Come, come, Joyce junior, you can do better than this. Your brother—'

It was when I failed Matric for the third time that my life first began to go to pieces, I think. After that even my father, most sanguine of parents, could no longer conceive a future of academic brilliance for me. He had had it all mapped out for years; Andy, big and strong, endowed with rapid reflexes, was to be the man of action; I, by no means a weakling, but more studiously inclined, was to win the intellectual honours. And for ten years I was dutiful enough to narrow my chest over my father's ambition for me. But then suddenly—

Suddenly around the age of fourteen I realized that I liked the sun outside my window far better than even the fattest book. I no longer wanted to narrow my chest over Shakespeare and Plato and all that gang, I wanted to expand it. For long my dreams had been Walter Mittyish and always there was a naked girl in them, usually some local wench years older than myself, and myself heroic amongst the roaring flames, or the icy seas, or the falling bombs, for her sake. And now these dreams became more important than books, they occupied all my thoughts even in the classroom. For the next three years the headmaster's reports grew progressively more anxious: 'Not concentrating.' 'Must apply himself more diligently to the subjects he dislikes.' 'Must realize that the time has now come to make a final effort.'

The list is up on the board. I approach with dread in my bowels. My eyes are so glazed with apprehension I can't sort out the letters that form the names. And there's no need. Amongst the press of excited boys, all my juniors (for my own year has passed out either to the university or into the great big busy world where I shall never do any good), I hear the voice of Bambridge, that never-to-be-forgotten voice: 'Crikey, look where old Joyce is. Still running true to form.' And then the burst of laughter, but some faces reddening and growing apologetic as they turned and saw me standing ...

So they put me down in Fourth Commercial, which was a disgrace, especially for Joyce major's brother. (By then he was a planter in Kenya and therefore still a heroic figure.) And I was two years older than the next oldest boy in the form ...

Christ Jesus, why go through that again?

I get up and go across the room. On the table is my mail. Only six letters—one per week. One from the bank. One from my mother. One from old Slither Higson, who used to ride with me on the cinders. And three from Lena.

I sit down on one of the hard wooden chairs. When I receive more than one letter at a time I like to read them in an ascending order of interest. I sort these out carefully. First the bank statement—that will only confirm what I already know. Then my mother's—that will be only parish small-talk. Third, Lena's—what sort of letters will she write? Finally Slither's, which is bound to be good and full of speedway news.

The bank statement is certainly gratifying. Although I have not stinted myself since I arrived in this country, I have saved more than one third of that part of my income which is being paid here.

I slit open my mother's sixpenny airmail form. It begins more or less as I expect:

Dear Reginald,

It is time I wrote to you to say thank you for your letters telling us about your aeroplane journey and your life in Bangkok. I am sorry you are having to live in a hotel. I have never stayed in a hotel in my life but I am sure it must be very uncomfortable. Aren't there any good boarding houses there where you can get good English food and proper attention? I know you are grown-up now and able to look after yourself but I cannot help feeling that the most undesirable characters live in hotels and I expect it is much worse in a foreign country than it is in England. You must also be careful with the food—the Chinese meal you described sounded quite dangerous to me, especially as you ate it in a shop which you said was very dirty.

Bangkok sounds a beautiful city from your description but I am sure really nice girls would not bath in canals in full view of the public even with all their clothes on as you describe.

Last Sunday your father was unable to take the services as he had a very bad night with pain round the heart caused by wind. I had to ring up Mr. Pottle the curate at Cotters Green who came over and did his best.

Your father is all right again now. I can't think what upset him. We only had cold beef and apple pie for supper.

We had the first fog of the winter yesterday, then it rained and the fog cleared. This morning when we got up it was snowing—much to our surprise. We don't often get snow so early in Malderbury. It didn't last long but has been cold and dull all day: but I expect you are sweltering in the heat and have almost forgotten what snow looks like.

Last Wednesday, I went down to Bantingham to see Andy and his good lady. As I expect you have heard, Sheila has been very ill. She was going to have a baby but shortly after you left something went wrong. Of course it happened in the middle of the night and the farm is miles from anywhere and not on the phone and there was only their two selves in it so Andy had to do everything himself. It wasn't until about ten the next morning that the policeman providentially called with a summons because Andy's pigs had got into Mr. Templeton's winter oats—that horrid man next door—and they were able to send Sheila to hospital. She's up and about again now but very pale and thin and she won't be able to help Andy with the milking all through the winter ...

Follows parish gossip, and then at the end:

By the way, Sheila asked to be remembered to you. She looked dreadful, poor girl. I'm sure Andy has some very bad luck, and he works so hard.

Poor girl, she looked dreadful. I had intended to spend the evening in the hotel but after reading those words the room seems intolerable, so I dress and go out.

I feed in Rajadamnoen Avenue. That is the Pall Mall of Bangkok. I think it is even wider than London's, and night augments the amplitude of its proportions. I sit at a table on the pavement outside a restaurant which has the seductive word DOUGH set up in modernistic wrought-iron lettering at the door. Enormous bats dive past my head and puzzled frogs jump and ponder, jump and ponder, between the chair legs. I order chicken salad, scrambled eggs on fried bread, cheese sandwiches, banana in cream, and beer. It is my first western food for weeks and in spite of my concern for Sheila—poor girl, poor girl—I enjoy it. A cool breeze is blowing down the desert of concrete; it stirs the leaves that catch the light of the lamps and my hair too and the folds of my shirt. The cars speed by, long streaks of smooth tinselled dimness, and in that vast expanse of thoroughfare their horns are muted and sound pleasant like a chorus of bullfrogs in paddyfields far away.

Poor girl. She looked ghastly. A conversational formula. The first two phrases that occurred to the speeding pen. Dead verbiage. Yet they have brought Sheila back to life again, made her as real as if she was sitting at the other side of the table ...

Damn and blast the poor girl ...

For the fact is that during these last few weeks I have been getting my obsession under control. For the first time in four long years, ever since I first met her—

What did she see in me in the first place, I wonder? She came to that hospital to see Greg who was sick in the next bed. Nothing much the matter with him: just an appendix. I was in that time with a fractured knee-cap. Literally tied to the bed with a ton-weight, as it seemed, on my left leg. She was wearing a pale blue jacket and skirt and a cream blouse and her cloud of hair, hardly less pale than the blouse, fell over her shoulders in an ordered sequence of shallow waves. Shc kissed Greg and made him blush.

I was staring at her pretty frankly and I saw her cast more than one covert glance my way and when Greg finally got round to introducing us—'Sheila, I'd like you to meet Reggie Joyce'—she wasn't merely polite, she was pleased.

'Reggie Joyce? The name sounds familiar.'

'Of course it does. He rides for the Leopards. He's ridden for England twice.'

She had half-risen from her chair by Greg's bed to cross to me and shake hands but at these words her face clouded and she sat down again. 'Are you really a dirt-track rider?' For the first time I felt the force of that ice-blue candid gaze bent full upon me. Clearly I was being measured against some preconceived notion of my breed. 'I think it's a horrible sport.'

It was my living. 'Have you ever seen any?'

'Yes. Once.'

'I took her,' said Greg. 'It was an unlucky night. There was a bad pile-up. You remember Lanky Spence—'

'Somebody ran into him and broke his back,' Sheila interjected angrily. 'He died next day.'

'Not next day. Three days later.'

'It was murder,' Sheila said. 'Men killing each other for just a few pounds.'

It wasn't murder at all. Lanky was my friend. We rode as a pair and shared our point-money.

'I think it was an accident,' I said. I hated anyone to remind me of that night. It was the biggest blot on my copybook, then. But—'Did you stay to the end of the meeting?' I asked at length, when I'd managed to master my feelings. Because if she had, she was overstating her aversion.

'No. I just stayed till the next time that man—the one that did it—was supposed to race again.'

'Why'd you do that?'

'I wanted to see if he would.'

'And did he?' I did like hell, chased by my fears for Lanky, hoping I'd crash heavily and expiate my—

'Yes. And he won. But nobody cheered him. Nobody booed him either. When the announcer announced the result, there was just dead silence.'

The well-chosen word ...

'You hate the chap so much, I wonder you don't remember his name,' I said bitterly, and that gave Greg a clue, and his jaw dropped, and he put in hurriedly, trying to change the subject, 'D'you think Ma'll come to see me tomorrow, Shee?' She glanced at him in surprise at the interruption and then went on to finish what she had to say. Telling me off for the first time.

'Greg here wants to be a dirt-track rider. But if ever he did anything like that I'd never forgive him—even if he *is* my brother.'

Greg started to say something apologetic but I stopped him. 'Never mind, chum. She's right. It's a mug's game.' Then, to Sheila, 'So Greg's your brother, is he? I thought—I was afraid—'

Greg exploded in artificially hearty mirth. 'Heavens, no, Reggie. When I get engaged it will be to somebody really beautiful, not an old hag of twenty-three like this sister of mine ...'

That effectually changed the subject anyway.

I think of Slither's letter back in the hotel room. 'It's been my best season: Why the hell did you pack the game up Reggie? That last spill of yours wasnt too bad. What was it, six ribs and a collarbone. They are all bones that mend easy. Riding is more fun than slicing up bacon in a grosers in Islington I should think. Whats it like in Siam. What in hell are you selling to the natives anyway. The only injury I got this season was writers cramp from signing so many autograph albums. If you had any sense youd make a comeback next season. Honestly theres nothing to beat these days. All you have to do is stay in the sadle for 4 laps and youre in the money. One of the other 3 always falls off and that makes you a cert for a 3rd place at least ...'

I sit back awaiting the next course and Rajadamnoen Avenue fades and the pavement wide as a track becomes a track and I am riding round with both hands off the handlebars fixing my goggles (which was showing off but used to please the crowd) and coming up to the white line with my feet dragging, then with the other three moving up to the gate, revving up the engine with tense ringers on the clutch, eyes glued to the tapes. Suddenly they fly up, I let out the clutch and hurl myself forwards to keep my front wheel on the earth, that atavistic race for the first bend is on. In three seconds I am getting into my slide, cinders are peppering my face, it's Lanky and he's drifting away from the white line, he's going to fall, the others are too tight to me on my right, he's over in a cloud of sprawling limbs and stinking dust and I'm into him. I feel the soggy blow of his body stopping my front wheel and myself leaving the saddle and flying over him, a crack on my knee from my bike and the automatic relaxing of limbs to fall with as little damage as possible, the jar and double roll and looking up all right to see Lanky lying flat and still behind the two tumbled machines ... And that sick feeling in the heart: this time it's really bad.

'Bananas and cream, sir.' For the survivor, he might add.

Why the hell did you pack the game up, Reggie? Well, it wasn't because of Lanky. Nor because of half-a-dozen broken ribs. It was because of her. Her ultimatum. 'Either your career, as you call it, or me.'

I chose the better part as I thought but I chose wrong.

Women are such traitors. They fall in love with you because of what you are. But they think they would like you better still if they moulded you a little nearer their ideal. So they mould away and when you're thoroughly mouldy they wonder why they don't like you any more and lose interest in you.

For a fortnight after I sold my bikes and leathers she was more affectionate than she'd ever been. We got engaged. But it took me a long time to get a new job—no Matric, no special qualifications—and finally it was she who got me into her uncle's shop in Islington. She'd moulded me nearer her ideal, all right. I was miserable and she was disappointed in me.

Poor girl ...

Poor girl be damned. Poor Reggie, he's the real martyr.

I finish my beer. It's eight o'clock. Now what to do with the rest of the night?

I order another beer and cogitate. I wish now I'd accepted Somboon's invitation; I'm tired of entertaining and being entertained, but anything would be preferable to aloneness tonight. It's too hot to walk far. It's too hot to go to a movie. If I go back to the hotel I'll only brood some more. I don't want to go to the House: Frost will almost certainly be out; the others I can't abide. I don't know where Windmill lives, and anyway it would be a crime to disturb him tonight when once more he is submerging himself to the bosom of his family after six weeks of bemoaning his separation from them in the Northeast. And he's probably glad of a rest from me.

Sometimes the randiest bachelor envies the married man. If things had gone as heaven ordained, if there'd been no perfidy—

She asked to be remembered to you. Poor girl. She looked hideous.

God damn and blast the bitch and hurl her from my mind.

What is the antidote to obsession with one woman?

Some would say a hair of the dog that bit you.

The only cure for one hangover, they would say, is to acquire another.

And certainly for the first few days after I first saw Venus—

Yes, for the first few days after I saw Venus in that Korat dive she ousted Sheila from my mind. Her ghost drove Sheila's from the court where it had reigned unchallenged for four years. But as the week progressed and I didn't see her again the new vision faded. After all, my imagination hadn't much to feed on. So being a creature of habit I gradually returned to worship of the old goddess, though there still remained moments when Venus flared up real again and the heart thudded with sudden unholy desire.

One week and three prostitutes later I found her again, and one month and thirteen prostitutes after that I returned to Korat and slept with her for the first time. Sheila was obliterated: I didn't even raise her effigy to castigate it—'see what you've driven me to.'

For Venus herself is lovely. And not just physically so: she is frank and cheerful too. She remembers how many days it is since you last visited her, counting them on her fingers, visibly chiding you ...

Venus's kiss-creased nipples ...

A wail of dance music is wafted down Rajadamnoen Avenue. Of course, of course. The Bolero. It's eight-thirty, they've just started up there. I can saunter there and sprawl in an armchair and drink beer after beer and watch the antics of my fellow men when galvanized by lust. The expense of spirit in a waste of chairs. Maybe the Mongol will be there. The Mongol! Several times upcountry she has entered my mind, a vivid figure amongst the seventeen ghosts, as vivid sometimes as Sheila and Venus themselves. I don't want her tonight—I don't want any woman tonight, it would be blasphemy, with Sheila pale and thin, unable to help with the milking—but I can watch her. There was something about that whore—

'Boy! Bill.'

There was something about her that was fascinating. I hope to God she's there again. I enjoy watching her work as I enjoy watching any skilled workman on the job. A bungler myself—

I wonder what sort of drunken sot she'll get her claws into tonight ...

It's a queer place, the Bolero. It's like a share-cropper's shanty on Brobdingnagian scale. A raised wooden floor, acres in extent; no walls; a low gloomy roof. From the gloom hang dozens of tawdry paper lanterns, all very dim and dusty. In the middle of the floor is a circular space waxed for dancing; this is flanked by the rows of tiny desks at which the girls sit like amazingly exotic schoolgirls in a kindergarten. The rest of the place is strewn with wicker armchairs arranged in fours around small tables. There is a bar of sorts and a band, also of sorts. Prices are fantastically high. Beer costs ten bob a bottle instead of the normal Bangkok price of six. The girls are said to be expensive too. Certainly the famous ones will be, the ones Frost said were remembered with nostalgia from Greenland's icy mountains to India's immoral strand, wherever men with itching feet and another irritating itch silt up at bars for an hour or so before the next hop ...

I select an armchair and order a beer and try to pick out a woman who looks as if she might be famous. The one nearest me has roses in her hair and some sort of nasal obstruction which causes her mouth to hang open like a trout's with lipstick on. She is wearing an odd garment which is split up the sides like a Chinese gown but instead of fitting primly around her neck as a Chinese gown should, it stops short a bare inch above her breasts ... She is smoking a cigarette, but every time she catches my eye on her she stops to heave an ostentatious sigh, as if she were already burning with desire for me. Surely that's a little premature, sweetheart. My lips curl like the blue smoke.

Most of the ladies, so far as I can tell in the dim religious light, are more prepossessing than the Trout, but there is none who awakes a compelling interest. And where is the Mongol? I can't see her anywhere.

Encouraged by my entrance, which brings the number of customers up to about six, the band goes into action. A few of the girls get up and start dancing together. Gradually the tune identifies itself: that ubiquitous favourite, 'I won Der whooz skeesing her na-o-ow ...' The last time I heard that was in Korat. The soloist, Bing Boswell, popular UN playboy. The accompaniment; sounds of falling water. The night I too fell ...

Oddly the song, which a few weeks ago would have slid by my ears as a meaningless, not unpleasant dirge, is now moving. The words cause a pang in my heart, as if they were poetry. And not one pang, but three successive ones, all tumbling over each other.

The first and heaviest is for Venus. Poor girl, poor girl, and I mean it. She's one of the most popular, therefore one of the most overworked, in Chakri Road. Not much doubt that at this very instant she is engaged with tonight's third or fourth twenty-tics-worth of importunate desire. Is she by any chance casting her thoughts my way, as I am casting mine across the central lakeland and the low forested hills towards her? I have noticed that a professional girl exercises a lot of detachment even when the client is being most industrious. It was only the last two or three times, even with me—(good God, who the hell do I think I am?)—that she would drop the fan which she had been flapping over my back and take a proper interest in the proceedings. Then, 'Oh Letchie,' she would cry, remembering my name in the height of the storm, and her body would go rigid, and I would know that I was being paid the highest compliment that a girl of her calling can bestow on a man—that of being moved by him ...

'Letchie finiss?'

'Reggie finished.'

'Ratom finiss too.' She had a chuckling sort of laugh. I can hear it in my head now.

The second pang is for Sheila and quite perfunctory. Whooz skeesing *her* now? There's only one man that can be doing that, her lawfully wedded husband, my erstwhile esteemed elder brother. And that's unlikely too, for mid-evening in Bangkok is early afternoon in England, so doubtless Andy is out in his fields, doing whatever it is one does do in fields on one of the last afternoons in November. I don't waste time trying to visualize *him.* I do fabricate a quick mental picture of Sheila washing up after lunch, but it is confused and unsatisfactory. She's not Sheila any more; she's variations of Sheila. The Mongol is much more clear-cut in the memory, for her I saw only once.

And the third pang is for the Mongol. Where in hell is *she* tonight? Has she already grabbed tonight's victim elsewhere—is she not going to turn up? Suddenly I recall that the last time I was here the Bolero was dull until I noticed her and I realize it is going to be dull again if she doesn't materialize. Good heavens, what is this? Lust at first sight? Can one genuinely be so eager to see again a woman one has seen but once before and whose record one can guess? What on earth is happening to the idealist in me?

I'll finish off this beer. If she hasn't come by the time the last bubble has been imbibed I'll clear off back to the hotel and pass the night, till sleep descends, in adoration of the Venus whom I love ...

One of the more buxom and elderly of the schoolgirls gets up from her desk and walks past me humming. She is in a pink full-skirted practically backless frock and she looks familiar. One of the famous ones? But if so, where would I have seen her portrait? She proceeds aimlessly a few yards into the desert of empty chairs, then comes back, passing so close that her skirt brushes my arm. I look up and that amounts to a formal introduction.

'Hallo, honey.'

'Hallo.'

'You lemember me?'

'No.'

'I sink I see you some place before.'

'I sink not.' But actually I have somewhere.

'You want me sit down, talk wiss you?'

'No.'

'I sink you not like girl.'

'On the contrary I sink women are wonderful.'

'Before, I see you, you not like me, too. You not want d'ink, not want smoke, not want dance—'

Of course, of course. The tart Frost brought to the House that night, just before they booted me out.

She laughs. 'Now you lemember me, I sink. Why you run away that night, go to bed by you-self?'

'I wish *you'd* run away, sweetheart.'

'I sink you not boy, you girl dressed up like boy. You not know how enjoy you-self. I sink you no good for dance-girl.'

There's seventeen bloody women you don't know about, Daisy.

She laughs at me and goes back to her desk and with her first words has half the class convulsed. And women look so pretty when they laugh, their eyes and teeth sparkling, their frocks jerking about like flowers under a gust of wind ...

I flush under their amused glances and grab my glass and drain it. I look round for the boy and finally catch his eye. When I next steal a look at the girls their attention has shifted elsewhere.

It has shifted because another girl has arrived and she is—I recognize her with an incredible tumult in my chest—the Mongol.

Even better than I remembered her.

She displays no interest in me or in any other of the few men present. She seems to have a great number of lively things to tell the class. She stands amongst them like teacher. Some hang on her words, looking up to her. Others withhold their attention. The Trout for instance still has eyes for me alone and is sighing at such a rate that (if Ellen the maid was right when she used to say that every sigh you heave turns a spoonful of your blood to water) she'll soon be suffering from dropsy. Daisy also seems disinclined to pay court to the newcomer, indeed she makes a bid to divert some of the scholars' attention to herself, but she fails, and pouts, and sits tapping out on her desk with long red nails the rhythm of the rhumba the band is now murdering.

'Your change, sir.'

'Bring me another bottle.'

He eels away through the chairbacks.

She has her back to me now and is sitting sideways at one desk talking to the girls in the row behind. The conversation seems less absorbing than it was but it is still continuous and very one-sided. She eases her green woollen cardigan off her bare shoulders and gives her great weight of hair an expert toss or two from the nape of her neck, throwing the waves into good order. The play of muscles and shoulder-blades is exquisite. I wish to hell she'd look my way. But all I can see of her face is an occasional glimpse of one ear, small and well-designed, with a large gold hoop twinkling below its lobe, and the lean white plane of her profile stretched from the cheekbone's boss to the soft clean line of the jaw.

The boy brings more beer and pours it from a great height into my glass.

That woman is beautiful. She is not only physically superb, she has personality too. It radiates from her, so that even when she has her back to you, as now, she makes all the other girls despite their finery look dowdy and tame. They are sparrows: she is—a kingfisher. Then why—why doesn't she fish for kings? That last time I was here she could have had the pick of the men in the place. Several of the Yanks were not bad-looking, all were obviously well-heeled, two were almost fighting for her. Yet she picked that drunken middle-aged sot with his congested face, his pickled unfocussable eyes, his pearshaped nose, red with purple scratches on it, his lungeing gestures, his sudden shouts and incoherent mumbles, his wet shirt coming out of his trousers at the back …

I look at her and she is incomprehensible to me.

She is the most restless girl in the place. She is constantly getting up to go to the bar where she talks animatedly to a morose-looking man in a white coat, or to the dais where she talks animatedly to the bandleader, or to the

Ladies where possibly she talks animatedly to herself. In between whiles she returns to her desk and talks animatedly to her fellow students. Once she dances with the Trout and I wonder if their conversation, animated as it is, is about me. Two or three times she wanders past the chairs where other men are sitting—it is a flagrant attempt to attract attention—but she never so much as glances my way. But I happen to be strategically placed to watch her and my eyes seldom leave her.

Why is she almost pointedly cutting me? Refusing me a chance to beckon her?

But I'm forgetting. I've resolved to leave the women alone tonight. Sheila, my true love, is sick. And I have A Friend in Korat anyway.

All the same it is galling to be ignored.

Damn it, I'm a fairly presentable young man. At twenty-seven I'm in the prime of life. My blond hair stands up thick and strong from my skull. My face is considered handsome in its square-browed, Nordic mode. The cinder-rash on my cheek is a bit of a blemish, but it is an honourable scar: one can't slide for several yards on one's face without retaining some evidence of the experiment. As for my figure, I know that is good: not so big in the frame as Andy's, but even more athletic. My shoulders are, for my height, Herculean, thanks to my every-early-morning tussle with chest-expanders. My wrists and arms after three years of speedway racing are like a boxer's. And in spite of my soft life these last three years, doling out pats of butter, there's not an ounce of superfluous fat on me anywhere. Girls used to mill about me for my autograph, sighing like the Trout; my photo, signed by myself, was more in demand than any other Leopard rider's ...

I'm sure I'm a better proposition than any whisky-soddened pear-nosed—

She looked at me then. I raised my hand. But a second too late.

The Trout gets the wires crossed and stands up and comes and poses before me, sighing like a furnace.

'You'll bust your bra if you don't look out.'

'Please?'

'Go away.'

Rather curt for Ivanhoe.

The sighs stop as abruptly as light when you throw a switch. For a moment her expression is hideous. Then she swaggers back to her place, humming loudly, and says something to the Mongol.

The latter is smoking. She is sitting sideways at her desk again, but this time the other way round, facing me. She puts the cigarette to her mouth, drags on it hard and long and holds the smoke, then removes the cigarette and expels the smoke in a slow blue cloud. Very deliberately she rests her arm on the desk behind hers and taps the ash from the cigarette's tip with a slim, red-taloned finger. And all the time her eyes, narrowed, dark, unfathomable, are fixed on me. At last she is sizing me up, and like Windmill six weeks ago finding me wanting.

Shall I beckon to her now? What have I to lose? Would it be disloyalty to Sheila? Now Sheila's Andy's trouble and strife. If she's sick it's his headache, not mine. I can't be faithful to a ghost forever. And Ratom—Venus? She's just a fight of love. In somebody else's arms this goddamned minute. By being faithful to her I would just make myself look ludicrous.

She's turned her head away. Following the direction of her gaze I perceive a troupe of Americans entering. Obviously the lords of creation in their own opinions. They don't deliberately show off, the sense of personal pomp and circumstance is inborn in them, each feels that he is as good as any other three men. Choosing the right group of armchairs is a matter of life and death with them. They ponder and debate and make decisions and revoke them. In a few minutes she will be sitting with them, for with them ostentatiously is the power and the money. I've got to act at once if I'm really—

I gulp down more beer, pause undecidedly, my stomach taut around its churning contents, as on the top stair at that Korat hotel. When I move it is not as a result of a conscious decision to move. Abruptly I am lifted to my feet. To sit down again, as I want to do, would look silly.

On trembling legs I approach her. 'Excuse me—'

Seeing me coming she has deliberately turned away her head. As I address her she turns back with a very small smile for me.

'You want dance?'

I shake my head. I can't dance. 'I want you to—to talk to me.'

'Talk wiss you? You must pay me money.'

'How much?'

'Twenty-five tic.'

'Twenty-five tics! For how long?'

'One hour.'

'Just one hour?' I can sleep with Venus for less. It is exorbitant. My astonishment is born of parsimoniousness and she sees this and her small smile scoffs at me. I flush and say 'OK' hurriedly. I've got to talk to the bitch now. Make her respect me.

'OK?' Her smile is a little more cordial. 'OK, you giff me money now, zen I come and sit wiss you.'

I fumble in the breast-pocket of my shirt, standing there before her blushing, a schoolboy in front of thirty staring schoolgirls. I find a few notes and begin fitting them together, one ten, one five. I have plenty of ones, but it would be undignified to offer them to her, like paying for a five-guinea box at the theatre with a five-pound note and the rest in coppers. Suddenly I thrust the whole lot back in my shirt and fish for my wallet which is in my trousers. The girls titter.

'Maybe you no have?' she says, and she laughs in real amusement, a rather delightful tee-hee sort of laugh. 'I sink boy not have twenty-five tic must not come Bolero. Here very high girl, must—'

'Here.' I've got my wallet out and opened it and withdrawn a wad of notes—hundreds. I peel off one and thrust it into her hand. She takes it without any sign of diffidence, there in full view of the whole place. Without enthusiasm either. 'OK. Go back your chair. Soon I come sit wiss you.'

'Why not now?'

'Eh?' Her eyes widen as if in anger. 'Must give zis money to manager, darling. Buy ticket. Zen I sit wiss you one hour.' So she isn't going to cheat me. 'Go back you chair, darling.' She drops her cigarette on the floor, only half-finished, and puts her heel on it.

I give one look at her, then at the ranks of grinning tarts before whom I have been made to look small. Ten bob just to talk to a floozie for one hour. I feel I have been cheated. I lumber back to my chair, empty my glass, look around for the boy. How many today? Three on the train and God knows how many since. Well, might as well be hanged for a gallon as a pint.

'Boy. Boy! Beer—*ick kort.*' The service is dreadful here. Or do they just despise me—as they must despise all their clientele? Suckers dragged in by their testicles to be fleeced by brewers and harlots?

It is ten minutes before she comes to me. In the interval she succeeds in establishing contact with the newcomers. I sit fuming: she is not only insulting me, she is a cheat. In my rage I sink half a bottle almost without thinking about it.

But at last she comes, and drags back the chair on the far side of the table and seats herself in it. She makes no apology for her tardiness in arriving and shows no affability.

I lift my wrist and pointedly study my watch. 'Nine-ten,' I call: I'm going to be hoarse by the end of my hour unless we can contrive to get closer together. 'That means I've got you till ten-ten.'

As I say it I realize it's hardly the most tactful way of opening the conversation, but I have noticed before that alcohol inspires me to give expression to the bitter thoughts in my mind which sober I would keep to myself. It doesn't seem to worry her much; she glances indifferently at the tiny gold watch on her own wrist and then lets her hands fall into her lap again with a jingle of bracelets.

How does one talk to a whore, I mean in any other circumstances but when one is sitting on the edge of her bed? 'What is your name?' I try first.

'Why you say zat?'

'Because I want to know what to call you.'

'Call me honey. All American call girl honey.'

'But I'm not American. I'm English.'

'You Ing-liss?' At last there is a spark of interest but it is a very dim fleeting one. 'I sink you American boy.'

'Why did you think that?'

'I not know.' She shrugs those splendid bare shoulders. 'I just sink.'

'Which d'you like best—Americans or Englishmen?'

She shrugs again. 'I like any boy who good to me. Sometime he American, sometime he Ing-liss, sometime he Dutss, sometime he Flenss. Many good boy come Bangkok.' She yawns without subterfuge, then leans forward with her elbows on her knees. She says wheedlingly: 'You buy d'ink for me, darling?'

More expense. And am I getting anywhere? 'If you come and sit a bit nearer.' I don't know whether she understands or not. Fearful of antagonizing her further I say quickly, 'What d'you want?'

'I call boy. I want peppermint.'

She begins to get up but I shout, 'Hey, where d'you think you're going now?'

'Go fetss boy.'

'Sit down. I'll call him.' I do.

Obediently she has sat down again, but still far away and looking mutinous. She leans far back in the armchair with her body almost supine and her head at right angles to it, propped up by the back of the chair. There is a frown on her low rather narrow forehead and her rather small eyes have gone smaller and are black with resentment. Her lips, tomato-red, are pushed forwards like a sulky child's.

What can I say? The more I annoy her the more I want to make friends with her. But I am always too abject with women. When they are cheerful, I am. When they're moody, I can't be happy. So I say ineptly, 'You still haven't told me your name, you know. What is it?'

She takes less notice of me than she would of a mosquito for the boy unseen by me has arrived and they are being voluble with each other in their own language.

I realize that I am getting nowhere with the girl—in fact I am apparently antagonizing her—but I get up and transfer myself to the seat nearest her on her right.

'It seems you can't hear me from over there,' I say with a sort of weak fury.

She catches someone's eye and waves and smiles and that smile is far more gorgeous than any she has bent on me. I peer round blearily to see what manner of man the lucky recipient is but I can see nothing but empty chairs. Perhaps I'm getting too drunk to see clearly. And certainly anger can blur the sight too.

'Pray confine your attention to this table for the next fifty minutes.'

She looks at me in surprise. 'What you say? I not unnerstan'.' I think it can only be the words she missed, the tone must have been unmistakable: that of an exasperated dictator.

Yet when I've got her attention I don't know what to do with it. I can only think of the same old question: 'What did you say your name was?'

She clicks her tongue and sighs. At last she says unwillingly, 'Lily.'

I laugh at that. No name on Earth could be more inappropriate, I feel. I laugh some more and say, 'That's only a nickname. And a wrong name at that. I mean your real name. What is your real Siamese name?'

Realizing that I'm going to keep nagging at the same point till dawn if need be she says indifferently, 'Vilai.'

'Vilai? Did you say Vilai or Virai?'

She doesn't answer.

I tap her knee. Determination pays with this one. 'Virai or Vilai?'

Suddenly her eyes narrow and blaze. 'What you mean, Vilai or Vilai? Not differnunt, I sink. I sink you very silly boy,' she adds as an afterthought. 'You talk too much.'

'My name is Reggie Joyce,' I tell her. The information is hardly relevant at that moment but I am at that stage of intoxication where one has to compose one's next contribution to the conversation several seconds in advance and allow no side-issues—least of all remarks from one's interlocutor—to interfere with their enunciation.

She ignores me completely again. For the boy has arrived with her peppermint. I am surprised to see there is another bottle of beer for me too.

'Did I order that?'

She gives me a hard look. 'Yes, I hear you.'

I must be getting really stinking.

'Pour some out for me,' I say, my tone lordly, for I have an obscure feeling that a dance-hostess who was really trying to play the hostess would perform this little office without being asked. When she makes no response I snatch up the bottle and pour some of its contents furiously into my glass. It is then that I find out that the boy has already filled it. The beer shoots across the table as if the glass had exploded and of course some goes on her skirt. She switches her knees away with a cry of annoyance. I cry out too in mixed annoyance and shame. I expect her to be enraged with me but she says nothing. She pulls up her skirt a bit and flicks off the liquid with her fingernails; then she opens her little square raffia evening bag and pulls out a handkerchief. It is neatly folded and she unfolds it with deliberation before using it as a mop.

'I'm sorry.'

She says nothing.

'I said I'm sorry.'

My voice is so querulous that she has to reply but her own is quite expressionless. 'Never mind. Forget about.'

But that's just what I don't want to do. I feel that a good way to demonstrate her importance to me is by an excessive vehemence of contrition over this piffling accident, this minikin catastrophe of bubbles and cloth. But before I can protest some more she changes the subject by standing up.

'Where are you going this time?'

'I go ex-cuse.'

'But dammit, you can't want to go excuse again already. You've been there three times in the last half-hour as it is.'

'How you know?'

'Because I saw you.'

'Why you look me all the time?'

Suddenly my tongue takes wings. 'Because you are the most beautiful girl in the place. Because there's nothing else to look at in this dump. Because ever since I first saw you here six weeks ago I've been longing and longing to see you again. Because—'

She's pleased all right but she states an objection. 'Just now you talk Black Leopard.'

'Black what?'

'Black Leopard. You know her very well, I sink. Fat girl. Very black here.' (Touching bicep). 'Her dress not rad colour but littun like rad colour.'

Good God, does she mean Daisy, the virago in pink? 'Her?' I cry in amazement.

'You know her, yes? Perhaps you like her very much? More zan me, I sink?'

'Like her? Good heavens, not me! She's—she's—hideous, that's what she is.'

'What you mean?'

'She's—oh, what the hell's the word—' and then I get it—

'she's *na-gliet.*'

Usually the farthest that a Thai will go in disparagement of a lady's looks is the mildly negative *'mai suei'*—not beautiful. To call her *na-gliet*—ugly—is to be almost violently over-emphatic. The Mongol—Lily—Vilai—is greatly amused. Her laugh tinkles out, that delicious little tee-hee tee-hee which before was at my expense.

'You say Black Leopard *na-gliet*?'

'Yes.'

'I sink I go tell her now.'

'OK. Go and tell her.'

'Tee-hee. Tee-hee.'

'But be sure you come back. Quick.'

She has started to go but she wheels and returns her face clouded again. 'Why you fray all the time I not come back? You sink I cheating girl?'

'No, no, sorry—I didn't mean—'

'I very good girl. I *must* come back your table. Not have finiss my d'ink yet.' That's a point of course. 'I come back as soon as I finiss pee-pee, darling. Don't worry.'

Surprisingly she's soon back. That makes me happy of course. And no sooner is she seated than the boy brings her another peppermint thoughtfully ordered by me during her absence. That makes *her* happy, too. In fact she is so pleased that she insists on ordering another beer for me. An air of bonhomie encompasses us like warm steam. We talk as easily as—well, as two men would. As Slither and I would do, if it was he that was sitting next to me.

I can't remember what we talk about. There is a lot of beery persiflage. I have the impression that I am at my wittiest best and better still, that my audience is unusually appreciative. We both laugh a great deal and drinks vanish and re-appear as if a conjurer were at work on them.

At one stage a bent brown ugly old woman with straggly hair and disturbingly sober eyes tries to sell me flowers. The Mongol— I still think of her as that—selects the largest bloom from the basket and fixes it in her hair. It is white. She also buys a wreath of small white flowers with a sweet penetrating scent and this wreath she insists on slipping over our wrists, hers and mine. When it is on she looks towards the kindergarten and raises our arms so that the girls over there can see us thus bucolically entwined. 'Give me ten tic for the old girl, darling.' I throw her a hundred-tic note and have to ask five times for the change. Dimly I am aware that a few minutes after I have paid for the flowers they vanish just as if a conjurer were at work on them too. Dimly I suspect that the Mongol is the conjurer; that she only borrowed the flowers from the old woman for as long as it took her to charm ten tics out of my pocket and into her handbag. But the perfidy of this creature, unlike the perfidy of other women—for a fleeting moment I think of Sheila and I chuckle—this Mongolian perfidy is a joke and I don't resent it at all, rather I enjoy the ruses by which I am being rooked. I am laughing at everything and anything and sometimes at nothing at all, just laughing, laughing, because I feel so exhilarated, so emancipated, such a dog, such a whale of a dog. I have never enjoyed female company so much as this before. Not even Venus's, not even Sheila's. For with Sheila I was always under restraint as of course a parfit gentil knight must inevitably be in the presence of his queen, the beldam sans mercy; thus Ivanhoe was always on his best behaviour with Rowena. As for poor dear Venus, excellent wench that she is, she remains when all is said and done a pro: our bodies are mighty orators in their lust but when they have thundered out their hackneyed speeches our tongues stammer; one hour of dalliance exhausts all our invention; our brains yawn at each other almost without attempt at concealment or apology. But with this animal I feel I could chatter cheerily till dawn and then after a short slumber resume the conversation at the breakfast table just as spontaneously as now after a swig of beer. For once, I feel, my instincts have not erred: when I picked the Mongol out as the girl for me I was inspired.

In a moment of clarity I try to focus my eyes on this woman, try desperately, for I must exercise my mind if I am to keep it alert and this is the chore I choose for it, a problem, trying to analyse her charm for me.

Lovely. Depraved. Mongoloid.

Those were the words that occurred to me whenever I recalled her upcountry and those are the words that recur now when she is so close that her knee is actually thrust against mine.

Lovely is not a word, it is more like a sigh.

And depraved?

But I become aware that she is kneading my arm and that she has been kneading it for quite a time.

'Eh?'

'Darling, you want take me home?'

I don't really know—I've just been living in the present. While I'm hesitating—there was some reason why I'd sworn off women for tonight—she changes her tack a little. 'Darling, I like you very much. You nice boy, I sink. I want very much you take me home, give me two hundred tic.'

I laugh at that 'If *you* want *me* to take *you* home, *you* must give *me* two hundred tics.'

She frowns and looks bothered; it seems this matter is too serious to joke about. 'No, you give *me,'* she says, earnestly. She puts on a whining tone. 'Honey, I love you so much. Please take me home, honey.'

'Don't call me honey. I'm not American.'

'Darling, what you say? You take me home, darling, give me two hundred tic?' Kneading my arm some more.

She looks worse than depraved now, she looks downright evil, with her face all screwed up by cupidity. I say, not trusting her—who could be so serious over two hundred tics?—'How do I know it's going to be safe to take you home? Maybe you have a husband there. Maybe when you get me to your home your husband will hit me on the head with a blunt instrument.' I feel my cunning matches hers.

'I not have husband. Why you say that? You safe with me, darling. If anysing happen tonight, bad for you, at my home, tomollow I cannot come work at Bolero. Manager say, You bad girl, man go your house get hurt, you cannot work here, get my place very bad name ... You not want be fray, darling.' She is still massaging my arm, and she has a strangely skilful way of doing it, she somehow sinks the balls of her fingertips between the ligaments and finds nerves that respond to her touch at once soothed and stimulated. 'Darling, you come now, give me two hundred tics?'

I wish she wouldn't keep harping on the financial aspect but all I say is, 'I'll give you one hundred and eighty. I'll take twenty off because they'—motioning towards her chest—'aren't real.'

It's been a joke between us for the last hour, I insisting her breasts are artificial—'no girl could have real ones that good: they must be rubber'—she denying; but now she can't see any humour in this topic either.

'Darling, darling—'

'OK.' If you don't want to play. 'Don't worry.'

'You give me two hundred tic?'

'And something else besides.'

She's so relieved she's almost purring. She pats my arm in companionable fashion, her face quite glowing.

I wonder whether it is the prospect of sleeping with Mr. R. E. Joyce or just the prospect of getting money. I haven't many doubts. 'You want another drink?' I ask, 'or shall we go now?'

She says, 'Not want go now. You sit here, darling, have one more beer. I go speak my frand. By and by I come back.'

'You going to walk out on me?'

'You not trust me?'

'What if some other bloke offers you three hundred tics?'

'Who?' It is supposed to be a joke but she takes it seriously. She believes the world contains a fool who would be daft enough to give her, a common whore, six pounds for her favours. 'If my frand say he give me three hundred tic, I come to you, ask you give me four hundred. I not go with my frand, darling, unless he give me more money than you. I like you very mutss.'

'I'm honoured.'

'You want me order you one more beer?'

'As you like. One for the road. One for the bed, honey.'

It is now my turn to go excuse. I find a baffling difficulty in getting out of my chair and when I do finally get erect, my head spins and rings and everything goes black: clearly I've been sitting too long. Then my eyes re-open and I set off. The armchairs are too close together and I stumble over several before I reach the dancefloor. I don't venture onto that, of course: I have an idea that it is slippery like a skating rink, and I don't want to fall over and make myself look silly. As I skirt it I think I hear people tittering at me but at the same time I admit to myself that I am too self-conscious in public: people come to nightclubs to have a good time and of course they are all laughing, but not at me; they are laughing because they are having a good time. But I always feel embarrassed when I go excuse in a public place.

The lavatory door—'inswinging on perpetual creosote.' That's William Faulkner. This one inswings on other matter, and so precipitantly that I almost go headfirst into it.

Over the partition I can hear two girls chattering. I am almost certain that one of them is the Mongol.

Depraved. At any rate that's a word, not just a burp, like 'lovely'. It implies Lavater and a science of reading character from physiognomy, and it implies that I know something of that science, or think that I do. It implies that to me the Mongol is anything but the personification of chastity: that blonde bloodless blue-eyed milksop who is set before us in our childhood days as the ideal to seek out and adore. It implies a lot of other things and where in hell is the door?

Re-finding my own table presents some difficulties but in the end one of the boys takes me by the arm and guides me in the right direction. I give him ten tics. There's a full glass and a full bottle but really I've had enough to drink. However, since it's here—

Mongoloid was the other word. It is the best because it is the most concrete. And it can be justified. There are plenty of suds on the table-top and I lean forward and try to draw with my finger the essential Mongoloidity of that face. Under the dark rich canopy of hair the low narrow forehead widens downward like this to the outwings of the eye-sockets. The cheekbones are wider still, but jutting inwards and obliquely downwards to the nose. From their roots, where the ears are delicately perched, the cheeks descend vertically to the angles of the jaw, which are as wide as the cheekbones at their widest; but from those angles the jaw turns in almost horizontally to the chin which is square, and the cheeks above the jawline are slightly hollowed. The nose is practically bridgeless, very wide, and tip-tilted, so that the nostrils aim forwards; it is a poor nose seen from the front, but in profile it is straight, delicate, ineffably refined—a perfect jewel of a nose. I have mucked up the drawing but the rest would be too hard to do anyway, for it is in the mouth and the modelling around it, and in the eyes, which are placed wide apart in their shallow sockets, small, honey-brown, with thick short lashes and little white, that the real life and individuality of her beauty lies. She has the slightest suggestion of double chin—all Thai beauties have it, cannot hope to become Miss Thailand without it—and between that double chin and her collarbones there are horizontal folds in her neck, three or four; and even across her chest, first round the base of the neck, then from shoulder to shoulder, there are long faint sweeping semi-elliptic creases in the flesh—lines that would be blemishes on a western woman but here suggest only opulent maturity. Oh, she's beautiful without a doubt, a noble woman nobly—

'Hey. You. Han-sum.'

I look up. There is a reddish blur as if a blood-vessel had burst in my eyeball. Gradually it resolves itself into—Frost's girl, the plump one in pink.

'What in hell do you want?'

'Why you sit alone?'

I shrug.

She comes nearer. 'That girl'—with a toss of her head—'she no good. She leave you. She have 'nother frand, old frand, give her much money. You not want trust her, darling. I know her long time. She very bad girl.' She seats herself on the arm of my chair. I shrink away from her. I don't want anything to do with her. She is just clay whereas the Mongol is fire. Her chest and shoulders are as opulent as the Mongol's, she has two double chins as against one, her breasts are huge but not unsightly, as well I know, for have I not seen her stripped to her bra and knickers, dancing with Frost?—but—

I put out my hand to push her away. She grabs it and holds it.

'Honey—dream boy—' Her voice is thick with simulated passion.

But suddenly there is a swirl and flash of cloth and the Mongol is back. Her voice is like a lash whistling through the air. Daisy gets up hastily off the arm of my chair and shouts back, her voice fraught with a different sort of passion from a few seconds ago and this sort genuine. From being a couple of magnificent oriental beauties, fit for a sultan's palace you would think, they are suddenly a couple of fishwives brawling outside a pub.

The Mongol is the accuser, speaking evenly in a low voice, in English. 'Why you must steal my man? Every time you must try steal my man from me. Why you not find man for you-self? Plenty men in Bangkok will go with very low cheap girl like you I sink.'

The answer is shouted in Thai.

The Mongol says, 'So, you want fight, eh? OK, I very fighting girl. You want fight, I fight you anywhere, any time. But not here, in Bolero. Too many pipple look what we do. Make manager angly to us. Only silly girl fight here, maybe lose job.' She looks at her watch. 'Now we go back work, make money. Twalf o'c'ock, when we finiss work, we go fight, OK?'

More shouted Thai, not quite so choleric.

'So you not want fight, eh? You only want fight wiss mouse.' I presume she means mouth. She laughs. 'You lemember last time, eh? And many times before.' Laughing. 'I very good fighting girl, I sink. I fighting good more zan you.'

It occurs to me that for the first time in my life women are quarrelling over me and that makes *me* laugh.

The Mongol turns on me with eyes blazing. 'Why you talk this girl? You like her, I sink. You like her more zan me.'

I answer sullenly, '*Mai chob.*' I don't like her at all. 'I told you before, she's *na-gliet.* She's *na-gliet* as sin.'

At that the Mongol laughs. She turns on Daisy again. 'You hear what my frand say? He speak Thai very good. He say you *mai suei,* you *na-gliet.*' She turns to the handful of girls who have gathered round. 'My boy not like Black Leopard. He say she *na-gliet.*'

The girls titter. Daisy gives me a furious look and fills her lungs for another blast. But just at that moment a boy appears and speaks to her urgently. Her face goes black with rage but she shrugs her shoulders and stalks away. The Mongol calls after her, 'You see? What I tell you? All the time you make tlouble. Manager no like girl who make tlouble. Maybe he make you stop work three day.'

She slumps into a chair. It is the one nearest to me but she doesn't look at all happy.

'What a cow—' I begin but she snaps my head off:

'Don't speak me.'

She sits frowning darkly for a few more moments until I venture to reach for my drink, then she bursts out: 'She very bad girl. All the time try to steal my man. If she can steal my man from me, she sink very good, she sink she make her face very big. But I know she low girl, very low. If she take my man, if he go with her, I no want speak him again. She very low, she make him low too.'

'*I* didn't speak to her, she—'

'You very low man, too, I sink. I leave you here short time, straight way you make eye to Black Leopard.'

The injustice of that!

'I not like man who make eye to other girl when I go ex-cuse.'

'You didn't go excuse. You went to talk to some other man. You've got no right—'

'I only like man who good to me.'

'Sweetheart!'—trying to capture her hand. But she snatches it away.

I feel miserable. For a start things went badly between us but then they picked up and everything seemed to be going swimmingly; but now it's all a mess again; probably everything is ruined. Any other man, I feel, would be able to do something decisive or at least say something decisive at this juncture. He would have the courage to show his feelings—'aw, go to hell'— stake everything on the chance of her reacting the right way, nor care very much if she didn't. But I as always am utterly under the dominion of the girl's mood: because she is angry I can't be anything but submissive and wary, dumbly, miserably hoping that my sympathy will touch her, uneasily waiting to see which way her rage will flare out next.

Finally, the silence becoming unbearable, I whisper, 'Sweetheart—Vilai—' She makes an impatient gesture but says nothing. Encouraged I continue, 'Dearest, let's get out of this dump. Let's pay the bill and clear off to your home. I want to go with you, darling, I really do.'

She looks at her watch. 'If we go now, you must give me sixty tic more.'

'Why?' Always that wounded yelp.

'Because not twalf o'c'ock, darling. I not finiss work. Any girl go out of Bolero before twalf, her boy must pay manager sixty tic.'

I toss over another hundred. At the same time I say, 'Call the boy.' I too can be a man of action.

As it happens the boy is already at my elbow with two or three bills on his tray. I pick them up and look at them stupidly. He tells me the total and I almost faint.

'How much?'

He repeats the same figure. It is over three hundred tics.

'That's impossible!' I exclaim. I propose to go through the bills item by item, but then I notice that the Mongol is looking at me critically. At all costs I must prevent her from getting the idea that I am miserly: even at a cost of three hundred tics I want to avoid that. I peel off four more notes. The wad is a lot slimmer than it was.

'I sink you not have mutss money,' she says.

'Why?'

''Cause tears come your eye every time you must pay.'

'I've got plenty of dough. You've seen it.'

'Maybe you have plenty money, not like spand, then. I not like man who want to keep he money for he-self. Man truly like me, he not care how mutss money he spand when he sit wiss me.'

'Have I complained yet?' Of course I have, but an oratorical question doesn't have to be founded on fact to sound good to the orator. 'Come on. Less go.' Shades of Boswell.

'Must wait your change, darling.'

'Why? *You* haven't given me any change.'

'What you mean?'

'Seventy five tics from the hundred I gave you to sit with me. Forty from the second one to take you out early.' Hazily I am aware that everybody is getting up and that the band is romping through the shorter of the two Siamese national anthems. 'Why'd you make me pay sixty tics to take you out anyway? It's midnight now.'

'When you want go it still ten to twalf. You take long long time pay your bill, darling, 'cause you d'unk.'

The fact that I could have saved myself that sixty by just looking at my watch doesn't make me feel any happier. 'Come on. Less go. Less go. Damn the change.'

'Boy coming now, darling. Wait. Must get your money back from him. Money you give me differnunt. You give me money 'cause you love me. You not love boy, do you?' Tee-hee, tee-hee. 'Here boy now, darling.

Take your change quick.'

I have no recollection of getting to the door, or through it, or getting into the *samlor.* The next thing I remember is riding in the *samlor* down the windy stretches of Rajadamnoen Avenue. A *samlor* is about the same size and shape as one of those double seats in the back rows of some cinemas which incidentally I have never occupied. I am aware that I am attacking her from all angles and that she is repulsing me with skill and that the *samlor* boy is pedalling like mad and it is all a great joke under the blazing stars and the streetlamps that go by like long yellow streaks. I haven't the faintest idea where we are going and I don't care. I wish I knew some of the arts of love-making instead of only being able to paw her about like a farm-boy at home getting rid of his first pay-packet after leaving school. I am crazy about this girl tonight, crazy as I have never been about any girl before, not even Sheila, and I wish that I could express the overwhelming feelings within me ... Then abruptly we are squealing to a halt.

'Hey, Joycey!'

I imagine we have arrived and start trying to get out of the *samlor* but then I realize that the girl isn't moving but is looking across me and upwards at an angle. I turn and there is Frost standing in the road.

'Hey, Joycey, what the hell d'you think you're doing?'

'Hey.' I'm quite bewildered. 'Hey, Frosty.'

'What are you up to, chum?'

I wink.

'You've been to the Bolero,' he says accusingly.

'That's right. Where you been?'

'Oh, around. I'm just going home. D'you know what you've got in that *samlor* with you?'

'She's my girl.'

'She's the one they call the White Leopard. She's the worst of the lot.'

'Goddam,' the Mongol screams, 'you talk too mutss.'

'I think she's the best of the lot,' I say. 'There wasn't another one there that I'd touch with Ivanhoe's bargepole.'

'*Bai,*' says the Mongol to the *samlor*-man.

We begin to move. 'You be careful,' Frost calls after us. 'I'm warning you, you silly sod. She's—'

I turn round and try to speak to him with severity, with dignity. 'I think I can look after myself. Seventeen bloody women you know, old man.'

'He very bad boy,' the Mongol says, as the cool air begins to pour round our faces again. 'All the time he talk too mutss.'

'He's a friend of the Black Leopard, if that's what you mean,' I say, with remarkable penetration for one so near drunk as I am, and then I put my arm round her again. 'What do I care if they call you the White Leopard or the White Elephant for that matter? I love you, sweetheart, love you, love you, do you understand, and the sooner we get to your home where I can show you how much I love you ...'

Part Two

THE LEOPARD

'Better to reign in Hell than serve in Heaven'
Satan, as reported by John Milton

'What we call "morals" is simply blind obedience to words of command'
Havelock Ellis

'Do you think that Nature gave women nipples as beauty spots, rather than for the purpose of nourishing their children?'
Ancient Roman Author

Five

There was a wild tattoo of ladle on stove and a jubilant yell; it could have been the start of another *coup d'état;* but she recognized it for what it was; the cook in the Chinese shop beneath her window proclaiming to all the world the emergence of a new wonder from his smoke-blackened *kuo*. And the rattle bong boom, and then the falsetto recitative, and then the bong rattlerattle bongbong boom of Chinese opera, competing as it alone could not only with a prodigious amount of static, but with the breathless descending xylophone runs of several different Siamese operas all being simultaneously purveyed by half a dozen radios within earshot. And the sweet, clear, inhibited voices of Siamese girl singers experimenting (as it always seemed to her when she was too sleepy to unravel the tune) first with this half-note and then with that, but never quite able to break free into a recognizable melody.

And the sound of ice being pounded up in wooden troughs, and of motor *samlors* poppeting down the lane, and of a dog fracas dying out in prolonged heartfelt snarls and hysterical yappings, and of boys shouting 'Lotter-lee, lotter-lee' on behalf of their chronically insolvent government, and of Bochang the cook, screaming amicably at Siput the maid, and of somewhere a child bawling—bawling persistently but without conviction, as if he'd been bawling so long he'd forgotten the cause of his woe, but knew the wrong had yet to be righted. And over and under and round and through all else, as pervasive as the roar of a not-so-far-off waterfall, the continuous, low-pitched thunder of the traffic in the New Road.

It was all as familiar as the face she examined twenty times a day in her mirrors. It was so familiar that by now she ought to have grown used to it, as one does to the beating of one's own heart. And most of the time she *was* quite unconscious of it: it was just a cradle of noise in which she lay swaddled and unaware like a newborn baby. Yet once every day what was familiar became alien; once every day the cradle exploded upon her like a bursting bomb. And that was in the moment of her awaking.

Somehow, although she had lived in this room for years—almost since she had first become a dancing-girl—she had never learned the art of waking up in it. But always she must start up with this violent jerk, and then lie tense and rigid, all ears, her breath held in. Only for a moment would the terror last, then something—perhaps the feel of the same old bed, or perhaps nothing physical at all, but just memory waking up a few moments after her body and reidentifying her to herself, would send reassurance in a great wave through her limbs. She would relax with a sob and collapse into the bed again, yearningly, as if the bed were sleep and sleep heaven, and all her desire to be merged and smothered in them forevermore.

Today, perhaps for the two thousandth time (for that was a stupefying calculation the fair-haired English boy had done the night before last) the pattern had repeated itself, and she was now lying as she best liked to lie when alone, diagonally across the bed, face down, with limbs flung all ways. But of course there was no pleasure in the posture now, nor for that matter in the aloneness, for alas, she was no longer asleep. And, being awake, she was becoming aware of annoyances that only sleep had the power to blot out. Her hair had got under her face and a hairclip was biting into her cheek. Her brassiere was too tight and constricting her painfully. Her head was aching, her mouth foul, her stomach raw and unsettled, as so often after she'd drunk too much. Naturally, she wanted to go to the *hongnam*. And wasn't today Friday, and therefore one of her shampoo and movie days, one of the two days in the week when she had to be up betimes? In a minute she'd have to open her eyes and look at her watch, and then, irreparably, the day would have begun.

So, accepting the inevitable in her usual realistic way, she opened her eyes on the blanched, blinding light inside her mosquito net and blinked them very deliberately four or five times.

First she put her hands behind her back and undid the brassiere. She pulled a pillow towards her, swept her hair from under her face and laid skin to linen. The hairclip which had been cutting her cheek fell out and lay on the sheet like a legless centipede. She felt so much more comfortable that she was tempted to try to doze off again, but she told herself it was Friday and she mustn't. Stifling a yawn, she drew up her arm and glanced at the tiny gold watch which was clasped by a bracelet of tiny gold hearts to her wrist. The hands were in a straight line across the dial, with the hour-hand just past ten—it was in fact twenty-two minutes past—but she didn't read the time as accurately as a foreigner would; she only looked at the hour-hand and to her it said approximately *'Si mong chao'*—the fourth hour of the morning—near enough her normal time of resurrection.

Keeping her cheek to the pillow, she heaved herself over onto her back and lay with her legs spread and her eyes again closed. The brassiere still fitted cosily because she kept its wings pinched between arms and sides but her sarong had come undone and only a corner of it lay across her legs. Without opening her eyes or moving her head, she fished around for it and spread it more tidily over herself, her jewellery jingling. For she was Siamese and in spite of being also, as she liked to boast, the Number One Bad Girl of Bangkok, she retained a lot of her national, Buddhist, no even more fundamental than that, her feminine modesty, and especially she abhorred exposure of the lower part of her body except in the acts where such exposure was practically unavoidable.

She had kept her head still because when she let it lie to one side like this the ache didn't see-saw round her skull so much, but as the pain in her head subsided, other discomforts become more noticeable and with a sudden groan she sat up, tore the mosquito-net apart and swung out her legs. She fished with her feet under the bed until she found the special sandals which the Siamese wear when they go to the bathroom and with agile toes fetched them forth and manœuvred them on. Then, snatching up the sarong and throwing it loosely round herself, and keeping the brassiere still nipped in place, she crossed to the door, unbolted it, and went out.

Clapping down the wooden ladder on her wooden soles she called, 'Bo! Bochang!' loudly several times, her voice harsh and rising. At first nobody seemed to hear but just as she reached the bathroom door and was filling her lungs for a real bellow the volubility below stairs ceased, there was a pause, and then Bochang's voice, politely modulated, floated upwards. '*Arai?*' What?

'*Oliang yen, keow.*' A glass of iced black coffee.

'Oh.'

The first today. She shoved open the *hongnam* door and shoved it half-shut behind her. Sunbeams slanting through the roof lit up the familiar equipment of a Siamese bathroom—on a raised square concrete throne the oval squatter, with a small round hole at the deep end and corrugated footrests like those on vintage motorcycles; the small jar of water beside it, a substitute for toilet paper; the old petrol tin full of soiled pieces of paper and flies; the huge earthenware vat of bathwater with its own clean dipper; and that fantastic system of tiny gutters and holes like mouse-holes which testify to the ingenuity of Siamese plumbers and also perhaps to their whimsical humour. Whipping off the sarong she squatted on her heels and relieved herself on the floor. Reaching for the dipper in the big vat she threw a little water between her legs and over her feet and then, filling it again, sluiced her urine down the nearest mouse-holes. She wiped herself sketchily on the sarong, re-donned it, this time doing it up securely round her waist. Then she went out, wrenching the door open and dragging it to behind her, all her movements being neat, rapid, and unnecessarily violent.

Back in her room she went automatically to her dressing table and seated herself on the stool in front of her three mirrors. First she took a general view of herself and then, thrusting her face towards the middle glass, a more detailed one of her face. The first showed her a statuesque body that was already well-fleshed and likely any day now (she feared) to topple over into grossness and unsightly folds. The second showed that her lipstick like the mascara was smudged (but that was only to be expected), that a new pimple was coming on her chin, that the whites of her eyes were anything but clear this morning and that the skin below them was not taut but puffy and discoloured. It was here, around the eyes, and in the two lines which curved deeper month by month from the wings of her nostrils down to and around the corners of her mouth that she saw most clearly the advances of age. She writhed back the smudged lips from her teeth and examined them closely. They at any rate were always in tip-top condition. But her tongue was like an autumn leaf, pink round the edges but yellow down the centre, down and round that central groove which was like the spine of a dying leaf. She sighed, got up, and, as all Siamese women do all day long, undid and did up her sarong again. Then she went to the bed and pulled the two pillows together and plumped them up and set them against the headrail, and she was just going to lie back against them when it occurred to her that Bochang was being a long time—goddam—so she went to the door and shouted 'Bochang!' and getting no reply, 'Siput!'

'Mem?' came Siput's voice from belowstairs.

'Where is my coffee?'

'Coming. Coming.'

'I want it now. You know when I want a thing I must have it at once. Why do you make me wait?'

'Bochang is so old. She walks slowly like a water buffalo.'

'I think a water buffalo is like a racehorse compared with Bochang. She is as slow as one of those creatures that carries its whole house on its back.'

'A crab?'

'Yes. Or a snail. Or a tortoise.'

This exchange made her immediately feel better. Conversation was one of the chief pleasures of her life. She delighted to egg Siput on to criticize Bochang. She delighted to make fun of Bochang whom actually she liked better than anyone else under her roof except her son. And this thinking of nice girlhood things like water buffalo and horses and tortoises—it was a chance word of Siput's that had opened up that vista. Life was not all fun by any means and waking up into it was a daily trial; but since the trial was a daily one and unavoidable while you had breath in your body you might as well make the best of it; there was plenty of time yet before things became unbearable and you did away with yourself—that end to which you would come, according to all the priests and soothsayers in whom you believed, not until you were fifty years old—many, many years yet, or at least quite a good few ...

Going back to the dressing table she searched in the handbag she had used last night until she found her compact and a pair of tweezers. Then, lying on the bed, she re-arranged the pillows, one under her sideways-turned head and the other a few inches in front of her face with the compact-lid propped against it. She raised one arm under her head and fiddled with the compact until the mirror in its lid was reflecting her armpit to her eyes. Then with the tweezers she began plucking out the small hairs which were sprouting in it.

This was a weekly chore and one she liked. While she worked she was wholly absorbed in the job. To her it seemed that her life was one long round of duties, from finding fault with her servants, which was her idea of housekeeping, to parting men from their money at the Bolero, and all these jobs she did, in her opinion, well: she was a good worker. But none of those other jobs was as agreeable to her as this one of making herself beautiful. For every day she must begin afresh, like a potter, her material nothing but clay. And every day, at last, sometimes after hours of labour, she would turn out another work of art. To be sure it was always the same subject—the White Leopard, the far-famed dancing-girl, an idealization of her actual clay achieved with cloth and cosmetics—and to be sure beauty was becoming harder to achieve and never again would attain to the heights it had sometimes reached in the past—but it was not in the finished product she found her joy so much as in the processes of creation. Counting baths, she never spent less than three hours a day on her toilet; often, on days when she had a shampoo or a massage, it was more like five; but they were always the happiest hours of all, and nothing would induce her to skimp them.

And this plucking of the armpits was one of the nicest of the various rites. For first of all you could do it in bed. Secondly there was an artist's pleasure in sliding the blunt nose of the tweezers over the skin towards the quarry and then with a sharp flick uprooting it and laying it alongside all the other hairs which had likewise been individually uprooted and laid out on the sheet. Neatness and deftness were required, such as were possessed by the little lizards that lived behind her mirrors: just so they would creep up to a mosquito on the walls and then with a sharp stab of head and tongue dexterously, unerringly, snatch it. Thinking of the tweezers as *chinchocks* and the hated hairs as mosquitoes amused her and added to her enjoyment of her work. And then there was the pain. No question but that that pain—that succession of small stinging ant-bites all confined to one small area of the body—was a pleasureable sensation; it was stimulating, and she liked inflicting it on herself. A counter-irritant, it diminished the throb in the temples and the staleness of whisky in the guts. In fact, if only she could get a draught of iced-coffee down her gullet ...

With abrupt impatience she raised her head to shout but at that moment she heard the old woman shuffling and groaning on the stairs so she relaxed, setting up the compact-lid again because her movement had toppled it. And before Bochang appeared she began banteringly, 'Goddam, old crock, have you been all the way to London by bullock-cart to fetch my coffee?'

'Truly, Mem, it is not I that am slow. It is that pig of a Chinese in the shop. If I were still young and beautiful like Mem he would doubtless serve me in my proper turn, for what man can be discourteous to one who is young and beautiful like Mem? But because I am somewhat past my best—'

'Somewhat? Your backside has been less wrinkled than your brow these twenty years, I think.'

Bochang realized that the words had no cruel intent: her Mem knew only too well that in a few years now her own face would start to crack all over like an old vase too: for the Buddha was like all men in this one particular; he was very hard on women. She placed the coffee on the table by the bed and stood looking down at her mistress through the mosquito-net, an affectionate smile on her brown homely face. 'Is my Mem suggesting that next time I go to the coffee-shop I show the Chinese pig not my face but my—?' and she slapped her behind.

The Leopard threw down her tweezers and laughed and laughed. Together they enlarged on the joke with shrieks of merriment. But servants have to be kept up to scratch so in the end she went back to her grievance again. 'Are you not a good customer of that shop?'

'Truly, yes, Mem. Twelve times a day I go at least, ten times for coffee for my Mem and once for coffee for myself.'

'And every time you go to the shop you give the Chinese my money, don't you?'

'Truly, truly, Mem. One tic for every glass.'

'And be sure he wants my money. Everybody wants my money. Money is everything and no man will be slow to serve you once he has seen it in your hand. No, Bochang: it is not your ugliness which is to blame for your slowness with my coffee. Rather it is the remains of your beauty. How long did you pause to pass the time of day with the seller of dried squid who is even now frying his squid on the pavement outside my door and it stinks like hell? I think you are a little sweet on that seller of dried squid and that is why it always takes you so long to fetch my coffee.'

'The seller of dried squid is old and I think probably his own personal squid is as shrivelled as those he sells.'

Again the Leopard had to laugh for this was the humour of the older women attached to her father's house and she'd learned to appreciate it while her chest was still flat as a boy's.

Bochang saw that her Mem was feeling good because of the jokes so she ventured, 'Mem was very drunk when she came home last night. She quarrelled very long and loudly with the American. The Python and the Black Mamba were made angry. They said they can no longer get any sleep in this house because every night the White Leopard fights with her men.'

'What do I care what the Python and the Black Mamba say? I pay the rent for this room. When I am old or sick and have no money to pay my rent, then it will be time for those snakes to hiss and try to sting me.'

Bochang nodded her tousled head. 'Today is the last day of November. Tomorrow Mem must pay her rent again.'

The White Leopard laughed, her tee-hee-hee laugh, full of mockery and delight. 'And tomorrow I must pay you too, eh, Bochang? That's what's really worrying you, eh? Are you getting anxious, you poor old girl?' And she laughed again, so much so that she shook the bed and the compact-lid fell forward with a flash of gold.

'I fear nothing. Since her last monthly sickness Mem has been lucky and had a man almost every night. And last night the American who came was an old friend of Mem's and doubtless paid exceedingly well as always before.'

'That is where you are wrong.' She set up the compact-lid with a vicious movement as it all came back to her. Her face was dark with anger. 'Last night that American was not good to me. He said that he had been with me many times before and had always paid me well, which was true. But this time, he said, he had no money and he wished to sleep with me for love. That is why we quarrelled.'

'But in the end he must have paid Mem, for Mem slept with him, and my Mem does not sleep with a man until he has paid her.'

'He said he will pay me when he sees me next week.'

'All the same—'

'And I was drunk.'

But this excuse carried no weight with Bochang. 'But my Mem never gets so drunk that she omits to collect what is due before she lies with a man. Only when the money is safely locked away in the top-left-hand-drawer of the dressing-table—'

The Leopard suddenly sat up. 'You talk too much,' she snarled. 'Go back to the kitchen, where your silly chatter will annoy only Siput.' She reached over for the coffee and sucked lustily at the straw. Then she returned to her work again, once more alone.

The first armpit was soon finished. She rubbed it with her fingertips. The skin, a little browner than on the rest of her body, and now slightly reddened, was rough like a plucked chicken's (but warm, not clammily cold in death, like a chicken's). The hair follicles stood up like minute white volcanoes with minute black craters to them, but shortly these would disappear, as they always did, along with the inflammation. Just below the armpit proper, where her side began, on the finer-textured skin which covered most of her body, a few long silky-soft hairs remained. She hated them but she couldn't pull them out, for they stolidly resisted efforts to remove them. Sometimes she shaved them off, as twice a week she shaved off the coarse black hairs that these days disfigured her shins. For she hated all hair on the face or body, considering it ugly and a source of bad odours, and she was perturbed because the more she made war on it the more widely it spread on her person. She would gladly have shaved herself all over, apart from her pate, except that to do so would have been unbusiness-like: most men preferred there to be at least some hair, and what men preferred it was her rice and jewellery to provide. Yet maybe too, when the time came—when men no longer wanted her and her son too had deserted her to live with some other woman—she might shave off even this hair on her head, of which she was so proud, and go about in a white gown, a nun. She considered the possibility for a moment, as she frequently did, but only for a moment; for she gave little heed to the morrow: time enough to worry about that when it arrived.

Sitting up she swept the little cluster of quarter-inch-long hairs off the sheet on to the floor, re-arranged the pillows and the compact and lay down on her other side to deal with her other armpit.

Last night had been a mess and she knew it. It had been a mess from the start and she wasn't quite sure why. Perhaps the Buddha thought he'd been giving her more than her fair share of good luck of late and had decided it was time to teach her a lesson. The odd thing was that she'd been wearing her yellow dress—the lucky one. All her clothes had definite personalities for her: they were much realer than most people; for if that nice English boy had been right the other night and she had actually slept with more than two thousand men she'd completely forgotten one thousand nine hundred of them, but she'd never forgotten a single blouse, sarong or dress she'd had since she was a schoolgirl, no, not one. And this yellow one was one of the most important. She marvelled now that she could ever have hesitated about buying it. But she'd never worn yellow before, and she'd been troubled about whether the colour would suit her, at night, at the Bolero, under the dusty lanterns. On the other hand yellow was her colour—for she'd been born on a Monday—and also it was the colour the priests wore, so she's taken the plunge, though still with misgivings.

The first time she'd worn the dress was almost two years ago, at Clissmuss, that festival which Americans and Europeans seemed to consider so important. She had entered the Bolero with her usual confidence, prepared for a big night. But something had gone wrong. She didn't like thinking about that night but quite often her mind would revert to it in spite of herself because she'd never been able to puzzle out just why things had fallen out as they did. The Bolero had been reasonably full—that is to say, plenty of foreign men—but incredibly, astoundingly, she hadn't been able to get one for herself. Not any man at all. Usually she could pick and choose, playing off one candidate against another until she had decided which was the best proposition—and then she distributed the also-rans amongst her best friends. But that night of all nights she'd had to sit at her desk and watch the other girls, all thirty of them, the plain ones as well as the pretty ones, the foolish no less than the experienced, one after another fixed up with men who could pay good money but herself neglected, almost reduced to buying a drink for herself, a nadir she had never reached before. And when the Black Leopard had walked off with an old regular customer of her own the nadir of nadirs had been reached. Nor had the Black Leopard missed the opportunity, of course. She had come up to the desk, her dark face, still very beautiful, filled with infuriatingly kindly concern.

'Dear Vilai, you seem so quiet tonight. Are you sick?'

She hadn't fallen into that trap, of course. All the girls watched each other like lynxes and none of them would have missed the significance of the fact that the previous week she had gone home three nights running unaccompanied.

'Not sick.' What excuse could she make? 'I don't much like to work at holiday times. I just like to show myself everywhere and have a good time.'

'But you aren't even drinking.' Then she'd become confidential and even more offensive. 'My friend, who is very nice' (as of course you know, her voice implied, since until tonight he was your friend, but now he has tired of the old favourite as men will and seen who can really give him a good time)—'my friend has a friend who is rather nice too, and *he* told me to ask you—'

But she'd shaken her head furiously. She didn't need the helping hand yet, never would, she'd die first. With an effort she'd controlled her temper. For she'd had to deposit a thousand tics with the manager—so had the Black Leopard for that matter—and all those tics they would forfeit if they fought on the floor again. She said, 'No thanks. I don't particularly want a man tonight. One gets so tired, night after night.' (That blow told: for the Black Leopard had drawn a few blanks recently.) 'And anyway I am half-expecting a friend—'

'American?' The Black Leopard pounced. It was already ten o'clock. The Bolero closed at twelve. There were only two hours left in which this rescuer, in whom she didn't believe, could materialize to save her enemy's face. But the White Leopard had been too wily to commit herself.

'A very old friend, but nobody you know, I think,' she had said, praying, 'Buddha, dear Buddha, send somebody, please, oh, please. Do not let me down before this low woman.' And she had gone on praying for almost two humiliating hours, praying for an unknown angel to appear.

And at the last possible moment he had come, a Chinese angel, monstrously fat, appallingly drunk, ugly and old. It was part of her code never to go with Chinese men and in fact she never did so except once in a blue moon with one that was very rich, rather nice, and obviously infatuated. For the Chinese exploited her own people and moreover they weren't so afraid of catching things as white men were and so they were less likely to be clean, and she had never been sick yet and had no desire to be so and have to go to the doctor and pay him good money for injections and possibly have to stop sleeping with men for ten days or two weeks and lose all that money too. But that night she'd had to swallow her scruples, and the fat old man (and she hated fat men of any nationality) had made her look cheap there in front of all the western men, they out of whom it was legitimate to make money, they who normally clamoured for her favours ...

Remembering that fiasco she caught skin as well as hair in the tweezers and hurt herself, goddam.

She licked her finger and applied saliva to the sore spot. After that Clissmuss she had hated that dress. She had put all the blame for the disaster on it, for what else could have been responsible? For six months it had hung behind luckier garments, unworn and despised. But then, having been unable to sell it to any of the other girls or even give it away to her sister, she had decided to give it one more chance. After all it had cost a lot of money. And on this second outing it had done exceedingly well—four hundred tics for nothing—just a 'short time' at the Cottages with a charming American airman. And every time she'd worn it since it had done well, never less than two hundred tics, sometimes double that, and once sixty American dollars, at a time when the exchange rate was much better than it was now, too. She had come to trust in that dress, wearing it every month twice, on the two nights before her rent fell due, relying on it to pay her rent. And up till last night it had never again failed. But last night—

'It's because I wore it a day too soon,' she reasoned. 'The Buddha must have thought I was being overeager. If I'd left it till tonight, the proper night to wear it, the night before I have to pay for my room—But I wanted to get good money a day early to make sure of it. And the Buddha thought I didn't trust my luck and punished me.

'I ought to have got up this morning to make an offering to the priests,' she thought guiltily. 'But alas I was asleep when they came round with their begging bowls.'

Her thoughts had become unpleasant so she did with them what she did with all unpleasant thoughts, she banished them from her mind. For the next five minutes her brain dwelt in her armpit. Then all at once the job was finished and her mind could wander again.

She was always tidy in her habits and the first thing she did after sitting up was to sweep the new collection of little crescentic fibrils over the edge of the bed. Then she finished the coffee. Her clothes had come undone and for a short time she sat on the bed naked with her legs angled under her in the Siamese style. With one hand in her pubic hair pulling upwards and backwards she gave herself a quick inspection. There was a tiny pimple on the inner aspect of one thigh which she attempted to burst with her almond-shaped nails but it wasn't ripe. Two hairs growing in her opinion too close to her groin she plucked out with her fingers: a sharp gasp accompanied each successful tug. Then she gave herself the sort of friendly pat-pat-pat which a man will bestow on his son's shoulder when the boy has given him reason to feel pleased and proud. She inspected her nipples and brushed them swiftly and lightly with a rapid up and down motion of fingers. And then a plane roared over the house, low and fast, and she jumped up and went to the window to see if she could see it. Cautiously parting the white curtains which were drawn across the lower half of the window and assuring herself that no men were getting a free treat she looked up at the dazzling strip of sky, very narrow, which was all that the high wall of the houses opposite allowed her. The plane had vanished but she continued to stare at the sky, smiling. Americans, perhaps. And flyers, the best sort of Americans in her opinion.

By and large she preferred American to all the rest. The English were too sentimental: they always fell a little bit in love with even a dancing-girl, even though they were going to be in town only the one night and never see her again; they were terribly possessive, would show signs of wanting to fight all the other men she had to smile at (for business reasons) even though she *was* temporarily attached, by a small fee, to them. As for the Dutch, they were always fat and quarrelsome about money. The French paid too little and never gave a girl any peace all night and also they always wanted to do things that the Buddha doesn't approve of. But the Americans knew how to treat a girl like her. They had plenty of money and were free with it when out to enjoy themselves. They never fell in love: they hated personal involvements like that. They took their women as they took their drinks and cigarettes: women were just one more pleasure to which they were addicted but which they didn't get emotional about. The world was scattered with girls they'd had as it was with the bottles and cigarette packets they'd emptied. And often, in fact usually, they were drunker than the English or the French (but not the Dutch), so they soon rolled over to snore. Sometimes in fact the snores began before the game had been played, but never before it had been paid for. And whether they had been cheated or not they seldom cut up rough in the morning, for with them getting drunk was always more important than the other thing. Sometimes the cheated ones had been too drunk to remember that nothing had happened, and they'd be grateful to her in the morning for the good time they thought she'd given them. These she would see off the premises with her little charming giggles and when the door was bolted behind them she and Bochang would laugh till they cried almost. But at other times, if the man was especially nice, she might relent in the morning, for although as a general rule she was indifferent to the sexual act, regarding it as just a way to make money, sometimes around dawn, warm and blurry with sleep, she would feel the need for it; she would crave for it then, as waking some stifling night she might crave a drink of water; and having drunk she would sleep more soundly, more refreshingly, than if her thirst had not been slaked.

Well, if it was Friday she'd got a lot to do.

But even as she turned from the window she realized it wasn't Friday, it couldn't be. For the man who had cheated her last night was Dick, and Dick came, when he did come, invariably on a Friday, for it was on Fridays that his plane did a one-night stopover in Bangkok. Possibly that plane which had just gone over had been Dick's plane making a delayed start for Tokyo. If so, good riddance to it. She must see Dick once again, to get the money he owed her, but after that she didn't care. He'd slept with her eight or nine times, she supposed, during the last few months, and been very nice, but eight or nine times was the most you could expect even with the nicest of men, then some other girl would catch their eyes, or something else would happen to end the affair. Fortunately the supply of new men never dwindled, nor would it for the next two or three years, or possibly even five with luck; for her Mama was still very beautiful at fifty—oh, it must be more than that now—and with luck her daughter too could hope to be desirable to men for a long while yet.

She stood in the middle of the room twisting her hair into a knot on top of her head. She was disappointed in Dick. Sooner or later he would have been bound to let her down, of course: every man let you down sooner or later, not one of them was to be trusted, and that was the first thing a dancing-girl learned if she had any brains at all. But Dick ought to have lasted a little longer: after all she had been exceptionally good to him, giving him a fine time, invariably dropping other prospects, however promising they were, however much trouble it caused, whenever he had come lounging into the Bolero. And then he had rewarded her with this insult. Asking her to sleep with him for nothing. As if she were a very low girl with no self-respect at all. Only the lowest girls slept with men for nothing—for love, as the foreigners said—but she was a very high girl, she had a price, and if a man liked her he would show his respect by paying that price. Even Bochang, old and dried-up as she was, doubtless had her price: she'd demand her five tics of the seller of dried squid, and if he balked at the sum he could take his dried squid elsewhere as far as Bochang was concerned.

Once again she snatched up her sarong but this time she fixed it differently, tightening it round her chest so that it swathed her cylindrically from her chest to her knees. Her moods were very variable and from being a bit dejected a moment ago she had suddenly turned angry. Too many white men after they had slept with her a few times would suddenly take up this nasty attitude, and the queer thing was it was often the ones that had seemed to like her the most, the ones she herself was most drawn to, who did so. That just showed how little you could trust men, even the most charming of them. She conjured up a picture of Dick holding her last night with her arms pinned against her sides, breathing down great gusts of whisky smell into her face. 'Why must I give you money every time, honey? This is love, don't you understand? Just this once you can give it a guy for free, for Cry sake.' Would he have spoken to one of his own white women like that? No, of course not. He would never have dreamed of insulting a white girl so badly. But with her it was different. She was only a Siamese. He thought she wasn't as good as he was. He thought he could do anything he liked with her. He had tired of her and this was the way he chose to make her hate him. But he hadn't succeeded. For she was Siamese and as good as anyone else in the world. She'd never hate him—you can only hate someone you could love. But from that moment she'd begun to despise him.

She despised all men. And especially she despised white men because they despised her own race. There was only one good thing about white men: they had more money than any one else. And it was her duty to get as much of that money off them as she could. For money was important: it was the most important thing in the world. If you had money you could do anything. If you had enough money no one dare look down on you. If you were really very rich even white men would respect you—and you would be able to spit in their arrogant faces. And that would make you feel strong and happy, and better, much better, than they were ...

She picked up her personal dipper of solid silver and a cake of expensive American soap and once more descended to the *hongnam*. This time she shut herself in securely, bolting the door.

She hung the sarong on a nail. A few years ago, like any other modest Siamese woman, she would have kept it on while she bathed, but dancing-girls like prostitutes soon get accustomed to the idea of their own nudity and once that premise had been established her practical mind quickly grasped the advantages of bathing in the western style, stark naked, except of course for the sandals, which were indispensable.

So she stood in a shaft of sunlight coming through the skylight and tossed bowlfuls of water over herself. There was nothing methodical about the process. She didn't do her arms and then her torso and then her legs, or follow any other pattern, but just as the whim took her she would rub her face, or an arm, or her front, or her back, using the soap sparingly, and stopping frequently to throw fresh bowlfuls of cold water over herself. And as she rubbed and rinsed her spirits rose. For bathing was another of the beautifying rites she enjoyed and soon she had forgotten about Dick and her resentment against the white race generally and had begun to sing in a dry high rather pleasant voice, but a little uncertain of the notes.

'I—wonter—whooss—skeessing—hernow,' she sang, and then stopped while she concentrated on a knee, and then she sang the same line over again, and then stopped while she did the back of her neck, and then, very loudly, happily, she sang the same line again. It was one of her favourite tunes, played every night at the Bolero, but she seldom sang it all the way through, partly because she had some difficulty in remembering the western sequence of notes, but more because her mind would always fly off the tune to some other matter and then return to the tune only to fly off again: she never disciplined her thoughts: who did? why should they? Her brain was very good, and in moments of crisis she could think quickly what to do for the best, but crises seldom occurred in the *hongnam:* there your mind could run free, as when you were a very young girl, your body had run free about the country, never imagining what was in store for it.

She thought fleetingly of childhood. It had been almost the best part of her life, but not quite: young girlhood had been the best, from ten, say, to sixteen-and-a-half; the years when you had known that every hour was increasing your beauty, that one day this beauty would surpass that of all other girls in the *ampur,* and that finally when it was supreme you would donate it to some man, rich, good-looking, young, benevolent, and captivated, a paragon of a man, a perfect lover, yet faithful to you alone; playing around with prostitutes, of course, as any man must, but never seeking to introduce rivals into your house. Those had been the best years, for then too Jamnien had been her friend, Jamnien who had been the naughtiest girl in the village next to herself, who had led to all this, and was probably in Bangkok still, if she wasn't dead.

'But I don't want to think about my story,' she told herself. 'It only makes me sad.'

But the annoying thing was that once you began thinking about your story you couldn't put it out of your head. And especially if something had gone wrong, like this business with Dick, you would get into a morbid mood and then there would be no escape from memories that hurt until—well, until you went on a drunk. And getting drunk was dangerous for a dancing-girl—goddam, look where it had landed her last night, yielding to a man who (she'd gone through his pockets) had only sixty-six tics in the world, and forty of those she'd had to give back so he could take a taxi out to Don Muaag in the small hours. No, she mustn't start thinking about her story again, but even as she made the resolution she knew it was hopeless; it had been hopeless from the moment that, turning from the window in her bedroom, she had thought of her Mama back there in the province of Korat; today was going to be bad, bad, bad, there would be rows with Bochang and Siput and maybe with Udom too, there would be rows with the men at the Bolero tonight, and no way out of her misery until about three o'clock tomorrow morning when exhausted and with head swirling she would drop into her bed, too drunk, too drugged with weariness, too much molested by whatever man she had picked up, to care any more until about this time—noon— tomorrow.

If only I could go home for a few days, she thought.

She slumped on the stool in front of her mirrors. She began taking her hairclips out and shaking and freeing and frothing up her hair. But she wasn't thinking about what she was doing. She was staring straight at her image in the glass but for once it was powerless to hold her attention. She was seeing instead her home, her Mama, her sisters when they were all young together, before life had got amongst them like a whirlwind on a hot afternoon, and sent them all spinning crazily across the face of the world.

She picked up a strong blue comb and began to drag it cracklingly through her tangled mane, though it wasn't time to do her hair yet, that item came a good deal further down the programme.

Home—that was the only heaven she had known, the only one she would ever know in this life. As she told herself this she deliberately suppressed the memory that before she had escaped from it often enough home had seemed less like heaven than like a prison. Deliberately she forgot her old grandmother's acid tongue and the squabbles with her sisters and the hours and hours of sulky mutiny against her mother. She thought only of the good things—food that was always just right, the fun at times of Buddhist festival, the utter absence of worry, the famous salad her mother made of coconut, mango, peanuts, chili, and sugar all grated together, the wonderful curries flavoured with powdered waterbugs, great white juicy woodlice ...

Her thoughts seemed to have a recognizable drift. She ran to the door. 'Bochang! Bochang!'

'What?'

'Is my lunch ready?'

'Not yet.'

'I want it immediately.'

'It'll only be a few minutes.'

'I want it *now.* I'm hungry.'

Like sleep and whisky, a good meal could usually be relied on to put worries and spectres to rout, at least temporarily. It might work today.

Meanwhile she returned to the mirror and got busy. First she undid and did up the sarong more securely. Then she began to work cold cream into face, neck, shoulders and arms. She worked swiftly and vigorously, her eyes never leaving her image in the glass, and often she would step back like an artist from his easel to judge how the work was progressing. Especially when she was doing her back and chest and shoulders her hands moved caressingly over herself, almost like a lover's hands, and like the beloved she responded to the caress, she felt soothed and pleasantly stimulated. When she had greased herself enough she wiped off the excess with tissue and stood back and admired herself and then peppered her face and shoulders with powder until she stood in a thin perfumed cloud. Then she stood back from the mirror again, took off the sarong and shook it and whirled it as a toreador whirls his cloak and refixed it. And all the time she watched herself, enamoured of her own beauty, her grace of movement, this lovely living body which was hers. Why had she felt dreary on and off this morning? There was still nothing to worry about; the mirror did not deceive ...

Thus the foundation was laid, and now on it the face had to be built. Unlike many dancing-girls—for instance, the Black Leopard—she wasn't completely made up all day long. *Neung chu-um*—the first hour of the evening—seven o'clock, according to her Lolex—was early enough to don the full regalia. In the day time it was better to take it easy, to give seduction a rest, to put on just enough stuff to make yourself look passable at impersonal daylight distances and smell good to yourself and others. Many dancing-girls of course made themselves miserable, never daring to be themselves for a single minute, always over-made-up, overdressed, over-refined, pecking at their food (even when it had been bought for them by an escort) because they thought it unladylike to appear hungry, always asking for, when invited by a foreigner to eat, European food that you just toyed with with knife and fork, never, like her, demanding say chicken giblets and a Thai salad and glutinous rice and wolfing them down, as she did, with her fingers, confident that if the man really liked her he wouldn't mind, and if he did mind, well, to hell with him, he could only too easily be replaced with someone who didn't. The Black Leopard was like that, a low low creature who would sleep with *samlor*-boys or waiters or taxi-drivers if they brought foreigners to her house and were handsome enough and demanded that as their fee; she was as low as that; yet always, when out with a foreigner, she must act very high, as if she'd never eaten with her fingers off a banana-leaf in her life ...

So she pencilled on in black a little emphasis for her eyebrows and in red today's lips. She never gave herself quite the same mouth two days running. This wasn't because her hand faltered: her hand was her servant, it had to be obedient as Bochang and Siput were. But it amused her to experiment with her mouth. One day it would be Lita Hayworse', another day Lady Lamarr's, a third day Yvonne de Carlo's. Dearly she would have liked to be able to adopt the Yune Allyson mouth, for of all feminine filmstars Yune Allyson was her favourite; 'a pewty, pewty girl' she would say in English, running 'pretty' and 'beautiful' into one of her numerous portmanteau words. But she had enough taste to know that the Yune Allyson mouth would not sit comfortably on her oriental, life-worn countenance; it was altogether too young and western and sweet; oh, the whole girl was too young and sweet to accord in any way with the Number One Bad Girl of Bangkok. That was a dream of beauty beyond attainment ... Today, she decided, after running her mind through the movies at present showing in town, she would be Mor-leen O'Hala. The Mor-leen O'Hala mouth fitted easily over her own; she had merely to run the red a little less widely into the corners than usual and play down the two lobes of the upper lip under the nostrils. And there it was. She pulled back her lips while she crayoned the inner part that faced her teeth: it showed when she smiled, and she hated a two-coloured smile with bloody edges and an anaemic core. When she let her lips return to normal again, she saw that today's mouth was a success.

Open the sarong and shut and lock it again.

What else was there to do? Curl the eyelashes with the twenty-five-tic gadget. Rub scent into your armpits. Drop a little Lurine into each eye. And then, except for doing your hair, you were temporarily finished.

While she was combing and combing her hair, leaning over forwards with it all hanging down in front of her face, then hurling it back and leaning to one side with it all falling down sideways, her son came into the room. She looked at him in surprise.

'Goddam, why you not go school?'

She often talked to him in English, for the more he knew of that language the better: there was money in it. But to her distress he was quite ambitionless, or rather his only ambition was to drive a *motor-samlor* and that was worse than having no ambition at all. For the traffic was dreadfully dangerous and he would certainly be killed: moreover too many of the *samlor*-men were cowboys (she used the modern Thai word for criminal type) and she had no desire for her son to become that. Not at any rate the petty *samlor*-type cowboy.

'You hear what I say? Why you not go school?'

He spoke wearily in Siamese. 'Don't be stupid, Mama. Today's Saturday. School's finished early.'

'Oh, Saturday. I forget.'

She stared intently in the mirror while she made the parting and then seated herself on the stool again. The energetic combing had loosened the sarong and it was slipping down, but she disregarded this. One hand was raised to her scalp to keep a mass of hair in position whilst the other went to and fro between toilet-table and head, picking up clips and inserting them in a vertical line above the ear. As she pushed in each clip she either shut her eyes or looked sideways but the rest of the time she stared in the glass, either at her reflected head or past it at the reflection of her son wandering aimlessly round the room.

Only the Buddha knew how much she loved this boy, only the Buddha and herself. Sometimes she loved him so much that she almost gave the game away. Like two nights ago, when that handsome fair-haired English boy who'd been so free with his money had left unexpectedly early, about two or three o'clock. Instead of returning to her own room she had crept first into her son's, next to the maids', downstairs. She had parted the mosquito net and stared down at him, her heart, expanded by numerous peppermints and the thought of good money easily earned, suddenly filled with an almost intolerable love for this child who was hers, unquestionably hers, the one good thing remaining to her from her three marriages. How handsome he was! Exactly like his father, except that he had unfortunately inherited her own flat nose. He was lying sprawled on his back with his mouth open, breathing noisily, because his tonsils were bad and one day he'd have to have them out. Sometimes he could hardly speak or breathe. But she was always putting off the operation, always thinking up fresh excuses for delaying it; it would interfere with his schooling, he was frightened of the doctor, she couldn't afford to spend two weeks looking after him at the hospital, she couldn't spare Bochang to go with him either, that would mean the house would be left unguarded whilst she was at the Bolero and out and about, and as for Siput, who would wash and clean at home if *she* went to the hospital?—and anyway Udom was too thick with her as it was. Right now it was winter, and too cold for an operation on the throat—yet here he was lying almost naked with his blanket kicked off. She could hardly resist the desire to draw the blanket over him again. But if she had done so she might have awakened him, and if he had awakened and seen what she was doing he would have guessed her secret, that she loved him, and that would have been fatal. For then he would have lost his fear of her. He would have thought, 'She's weak after all, she's weak enough to love me as other silly weak women love their sons' and then he would have begun to take advantage of her, as other sons do of their mothers; his natural male badness would have asserted itself, and never again would she have had any control over him. But while he was frightened of her she could exercise authority and that discipline was good for him. But every day he was getting harder to hold down—more 'nerty', as she expressed it to herself using another of her original contributions to the English language, this one consisting of 'naughty' and 'dirty'—and more resentful of her continual nagging. He didn't realize that she had only his own good at heart, that she was doing her best to fit him for a world which only too well she knew to be cruel and unhappy ...

She could see that he had picked up a women's magazine and was flicking through its pages without hope of finding anything of interest in them. And as he stood there with his thin eyebrows drawn down over the huge dark eyes which were so like his father's she felt her love for him come over her again in another dangerous tidal surge such as that night's. She had a sudden insane desire to hurl herself across the room and sweep him into her arms and hug him till he broke free. But that would have been madness: he was fourteen years old: both he and she would have been deeply disgraced by such a scene of weakness ...

'Udom.'

'What?'

'Come here.'

He put down the magazine and approached on his bare brown feet. 'What do you want, Mama?'

She was intent on her work with her head jutted toward the mirror and did not immediately answer.

Suddenly he blurted, 'Mama, why don't you cover yourself up?'

She was astounded. 'What you mean?'

He made a gesture towards the slipped sarong. 'You are not an old countrywoman,' he muttered sullenly.

She glanced down at herself in surprise, as if she hadn't realized that there was anything there that could be offensive to anyone's sight, and made a move as if to lift and fasten the cloth. But her hand stopped and she laughed instead. It was not a laugh of amusement. 'What is matter?' she enquired, returning her attention to the mirror and putting the finishing touches to her hair. 'Why you not want look my—' she couldn't remember the English word—'my *num*? Maybe you sink not pewty, eh?

You big man now, you know all 'bout *num,* you know some girl have *num* pewty more than me, yes?'

'It isn't that.' He was deeply abashed. He knew he shouldn't have said anything.

And she was deeply abashed too. For she knew he was right. Nursing mothers could be excused, for it was too much trouble to be particular when the body had to be exposed every ten minutes or so, every time the baby cried. And really old women with grey cropped hair and betel-stained mouths and their sarongs put on in the old-fashioned way could be excused too for they had earned any comfort they could obtain. But she wasn't a nursing mother—hadn't been these twelve years—and wasn't old yet and probably never would be. She was just coarse. She was becoming so coarsened by this almost nightly ritual of undressing to total strangers that she forgot the proprieties even before this son whom she wished to honour her.

She was in the wrong but she couldn't, she mustn't, admit it. That would have looked weak, too. That was why she had begun to flog herself into a tantrum.

He began to move away but she halted him sharply in Thai. He stopped because he still dare not disobey. He stood as though he were manacled by the feet, staring at the floor. He couldn't conceal his shame and misery. 'Udom, look me.' Obstinately he kept his eyes downturned. 'U-dom—' There was still something in that tone which he couldn't oppose. He raised his eyes. She was winning once more. Perhaps for the last time. She said, less steelily, 'Look me here.' She turned towards him and opened the sarong wide before securing it firmly. 'Man see me at Bolero, he say, "That girl must have body very good, I sink I must have." He come zis house, he want kiss, he want play. I say, "No, no: you cannot: must giff me money first." Zen he giff me money.' It was an old line: she never let any of them, Udom, Bochang, or Siput, forget for a single day that it was she by the labours of her body that kept them fed and clothed and sheltered. 'I sink you not want hate anysing in your Mama's body,' she concluded. 'If your Mama die, I sink you die too very quick ... Now look my hair, see if you can see white.'

He came nearer reluctantly. Out of the corner of her eye she could see that he was trembling. Fear—or some other emotion? A boy was not like a man: he was much harder to understand.

He gave her head a cursory inspection. 'There's none.'

'Again look.' And as he still hung back she said in Thai: 'Udom, please examine your Mama's hair thoroughly, as she asks you.'

It was only an excuse to have him stand close to her, of course. To feel his hands, however clumsy and indifferent they might be, laid on some part of her body. But there was a practical justification for the self-indulgence too (in case anyone should think she was yielding to sentiment). There *were* two white hairs, two which sprouted perennially, defying constant plucking, and in two weeks they could achieve almost an inch of growth. Dozens of times before he'd tracked them down, sometimes cheerily, chattering of school or the movies or his latest fishing expedition, sometimes surlily, deeply resentful of being forced into such an unmanly occupation, women's work, a job Bochang should have done (and would have done) if only she hadn't been half-blind ...

It was like life, she thought, that these two white hairs, which augured what she feared most of all, the loss of her power to attract and fleece men, should be the means of bringing her into this close communion with her son. She never felt nearer to him except on those rare occasions when he could be induced to pluck her armpits (and she could endure the pain of his clumsy efforts). But they had to be in love with each other for there to be any real warming satisfaction in such passages, and today they were put out with each other. She looked down sideways at his thin wiry brown legs sprouting out of his khaki shorts, at his broad flat feet with their spread toes—she felt his fingers amongst the roots of her hair, making temporary partings this way and that—but they could have been anybody's legs, feet, ringers: they were as ugly, as unlovable, as those of the night ...

Bochang came in with the rice in a big white enamel tureen and a handful of plates and cutlery. She stooped with an exaggerated groan to place them on the floor. As she set out the three plates at the three corners of a triangle with a fork and spoon on each she said in her jocular way, 'So! Now we have a new lady's maid. And a very pretty little lass she is too.'

She was of course joking and anyway Udom was too slow in the uptake or too absorbed in his quest to realize that he'd been insulted. But his mother was promptly ablaze.

'Take care what you say, you old hag, or very soon we may have a new cook too.'

She shook her head violently to free it from Udom's hands. He looked down at her blankly: 'But Mama—' He'd only just started to pry. He'd thought that by searching diligently he would do his share towards restoring peace. But here was Mama apparently angrier than ever.

She understood his bewilderment but it only increased her fury. She pushed him roughly away. One should be quick to take offence, to realize that one was being debased. Otherwise folk would think one was soft, would despise one. He should have sprung at Bochang with a maddened snarl.

'Get out, both of you. I want to dress.' To Udom she added venomously, 'Or do you want to stay and see you Mama naked again?'

He flushed with anger and defied her by taking his time about leaving. She took no notice of him, busying herself searching for underwear in a drawer, but in her heart of hearts she was pleased. If he had scuttled out cravenly like Bochang she would have been disappointed. But he had stopped to pick up the magazine, then sauntered across to the door, his face still angry. He had obeyed her, but not meekly. Her tyranny was harsh but it wasn't breaking his spirit. When the time came he would throw off her yoke. But he wouldn't just slip it and disappear by night. He would metaphorically beat her brains out with it. And in that moment he would become a man.

She was being a good Mama to him. She was bringing him up the right way, so that he could face life and triumph over it ...

These would do for today ... The panties were very brief, pink, with TUESDAY embroidered on them in silk. She put them on in the Thai style, before removing the sarong.

After the sarong was off, she put on the brassiere. She put it on back to front round her waist, fastened it, then twisted it round and hoisted it into position. She squirmed like an eel to get her arms through the shoulder-straps and then spent a long time pinching her breasts and adjusting them inside the cups until they were settled to her satisfaction.

Posing before the glass she turned this way and that, admiring the smooth fit of the pink cloth over her hips and bottom and the way the golden-brown flesh swelled out of the white cloth of the brassiere. Both garments were well-worn, but what did that matter? It was the outer trappings that caught the male eye. It was they that inveigled him into your room and once he was there a few holes in your pants didn't worry him much. As long as they were clean he couldn't care less, and hers were always scrupulously clean. Her daytime underclothes she wore only two days before Siput washed them, the evening ones were fresh every night.

She took out a clean sarong, red, with a traditional design in silver thread worked all over it. It was the sort of thing she had worn at home, when she was still a young girl, still good, still full of ignorant dreams that included one man, a big house, plenty of servants, one son and one daughter, jewels, good food, everlasting beauty, endless glorious leisure and no troubles from year to year until seventy years were spent. She fastened it nostalgically around her waist and squatted on the floor before one of the places to await her meal.

Every day she gave Bochang fifteen tics to buy food. This was for fish, meat, vegetables, eggs, and sauces only: the rice she bought separately twice a month by the sackful. Fifteen tics a day came to about four hundred and fifty tics a month or more than most people in Thailand earned in that time, but she could afford to spend that much on food because she could earn it in one night with a bit of luck: certainly it seldom took her more than three nights to net that much ...

The economics of her life seemed to her simple. One source of her income was the Bolero. Every time a man paid ten tics to dance with her she got five of them. Every time he paid twenty-five to sit with her she got twelve of them. Every time he purchased a drink in her company she got five tics' commission on it, no matter what it was. And if he paid sixty tics to take her out of the Bolero before midnight she got twenty of them. These were her wages, handed over every week by the cashier at the Bolero. In a good month they amounted to two thousand tics, for she was very famous and in great demand.

The rest of her income came from sleeping with men. The amount of money you made this way varied a great deal from man to man. In her early days at the Bolero, when she had been so beautiful that almost every man who saw her had wanted her, she hadn't known how to worm money out of them: she'd been content with fifty tics for a short time or a hundred tics for all night like any other high-class girl. Thinking of all the thousands she could have made if she hadn't been so green she wanted to cry. Nowadays she never dreamed of sleeping with a man for less than two hundred (except on the rare occasions when he was a pewty pewty men but impecunious or when it was a matter of face to win him off some other girl), and usually she stuck out for, and got, three. The price, all other things being equal, went up in inverse proportion to the attractiveness of the man. Fat ones had to pay more than thin ones, and the bald had to fork out quite exorbitant sums. And if the intended victim proved recalcitrant what did she care? He was never any match for her in a quarrel; he paid her price, or he went. Too many men were bad for a girl, anyway. Twenty a month was enough, about half of them short time; that would net her another four thousand or so these days.

Thus on an average she made about six thousand tics a month as near as she knew. At the present exchange rate—the dollar was going down as the baht strengthened—that worked out at about three hundred and fifty American dollars a month, a reasonable income anywhere, she thought, and in Thailand, for a woman, a small fortune.

But of course her expenses were dreadfully high. First of all there was the rent for the room. Nothing vexed her more than having to hand over three hundred tics twice a month—on the fifteenth and the thirtieth—to the Python's uncle, for the privilege of living in this hole. That fair-haired English boy two nights ago—she'd forgotten his name and soon she'd forget him too, as she forgot every man she only saw once—he'd been interested in her budget, and good at mental arithmetic, and he'd worked out a lot of sums for her, in his head, sitting naked in the deckchair while she, naked on the stool, handed him slices of mango to eat. He'd told her she was paying seven thousand two hundred every year for her room and that in the four years she'd been here she'd practically bought the whole house. Yet there was nothing to show for all those thousands of baht. Indeed, a few nights ago, when she'd come home drunk from the Champagne Bucket followed by two Danes she didn't want, and

Bochang had been slow opening up and she'd kicked in the door in her fury, the Python's uncle had made her fork out an extra four hundred for repairs to the door. If she couldn't pay her rent tomorrow she and Udom and Bochang and Siput and her toilet-table and bed and deckchair and her few other sticks would all be dumped into the alley. Nor—now that a certain General who was powerful in the police force was so scared of assassination that he no longer went to places like the Bolero or admitted girls to his house or office—could there be any redress. Once she was thrown out she'd be thrown out forever, and the Python (who didn't have to pay any rent because it was her uncle's house) conscious of her own security would put on airs over the eviction. Anyway the General probably wouldn't be sympathetic these days, she told herself, though once he had been a damned nuisance—a Thai she dare not refuse to sleep with, and he'd taken advantage of that fact, and slept with her 'for love,' not once, but a dozen times, giving her a certain temporary prestige but cheating her of thousands of baht ...

Always if you sat still for a minute doing nothing your mind went into unpleasant channels like that. She jumped up and went to the mirror to take a quick reassuring look at herself.

Six hundred for the room. Five hundred for household food, including rice. Fifty for Bochang, who was so old and feebleminded that she couldn't get a job anywhere else and indeed was glad to get this one. Another hundred for Siput, who was fat and only early-middle-aged and a grouser but who washed things so well that she had survived upheaval after upheaval. Five tics a day to her son for his fares to school and his midday meal, but he saved on it somehow and had started smoking she was sure. At least four hundred a month for her own fares, for she went everywhere by *samlor,* not only to the Bolero nightly at a cost of six tics, but, if she failed to pick up anyone there, then right across town to the Champagne Bucket, which kept open till dawn and admitted unescorted girls; and then there were all the daytime jaunts to cinemas, beauticians, hairdressers, goldsmiths and the like—oh, certainly her fares came to four hundred a month, probably more. And then there was all the money she *enjoyed* spending (as against the money she was forced to spend)—for coffee, for fruit (she had a passion for durian which tastes like toffee and stinks like rotten eggs and costs fifty tics per thorny football-size pod), for clothes and cosmetics, for having her fortune told, for lottery tickets—anything she fancied she bought immediately, for now she had money and could spend as she liked, but the day was coming when she would be more or less penniless, and she would be most unhappy then, but at least she would be able to look back with satisfaction to these days when she'd had money to burn and hadn't stinted herself—another heaven in the past. She never stopped to calculate how much she threw away every month, maybe one thousand tics, maybe two, but anything that was left over she invested in gold and diamonds, partly because they never lost their value but also because she loved them. She reckoned that all the jewellery she possessed this morning was worth twenty thousand tics. Enough to get even the most greedy policeman on her side in the event of trouble, or to tide her over a quite lengthy sickness.

Bochang had brought in three dishes and set them on the floor and she was now down on her knees ladling big heaps of rice out of the tureen on to the three empty plates. The Leopard went to the door and called for Udom—that was a peace-overture: he could have starved to death for all she cared if she hadn't known he'd been in the right—and then subsided cross-legged before her plate. As she arranged her sarong decently about her legs she ran a greedy eye over the food.

There were the inevitable prawns which she loved, today served up in a blazing paprika soup. There were curried bananas—the cheapest sort of curry this time of year—the curry being flavoured with powdered water-bug. There was a Thai salad containing cucumber, onions, white cabbage as hard and crisp as crackers, mint, the leaves of two different sorts of tree and a weed that grew in ponds, a big coarse-looking tomato, and *me-krua* which looks like a small green tomato but has a hard rind which bursts in the mouth and floods the whole cranium with a delicious spicy essence. The Leopard felt her saliva begin to flow. She seized a spring onion and began to munch along its stalk with relish.

'What else is there?' she asked eagerly, accepting the plate of rice Bochang handed her. 'And where's all the sauces?'

'Have patience, please.' Bochang's tone was more that of a mother to a greedy child than of a poor old servant to her Mem.

Soon Siput arrived with the rest. Seeing that the Mem was already seated and eating she didn't presume to enter the room: she sank to her knees in the doorway and then leaning forwards on all fours pushed the dishes across the linoleum to Bochang, who, crouched down too, took them and arranged them before the Leopard.

There were only two more—shreds of fried beef and an omelette. But more important than these were the condiments, five in all: a mauve sauce that is inseparable from salads, a black Chinese one made from soya beans, a brown Siamese one made from fish-salt, a red chilli one that was hot as fire and finally sliced green chilli in vinegar. Anything with chilli in it the Leopard placed close to her own plate and during the next few minutes she took such enormous quantities of pure fire into her mouth that she had to stop every now and then to blow on her tongue to cool it.

Siput remained on all fours for a few moments with her paps (which were offensive to the Leopard's sight because they were fat and no longer firm and presaged what her own might soon become) squashed together more out of the skimpy white slip than in it; then she slowly drew back onto her heels and as slowly rose to her feet just outside the door. There, having first pulled one shoulder strap up her podgy dark-brown arm she undid her sarong, held it extended in her hands and waggled it from side to side to remove creases and folds, and then did it up again as if she were doing it up forever. And all the time her dark face, fat, fortyish, and disagreeable, but still not really ugly, watched her Mem speculatively.

The Leopard of course was aware that she was being watched, but she feigned not to notice.

She knew what was going on in Siput's mind. Udom was a growing boy. He had the normal growing boy's concern to be in at the very beginning of a meal. With that idea in view he had come up to his Mama's room while she was still dressing, before Bochang had even brought the plates up. But at the present moment, when he ought to have been stuffing himself with good fare, he was sulking downstairs, pretending to read a magazine. It was obvious to Siput that mother and son had had words. But what about? And could she make any capital out of it?

That, the Leopard was quite sure, was the gist of Siput's thoughts.

There was no love lost between her and this rotund maidservant of hers. Besides being revoltingly fat, Siput was sulky, quarrelsome and expensive. It pained the Leopard that she had to pay a hundred tics a month to such an unlovable creature when Bochang who was good fun and loyal and industrious in her slow muddling way was available for half that amount. The trouble with Siput was that she wasn't beaten by life yet. She believed that if she lost this job she could get another. She was always threatening to leave. She even sometimes started looking round for a new place. But not very diligently. For, when all was said and done, she was well off in the Leopard's service. The work was not hard, just washing and ironing for the four of them, keeping their quarters clean, and helping Bochang prepare the food, but that was not the point: she could have got an equally easy job elsewhere for just as good pay if not better. What kept her clinging to this place was the vicarious thrill she got out of serving in a house which contained three such women as the White Leopard, the Black Mamba and the Python. In a dim way the Leopard understood how Siput's mind worked. All her life had been blameless because her husband had cherished her and supported her until so much of her beauty had gone that she'd lost all chance of going into a brothel, and when he'd finally taken up with someone younger and prettier, someone who wouldn't presume so much upon old acquaintance as an old wife did, it had been too late for her to take up anything but sewing or washing. Yet she'd always been a woman of normal instincts and she naturally thought she'd missed a lot of the fun in life and now she tried to make up for years of dullness as best she could by living, continuously mildly scandalized, in this house where women were indubitably women ...

In addition there was the matter of Udom. As the boy had become more nerty, and his Mama consequently harsher, he had veered away from her to other things—to more nertiness, like smoking, and going on prolonged fishing expeditions, and coming home very late from school and refusing to say where he'd been. She hadn't realized that he'd veered away in search of sympathy too, and found it. When he pointedly refused to eat with her for a few days and took all his meals downstairs she'd thought his motive was disgust with her, not love of Siput. It was the eels that finally opened her eyes. That day the squabble was particularly violent. It was a Sunday and he'd been out all day from before she was up until when she was getting ready to go to the Bolero. When he'd come in there'd been a great commotion downstairs and she'd found him proudly exhibiting an enormous eel and some smaller ones. His face was shining with pride and joy and Bochang and Siput were making as much fuss of him as if he'd just won first prize in the lottery.

'Look, Mama, a great big eel. I caught it myself.'

'I'll cook it tomorrow,' Bochang was saying. 'It will be wonderful curried.'

Without a word to any of them the Leopard had taken the eels from his hand, gone to the door and hurled them into the lane. Returning to the trio she'd burst into a storm of fury. 'Do you want to bring shame on your Mama?' she'd yelled at the boy. 'Do you want all the people in the street to think that your Mama is poor, so poor that she has to send out her little son to fish for eels for her to eat? When I am sick, when I can no longer eff eff eff to keep you clothed and fed and at school, then it will be time for you to go out fishing for eels. Then maybe I shall not be ashamed to see you come home laden with eels, for a hungry belly knows no shame ...'

'Everything I do is wrong,' he stormed back. 'I wish I was dead.' And then suddenly he'd started to cry and had buried his head in Siput's dirty sarong.

Even then the Leopard hadn't wholly grasped the fact that that dirty sarong was comfort. She'd continued to shout, 'Never go fishing again, and if you do, give everything you catch to your friends, not to me. Their mothers are not high girls like the White Leopard: doubtless they will accept your gifts without shame.'

Back in her room, trying to get on with her making up, she'd been bothered by tears obscuring her sight. He was so young, he just did what he wanted to do without considering how his pranks would be construed. He'd brought shame on his mother but instead of being repentant ... She'd heard the door opened and slammed and her heart had gone cold: perhaps he'd run away for ever ... When Bochang had brought up that night's dress, freshly ironed by Siput, she'd asked, far too soon, far too obviously anxious, where he'd gone ...

'He's gone nowhere. He's downstairs with his Mama.'

'What do you mean, idiot? I am his Mama.'

'I think that is not so any longer. Once my Mem had a son who lóved her very much but she did nothing but scold him. But Siput has borne and lost three sons and her heart is soft.'

'It is your head that is soft, not her heart, you old buffalo. Your head is so soft today I can't understand what you say.'

'I am soft in the head, as Mem says, and moreover I am half-blind, but this much I can see with my poor eyes and understand with my soft head. My Mem is losing a son while her washerwoman gains one.'

She'd screamed at the old fool until her throat could scream no more but all the screaming hadn't been enough to frighten the terror from her heart.

Why hadn't she sacked Siput on the spot? The immediate reason had been that there wasn't time, she was late for the Bolero already. Then there she'd met an old friend and fallen into a mellow mood. Over her third whisky she'd had a brainwave about the door slamming. Of course, Udom or Bochang retrieving the eels! She'd laughed so much that her friend had thought she was drunk already. And very sincerely she'd hoped that no one had forestalled them, for it would have been a pity to waste good food, a bigger pity still to make a gift of it to a complete stranger ...

Well, she'd never seen any signs of their feast, but she knew they'd had it. And Siput had stayed on. Stayed on to annoy her on a good many subsequent occasions such as now. Why hadn't she thrown her out? She was a snake, a fat snake, coiling herself around the innocent heart of a boy ...

They were a mixed lot of reasons. Paramount was the knowledge that Siput was good at her work. Those square hands with their hard heels and short fingers worked wonders with the tears and stains to which a dancing-girl's clothes are subject: it would have been stupid to get rid of their owner except over something vital. Then there was an obscure but comforting feeling she had that blood was thicker than water; no son of hers, she thought, could really, if it came to a showdown, prefer so common a creature as Siput to herself. But there was always the danger that he might, and that was the third most important reason. She could never resist playing with fire. Just because Siput was a threat to her peace of mind it was a pleasure to keep her in the house. To expel her—to obliterate her—would have been easy, but it was better to have her there to fight, a constant challenge, an enemy she must grapple with and defeat at every opportunity.

And here was another crisis in the long-drawn battle.

What to do? Ignore Siput? Then she might go to Udom and he in his childish inexperience might not be able to lie effectively, might even blurt out the true story—'the sarong was undone; my Mama is not an old country woman; why—?' No, she must not just let the matter drift; that wouldn't do.

Tell Siput to call Udom? But he might not come. That would be a victory for Siput. That wouldn't do either.

Go and fetch him herself? But again he might refuse to come. That would be not only a victory for Siput, but an additional loss of face for herself.

What to do? Dear Buddha, what to do?

Udom solved the difficulty by appearing in the doorway.

She felt a queer little halt, then a speeding of blood through her heart; her whole chest seemed to swell up with a pleasurable pain.

'Eh, Udom, you silly boy, where have you been? The food is getting cold. Sit down and eat before Bochang gobbles it all up.' And she wriggled a little to one side as if to make more room for him before his plate.

But he just stood in the doorway, first on one foot, then on the other, his head hanging. With Siput dark in the background.

'Come on, come on,' she said in English, which was a private language between them and excluded Siput. 'Why you waiting for?' She blew on her tongue to show how much she was enjoying the food, then leaned forward to pick up a whole stalk of mint.

'Mama, I do not want to eat. I want—'

'Don't be foolish, Udom. Sit down and eat. I have spent my money so that there shall be food for you too.'

It came out with a rush. 'Mama, give me five tics. I want to go to the movie.'

She could hardly prevent herself from laughing. How guileless children were! He had handcuffed himself before he started to box with her. She said, 'Eat first. Then I will give you the money. Perhaps.'

'But I don't want anything to eat.'

'If you don't eat I won't give you any money, that's certain.' To show that she was not just being tyrannical she added, 'You are a growing boy, Udom, and already today you have been up for many hours and gone to school and worked there very hard, or so I hope. If you do not eat you will not be strong. And I want my son to be strong, so that when I am old—'

She saw him look round over his shoulder in misery at Siput and she knew the thought was in his mind to refuse the food and the money with it. But the stakes were too high for him. He was furious enough to forego his food but he couldn't forego that and his movie too, that was too big a price to pay for his pride. Unwillingly he came across the room and awkwardly squatted in front of his plate.

Siput sniffed and tossed her head and went heavily downstairs.

With a sigh he picked up his spoon and fork and began turning the rice over and over. Soon he couldn't resist putting a little in his mouth, just to taste it. In another instant he had started eating voraciously.

The Leopard laughed. She was aglow with chilli and triumph. She was a match for all of them. Nothing could defeat her; her heart was so strong.

She passed her plate across to Bochang for another helping of rice. 'Give my son a fresh helping: what he has is not hot and flies may have walked on it,' she said, but when Bochang offered to take his plate he motioned her away, he couldn't even wait that long ...

The first almost unbearable pangs of her own hunger were now dulled. But she still had a long way to go before she was replete.

Eating, like sleeping, whisky, tending her beauty, talking, quarrelling, fooling men, and getting their money from them, was one of the major pleasures of life. But like all those others—there had been an example with whisky only last night—it had its drawbacks. Food was bad for you because it made you fat. It hastened the day when you would no longer be able to inflame men with desire. Yet on the other hand it was a necessity: it had to be taken, and in large quantities, in order to keep your strength up. The only solution to this quandary was in control. She had a theory that if you ate only once a day, like the priests, you weren't so liable to get fat—for whoever saw a fat priest? But at this one meal you must eat enormously to give yourself energy for the next twenty-four hours. And she had stuck to this regimen with strict self-discipline for two years, ever since she had begun to put on weight. The cakes she liked to eat at the Singsong Lounge in the afternoons, the occasional bowl of noodles she would have after a visit to the hairdresser's or a movie, the various little delicacies Bochang would bring her in the small hours when work was done—these were only snacks, not meals. They were too small to have an enlarging effect on the figure. But at this one meal of the day the risk must be taken. She must eat hugely now, to prevent herself from wanting to eat hugely between now and this time tomorrow ...

'Is not the food good?' she asked Udom.

His mouth was so full the reply was unintelligible.

Bochang, who never ate a big meal because she was preparing herself little treats all day long, got up to fill the silver dipper with drinking water and fetch the toothpicks off the toilet-table.

'Which movie do you wish to see, Udom?'

Again his words were indistinct but she gathered that the film was called *Iverhoe* and that it was showing at the Chalerm Krung theatre.

She made delighted noises. '*Iverhoe*? That is good. As it happens I wish to see that movie too. Lobber Taylor is in it, and I like Lobber Taylor very much.'

Bochang, running a toothpick in and out between her betel-blackened teeth, paused to spit noisily into the brass spittoon. 'What is the difference between one man and another?' she asked with the tone of a child that has outgrown the habit of playing with dolls. 'Personally I wouldn't go ten yards in a taxi to see any man on Earth.'

'But Lobber Taylor is an exceptional man. Many many men look like men but they do not act like men. Lobber Taylor—he looks like a man and he acts like a man too.' She accepted the silver dipper she had used at her bath and took a long gulping drink. 'I think if Lobber Taylor came to Bangkok,' she said when she'd finished, 'I should have to try to pass him once.'

She got up, filled her mouth with drinking water again, worked it around her teeth, and then ejected it in a long well-aimed stream into the spittoon. Coming back to the dishes and stooping to pick up half a dozen toothpicks she said, 'I even think, if he hadn't any money, I would let him come here for nothing.' Bochang snorted. 'I wonder if he'd buy me a new bed. This one is old and it creaks in a tell-tale manner and I am afraid one of these nights when someone is too rough and clumsy—' She sank onto it and began picking her teeth thoughtfully. 'Maybe he would take me back to America,' she added at length. Her dreams were often very rosy when she'd just finished her meal.

She looked down at Udom sitting alone on the linoleum with his thin brown legs tidied away under him and the soles of his feet pointing upwards in the proper Buddha style. He was tucking in with gusto, all his late huff forgotten.

'Udom.' He cocked an eyebrow but didn't stop eating. 'How about we go together to see the movie this afternoon? And I will buy you ice-cream and Cola afterwards.'

It was as if she had said, 'Tomorrow at dawn you will be taken out into the lane and shot dead.' He dropped his spoon and fork with a clatter. 'No, Mama, no.'

She was amazed at his vehemence. When an idea seemed good to her she always expected it to look equally good to others. 'What is the matter with you now?'

He picked up his spoon and began to toy with the food again but the boyhood had gone out of his appetite. He didn't answer.

She said, 'So. You do not want to go to the movie with your Mama. I suppose you would rather go with your friends. When you go to the movie with your friends, you can smoke cigarettes like a big man. But if you go with me you have to behave yourself. Is that why you don't want to go with me?'

'No. Not that.'

'Why then?'

Sullen silence.

She began to work herself into a passion for it was in her rages that she conquered and ruled. 'I work like hell to make your life good. I feed you. I buy you clothes. I give you money so that you can go to school and learn. I am a very good Mama to you. Yet when I ask you to do one little thing for me—'

'Give me five tics and let me go.' He had got to his feet and he wouldn't look at her.

'If you were a good boy—if you were grateful to your Mama—' She began to cry. For the Buddha in his kindly provision for her had given her this power to weep at the right moments and sometimes as a matter of fact she did it when she had no intention of so doing. On the other hand there were times when it would have been expedient to cry and she tried very hard to do so but she couldn't squeeze out a single tear. And right now she might have been dry-eyed for all the effect her weeping had on the boy. Seeing that tears would not melt his heart she wiped them away and said evenly, 'Tell me why you do not wish to go to the movie with your Mama. If your reason is good, I will let you go by yourself.'

'You know the reason. I have told you before.'

So that was it. 'Tell me again. I forgot.'

She was foolish to press the point, of course, for by shutting up she could save them both pain. But there was this urge in herself continually to hurt not only herself but this son whom she loved too. And she couldn't resist it. The pain was there all the time anyway. Words only brought it to the surface, like tearing the bandages from a raw wound.

'Well?'

He refused to say anything.

'U-dom—'

He burst out passionately, 'Why must you make me tell you over and over again? You know very well why I don't want to be seen in the street with you. Maybe we would meet some of my friends. I don't want them to know who my Mama is.'

Each syllable was like a dagger entering her heart. Her son was ashamed of her. He didn't regard her as a fine independent woman struggling to support him by the labours of her own body. He took the conventional view of dancing-girls, that they were bad. She said, mildly, 'I think your friends would not know me.'

'Of course they would. Everyone knows the White Leopard.'

It was the first time she'd ever heard him use that term. It sounded ghastly on his lips. 'Don't call me that,' she cried sharply, and it was a plea, not a command.

He went on, 'So far I think nobody knows my Mama is a dancing-girl. I have told them many lies—'

'What lies?'

'Oh, I don't want to tell you.'

Bochang was just going out with the last remains of the meal. The Leopard went to the dressing-table and took a ten-tic note from her handbag. 'I will give you not five tics but ten,' she said, 'but first, Udom, I want to know what lies you have been telling other boys. It is wrong to tell lies,' she added, suddenly remembering her role as Mama and mentor. 'The Buddha forbids us to tell lies, and so we should never do so, unless of course it is absolutely necessary. The Buddha will never blame anyone for doing wrong when it is absolutely necessary.' She lay down on the bed again. 'Now tell me what lies you tell your schoolmates.'

The knowledge that he was soon to be wealthy loosened his tongue and soon as any Thai would have done, he began to enjoy telling the story, it began to seem to him like a joke. 'When I first went to the school, when you had me sent up from the country one year ago, of course all the boys wanted to know where I came from, and who my father was. I said, 'My father is dead.' Then they asked, 'Who is your Mama?' and I said—' He hesitated as if frightened.

'You said, "My Mama is a dancing-girl at the Bolero"?'

'No, no. I said you were a princess.'

'What?' The Leopard jumped up on the bed and her face was the picture of delight. 'You told your friends your Mama was a princess? That was a very good lie, Udom. Very good indeed. It made your Mama look high, so of course it made you look high too.'

'Yes, but they did not believe me. They said, "If your Mama is a princess, why do you come to school in a tram? Why doesn't she bring you in a car?"'

The beastliness of children, not to let a good romantic lie like that stand on its own sturdy legs! 'So what did you say to that? I suppose you changed your story, and said I was a washerwoman like Siput.'

'Of course not. If you change your story, no one will ever believe anything else you say.'

'Then I am still a princess?'

'Yes.'

She felt like jumping out of bed and hugging him, but she contented herself with laughing happily into the pillow. Finally she said, 'So your friends still think I am a princess. But how do you explain the fact that you still go to school by tram at a cost of ten satang?'

'I tell them you are not only a princess but a doctor too.'

She was startled. 'A doctor? What sort of doctor?'

'A doctor of medicine. The sort that gives injections.'

'But why—?'

'Don't you see, Mama? You were a princess, but you were a doctor as well, and you'd had to go to America to study—'

'I don't like this lie so much,' she said. For she'd often dreamed of being a princess but had never had any desire to study medicine. The whole idea of injections was bound up in her mind with the hazards of her profession and she disliked it—from either end of the syringe. She couldn't identify herself with the dream. 'I think it is a silly lie.'

'Oh, you don't understand. If you had gone to America how could you drive me to school in the car? I said you'd had to sell the car so that you could have enough money to fly to America.'

'I don't like this lie either,' she said sharply. 'You must always make people think that your Mama is very rich.'

'Dear Buddha, how dense you are, Mama! It was a good lie. Everybody had to believe it, for how could they show it was a lie? But then you gave me this watch—'

'What, does that come into the story too?'

'If you had bought me a gold one as I wished everything would have been all right. But the first time I wore this one everybody of course crowded round to look and they asked where I had got it and I said my Mama had given it to me. Then Chalow—'

'Who's he?'

'Oh, one of the boys—I don't like him—he said, "But how can your Mama have given you this watch? Your Mama is in America but this watch is not an American watch. It is an Ernest Borel such as can be bought anywhere in Bangkok for five hundred tics."' His face twisted. 'Then again everybody thought I was lying. So I had to think quick what to say.'

'And what did you say, Udom, my son?' (Even her gifts made trouble for him.)

'I said you'd just come home again, and you'd brought me a lovely gold watch from America, but the customs man stole it—'

'Good. Lies should always be easy to believe.'

'And—and—you still wouldn't be able to take me to school in your car, because now you were a very famous doctor and you had so many patients to go and see—'

The Leopard couldn't bear it any longer. She leaped off the bed, threw her arms round her son and hugged him.

He was scandalized. 'Mama—' He struggled to break free and she had sense enough not to hold him against his will. 'Mama,' he cried, 'give me the ten tics and let me go to the movie.'

At that moment she'd probably have given him a thousand if he'd asked for it. Well, a hundred anyway. She handed the note over without any further hesitation. And with it she gave her commendation. 'Udom, sometimes you are very naughty and make your Mama angry, but in this matter you have been a good boy. You have lied well. If you are going to be a liar, you must be the Number One Liar in Bangkok. It is the same if you're going to be a cowboy, or if you're going to be good. I would rather you were going to be good, but I don't want you to be just a little bit good; if you are going to be good you must be the Number One Good Man in Bangkok, you must not be number fifteen or sixteen at anything, for you Mama is Number One Bad Girl in the world I think, and you must always be Number One too, or you will put your Mama to shame.' But he'd already gone. She followed him onto the landing and shouted, 'Don't be late. Get home before I go to the Bolero.' The only answer was from the front door, which slammed.

For once she didn't drift automatically to her mirror. She went straight to the bed and lay down. Already her mind was beginning to gloss over the pain of the scene, to make it more acceptable to the memory. She said to herself, 'My son doesn't want to be seen on the street with me, but it isn't because he is ashamed of his Mama, it is because he has made all his friends think I am a princess ...' She tried to laugh at the absurdity of children, but suddenly tears came instead and poured down her cheeks into the pillow.

Six

A sparrow slapped onto a window spar and stuck; examined the room with bead-like eye.

The Leopard didn't stir. The tears had long since dried amongst the mascara. The second-hand of her watch was scurrying round and round the dial. An artery in her throat pulsed visibly, rhythmically, sturdily, as if it too were keeping track of the time. But for two hours she had been letting her beauty run away without caring. She had temporarily died.

She was dreaming that she was at home again, a young girl. It was evening; Jamnien and she were sauntering back from the river in the twilight; there was a purple cloud in the West dividing the dull gold below from the silver and blue above. They were both in fresh sarongs; the wet ones they carried in their hands; they had towels over their shoulders; their hair curled damp against their cheeks. They walked carelessly, sometimes bumping against each other, or scuffling with extravagant giggles, or stopping to muse hand in hand or with their arms round each other's waists, watching the green parrots arrowing nestwards over the treetops with their wild remote cries like those of ghosts in the dusk, or the bats, swift and erratic as thoughts, wheeling noiselessly in and out of the lower branches. Jamnien was excited about something; this time it was about a letter that some boy had slipped her on the way home from school; it was a love-letter, of course; it contained a lot of poetry and one quite outrageous proposal. Vilai, felt very superior to Jamnien—how gullible the girl was! Obviously half a dozen boys had worked on the letter in committee—but at the same time she felt a pang of envy: why didn't she ever receive any love-letters herself? Could it be that she was unattractive to men?

Then suddenly, as if to scotch that doubt, the scene shifted to the Bolero; men were milling about her in an importunate ring; most of them were Americans, very tall and handsome, with clean lines to their loins except where their wallets bulged their hip-pockets; and there wasn't one of them who wouldn't have given his whole right arm clean up to the shoulder, *and* his wallet, to win her for that night. She was dawdling over her selection, trying to determine which candidate combined in himself the most money with the best looks and the pleasantest disposition, so that she'd have no regrets on any grounds whatever, when suddenly there was a stir and they all cleared off; she was left deserted at her table; and looking round ... Looking round she found Jamnien had appeared; Jamnien, still young and straight from the river in nothing but a sodden black sarong; Jamnien, looking lost and childish, yet all the men had run to her and kneeling before her were casting jewellery and wallets as big as briefcases at her bare brown feet, and not one of them had eyes for any other woman, although she was still only a kid without a vestige of bust or make-up. Then the knife really twisted in her heart, but she got out her compact as if she didn't care, and sprung the lid to powder her nose; and there, shatteringly, horrifyingly, in the mirror was her own face, gone to pieces all of a sudden without her realizing, overpainted, creased, with cheekbones jutting like boulders and a great oozing sore on the chin ...

She awoke with a tearing sob. For a little while she lay quaking while the phantoms dissolved in the light. Then with a curse she brought up her wrist to look at her watch. She stared at it incredulously. Past two o'clock? With another curse she leapt off the bed and rushed downstairs, ready to murder the first person she encountered because she'd been left to lie so long.

Her victim was Udom's new pup. Udom was always getting new pups, creatures that began sweet and kissable but too soon turned gaunt and mangy and so were inevitably kicked out by Bochang or herself. But Chokchai had barely started this cycle yet. He was still about the size and shape of a ball of brown wool, and irritatingly innocent. So now, instead of divining that she was in a temper and giving her a wide berth, he came cavorting up, and when he smelled the red toenails, which were associated in his mind with several ecstatic slobberings and ticklings in the past, he wagged his tail so hard he fell over. And he was still on his side, struggling to right himself, when five of the red toenails caught him just where he was fattest.

He sailed through the air, obviously almost enjoying the new sensation, until he hit a corrugated iron partition and fell to the ground in a welter of dismay and shrill puppy howls of shock.

He then scooted away as fast as he could, tumbling over twice with frantically-scrabbling legs before he finally managed to round the corner of the partition. She smiled in spite of herself at his comical anxiety to get away from trouble—just so sometimes she couldn't run away fast enough from some horror in her dreams—and she followed him to make peace, but he'd gone to earth behind the kitchen water-vat and it was damp and smelly there, so she couldn't be bothered with him any more.

Besides, there was something else to think about. She was now in the grip of a new importunity. Every day you had to go through the same sequence of events, it seemed. You woke up, had a coffee, bathed, fed, dozed a few minutes, then this ... She ran upstairs, hoping to have time to fetch a cigarette, but there wasn't even time to get her sandals. She had to enter the *hongnam* just as she was, bare-footed: a revolting business.

She tossed bowlfuls of water all over the squatter, tore at her clothes and plumped down.

The pain got worse, so bad she started to groan.

She never thought of putting the blame on too much chilli. She cast her mind over the last few days, trying to recall a single sin that the Lord Buddha, knowing the full circumstances of her life, could possibly hold against her. She judged her actions in the light of the five normal precepts which are all that the Buddha, knowing we have to make a go of it in a wicked world, expects the laity to observe. Thou shalt not kill, lie, steal, commit adultery or get tight. Where had she transgressed? Certainly she hadn't killed anyone, though she'd felt like killing Siput and of course the Black Leopard more than once. She hadn't lied either, except forgivably in the routine of business, like telling that nice English boy she was only twenty-nine and that her real name was Vilai and that she never slept with a man all night for less than five hundred tics (but instead of coughing up another three hundred he'd gone home early). Again, she hadn't stolen anything—in fact when she'd emptied Dick's pockets she'd returned forty of the sixty-six tics she'd found in them, though morally they were hers: it was he who was the thief, he'd slept with her and not paid: what was that but out and out robbery? Then adultery. How could she commit that? She'd been finished with her third and last husband for seven years at least ... Only drunkenness was left, then. Well, admittedly she'd got drunk in the last few days, twice. But surely the Buddha wouldn't blame her for either lapse. It was part of her job to get drunk. Every drink she put into her own belly at the Bolero put five more tics commission into her handbag. The Buddha knew she had to have that money, for who in the world would give her a single satang? She had to earn every one herself. Those six peppermints which—what was his name? Wretch, or something like that—had forced down her throat, were not in the circumstances so much six peppermints as thirty tics: the price of a bag of rice; she'd had to drink them so that Udom wouldn't starve. And last night she'd only guzzled because Dick liked her to. In fact the Buddha, being just, *must* realize that she'd already been paid out for getting drunk last night, thoroughly. Her present misery must be a reprisal for some other misdemeanour, committed, perhaps, weeks ago ...

There was one more bout of pain but it was fairly mild and came to nothing. She tore a piece of paper from a wad that hung on a nail and with it picked up the dipper in the smaller of the two vats. Quickly she washed herself clean, dropped the dipper back in the vat and threw the piece of paper into the old petrol can. She dipped up clean water out of the big vat and washed her feet and fingers in it, dried herself on the sarong, and pulled TUESDAY up into place. Then she hurried to her room. It was time she went out: the day was half gone; too soon it would be time to be getting ready for work ...

Half an hour later she entered the Singsong Lounge. The first person she saw there was Dick. The next was Wretch. And they were sitting at the same table together, talking, as if they were friends.

She didn't give any indication that she'd seen them, of course. She walked unhurriedly to the bar and seated herself on one of the high stools. There was a mirror running the full length of the bar; in it she could keep Dick under observation, also anyone else who might be interesting. And they wouldn't know they were being watched, or alternatively, if she wanted them to, they would. She knew how to use that mirror ...

The barman didn't speak, he just raised his eyebrows,

acknowledging a customer who was regular but whom he didn't esteem—a tart who came in unescorted, flirted shamelessly with foreign men, and never gave a tip, unless her change happened to be negligible and she wanted some dupe to see her nonchalantly wave it away. She was so used to the expression it couldn't hurt her any more. She was almost too polite to him, for she had to be careful with waiters; they were legitimate sailors on the high seas where she committed her acts of piracy; like *samlor*-boys, they could be useful when friendly, but they were potentially dangerous if they disliked you. This one was a pig, but she had to treat him cordially, as if he were a fellow pirate.

'I think I'll have iced coffee with milk today, please, and three cream-puffs.'

Rich men had to pay for the smile she gave him free, but his expression didn't alter. He turned away to get what she wanted. She stole one glance in the mirror at Dick, then switched to her own reflection. She shook her head vigorously, not because her hair was falling between her shoulder blades in the wrong sort of disorder, but because any men who were already watching her would be fascinated by the movement. For the same reason, apparently quite forgetful of her surroundings, she preened herself in the mirror, straightening her back, placing her hands on her hips, and lifting and expanding her chest. She had put on a vivid red blouse, sleeveless and simple; it was perfectly cut for her purposes, loose enough to strike a good man as not immodest, yet not so loose that it wouldn't reveal some of the modelling when she wanted it to, as now. Her sharkskin slacks were just right too, dazzlingly white, and moulded in unwrinkled relief to some of the best parts of her figure. Only the handbag was not quite what she wanted; it should have been white plastic but it was mere raffia and besides she'd had it for months; but perhaps if she worked Wretch right ... He seemed like the best bet.

The barman brought her order. 'Things seem quiet today,' she said, 'or perhaps it's because I'm later than usual.' She spoke brightly and he heard all right but he refused to respond to her sociableness, turning away wooden-faced without a word. Then she lowered her head for a long refreshing drink.

With her head down she looked up artfully under her lashes to study Dick in the mirror. What with the dim cool greenish sub-aquatic light, the confusion of heads and tables and palms and posturing waiters and pirouetting fans, and the state of her eyes, which were not so good as they had once been, she couldn't make out the features of his face, but she could tell a lot from its angle. She was sure he had seen her and was hoping she hadn't seen him, sure that in a minute or two he would try to make an unobtrusive getaway. She could make out that much as clearly she thought, as if he'd spoken his thoughts in her ear.

She bit a cream-puff in half and the cream blupped richly onto her tongue but she hardly noticed how delicious it was.

What a cad Dick was turning out to be! Just like all the other men. Talking all that nonsense about love—but it never meant anything. Cheating her last night. Lying too—saying he'd fly at dawn—yet here he was at midday as large as life at the Singsong. He must have had more money than he'd declared all along too, for the Singsong was expensive. Or had he contrived to raise a few dollars this morning? If so why hadn't he come straight to her house to pay his debts? He knew the place all right and it was only three minutes' walk from here. Once before when his plane had been delayed by engine-trouble he'd knocked on her door before she was up and spent all day with her, and that time—it was in the days when he was still being good to her—he'd given her five hundred tics, so they'd both been very happy.

She felt like spitting but you weren't supposed to do that when there were foreigners around, even in a public place like this.

Why didn't Dick go?

Did he think he was safer here, amongst his own kind, than he would be if he attempted to flee? Was he afraid she'd chase him? Her lip curled. He ought to know her better than that by now. She was the White Leopard: men ran after her, not she after them. He was free to beat it if he wanted to.

Besides, trying to run away wouldn't do him any good. He'd been silly enough to tell her the name of the airline he worked for. Somebody in the office would be bound to tell her where he was staying. They might not want to at first, but a tip would soon loosen their tongues. Afterwards Dick would have to refund the tip, besides paying up what he already owed, plus another thousand tics for having given her so much trouble.

'Go,' she whispered fiercely at his reflection. 'You're in my way. Wretch would give me a handbag.'

She finished her second cream-puff and called to the waiter for tissue to wipe her mouth and fingers. She sought out Wretch's reflection in the mirror. He couldn't take his eyes off her, it seemed, was hungering for her to look round and recognize him. It was a pity not to be able to turn such devotion to account and she cursed Dick again.

'Goddam you, Dick, Goddam.'

It had already occurred to her that the Lounge might contain a better proposition than either Dick or Wretch—since they temporarily cancelled each other out—but that was something she couldn't determine from the mirror; she'd have to turn sideways on the stool and give the place a careful survey, or maybe even go for an exploratory walk amongst the tables.

She left half a cream-puff on her plate—only the poor cleaned their plates as if they couldn't afford to waste a single crumb—shovelled ice into her mouth with the straw and still crunching, swivelled round.

Her face wore a smile, one of her professional smiles. It was as discreet, and yet at the same time as indiscreet to those in the know, as the red lamp over a French doorway. It said, 'I am a high-class girl enjoying my hours of leisure. I am certainly not looking for men in the streetwalker sense: I am not on duty now. But I thrive on the admiration of men, and if there is a really nice one in this assemblage who wishes to strike up an acquaintance with me and can do so in a gentlemanly manner that won't make me look cheap and too easy in the sight of all these rich nice people ...'

But the survey was unpromising. There was a group of American naval ratings at one table—'narvy' she called them—but she had a low opinion of the American narvy; either they were genuinely short of cash or they were close-fisted; they seemed to have the idea that they were heroes and that girls should be honoured to lie with them for nothing, whereas in peace-time they were no braver than other sailors and ought to pay market prices as other sailors did. Only a few months ago when an American narvy boat had brought fifty new planes for the Thai air-force she'd had serious trouble with one officer, not at her home thank God but at the Cottages; the naval MPs had wanted the Thai police to lock her up, and all over a measly hundred tics she'd extracted from his pocket because he hadn't given her enough seeing he was an officer ... There was a little gibbon-faced man who was devouring her with his eyes whenever he got a chance; he looked vaguely familiar and she thought she might have slept with him sometime once; but he was with two large ugly superbly-well-got-up foreign women and anyway he didn't look like a good spender ... There were also a few bad eggs, regular Bolero-ites and Champagne Bucketeers; they recognized her and she them; but they only cracked smutty jokes about her amongst themselves and she hated them all; they would go with the Black Leopard or any of the other girls as soon as with her, they were too coarse to be able to appreciate the difference ...

She shrugged round again, called the barman and ordered another coffee. While it was on the way she took out her compact and examined her face with care, including her teeth. Everything was in order, though a gold locket would have gone well in the deep neck of this blouse. Gold lockets didn't grow in the *klongs* like water lilies though ...

When her coffee came she slipped off the stool and carried it between the tables. At one point she deliberately paused looking from side to side with lowered eyes but nobody hailed her, and finally she sank onto a sofa in an alcove between two pillars. She was only twenty feet away from the table that interested her most and directly in front of Wretch. Playing with fire again. In a few minutes she would be at the table or they would be on her sofa. And she was so incensed with Dick that inevitably the topic of money would come up, and with it trouble. For Dick would resent being accused of welshing in front of his friend. As for Wretch, he seemed like an idealistic type: it was quite possible he would be nauseated by the idea of there being an understanding between her and Dick. They might even fight. Men were so stupid: they never seemed to realize that a girl was always willing to be as good to one man as to another as long as both were equally good to her. Well, if it came to blows, never mind: it was always reassuring to find men still thought you worth fighting over, and the Singsong was dull today; goddam, she'd been here more than a quarter of an hour and she hadn't had any fun at all yet.

Although she hadn't once looked straight at him (naturally) she'd been well aware of Wretch's mounting excitement as her meanderings between the tables brought her nearer. She could now see out of the corner of her eye that her proximity was so distracting to him that he couldn't pay any attention to Dick's drawl. He was shivering with anxiety to catch her eye. So young, she thought, and so poor at hiding his feelings: it was pathetic.

She considered him as dispassionately as if he were a cream-puff. One more of the two thousand. No more important to her than the little gibbon-faced imp who had also had his hour with her and continued on his march into oblivion. He'd been a lot nicer than some, of course—uncommonly free with his money, humble and worshipful in her room, an earnest if uninspired performer in bed. To be honest, she would have welcomed further attentions from him, for she had been just pleasantly tipsy while he was young and clean and unvicious and good-looking, but when she'd hinted at more money he'd taken her seriously, got into a huff, got dressed, and had stupidly given Bochang ten tics though she'd done nothing for him and departed. It was only because these incidents were so recent that she recalled them; in a week he would be forgotten, for she deliberately erased from her memory those who paid only once; they weren't worth remembering. There was little likelihood that he'd ever become A Friend, as Dick had been. His youth was against him. Young men seldom have much money—how can they? they are just setting out in the world; their pay is low and furthermore their appetites are insatiable. Ten to one next time he tried to get her he'd only want to give her a hundred tics, and that would be the end of him as far as she was concerned.

But in the meantime she must give him the chance to make good ...

She lifted her eyes and recognized him with a start of surprise and pleasure and clung to his gaze for a moment and then looked meaningly from side to side and dropped her eyes. He understood perfectly: she was delighted to meet him again but she didn't want any of his acquaintances who might be present to see him exchanging glances with her: he might go down in their estimation. Next time she looked at him she saw he was in a turmoil of pleasure at being recognized and deeply touched by her discretion. He was in fact as innocent as Udom's pup and a predestined purchaser of handbags ...

She was just running her mind over the current shop displays and wondering how deep his hand would go into his pocket when Dick, who was getting to be a goddam nuisance, went and spoiled everything.

Presumably he wondered what Wretch was goggling at and glanced over his shoulder to see. When he saw her he couldn't prevent himself from starting slightly but he acted very well, there was nothing guilty-looking about him, his expression could easily have passed for honest surprise. He raised his hand in an informal salute and grinned. Then he beckoned to her, in the crude western way, with his finger up, instead of with the hand turned tastefully downwards.

She looked away stonily, her eyebrows depressed in a frown.

Dick laughed and excused himself to Wretch and rose to his feet. He was really a most handsome man in his airline uniform, broad-shouldered, narrow-pelvised, long-legged; the crinkled brow, the bent nose, the smile that went further into his right cheek than into the left, were all very engaging; it was a naughty-boy face, full of self-confidence and good-humour. She couldn't help feeling a little more forgiving as he came towards her, lounging along as unconcernedly as if there were only themselves in the whole place. He was a man that even a Miss Thailand would have felt proud to stand beside. Compared with him, Wretch, though even handsomer, was distressingly adolescent. But in spite of his looks this Dick was bad, like all men, and she steeled her heart against him.

'Hi, Leopard, I didn't know you prowled by daylight too. Why don't you come on over to our part of the jungle, meet my friend?'

'Give me my money.'

'What?'

'I want one t'ou-sand tic.'

'*What!*' He stared at her incredulously, then broke into a laugh. 'One—thousand—tics! You must be crazy, kid. Jesus, that's more than sixty dollars!'

'OK. Give me cheque for eighty dollar, enough.' She shot him a dazzling smile, not because he deserved it, but because she'd noticed a few people watching them, and she didn't want them to get the impression that the colloquy was anything but friendly and casual.

He clapped his hand to his head in a helpless gesture that had often seemed captivating before. Then he said earnestly, in a low voice, 'Look, honey, my friend's waiting and I've gotta get back to him. But I'll see you some place else and pay you something, honest I will. Maybe I'll come to your house. Or maybe I'll go to the Bolero tonight—'

'I must go my home, wait you all day? And *then* maybe you not come?' She almost choked with rage—now he was really beginning to treat her shabbily—but she forced another incongruous smile, and it was so enchanting that it deceived not only the people it was intended to deceive but him too. He jumped to the conclusion that she'd been joking and his relief showed in his face.

'Did I ever double-cross you, honey? You ought to know me by now. I'm one of the best friends you ever had.' He smiled down at her. 'Come on, kid. Let me introduce you to my new buddy. He's a good guy, did me a damn' good turn this morning.' He tried to catch her hand but she eluded him. 'Come on. Come on.' Half plea. Half command. The conjugal tone. It infuriated her. It made her look cheap in front of everyone, as if she were a dancing-girl even now, when off duty.

'I sink your frand go,' she said coldly.

'Eh?' He whipped round in consternation. 'Hey, Reggie, what's the big idea? You're not walking out on me, are you, bud? I thought we were all set for a beery afternoon.'

Wretch gave him a haggard grin and subsided into his seat. And as he settled himself he looked at her. Just like Udom's pup again. After he'd been kicked.

Now Dick would have to buy that handbag.

Suddenly she was in a blind fury. She could have torn Dick's cheeks to shreds with her Leopard's claws, there in front of everybody. If she'd had a gun she'd have shot him and cheerfully done her ten years. Cheated. Brushed off. Made to look mean in this public place. And before a man who honoured her and might have turned out unexpectedly generous—

She jumped up, knocking over the coffee.

'That's the stuff, kid. Come and meet—'

But she swept past him like an empress. She was too incensed even to give Wretch a promising glance. She marched to the bar and demanded her bill. Nine tics fifty satang. She threw a ten-tic note at the barman and stalked out. Near the door she threw one look backwards. Dick had gone back to Wretch. His back was towards her but he appeared to be saying something about her and laughing. Wretch wasn't paying any attention; he was craning his neck to watch her. She couldn't make out whether it was from desire still, or just curiosity.

Outside the revolving doors she stood undecided for a minute. For one thing it was always good policy to wait a little and see if anyone followed you out. For another she wasn't sure what to do next. She'd intended to spend about an hour in the Singsong, then study handbags, then buy a magazine and go home and read. Well, that was one thing she was definitely *not* going to do now: supposing Dick went to her house he must not find her there meekly awaiting his appearance. Handbags would be depressing objects for contemplation too, since they'd only remind her of the miscarriage of her plans for Wretch. She'd have to think of something else to kill time, if she could.

She stopped and looked up and down the street for inspiration but it only confused her further. It was choked with the usual traffic; overloaded, lopsided buses with battered tinwork and radiators pouring steam and water; wooden-wheeled rickshaws tugged by Chinese men in wheel-like hats, their black shirts plastered to their sweating shoulders and their black pants rolled up high on their knotted thighs; sleek luxurious private cars transporting the rich from homes that lacked nothing the heart could desire to resorts where they could throw away their inexhaustible wealth; *samlors* with strident bells; bicycles, trams, motor-scooters—everything except bullock-carts, it seemed ... (Oh if only she could go back to the country once more where the bullock carts creaked through the forest—the ambling bullocks with their necks bowed under the massive beam, and the carter sprawled on top of his load, cattle and man alike in a heavenly dream, a million miles away from pain and racket and jealousies and unfulfilled desires!) ... For here peace was impossible. The pavements were no less crowded than the road; the shops obtruded their wares upon them; in every shaded nook were stalls for the sale of mangoes, noodles, dried squid and lottery tickets; little naked urchins of both sexes went dodging and shrieking amongst the forest of legs. There were male legs in shorts or trousers or Indian *dhotis;* female legs sprouting naked from the hems of neat blue western skirts, or swathed in *passin* that made the road a rainbow, or merely hinted at in Chinese pyjamas of shimmering silk ... And everywhere was a roar of voices that even the chorus of horns and grinding gears could not completely drown—everyone trying to make his own little individual voice heard above the universal thunder. Suddenly, the racket was overpowering and she turned giddy ...

She moved into the shade. She stood studying the lottery tickets on a folding table while she recovered. It was silly to have got so angry. It was bad for you when it was hot.

She idly thumbed through the booklets. She couldn't find anything attractive. 344193. 601995. 838371. None of them was particularly shapely. None of them struck her immediately as a number with a good chance.

'How much?' she asked the woman, for something to say.

The woman told her, staring: surely everyone in the world knew the weekly state lottery tickets were ten tics! She was a country type, this woman, very brown, with a roughened face but permed hair. She had a baby girl in her lap. Her dirty white slip was pulled up, and she was absent-mindedly massaging one breast. When the baby kicked and cried, she automatically lifted it into position. It sucked briefly, then pulled its head away and bawled. A pearl formed on the nipple and clung there, trembling.

The Leopard said, 'It is a beautiful child.' Actually she thought it was ugly. It was rather thin and completely bald. It was not half so beautiful as Mam, Udom's sister, had been. 'Why does it cry so much?'

'The day is so hot.'

'But not here. You sit in a cool place. There is a constant breeze.'

'Babies always cry.'

'But not without reason. Everyone likes to be happy. If one is without pain or trouble one laughs all the time. That is as true of babies as it is of adults. Or puppies.' (Chokchai). 'Or even birds, I imagine.' (Had Chokchai come out from behind the water-vat yet?)

'Does Madame know she has a stain on her trousers?'

The Leopard glanced down with annoyance. It was true. She must have done it when she knocked the coffee over. There was a string of brown blobs across the dazzling white. It looked dreadful. But there was nothing she could do about it now. It had already dried.

The Leopard threw down the booklets and her lips tightened. What was the use of her buying lottery tickets? She never had any luck. She'd never had any since the day she left home.

As she moved away, the woman was trying to make the baby suck again. That had been the first sign of fat little Mam's decline, when she'd begun to refuse the breast.

Luck is like money—to him who already has plenty, more is given. The Lord Buddha dispenses it, meting out much to those whom he thinks merit it, withholding it from those who by their acts displease him. But the trouble is that a mere woman cannot understand the workings of the divine mind. She herself for instance was a good woman, and the Buddha must know that; she never did anything wrong for the sake of doing it, but only to make money or because some evil spirit had temporarily taken control of her. Yet all her life her luck had been bad, as if the Buddha disliked her.

Was there ever going to be a change in her fate? Most of the time she faced the future unflinchingly, knowing it would be grim, and increasingly grim. But once in a while she liked to amuse herself with happier dreams. And it occurred to her now that she hadn't been to a fortune-teller for weeks ...

She signalled for a *samlor,* and five hurled themselves at her. She sized them up in her usual lightning style, selecting the best combination of man and vehicle just as at the Bolero she would select the best combination of man and money. The vehicle she got was sound enough though short on chromium and coloured lights. The man was rather old but he looked the hard-pedalling type and fairly tidy.

She asked the price and gasped at it and suggested an amendment and of course the man knew the amendment was correct and accepted it at once without rancour. She got in and arranged her legs to one side as if she'd got skirts on and they set off.

It was quite a long way to the fortune-teller's she'd chosen. The *samlor*-boy was fast, daringly dodging in and out of danger, and continuously ringing his bell, as if trying to draw attention to himself with this dazzling cargo behind him. She assisted all she could with the navigation but he took no notice of anything she said. She also kept a bright eye on the shops, pedestrians, cars, and passengers in other *samlors,* for she was eternally vigilant, eternally on the hunt; you never knew when a chance to do yourself a bit of good would present itself.

Yet all the time she couldn't keep the memory of that thin bawling baby from troubling her. And all the time it reminded her of another little golden-brown baby she had loved.

Mam would have been twelve or thirteen by now. That is the age when a mother really has to take her daughter in hand. Up till now she would have been a child, sexless, hardly distinguishable from a boy, always in mischief, like Udom, unconscious of herself, climbing trees to get her own green mangoes and blossoms and cicadas, never thinking of inducing the boys to fetch them for her. But at thirteen a girl starts to look at herself in the glass. By then she has learned all the useful stuff that a schoolteacher can impart, how to read and write and add up baht and satang. By then she is ready for the real education which only an experienced woman can give her. The Leopard was certain that no one could train a daughter better than she would have done. No daughter of hers would ever have suffered want. She'd have taught her how to make money and be happy. If she'd fancied marriage (and most girls did, for a start) she'd have made the right sort of marriages, to men who could have given her cars and prestige and set her up in businesses; and later, when they left her, she'd have known how to fix things so that her future needs were looked after. Mam wouldn't have got married to men like Keo and Pichar, her own second and third husbands, the one already married to a bad woman and the other a drunkard. Nor would she ever have become a dancing-girl. She'd have lived an easy life and at forty—which was to say almost another thirty years on—she'd still have been miraculously beautiful. She might even have married a millionaire by that time. And then her Mama could have lived with her in comfort during the last days.

Udom was wonderful of course but a son was not like a daughter. A son never seemed to belong to his mother, to be part of her, in the same intimate, inalienable way that a daughter did. He was male and therefore he was apt to do incomprehensible things, and the bigger he got the further away he moved into a sort of fog. He went fishing all day for eels with very low naughty boys and his highest desire was to drive a *motor-samlor.* 'Mama, I know where you can buy one for me, only three thousand tics.' What sort of future was there in that? A man had to be born rich, it seemed, or the chances were he'd die poor. He even seemed to prefer it that way. But the most penniless girl could always better herself if she'd been taught by her mother how. All that was required was beauty, plus, if possible, a predilection for a life of pleasure, wit, charm, and brains—or at least hardheadedness. All these Mam would have had without a doubt. And throughout a splendid career she would have done credit to her Mama.

The *samlor*-boy screwed round on his saddle, still pedalling. 'Is this the road Madame wants?'

'Yes. Stop here.'

The prophet was snoring on a bench at the back of his office. Even the stars hadn't been able to foresee a client on such a hot afternoon and he awoke with great reluctance. Then he was hawking and spitting for five minutes behind the curtain and between spits he cursed and grumbled a great deal. She waited tranquilly. At least it was cool in the darkened office. A small boy brought her a glass of iced tea. And the charts and globes and wheels of fortune were fascinating.

Finally the seer shuffled in. His spirits visibly rose when he saw what his client was like.

'You were sleeping, doctor?'

'Never mind. It is always a delight to be awakened by a beauteous woman.'

'But not such a delight as to go to sleep with one, eh?'

They both laughed. He rubbed the sleep out of his eyes. Then he spat juicily on the floor, and seated himself opposite her across a loose-jointed table.

He was a fat dwarf of a man with close-cropped skull and a face, that was more shrewd than mystical. His ears were enormous, and of course it was primarily they that inspired her confidence, for everyone knows that big ears with fat jutting lobes to them denote infinite wisdom—the Buddha has ears like that too, as you can see in every temple. Moreover, this man had a wart on his chin, and out of it were growing a few whiskers which had never been shaved; they were now about four inches long, and they denoted wisdom too, also good luck. In fact the man, in spite of his short fat body and soiled singlet and shorts, was plainly endowed with supernatural gifts, and she ought to come to see him more often. But he lived rather far from her house—at least five tics by a *samlor.* And since you had to pay him at least ten tics if you wanted a reliable forecast ...

She extracted that much from her bag and laid it on the table.

The seer joined his palms under his chin and did a moderate obeisance to her, but he didn't deign to pick the money up—not yet. 'What does Madame wish to know?'

'The future.'

She stretched her hand across the table and he got hold of it with his, which was hot and rather grimy. He pored over it for a considerable time. Eventually he heaved a sigh. 'Madame has suffered greatly.' His voice was deep with sympathy.

She thought his fingers had stiffened on hers until she realized it was hers in his. She relaxed them but remained moved. Practically all the doctors began by telling her this, and it never failed to impress her. For she was absolutely certain that her fundamental unhappiness did not show in her appearance. A tragic-looking dancing-girl would get nowhere. The truth could only be written in her palm, and there, apparently, it was written as clearly as the sentences in a confession—for those who could read the script.

He went on, his voice still deep, in measured cadences, rather priest-like, 'There have been periods of distressing poverty. There have been periods of terrifying sickness. There have been periods of friction with relatives. There has been the infidelity of loved ones. There has been a most unhappy marriage—'

'Two.'

He turned her palm towards the door and examined it closely, 'Yes, two,' he concurred. He emitted another sigh, this one tremendous. 'Truly the sufferings of some women—'

But this was just wasting time. 'I know you can read my past, Doctor,' she said; 'you've read it before. But I have given you these ten tics'—she picked up the note and put it down again—'to tell me about the future. And please will you make haste, as I want to go to the movie at four o'clock.'

'At Chalerm Krung?'

'Yes.'

'It is only a minute's walk away.' He returned to his studies for a time, then looked up at her. 'Much is revealed here to such a man as myself. What in particular does Madame wish to know?'

She could hardly control her exasperation. He shouldn't be hedging like this. For ten tics—

He must have sensed her impatience, for he went on rather hastily, 'Many are the women who come to me asking what joys and afflictions will be theirs in the days to come, and I tell them the truth as I see it. But Madame is not like those women. They are poor, but Madame can afford jewels and fine clothes. They are sick, but Madame is in the best of health. They are tormented by faithless husbands, or jealous husbands, or cruel husbands, or impotent ones, or they are temporarily husbandless and anxious; but Madame (I see from her hand) is indifferent to husbands, jealous, faithful, past or to come. There is much in this hand which is of consuming interest, but I am at a loss to understand why Madame desires to have time's secrets divulged. She has so much—what more can she possibly desire? Or if she fears—what can she possibly fear?'

She kept silent. He must know the answer to his own questions. If he didn't, she'd wasted her ten tics.

He sighed again, but differently: this time it was less over her unhappy past than over his unhappy present. When he resumed prognosticating it was in a grumpy tone. 'Take the question of health. Many women worry about their health, most of them needlessly. Madame does not worry, and that shows how wise she is. Her health will be perfect for years. Not until she is about forty years of age will she have any worries on that score. Then she will be sick. In fact she will be very sick—'

'Will I die?'

He deliberated before replying. Then he said, 'No. You will be dreadfully sick but you will not die.' She sighed with relief. At forty she would still be beautiful, with luck. 'You could live to be exceedingly old—'

'But I don't want—'

'And you won't. Your body is not destined to outlast its beauty entirely. At some point before the sunset glory finally fades—but this is not pleasant to talk about—'

'I shall kill myself?'

He seemed surprised at her foreknowledge. He bowed his head without speaking.

'And when will this be?'

'The palm is not a calendar—'

'I shall be fifty when I do it.' She spoke in a matter-of-fact tone that had a hint of satisfaction in it. It was common knowledge amongst fortune-tellers that this was how and when she would end up. And it suited her perfectly. At fifty she would have ceased to be attractive to men. What would be the use of living after that? She wouldn't be able to make any more money, would just have to sit around chewing betel-nut and occasionally getting drunk on fermented rice-water which was cheap, watching the young girls have the time of their lives and make their fortunes while she herself got uglier and poorer by the hour. Death would be infinitely preferable to that hell—that death in life which would be devoid of the one great advantage of death, peace, the utter cessation of all desires ...

The doctor was saying, 'There is something here about love which may be of interest to you.'

'I am not interested in love. I am only interest in money.'

'That is exactly what is written in your palm. Even now there is a man who loves you to distraction, but he is not rich—'

'Then I don't want to hear about him.'

'And that is where you are making your big mistake. In this poor man lies your one chance of happiness on earth. If only—'

'A man without money is incapable of giving happiness.'

'That is untrue. A poor man is no less capable of giving and inciting love—'

She snorted 'Love! All the time men talk about love. Even a wise man like yourself—I think you understand about the stars and cards and hands, but in this other matter you are a child. Once perhaps I believed in love myself, but then I was a young silly girl. Now I have my head screwed on right, and I know—'

'All this is shown in your hand. Your heart is hardened. Love will come, happiness will knock at your door, but you will turn it away. And you will never know—'

She said firmly, 'I am an experienced woman now, I am not a young girl. Everything that can happen to a woman has happened to me: there is nothing that I do not know about life. And one thing I have learned very clearly. Sometimes perhaps money can create love. But love cannot create money. And without money, happiness is impossible. Money *is* happiness. If you have money you can do anything. Without it—' She shrugged her shoulders. 'Tell me something more interesting. What about my son?'

'Your son?' The question seemed to startle him.

'My son is more important to me than any lover, rich or poor. Sometimes I think he is even more important to me than money.'

The doctor raised his eyebrows. He turned her palm this way and that, obviously scrutinizing minute details. Once he started to speak but stopped. At a second attempt, after a quick look at her face, he blurted it out. 'It is the darkest thing in your hand. Your son is in danger.'

Her blood ran cold. She couldn't believe her ears. She snatched her hand out of his grip and stared at it with furious eyes, trying to make out where such blasphemy was written. Finally she said in a low tense voice, 'You are lying.'

He lifted his shoulders but said nothing. His eyes fell on the ten-tic note and he absentmindedly picked it up and put it in his shirt pocket.

She burst out fiercely, 'What is the danger?' She thought of the Black Leopard. 'Does somebody want to kill him—to hurt *me*?' But the Black Leopard was likely to be more direct in her methods than that. Bochang—poisoning his food? But Bochang loved him most of the time. She was getting hysterical. She calmed herself with an effort. 'Or is he going to be sick?'

'It is difficult to tell. All I can see is danger, serious danger.' He leaned back on his stool, picking his teeth with a toothpick he'd found in his pocket when he put the money in it.

She snatched up her bag and slapped down a five-tic note on the table, 'Will he die?'

'It is probable. But those who love him can save him. If you strive to avert danger—'

'All the time you talk danger, danger. Tell me what the danger is, then I will save my son.'

'You must be vigilant, Madame. Danger comes in many forms. Tainted crab. The atom bomb. Communists—'

Suddenly she guessed the truth and laughed in relief. 'It's his tonsils, that's what it is! I've known for months that he ought to have them out. As soon as the warm weather comes, as soon as it's the school holidays—' But then another fear smote her. 'But perhaps that is where the danger lies—in the hospital. Perhaps I will send him to the hospital to make him better, and they will make him worse. Perhaps the doctor or the nurse will be careless. Why should they be otherwise? My boy does not belong to them. If he died they would shed no tears.' She drummed on the table with her long crimson nails. 'Tell me, doctor, what must I do? Shall I send him to hospital for the operation? If he doesn't go, he may die. And if he does go, still—'

The doctor said, 'I have warned you of the danger your son is in. It is up to you now to circumvent that danger. I feel sure that since you have been fortunate enough to receive my warning—'

She flashed him a brilliant smile. He was being deliberately unhelpful, but there were plenty of other doctors in Bangkok, and they could all read hands as well as he could, and surely one of them would be more willing to talk out straight. Certainly she was not going to go down on her knees to this one after giving him fifteen tics. She said, 'Well, thank you, Doctor, for your warning. I shall be very careful to protect my son from danger. And now I must be going, or I shall be late for the movie.'

He said, 'It is an excellent movie. Elissabees Taylor. And many horses, big like elephants. And much much fighting. I saw it last night, and if I had money enough ... But the prophet is a poorly paid man, and it is hard enough for me to get sufficient rice to eat, let alone go to the movies more than once a week ...'

Outside the sunlight dazzled her. She stood blinded on the brink of life which went roaring down the roadway between the high walls like a mountain torrent through a cleft in the rocks. She hung over it like a blossom on a branch, knowing that in a few moments she must drop onto the surface of the water and be swept helplessly along again, forever downstream ...

It was, as the palmist had said, only a minute's walk to the cinema. There was plenty of time and she walked slowly, swinging her bag by its strap.

Udom in danger? That man had frightened her terribly. In there, in the gloom full of shadows, it had been easy to believe in horrors.

But now she was out in the sun again. And the light banished fears just as it banished ghosts. Udom might be in danger, but out here in the brightness and realism of the afternoon you knew he could be protected. The world was thundering down this street as it had thundered down it yesterday and as it would still be thundering down it this time tomorrow; dreadful things happened to other people and you yourself sometimes suffered knocks it was hard to bear; but the catastrophic—the end of the world—and Udom's death would amount to that ... She almost laughed. It couldn't happen to *her*. The Buddha wouldn't let it happen. He knew that she tried to be good and that whenever she was awake in the early mornings she gave food to the priests. Such virtues were her safeguard against disaster.

She turned a corner and there, on the opposite one, beyond the traffic lights, was the cinema.

To her it was a magnificent building, loftier than a temple, strangely beautiful in the austere western style with its angles and parallelograms of bare white wall lifting the eyes, and the heart with them, up towards the heavens into which the oblong tower thrust like a white stone jetty into a blue sea. Over the porch this week was a tremendous gaudy portrait of Lobber Taylor looking sterner and more noble even than usual in rather odd clothes; not quite so odd as what he'd worn in Ko Wadis but still odd. Below him were smaller pictures of the other stars in the film and she recognized them all at once—Yoan Fontaine, a lady, but blonde; Elissabess Taylor, whom all the men were crazy about; and tall handsome Shorch Shander ... In the porch itself was a big cardboard figure of a rearing horse and, straddling it, Lobber Taylor again; this time he was completely encased in steel except for his lean and handsome face; there was fury in his eyes and she knew with a thrill that here was a man who would *kill* for her, if only she could make him love her enough. Ah, if only Lobber Taylor would come to Bangkok!

The traffic lights weren't working (as was often the case) and a policeman was standing beneath them directing the traffic. She waited for a chance to cross.

While she was waiting people started coming out of the cinema. They came at first singly or in pairs, lingering on the top step, turning, running together into groups, then dripping down step by step into the street. Like raindrops on a banana leaf. And soon the drizzle became a shower, and the whole leaf was wet with a wall of pouring water. The pavement before the steps filled up with the water, like a hoof-print on the ground beneath the leaf ...

She decided to stay where she was for a while. Udom was somewhere in that crowd. She had no desire to meet him face to face here. The lunch-time scene was still fresh in her mind. It would only embarrass him if he had to acknowledge her. At the same time she'd like to see these friends of his that believed she was a princess, these boys that must never know what his Mama really was ...

'Vilai. Vilai!'

She'd been so intent on trying to catch sight of Udom that she hadn't realized her name was being called. In any case it was a foreigner that was calling and he bungled the tones so badly the name was practically unrecognizable.

She automatically put on a brilliant smile before she located where the voice was coming from. She looked around her brightly.

'Vilai!'

He was in a car that had stopped by the kerb only a couple of yards away. A nice-looking boy, though blond, with eager eyes. His head was thrust out of the window.

'Why, hallo-o, how you do-o,' she said, dragging some of the vowels.

'Vilai, are you going to see *Ivanhoe?* I'm just going to see it myself. How about we go together?'

She took a step towards him, but then she suddenly recollected herself. Udom was somewhere close at hand, possibly watching her even now. And it wouldn't be good for him to catch her talking to a foreign man on the street. He'd never be able to look at the matter realistically—'My Mama is working'—and turn his face away. He'd be ashamed of her, hurt worse than ever. His attitude was stupid, but nothing would make him see that. He believed that there were depths she still hadn't plumbed, that she hadn't yet sunk to picking up men, on the street, in her hours off work. And it was most important that she should not betray this trust in her. She could never bear to see reproach in Udom's eyes.

So she erased her smile and glanced guiltily across the road.

Out of the corner of her eye she saw the young man's face drop. He pulled his head inside the window with a savage, insulted jerk. She felt a pang. She hadn't wanted to hurt him. He looked nice. And she knew him well too, if only she could place him.

Then she saw Udom.

He was crossing the street towards her. He was with two older boys. They were not walking nicely: they were swaggering, as if they thought themselves very big men. And all three of them were smoking.

Rage rushed into her throat, almost choking her. And she hurled her rage across the road like a death-ray to annihilate him. All day and half the night she slaved to make him happy. She suffered torments because of her love of him. Yet he did nothing but disobey her. Acting very low in public. Heaping shame on his mother. She could have killed him.

And such was the intensity of her wrath that it actually seemed as if she had somehow managed to project it across space and strike him with it as with an open hand. For she saw a sort of uneasiness come over him as he reached the island in the middle of the road. He took the cigarette from his mouth and looked about nervously as one does when one gets that uncanny feeling that one is being watched by unseen eyes. Then, as if inevitably, his stare swung round to her and she saw him trip with the shock of seeing her.

The policeman did some balletic movements, causing the traffic to cease flowing in two directions and begin flowing in two others. The car at the kerb got gratingly into gear. The cars on the far side of the crossroad, a handsome long green limousine at their head, moved forward with a surge of joy like children escaping from school.

And instantly she foresaw the events of the next five seconds as clearly as if they'd happened already. And because of this foreknowledge they seemed to develop with a goading slowness. Yet all her own actions were slowed down similarly, and she could do nothing to alter the course of fate.

Udom pretended he hadn't seen her. He pretended he'd found something of interest in a shop behind him. He called to his two friends who were already in the roadway coming towards her. Then he stepped off the island away from her without looking.

She screamed and leaped leadenly forwards. She heard a squeal of brakes as the nice boy in the near car avoided her. But she had eyes only for Udom. The long green beautiful car was gathering momentum as it escaped from under the policeman's arm. It moved with the silent deadly stealth of an arrow. It didn't really hit Udom. He blindly stepped into it somewhere near its tail. The impact sent him spinning back towards the island. He tripped over its edge, crashed against one of its iron posts, and fell in a little heap. And she was hung over the roadway, trying to run, but her numbed thighs were scarcely movable. And she would never reach him.

'Udom! Udom! Udom!' She was transfixed by the terror in her own voice.

Suddenly she was grabbed by the arm. An English voice shouted roughly in her ear, 'What the hell are you up to, you stupid bitch? Trying to commit suicide? I as near as dammit belted you.'

She couldn't answer. She raised a hand and pointed dumbly towards Udom.

'Well, what's *he* to you? He's a silly little bastard that tried to commit suicide too. Is he your brother, or something? Maybe it runs in the family.'

'He my son.'

'Your—*son*?' There was so much agony in his voice that she was compelled to throw him a glance. And of course seen full length he was unmistakable. No wonder his face had looked familiar, stuck out of the window. And now it was wearing an expression which was also becoming familiar, that Chokchai expression again—as if he'd just had another kick.

'Wretch!' she exclaimed, overwhelmed with relief. 'You here? You help me, honey—sweetheart?' He looked sick, and she added an unusual word for her—'please?' And then, suddenly breaking into tears, 'Oh, Wretch, come quick and help me with my son.'

Seven

Wretch was wonderful. It was he who proved to her that Udom wasn't dead. He did it in a brusque manner that under any other circumstances would have seemed insufferably rude. 'Stop squawking and feel his pulse.' He got hold of her hand and pressed two of her fingers against Udom's wrist. 'Feel it? He's nowhere near dead. Just knocked out, that's all.'

'But why he not speak? Why he shut eye, lie still like he d'ad?'

'He's knocked out, I tell you. Like in boxing ... What the hell does that bloke want?'

It was the traffic policeman. He'd left the traffic to fight its own battles and had come to see why a crowd was collecting here. She got up—for careless of the white slacks she'd fallen on her knees beside Udom—and began telling him. And all her seething emotions—horror at what she had witnessed, a sickening fear for Udom, fear for herself if Udom should die—gave added power to her natural eloquence. Words poured out of her in a passionate stream, fascinating the crowd but confusing the law.

For she told them all about Udom being a good boy except that sometimes he was disobedient and smoked and played around with the other boys instead of coming straight home from school. That this morning he had asked her for five tics but because he'd been specially good she'd given him ten and he'd come to see this movie over there, first house. That she had subsequently visited a palmist who had told her her son was in danger so she had immediately come to the cinema to save him. That the *samlor* had been slow and so she had actually arrived a few seconds too late to prevent the tragedy, with the result that her child now lay at their feet with blood pouring from his head (there actually was a small trickle from one ear) and every bone in his sweet little body broken.

As rhetoric it was magnificent, but as evidence it was worse than useless, it was misleading. The policeman even thought it was deliberately misleading.

For one thing was already crystal-clear to the policeman. He hadn't actually seen the accident happen, but he was positive that it was the foreigner who had caused it. Else why was he displaying so much interest in the case? Kneeling in the dust and applying a very fine clean handkerchief to the bleeding ear? Straightening the body out and feeling it all over for broken bones? Every gesture was a confession of guilt. In the middle of her testimony he went away to write down the number of Wretch's car.

Wretch became impatient. 'How much longer are we going to be fooling around here? Has that gamboge-topee'd prat sent for an ambulance yet, or not?'

'Who you mean?'

'That so-called policeman.'

'Send for what?'

'Am-byou-lance, darling. Don't you know what an ambulance is? A special motor for taking injured people to hospital.'

She couldn't understand all those long words and in reply to a question from the spectators now about forty strong, began giving another vivid but quite different account of what had happened and why and how.

In the midst of it, Wretch swore. He stooped and picked up Udom in his arms. She was startled by such abruptness. 'Where you go?'

'Go my car, darling. Take the kid to hospital. We can't hang around here all day. He's concussed. He needs a doctor.'

He strode away with Udom dangling limply across his chest. The spectators fell back from before him, looking up into his angry blue eyes with their mild brown ones. The policeman was crouching in front of the car examining it for dents or bloodstains. She ran after Wretch and got in front of him to open the door.

'No, the back one.'

He manoeuvred Udom through the narrow opening and laid him out on the back seat. All his movements were surprisingly gentle and careful. He might have been handling his own child.

'You going in the back with him? Or in the front with me?'

Her first impulse was to say 'In front wiss you.' For Udom was dirty after rolling in the road. Also he looked as if he were dying, and she was afraid of him. His face had gone yellowish white, his eyes were shut, his mouth hung open and out of it came an occasional choke or strangled gasp. She knew he was a great deal worse than Wretch appeared to think. And her legs had begun to shake uncontrollably, and she was afraid she might faint.

But she knew what was expected of a mother. 'I go back.'

'Good.' Wretch went in first and held up the boy's head while she seated herself, then lowered it into her lap. As he backed out of the far door he said, 'Keep him still. I'm an old dirt-track rider and I know about these things. Broken bones don't matter a damn, unless you ram a rib through your lungs: just get 'em properly aligned, and in a few weeks they're as good as new. But concussion's funny. You've got to keep the patient quiet, or else no telling what may happen.' She hadn't understood a word but she was comforted by the sound of his voice. It was confident, and it gave her confidence too.

She caught hold of one of Udom's limp hands. It was ten years since he'd last slept in her lap. How many times since then she'd longed to have his body nestled against hers, unresisting, in willing embrace! And now her wish was granted—but in what circumstances! She couldn't hold back her tears, for the second time today.

The policeman wrenched open the door and climbed into the front passenger seat. 'There are wheelmarks in the road,' he said, 'but they aren't very clear. Probably the brakes are defective. Tell him to go to the traffic police station for a brake test. This instant.'

Wretch, in the act of getting into the other front seat, exploded with wrath. 'Where does this sot think he's going?'

'He go wiss us, darling.'

'What for?'

'Because accident. Must go wiss us.'

'But *why*? *I* didn't run over the kid. Why the blazes doesn't he go and look for the car that did it?'

'He sink you do it, darling.'

'Then tell the twerp to think again.'

'I tell him before, darling, but he still sink not true. He sink why you worry to me, my son, if you not do? He sink maybe you, me, fix price very quick before he come. He sink you, me, fix price, then we not give policeman nussing for fix for us. He angly to us, he sink we try to cheat him.'

Wretch swore. Then he took a deep breath and started shouting at the policeman in Thai. It was such terrible Thai that the policeman didn't even realize he was being addressed in his own language. After a moment or two she interrupted.

'I am sorry to trouble you with these wearisome details, Officer. But truly it is not this foreigner who tried to kill my son. It was someone in a big green car going the other way. But this foreigner is a friend of my husband. That is why he wants to take my son to my home—because he is my husband's friend. He happened to be passing when the accident occurred, and so he came at once to help me—'

'Has he a driving licence?'

'He tells me he wants to thank you for your interest in the case—I do too—but we both feel it would be a waste of your time to bother about it any more. For unless we can find the green car that ran down my son there will be no satisfaction in it for anyone. I—I mean my husband—will have to pay the doctor's bills out of his own pocket, and as he is not rich—'

The policeman gave her jewels a hard stare. 'Who is your husband?'

She fixed a fictitious first name to a family one that is respected throughout the length and breadth of Thailand and gave the address of a rich American bachelor in Bankapi. While the policeman was jotting it all down she said to Wretch, 'Giff him twenty tic, darling.'

'What in blazes for?'

'Because he interest to us. We haff accident. He must reet in his littun book. We make trouble for him, much trouble.'

Wretch smiled grimly. 'You're a pewty girl. I'm a nerty boy. And the policeman must reet in his littun book. And meanwhile the kid's just about breathing his last ... So I give this sleuth twenty smackers, eh? The price of a maidenhead upcountry. Well, if you think he's earned it ...' He pulled a green note out of his breast-pocket and thrust it rudely at the policeman. 'Tell him I think your Thai policeman are wonderful.'

'My husband's friend says he thinks the Thai police are really wonderful because of their efficiency and their unfailing courtesy to all,' she translated. And she added a lot more designed to prevent the policeman from taking offence at the uncouth way in which the money had been shoved at him. It was touch and go too, for Wretch *would* keep on interrupting her pleasantries with cross reminders that Udom would soon be a corpse. She ignored these and finally got the law mollified. But it remained surly, quite omitting to bid Wretch farewell and giving herself only the most perfunctory obeisance, as if it thought she didn't amount to much, even though she *was* travelling in a private car, and had a husband with that distinguished family name she'd mentioned, and that address in Bangkok's most swanky suburb ...

They had a bit of unpleasantness in the car. Wretch was most unreasonable.

'Where do we take him, Vilai?'

'Go my home.'

'Don't be silly, darling. He's hurt. We've got to take him to hospital first.'

'No time. Must go my home now. Get ready to Bolero.'

'*What*?'

He threw a glance over his shoulder. It was angry and incredulous. She couldn't see any need for that and was annoyed. But he was being nice to Udom in his rough way so she kept the peace. She just said sensibly, 'More batter we go my home, darling. Then my cookee go fetss doctor—'

They'd crossed the intersection. He pulled up in the gutter and with the engine still running, turned to talk to her seriously. 'Look here, you callous bitch. If the Bolero is more important to you than your son, hop out and clear off there. *I'll* take the poor little sod to hospital.'

'Why you angly to me?' She was genuinely puzzled. His only reply was a snort. She grew resentful. 'I do not like you angly to me. Why you not take my son to my house, like I ask you? He not your son, he *my* son. Why you must take *your* house?'

He cried, 'God the All-Highest! Do you think I'm trying to kidnap the brat? I haven't got a home to take him to, as it happens—I live in a hotel. I want to take him to a *hospital.* Don't you know what a hospital is, dimwit? Doctors in long white gowns. Nurses in funny hats. Beds in rows—'

Doctors and beds were English words she was familiar with and she at last grasped what he was getting at. She was horrified. 'You mean *ron-piya-ban*?' she cried, and her tone expressed her consternation. 'Oh no, I not want my son go there, oh no, oh no.' She shook her head resolutely, her lips pursed.

'But why not, in Heaven's name?'

She couldn't remember the English for *anterai,* so she spoke the Thai.

'*Anterai*? Dangerous? What the hell do you mean? It's not dangerous to take your son to hospital, it's dangerous *not* to take him there.'

She still shook her head, muttering again '*Anterai mark*.'

'But what makes you say that? At the hospital they have trained personnel. They have equipment. They deal with hundreds of cases daily—'

And that was the point, exactly. 'Too many pipple go *ron-piya-ban*. What the doctor care my son? He not know me, not know my son. How can he care my son, when so many pipple go see him? He care *everybody*?' She laughed derisively.

'You care for plenty of men, don't you?'

It was like a backhanded blow across the mouth. She was dumbfounded by his bitterness and savagery. She was far too hurt to retaliate at once. She just said quietly, 'I not care man. I only care myself. And my son.' And subsided into silence.

Then suddenly Udom stopped his stertorous breathing, swallowed frantically, choked and gave a sort of groaning cry and then restarted breathing, but even more painfully than before.

'Oh, Wretch, Wretch—Udom—he die, I sink—'

'He's bad. We've got to hurry.'

'Before you say not bad, just knock out—'

'That was to stop you worrying. But you don't worry enough. Now tell me the way to the nearest *ron-piya-ban* if that's what you call it and I'll really open the taps—'

Udom was rolling his head on her knees. She could feel the writhing of his neck muscles through the sharkskin. She was terrified. He mustn't die in her lap—that would be the worst of bad luck forever. Nor did she want him to die in her house, for then it would be haunted by his ghost, and she'd have to move—but she couldn't afford to move, for if she changed her address how could that small but remunerative body of old friends who for various reasons—wives, mostly—couldn't come to the Bolero openly to pick her up, contact her when they got a chance? She'd lose not only a son, but business too ...

She began to cry. '*Bai ron-piya-ban, leu-leu bai*'—go to the hospital as quick as you can—she sobbed.

He'd already got the car moving. 'Which way from here?' 'Go straight, and when I ask, go *this* way.' She motioned with her arm, because she always muddled the English for *kwa* and *sai*.

The hospital turned out to be even worse than she'd feared it might be. She'd never been in one before. All her ideas about them were founded on those in the movies—aseptic palaces run by famous actors and extremely chic nurses. But the reality was dingy and and unswept and (especially disgusting to a Thai woman) it smelled bad. The doctor had a broken lens in his glasses and his coat, far from being brand-new and snow-white like those Lew Ayres wore, was grey from a thousand imperfect launderings and spotted with blood. The nurses stared at her out of insolent country eyes and she saw instantly that no sympathy for her son was to be expected from them. And to do him justice Wretch himself seemed disappointed in the place. He'd carried Udom in as if he was carrying him into heaven, brushing past clerks and porters and making for a side-room where he'd laid him on a high white bed, and it had been gratifying to see the way everybody jumped to it at the foreigner's entry—they'd have kept *her* waiting for a couple of hours, she knew. But then the clerks had started making a muddle of forms, the doctor had been clumsy and cruel in his examination, the nurses had got in each others' way and giggled, and Wretch had become more and more exasperated. When she judged that he was exasperated enough she had proposed that they bow out, taking Udom with them, but he had ignored the suggestion. Apparently in his opinion a bad hospital was better than no hospital at all. She had shrugged her shoulders then. It was all Wretch's idea, coming here. If anything went wrong he would be to blame, not she ...

The doctor, who had put off talking to her as long as possible because he was not quite sure where she stood in the social scale and was afraid of demeaning himself by being too courteous to someone of no account on the one hand, or of not being courteous enough to someone who really mattered on the other, finally found himself forced to address her. He did it as neutrally as possible. 'This is your son?'

'Yes.'

'The foreigner ran over him with his car?'

'Yes.'

'Why has no policeman accompanied you here?'

'None saw the accident.'

'The boy will have to be admitted for a few days. Will the foreigner guarantee the fees?'

'He will pay them.'

'Do you know his name? Where does he live? Whom does he work for?'

'I don't know, but I'll ask him.' To Wretch, in English, she said, 'What your name, darling? The doctor want to know.'

He said, 'The name's Joyce. But what's he want to know *my* name for? I don't think they've got the patient's down yet.'

She said, 'He want you—oh, I no know how you say.' She puzzled it out. 'I just woman, I Siamese—how doctor can trust me? Maybe I not tell him my truce name. He make my son well, then maybe he cannot get my money. But you foreigner—you alway say truce things—also foreigner always haff much money—'

'Bags and bags of it, yes.' He sniffed. 'So he wants me to stand guarantor, is that what you mean?'

'Yes, that what he want. Ab-solutely.'

Wretch with the queer recklessness of foreigners promptly gave his real name and the name of his firm. The doctor was much more impressed than she was. Blodderlick Peers. Everybody knew that name, of course. It belonged to one of the oldest and best-respected of the foreign firms. But the firm was British, not American. It employed nice boys but it paid them next to nothing. No wonder Wretch winced every time he parted from a hundred-tic note. He might have enough to pay the hospital bill, perhaps. He'd *have* to have enough, since he'd brought Udom here. But after that he'd be played out. However crazy he might be about her (and, in spite of all his tantrums, he was continually throwing infatuated glances her way) he'd be no more use to her ...

At last they were ready to leave. They left Udom lying on his back on a stretcher. Wretch had had a long talk with the doctor in English. When it was over he tried to take her arm to lead her out but she eluded his hand indignantly. These men! Acting like that in front of the doctor! Spoiling her story and making her look cheap! She threw a last glance at Udom. She wanted to hug him, but the doctor's and Wretch's insistence that he must be kept quiet had impressed her at last and she controlled the impulse: a kiss might kill him, she thought. 'You are quite sure he will be all right?' she asked the doctor doubtfully. The doctor was positive. 'Just a bump on the head. But we must keep him under observation for a few days. You will of course come back shortly, or will send somebody else to look after him?' It would have to be Bochang, she supposed. She nodded and just touched Udom's wrist. It was clammily cold. She was sure she'd never see him alive again.

Out in the hospital courtyard, while Wretch was opening the car door for her, she vomited. He had to help her into the front seat, because suddenly her legs were boneless.

In the car she laid her head on the back of the seat and gave herself over to her misery. Never before in her life had she known a prophecy come true with such alacrity. She had expected to have time to make plans and offerings at the temple, but horror had struck like lightning. And now she had more pain than ever to bear.

She was so overwhelmed by her troubles that she completely forgot about Wretch until she realized he was asking her which way to go at a crossroads. Then she quickly recollected herself.

'Stop here. I get out.'

'But can't I take you to your home?'

'No, no. I get out now. Go *samlor*.'

He turned nasty again. 'You mean you don't want to be seen getting out of my car at your house? Somebody else is waiting there for you?' He couldn't keep the suspicion to himself. 'Dick?'

'All the time you want to fight wiss me,' she complained. It was a serious blemish on an otherwise likeable boy. 'Stop car.' Dick had never entered her mind as it happened.

He pulled up with a jerk and as she opened the door, not giving him time to run round and be gentlemanly, he grabbed her elbow. His voice was quite broken. 'Vilai!'

'What matter?' His fingers round her arm were like manacles but they were trembling. She tried to shake herself free but he hung on. He was too emotional altogether and she clicked her tongue in disgust. 'Let go my arm—you not want me call policeman, do you?'

'Vilai. Sit here a minute. I want to talk to you.'

'No time now. Must hurry. Get ready go Bolero. Saturday night big night always. Many men. All want Leopard. Tee-hee.'

'You're going to the Bolero tonight?'

'Of course. I must go sair. It my shob. If not go, must pay manager eighty tic tomollow.'

'I should have thought your son was more important to you than eighty tics.'

'He is. He very important me. He only sing in world I love more than myself. I sink he sick at home I not go Bolero. But you take him *ron-piya-ban*—OK. What I must do? Sit in that place all night while he do like this'—she imitated his breathing—'all the time? I sink that no good. Only make me very unhappy. Not halp hem get well—'

'But, hell, tonight he may peg out. Have you thought of that?'

'Peg out—what mean?'

'Die.'

She didn't speak for a moment. Then she said, 'OK. He die tonight. I at Bolero. I d'unk. I forget he hurt. I forget maybe he die. I very happy.' Her heart felt like a hot stone in her breast. 'Tomollow I wake up late. My cookee say, 'Udom d'ad.' I sink I cry then. I sink I cry very mutss. Eye get fat here, and rad colour. But what is use? Not make Udom come back from d'ad. Only make Vilai not pewty. So tomollow night, I put powder here'—she demonstrated—'I put rad colour here, I dress very smart girl, I go Bolero, I get d'unk again, I meet nice man, I forget—' She laughed a hard laugh and as Wretch had released her arm, got out of the car. 'You not want sink so much, darling,' she said. 'Tonight I *must* go Bolero. Now you take my son *ron-piya-ban* I must have money more than before. Must pay for doctor, must pay for *samlor,* must pay for cookee go *ron-piya-ban* to look after him. But who giff me money if I not go Bolero, make for myself?' She gave him a teasing smile. 'You?' A youngster from Blodderlick Peers! She laughed at the absurdity of the thought. 'Bye-bye. I see you again sometime, maybe.'

'Vilai!' There was agony in his voice but she ignored it. Perhaps he'd been right at that. Perhaps Dick was at her home by now, with money.

She signalled a *samlor* and it swung to her with a squawl of brakes. She got in without giving Wretch another look and they set off, leaving the car on their left. A moment later it passed them, accelerating, on their right. Wretch refused to look at her and his chin was set at an offended angle. He muffed another gear change and nearly side-swiped a taxi in his anxiety to roar away from her.

Of course she was late for the Bolero and the manager fined her twenty tics. Ordinarily he fined the girls forty tics for being an hour or part of an hour late and the fact that he was so lenient meant that her story was getting good. With a few more revisions it would become a masterpiece. For even those who had only heard these imperfect early versions were held spellbound while she talked. And the manager, who heard women lying every night, was almost completely insensitive to women's troubles ...

She'd told the story now about a dozen times. And at each re-telling facts which did little to heighten the effect were dropped while fictions that heightened it considerably were added. Yet she was not just lying outrageously. She was only doing what the conscious artist must always do, attempting with whatever means were at her disposal to create in her listeners the full force of the emotions she had felt in herself. But since it was not *their* brother who had been knocked down before their own eyes and who now lay bleeding and insensible in a hospital ward, a bare recital of the facts of the case could not achieve that object. There had to be extra stimulation of their imaginations to bring their reactions up to the full pitch. She had to lie in order to make them understand. In fact she was an epic poet in style rather than a historian.

As usual she hypnotized herself with her own visions and it would now have taken a powerful intellectual effort, which she had no intention of making, to recall the actual drab facts of the accident. And the next time she told the tale—to Dick—she almost believed every word she said. She told him that Wretch had deliberately tried to mow her down with his car and that he had actually succeeded in laying her little brother low, that he was inspired by frantic spite because she'd consistently refused to sleep with him for weeks, that he'd driven off without stopping and left her to take the mangled child to hospital in a *samlor,* that the operation was going to cost five thousand tics and that even then it might not be successful, that the poor child had a broken back and a shorn-off leg and that they couldn't stop the blood from pouring out of both of his ears, that if he lived he would be a burden on her and if he died she'd kill herself, and that it was all in fulfillment of a prophecy a priest had made to her when she was fifteen years old and still an innocent girl in her mother's house.

But Dick was unresponsive. 'Who d'you say did all this?'

'Wretch. Boy wiss you at Singsong today.'

'Seemed like a hell of a nice guy to me.'

'You sink I not speak truce?'

'We-e-ell, I don't say that. He could have run over you easy— drives like he was at Indianapolis on Memorial Day. But he sure wouldn't have done it on purpose. And if he'd known he'd hit your brother he'd have stopped—'

'You not unnerstand. He *hate* me. Because I not—'

'Look, Willy. This morning my ship's still have trouble, see? They tell us to get the hell out till ten tonight. I get into the company bus to come to town. The other guys are worn out after last night; they can't face it again. Halfway to Bangkok the rear diff seizes up—not a drop of lubricant. There we are, stuck. Blazing hot and not a drink for miles. Then along comes this guy Reg. He's been out to Don Muang on business. He's barrelling like hell but he sees me. Those tyres really whinny when he slams on the brakes. He backs up. 'Having trouble? Can I give you a lift?' There was no need for him to do that. He'd never seen me before. But he's that kind of a guy. He's the sort that'll stop to turn a beetle over when it's fallen on its back and can't get righted again.'

'Maybe he OK wiss men. But wiss women, differnunt.'

'And now you're just talking like an oriental. A westerner that treats his fellow men right'll treat women better still—a hell of a lot better than they deserve, mostly. Women aren't just pieces of tail in the West. They go through a door ahead of the men. They don't tag along behind like in the Or-ree-ent, carrying the baby and all the baggage. They're right out there in front.'

She gave up. She'd found out years ago that it was waste of time telling stories to westerners. They never accepted a tale at its face value and enjoyed without questioning the thrills the narrator had set out to give them. They always started pulling it to pieces, like a customs man tapping a heel to see if it was hollow. They expected a story to be merely true and didn't care whether it was sensational or not ...

'You want dance wiss me?'

He looked at his watch. 'Yeah, I guess. But it'll have to be the last one, honey. Then I'll have to be hitting the trail for the airfield ...'

Just as she was accompanying him to the door (for he'd given her three hundred after all plus a few incidentals and though it wasn't as much as she'd wanted it was more than she'd expected and she was sorry to see him going) a boy brought her a note.

'What this?'

'A letter.'

'Who bring?'

He pointed with his chin. Another boy she'd never seen before was grinning at her from amongst the potted palms in the main doorway.

She turned the letter over. It was addressed in English.

'What it say?' she asked Dick.

'It says "Miss Vilai" in big letters, and underneath in brackets it says "The White Leopard." Do you want me to read it for you?'

She debated the point rapidly. The only Thai present whose translation she could trust would be the manager, but she didn't want him to know too much of her business. As for that, she didn't want Dick to know it either. She accosted the strange boy, who was smart and clean and rather good-looking. He did obeisance to her, which was extremely gratifying in front of Dick.

'Who sent this letter?'

'A foreigner.'

'What is his name?'

'I don't know.'

'Where does he live?'

He pointed with his chin and named a hotel she'd never heard of before.

Dick said, 'If you want me to read that billy-doo you gotta give it me quick. I'm running it mighty fine—'

She handed him the letter.

He opened it and unfolded a single piece of paper. As his eyes ran down the dozen or so lines his puckered eyes began to smile. Finally with a short laugh he handed the letter back to her. 'That guy sure does hate your guts,' he said drily.

'Who?'

'Reg. The guy that tried to bump you off with a car.'

'It from he?'

'Yes. Surprised?'

'What he say?'

He took the note back and read it quickly in a toneless voice. '"Dear Vilai: I hope you can get someone to read this to you. I am sorry I upset you this afternoon. I should have realized how upset you must have been by the accident to your son"—I guess he means your little brother—"and been more decent to you. Vilai, I can't bear the thought of your dancing at that goddamned Bolero, pretending to be gay and happy, getting drunk to make yourself forget, while all the time Udom is badly injured. I know you are not really as hard and bad as all that. Is it just the money you must have? I will pay all the bills for you, darling. But please, immediately, come here to this hotel, where you can rest decently, and tomorrow if you like I'll take you to the hospital to see the poor kid. Do please please come, Vilai. I can't come to the Bolero for you; I can't bear to see you working there, especially tonight. Reggie. PS. Please tell the bearer if you will come or not. It is torture waiting for you here."'

She took the note back again. 'He little bit mad, I sink.'

'He sure is. Well, you'd better cash in on it, kid. So long.'

She called a *samlor* to take Dick to the taxi-station and by the time he'd vanished waving into the wide dark spaces of Rajadamnoen Avenue she'd decided what to do. 'Go back to the hotel and tell the foreigner I must have sixty tics to pay the manager, else I cannot leave the Bolero until closing time,' she told the boy. Then she went back in the Bolero to augment her income if possible.

Not that she particularly needed any cash now that Dick had settled up with her. But making money was the most engrossing pursuit she knew of and it alone had the power to keep horror at bay until you were drunk. Already she had found it was unsafe to sit idle and alone for a single second. And one grisly idea kept jumping into her mind in the middle of a dance, a drink, or a laugh—'He may have died. He may already have died.' This idea had been even harder to keep off since just before Dick came in, for then, going towards the bar while the band played 'Sleepy Lagoon' she'd thought she heard a faint cry—'Mama'—up amongst the coloured lanterns—his ghost come seeking her here in the midst of all her shame. She'd nearly fallen, and against all her principles had had to order a whisky without having a prospective purchaser of it in view. Then Dick had come, and of course paid for this one and another. But she didn't want to hear that ghost again, or be left to herself for a single second: she must have her mind continually distracted.

Luckily there was no shortage of men tonight. The drinks had given her animation and she knew she was looking superb in her ivory-white full-skirted dress. (She'd had to be her own maid after Bochang had finally left for the hospital.) Several men danced with her and bought her drinks at the bar. None secured her to themselves for an hour and that was just as well, for there were always pauses in an hour-long tête-à-tête which tonight she was determined to avoid at all costs.

Almost an hour after Dick had left, the nice-looking hotel-boy returned with another envelope from Wretch. There was no letter this time but there *was* a hundred-tic note. She put it into her handbag with a sense of deep satisfaction. Four hundred already tonight for nothing. Plus all the chits for drinks and dances that were going down to her name. 'Tell him I will come as soon as I can,' she told the boy. 'I think twelve-thirty, but I may be late. And if I don't come tonight then definitely tomorrow ... What was the name of that hotel again?'

At two-thirty in the morning she kept her promise.

She'd had an excellent night. She'd danced and drunk and chattered till eleven-thirty. Then a group of business men who'd been pretty boisterous and had already made several attempts to get her to join them had jettisoned that Black Leopard from their midst and so she had yielded to their persuasions. She'd already noticed that money was abundant at their table and that bottles of bourbon were arriving full and being carried empty away with a speed and regularity that foretold easy pickings later on for even the dumbest type of girl. An old customer, a round-shouldered chinless blond with extremely high-powered spectacles, had made the introductions. He was quite tight. 'Hi, Leopard,' he'd shouted, staggering to his feet and grasping her hand and shaking it warmly but then trying to encircle her with a familiar arm—'Hi, Senator, hi, Senator—' He'd had a great deal of difficulty in disengaging the Senator's mind from another girl whose knee he'd got hold of but finally the flushed, moon-shaped face had swung round. 'Hi, Senator, she's here. The number one lay in Bangkok, in the Orient, in the world! The Whi' Leopard I been telling you about all ni'. Hi, Senator, meet the Whi' Leopard, the number one lay in Bangkok, in the Orient, in the world I figure—'

When midnight came the party had been divided about what it should do with itself next. Chinless had vociferously insisted that the Senator must be guided to the Leopard's den by himself. 'Only the great deserve the fair,' he had shouted, and as this had made the others laugh and clap the first time he said it, he'd repeated it twenty times getting no further laughs but his own. Some of the others had been of the opinion however that what the Senator needed first was a few more drinks. 'It's too early to go to bed, even with the number one lay in Bangkok, in the world, in the universe,' one of them had said—the nicest-looking of the lot—with a sly smile at her, which clearly set themselves as two individuals aside from and above this drunken rabble, and she'd returned the smile and said 'Why we not go Champagne Bucket?' and the suggestion had been jubilantly taken up.

She'd lost the Senator and Chinless but she herself had got into a big American car and after a crushed and dangerous ride during which her dress was torn at the waist she'd arrived with four or five men and a couple of other Bolero girls at the Champagne Bucket. And the man who'd taken the seat next to hers was the nice dark quiet one with the sleeked hair and the sly companionable grin, the one who was easily the pick of the bunch.

The party spirit hadn't survived transplantation any too well however and soon one man and one girl had disappeared and shortly after that everybody else went except for the nice dark man and another man who was almost as nice. Even these two kept on yawning and though they both danced with her once or twice they showed more inclination to talk together, mostly about what they thought about the Senator. She'd found she was getting left out and that was just what she couldn't stand tonight. She'd looked at her watch. One-thirty. Goddam early. Should she try for one of these two or someone else in the place? Or go to Wretch? It would be a bore going back across the city by *samlor* to search for that hotel. And then Wretch would be sympathetic instead of distracting. He'd tend to concentrate her mind on her troubles instead of diverting it from them. She groaned inwardly. This was the usual interlude of despondency that descended on her briefly in the small hours, only tonight it was worse than usual ...

Then another American had come up and clapped the other two on their shoulders and had his own clapped back and had asked if he might make use of the amenities since they seemed to be neglecting them. He'd trod on her toes and held her too low down. When the dance was over she'd gone to the toilet and after releasing a lot of beer and whisky characteristically examined herself in the glass. Her lips had needed renovation and there, when she opened the bag, on top of everything else had been Wretch's letter. She'd opened it and looked at it although it was incomprehensible to her. In a way he was nice. And he'd sent that money and here it was. And he might be good for more yet. And it would be wrong to break your word to a man who was good to you. The Buddha would be displeased. And He mustn't be displeased in any way whilst Udom was still in danger ...

She hadn't bothered to go back to the others to say goodbye. Let them gabble on about their fat old *assuin*! She'd slipped out of the side-door and into one of the fifty waiting *samlors*.

'Vilai!'

No doubt about his delight at seeing her. If he'd been Chokchai he'd have collapsed on his side wagging all over. And curiously she was pleased to see him too. His hair was tousled and his eyes were heavy with sleep and his torso soared nude and beautiful out of his western-style pyjama trousers which had green and white stripes on them. She didn't know why she was so drawn to him. He was blond and she hated blonds, he was too young, he was poor, and worst of all, he was romantically infatuated. He seemed dazed with his good fortune and didn't know what to do first. In the end he shut and locked the door and came and fell on his knees before her. 'Vilai,' he groaned, like a man who sees God.

She got up out of the chair she'd plumped into and pushed past him and examined the bed and the wash handbasin and the *hongnam* and herself in the full-length wardrobe mirror, 'This room nice,' she said, turning from side to side before the glass so that her skirts whirled back and forth.

'I suppose it is. But I never realized it till this minute.'

'Why you not have that?'—indicating the fan, and as he got up off his knees to start it, 'I go pee-pee.'

She did so on the tiled floor with the proper place to perform the function only a yard away. She threw water about and when she came back into the room he was combing his hair.

'You haff somesing for me to eat?'

'I'm sorry, no.'

'Not d'ink neither?'

'There's water.' He indicated a flagon with a tumbler on it.

She touched it. 'Not cold.'

'I'm sorry.'

'Never mind.'

She sat down on one of the hard wooden chairs. There were a few letters on the low wooden table and she riffled through them but there was nothing of interest—nothing in Thai, no pictures.He dragged the fan up on a stool so that it blew directly on her. Then once again he sank onto his knees before her.

She lifted and angled her legs and pulled her skirts up to her hips. She had on tight pink panties with white lace inserts. A hair or two emerged and she snatched one out with a gasp and a laugh, and then rubbed the injured spot.

'Vilai, have you had any news of Udom?'

It was just what she'd feared. He was going to try to make her face her troubles instead of helping her to ignore them. She flared up. 'I not want you talk Udom. He not your son—why you must worry to him? He *my* son, but I not worry.'

He said, 'Vilai, there's no need to act with me. I saw it happen and I know what you must be feeling. I asked you here because I can give you sympathy. I won't try to—to make you tonight, darling; I'm not so insensitive. I want you to get on the bed, and I'll just take the two blankets which you won't need. I'll be able to sleep on the floor quite comfortably, and in the morning—'

She said, 'How much you give me?'

His head jolted backwards. 'What for?'

'For come here tonight.'

He looked at her, hurt, a moment, then he said gently, 'You don't understand, darling. I've just said I don't want to—*do* anything tonight. I've asked you here because I'm your friend, to, to *save* you from all that—'

She said, sticking to her guns: 'You giff me five hunderd?'

Suddenly he was blazing with anger. He leapt to his feet and unlocked the door and flung it open. '*Lakon*,' he grated.

That meant 'Goodbye forever' but she continued to sit on the chair with her legs up and her skirts too, rolling her hips about and humming.

He shut the door with a slam again and marched up and down the room a few times and then stopped in front of her to harangue her furiously. 'God damn and blast you to all eternity! You haven't got a soft spot in your make-up anywhere. You don't care tuppence for your son, or for anyone else who loves you—'

She said, 'Please sit down.' She waved to the other armchair the other side of the table and in the end he dropped into it, though still fuming. Then she said rationally, 'Wretch, you nice boy, but all the time must angly to me. I not like that. Man like me, must be good to me. He not like, must not ask me come he house. Fight all the time, no good. No good him, no good me ... You haff cigalette giff me?'

He shook his head.

She laughed. 'Wretch good boy, I sink. Not haff nussing in he house for giff girl.' She found a cigarette in her bag and went on: 'Tonight Saturday night. Many men at the Bolero. Many men want White Leopard, I sink. I sink, I go wiss them, I get many hunderd tic. But Wretch send letter say he want me, so I not go wiss usser man. I come see Wretch—'

'And a damn' long time it took you to get here, too.'

'Could not find hotel, darling. *Samlor*-boy not know. He take me many place not right, I must pay him sirty tic. Much trouble to me.'

'What's the time now?' He could have looked at his own watch but he roughly grabbed at her wrist and she allowed him to hold it. 'Yes, you've certainly done some searching all right. Must have been all over Bangkok. It's taken you more than four hours to get here since I sent you that hundred tics. For which by the way you haven't said thank you yet.'

He jumped up and again started tramping about. She smoked quietly for a minute, then she said, 'If you my husband, yes, of course I come your house when you ask me, for nussing. But you not my husband—'

'Why d'you come here then?'

'Because last time you very good to me. Pay me well. Buy me many d'ink. I sink tonight maybe same. But you buy nussing. Not even cigalette.'

'I'm sorry about that.'

'And I come this hotel. Not good for me to come hotel, darling. If you not pay me what I do? I not know policeman here. But if at my house, you not pay, I call policeman, he come quick quick quick—' She laughed.

'He gets a cut off it too, does he?'

She had been casting her eyes around the room and now she located his discarded clothes on the towel rack. She got up and looked in his shirt pocket. Only small notes, as she'd expected. She felt his wallet in his trousers pocket and carried the garment back to the armchair and sat down again. He made an attempt to prevent her opening the wallet but it was only halfhearted. She began searching through the compartments for hundreds.

He said, 'I'm damned if I'll stand for this. Put that wallet back immediately.'

She laughed and lifted her legs up again. 'I not take nussing. I just look see.'

He resorted to force and that was of course poor strategy on his part for the moment his flesh brushed against her his energy was diverted from protecting his money to other matters. He was suddenly kissing her arms and legs and any other parts he could reach and while she wriggled to keep his interest up she got the wallet opened in the right place.

'A-a-ah ...'

She stopped wriggling and he buried his face in her belly, trembling.

There were six red notes. She took the five cleanest ones and put them in her bag. He never looked up.

While his head was still pressed into her stomach she crushed out her cigarette in his perfectly empty ashtray. She looked down at the back of his neck which was a choleric red, like so many fair men's, between the yellow hair and the whiteness of his back. Then she tapped his shoulder. 'Come on, Wretch. Take a bass. Clean your teece. Make your-self smell good.'

He seemed to think it was unnecessary but of course he did her bidding. When he emerged from the bathroom she was already under the mosquito netting. She had taken off her dress and was in pants and bra only, smiling at him.

'Christ, you've got a lovely figure, Vilai.'

'Yours good too. Turn fan this way, darling. It so hot.'

Fundamentally one man's love-making was exactly like another's and that increased the dullness of it. It very seldom happened that a man was able to stimulate in her a passion commensurate with his own. Usually she pretended successfully enough that they did, with the result that her fame had gone round the world. But the groans, the head-rollings, the beating of the bed with doubled fists, were all part of routine, like a dancer's movements in the classical dance, and if there was any emotion in them at all it was impatience.

But just occasionally some combination of circumstances would predispose her body unpredictably to be genuine in its responses. It was in these embraces that she had earned the name of Leopard, rather than in her ruthless prowlings at the Bolero. Any man who had happened to be the lucky *agent provocateur* on such an occasion was unlikely ever to forget his good fortune.

Tonight was such a night. She'd been dimly aware for some hours that it would be. The day had been one long assault on her emotions. Udom's ridiculous loyalty to his princess: that had made her cry in the first place, had filled her heart with pride and shame and consuming but thwarted love for her son. Then seeing him hurt before her eyes. And then all Wretch's goodness to her. Of course she didn't let that fool her altogether; she told herself he wasn't entirely disinterested; what man ever is when a beautiful woman is the object of his benevolence? He wanted to sleep with her again. And his attitude a few minutes ago had shown that he was hoping that in view of his helpfulness this afternoon he'd be let off paying for the privilege. Men were all the same: they thought if they put themselves out for you the slightest little bit they merited a reward. But such services were to be regarded strictly as extras, like handbags and tins of expensive cigarettes. They were no substitute for money. Usually she had difficulty in putting this point of view across, but Wretch seemed to have grasped it at once. That was another reason for her receptive state. Wretch was unutterably nice. He was short-tempered of course, but he was generous within his means, he was adoring, good-looking, clean, and humbler in his manner than most men. Chokchai came into her mind once again: this boy had the same innocence and the same unspeakable delight in pleasing. She wanted to cuddle and kiss him, as she would the pup, out of gratitude for his affection, his youth, and his beauty. So the minute he got into bed with her she put her arms round him and kissed him on the mouth. That was something she rarely did to any man. But tonight she'd known she must. And she'd already wiped her lipstick off in preparation, while he was bathing.

After she'd washed herself she put on her brassiere and tied one of his towels around her waist and lay down beside him again. He promptly rolled over and clasped her but she shook him off. 'No. Now I slip. What time now?'

'Nearly four.'

'Wake me five o'clock. Must go home before light.'

'Stay here, Vilai darling. I have the car this weekend. I can take you to the hospital—'

'Not haff clo'es.'

'We can send the boy. Or fetch them in the car.'

'No, I go home.' She took both pillows for herself and made herself comfortable. 'Not want you tutss me, darling. It so hot.'

'Anything you say.' He moved away but a few seconds later his body was touching hers again, unobtrusively but annoyingly.

She lay on her side, curled up, with her back to him. Completely tired out and sexually replete she'd expected to drop asleep at once but now she lay staring into the blackness outside the dim whitish smear of the net and she knew sleep was still a long way off. Wretch wasn't sleeping either. Every time she moved a little he made a reverent adjustment of his own body to fit hers lightly but persistently.

'Why you not slip?'

'Me? Good God, Vilai! Do you realize this is the first time in my twenty-seven years I've actually slept with a woman—I mean, just lying down peacefully beside her with my eyes closed? Do you think I'm going to waste a single precious second of such bliss in unconsciousness? This is the climax of my life, this is peace, this is what I've been seeking, without properly knowing it, ever since I first got impatient of my mother's fondlings when I was around six or seven, I suppose—'

She turned on to her back. 'Wretch, how mutss money you haff?'

That stopped the ravings. After a pause he said, 'How much did you take? There was six hundred in the wallet, I think.'

'I no mean that. I mean altogesser. In bank—'

He lay very quiet for a moment. Then he said, 'Haven't I given you enough? More than a thousand, counting in drinks, for just two—'

She tossed her body impatiently. 'I not sink that now. I sink Udom. Wretch, I not like he at *ron-piya-ban* all by he-salf. I sink all the time he call 'Mama, Mama' but Mama no come. Wretch, I want go *ron-piya-ban,* stay wiss my son till he well again.'

He got up on his elbow and stared down at her face through the darkness. 'You do?' She could tell he was thrilled. He was certain now that she had the right maternal instincts. He felt his love for her had not been misplaced.

'I want. But how can I do? Must pay for room. Must pay for food. Must pay for *samlor.*' She sighed, and rubbed her eyes—really, her lot was very hard and it was a wonder her tears weren't flowing. 'If I not go Bolero every night—' Suddenly she grabbed his hand and pressed it to her lips in such a way that his wrist touched her cheek. For it was wet ...

He said, thickly into her shoulder, 'Vilai, Vilai.' He was overcome with pity. Finally he lifted his head and said, 'Sweetheart, sometimes you act the tough guy so well you bamboozle even me. But I *know* you aren't bad, not right deep down. How could I love you if you were? And this proves it. You're good, good, good—'

She agreed with him, but practical as always, she said, 'How mutss you giff me?'

'How much do you think you need?'

She'd already made a guess at what she thought would be the utmost he could manage. 'I sink two t'ou-zand—but I know you very young boy—and young boy never haff mutss money—' She continued to cry softly in the darkness.

Finally he spoke. 'Vilai, if I give you a cheque for two thousand—*if* I do—do you swear you'll forget the Bolero for a few nights and go to be with Udom at the hospital?'

'You giff me two t'ou-zand, of course I not go Bolero. Who want to work when he haff money?'

This rejoinder was clinching, she thought, but it didn't seem to carry Wretch as it should have done. He lay silent for a long time. Then he said doubtfully, 'That's more than half of what I've saved. If I give it to you, do you promise—'

'I plomiss.'

'If you cheat me, Vilai—' He didn't complete the threat and if he *had* done so it wouldn't have interested her much. He hung over her for a long time, propped on one elbow, then he growled, 'I'm a chump,' and got off the bed. He snapped on the light and stark naked began searching for his pen and chequebook. At that moment, as she lay comfortably on the bed, he looked to her the handsomest of the two or three thousand men who had known the inmost chalice of her body ...

'I'll date it for Monday,' he was saying. 'The bank's not open tomorrow, or rather today. But if you cheat me, Vilai—'

'Of course I not cheat you, darling. Don't you unnerstand I in love wiss you?'

And she really was a little at that moment. Therefore she suffered without too much fretfulness the long kiss he came over to fix on her lips ...

Going home by *motor-samlor* in the waxing light of dawn it was only the thought of that cheque which kept her spirits up. The ribald comments of the early pedestrians who happened to catch sight of her bare shoulders and flowing skirts were mercifully drowned by the uneven explosiveness of the engine and the rush of air past her ears but nothing could drown her thoughts. She'd been betraying Udom all night long. He'd made his school fellows think she was a princess—and a princess who'd been to America and had medical qualifications into the bargain—and now, poor little child, he was sick. Yet instead of staying by his bedside, reciprocating his loyalty, she'd been determinedly thrusting him out of her mind all night, exerting herself to entertain foreigners who cared no more for her than she for them—men who made her as low as he'd made her high. She thought of him coming round in that dingy barn of a place and wondering where he was and seeing those dreary white nurses floating around—perhaps he would think he was dead and be terrified and start to cry out for her, but no one would take any notice. He might be screaming with terror at this very moment and probably Bochang was asleep ... Only she, his Mama, really knew how to look after him ...

She decided to do what she'd told Wretch she would do. Go to the hospital and keep Udom company till he was discharged. Wretch had made it possible for her to do so, and she wanted to do it ...

She paid the *samlor*-boy the exorbitant twenty tics he'd demanded and began pounding heavily on the corrugated iron door. Siput was always a sound sleeper.

The footsteps came unexpectedly soon. There was no reply to her shouts to hurry up. The lock was fumbled with and finally the door dragged open.

Bochang!

'Why aren't you at the hospital?' she began in a fury but then she saw Bochang's expression and she stopped. An agonizing pain opened in her heart and spread frighteningly through her breast. 'Udom—?' she quavered.

'Oh, Mem, Mem,' Bochang burst out, her voice hoarse and bewildered like a frog's. 'Why did you let the foreigner take our Udom to the hospital? Why did you not bring him home where we could have looked after him ourselves? Everybody knows hospitals are not to be trusted. Everybody knows that they will not trouble themselves about a little boy unless of course his family is exceedingly rich and can pay huge fees ...'

Part Three

THE SLAUGHTER

'Who rides a tiger cannot dismount'

Chinese Proverb

Eight

After she'd gone that Sunday morning I went back to bed. But I was too hungry and too stirred up to sleep.

Simultaneously I despised and admired myself. I despised myself because I'd allowed myself to be cheated so badly. What had I paid her during the previous few hours? Altogether two thousand six hundred tics. At the rates then prevailing that was fifty-four quid or one hundred and thirty US dollars. Ten weeks before, when I was still a grocer's assistant, it would have taken me the best part of three months to earn that much. And every few minutes that thought would bring me up aghast. For what was there to show for my money? Nothing—unless you counted a single strand of her hair I'd found on the pillow. And I'd had her body twice ... Ratom would have given me that much for a fiftieth of the cost. In fact I had allowed my lust and my sympathy, both riding me full-pelt, to stampede me into idiocy, and at intervals that thought would make me writhe.

But the rest of the time I had no compunction at all over what I'd done. On the contrary I was pleased with myself.

'At last I'm out of my adolescence,' I told myself. 'At last I'm man-size.' My muscles automatically flexed themselves. My body had come into its own. I could face adults now eye to eye.

I recalled various things she'd said. 'I like you, Wretch. You good boy, I sink. Why you not marry wiss me? What you do tomollow? How mutss money you get every munss? If you like, I marry wiss you, go everywhere—'

'I not bad girl. I not pross. I dancing-girl. I slip only wiss man I like. I not like you, you giff me one t'ou-zand tic, you cannot slip wiss me—'

She'd wanted me to escort her home because it was getting light and it was not nice, she'd said, for a girl to be seen out alone at that time of day in evening clothes. 'What, going to hide behind my big European nose?' I'd asked. She'd wanted me to take her to the hospital to see Udom, but later she'd decided it would be better if she went by herself. She wanted to know when she'd see me again—tomorrow, the next day after that? I'd remembered I must get another payday in first and suggested Thursday. She'd said sadly, 'You not like me, Wretch.' I'd protested that I did, that she'd given me a wonderful time, that she didn't know how much she'd done for me. She'd smiled, thrown her arms round my neck, and kissed me on the lips. An affectionate kiss, not a lustful one. Then she'd gone, lingering a little at the door as if she'd expected me to accompany her downstairs, but I was still in pyjama trousers only ...

As soon as I heard a boy slopping around in the passage I ordered coffee, ham and eggs, toast and marmalade for two, and gobbled the lot.

'Leopard, Leopard, burning bright
In the Bolero every night,
What immortal hand or eye
Could frame thy fearful symmetry?'

I repeated that quatrain many times. It seemed to fit.

After I'd eaten and the boy had straightened the bed I laid down on it again and tried to make up for lost sleep. But the Leopard was burning too bright in the forest of my mind. Sleep wouldn't come. In the end I got up and wrote letters to Lena and Slither.

Shortly after midday she shot into my room like a projectile. And exploded like one.

'Wretch, you no good, I sink. I hate you. You kill my son.'

'What?'

'Udom d'ad.'

'No, Vilai, no!'

'You sink I lie? Huh! I not lie 'bout sing like this, I sink. Udom d'ad, I tell you. Because you kill him. *You*!'

I'd got up when she'd burst in but now I had to sit down again because my knees had gone weak. 'What happened?'

'What you sink happen? Like I tell you must happen. *Ron-pi-ya-ban* no good. Not do nussing for my son. Not care he at all. Let he die. And now he d'ad, they all laugh very mutss, I sink.'

She had her elbows on the dressing table and was staring at herself in the glass. She had on no make-up except lipstick and it was easy to see she had been crying. I got up and stood just behind her, but I thought it would be desecration to touch her in her sorrow. 'Poor little Udom!' I said.

'What you mean—poor littun Udom?' She whirled round, her face angry. 'Nussing wrong for he, I sink. Now he d'ad. Not feel nussing. Not fray nussing. Not want, want, want all the time. Now he happy, I sink. No more trouble for he any more at all.' She went to one of the armchairs and flung herself into it. 'Poor Vilai! That the truce word, I sink. Why I want to live any more, now Udom d'ad? Why must work and unhappy all the time? I sink I d'ad too batter—'

'Vilai!' Although I'd once tried to kill myself I'm always shocked to hear anyone else repudiating life. I clasped her hand across the table.

All at once her eyes overflowed with tears. 'Wretch, why the God do this to me, you sink? I not bad girl. I *bad* girl, yes, but I *good* bad girl. I not bad 'cause I want bad. I bad 'cause I must haff money. If not bad, how can girl do, not haff huss-band? Every girl not haff huss-band *must* be bad. Unless she just work in s'op, for rice—'

I couldn't think of the right answers at that moment and simply squeezed her hand. She snatched it away impatiently and went into the bathroom. When she came out she was carrying her skirt, a red one with several hundred pleats in it. She arranged it tidily over the towel rack. Then she unbuttoned her white blouse and squirmed it off. She tied a towel round her middle and came and sat down again. 'Wretch eat yet?'

'Not yet.'

'What you will haff?'

'I don't know. Are you hungry?'

'Yes, a littun.'

I got up and rang the bell.

She ordered a very great mess of pottage and when it came attacked it with vigour. But after a few mouthfuls her appetite failed and she went and lay on the bed. I sat at the table eating a little while longer but in truth I was off my food too. I pushed my plate away and looked across at her.

She was lying with her legs spread, on her back, staring at the ceiling, lost in gloomy thought. But at length she became conscious of my gaze, looked down along her body at me and—laughed. I couldn't believe my ears. She rolled her hips from side to side, then lifted them, then let them drop back on the bed with an accompanying small grunt. I had learned the sign, but I couldn't move. It was blasphemy—like murder in a cathedral.

'What matter wiss you today? You not strong any more? You haff nusser girl in here since I go this morning? Tee-hee, tee-hee!'

For a moment I wondered whether she'd been fooling me. But then I recalled those tears that had poured down her cheeks—they'd been genuine all right. I went across to the bed and stood staring down at her. She seemed to me like some sort of monster.

'You angly to me again? Oh, Wretch, all the time you must angly to me. You not haff good heart, I sink. You want to fight all the time—'

'Vilai, if Udom's—dead—'

'What differnunt? Last night you—bam bam—like you mad. Udom d'ad then too. Only differnunt, then you not know. Now you know—'

'You're so hard. You're hard as—'

'Nusser sing. I not want you talk Udom again. Now he d'ad. He finiss. He neffer hear bird sing again. OK. Forget about. Forget about.' She had to struggle to check her tears again but succeeded. She thrashed around until the towel came undone and then began making the little anxious, querulous, exciting noises I knew so well. I was deeply ashamed of myself as I sat on the edge of the bed pulling my shorts off. Yet if her hands had been dripping with her son's blood I think I would still have been unable to resist her.

Afterwards she took my last hundred-tic note. 'You haff more on Sursday?' she asked. 'Now must pay more zan before. Must pay for burn Udom. Must pay for pliests sing for him. Must pay for feast. Everyone must get very d'unk, I sink. Haff man burn, always everybody must get very d'unk.' She was putting on the red skirt. 'You like? Siamese girl only wear red colour when she happy. That why I wear red colour today. Not want any pipple know I sad. Man see me sit in *samlor,* he must sink, "Oh, there go White Leopard. She very happy girl, I sink. She not haff any trouble in world ..."'

She didn't come Thursday and I spent an angry anxious time until three in the morning, when I finally gave up hope. I got up then and ate all the mangoes and spicy Siamese delicacies I had bought for her. I drank the beer I had provided for myself, though it was no longer cold, then went back to bed hoping to sleep. But the hope was vain.

Most of the thoughts that tormented me were unworthy of a man; I knew that even then, and it made them all the more galling. I thought, 'She thinks she's got all the money she can off me so she doesn't want anything more to do with me.' I thought, 'She's found another man she likes better than me. Maybe Dick's plane's having engine trouble again.' I thought, 'All women are cheats. Look at Sheila—' The images of my mother, Lena, and the Korat Venus popped into my mind, accusing me of being hysterical and unfair, but I bundled them out again. I sat up under the mosquito-net rehearsing the speeches I was going to make next time I saw her. I dreamed impossible dreams: that I'd won the Speedway World Championship before ninety thousand cheering spectators at Wembley Stadium, and that she was riding round the arena with me on my bike, waving the enormous gold cup to the throng; that I'd just conquered a mountain higher even than Everest, the first to do so, and having returned to civilization was sending off my first cable: 'Miss Vilai, c/o Bolero Bangkok Thailand I got there Vilai thanks for pushing all my love Wretch.' I prayed to her son. 'Udom, she loved you so much you must have loved her too. I love your Mamma as you did. I hate to have her live this horrible dangerous life she leads, just as you must have done. I want to save her from it. I *can* save her from it. But she doesn't recognize a true friend when she sees him. Oh, Udom, if you have any power over her now, if you can reach down or up from wherever you are and knock the scales from those lovely foolish eyes—' After daybreak I *did* drop off for a few minutes,—and dreamed about Ratom. I remember my last waking thought was, 'What an ass I am. Self-sacrificed upon an unchaste *mons veneris*—'

The next night I shook off Somboon after dining with him and went to look for her at the Bolero. She was there all right, looking no different, unless handsomer. She was perplexed when I went in, for there was a great tableful of Americans who all seemed to know her very well and out of whom I don't doubt she was making a good deal of money. When she came and sat with me for a few minutes some of them turned nasty: in fact one of the blighters came and joined us—'you don't mind, bud?' he said, 'there's sump'n I have to discuss with this lady'—and she was obviously alarmed. He monopolized her attention but I sat it out for a beer and a peppermint: total cost, with flowers, eighty-three tics. When I left she accompanied me to the door, talking in an earnest undertone. 'Neffer come Bolero again. I working girl. Must do my shob—'

'You never want to see me again?'

'Don't be silly. I in luff wiss you, darling. But when you want see me, must send hotel-boy. Any time you ask I come your hotel.'

'Tonight?'

'You want me come this night?'

'Yes. You're were *supposed* to show up last night. I had *pat-mi-han* and *khao-neu-mo-muang*—'

She said, slowly, 'I want to come tonight. But maybe can not.'

'You really love me very much, don't you?'

She stamped her foot. 'Now you mad again. Why you can not understand? I dancing-girl, darling. Sometimes can not do what I want to do. I must work—'

'Goodnight.'

'Goodni', darling. I come if I can, I plomiss.'

I walked home in near despair and spent another night of misery. It wasn't so much that she failed to show up. But the Calvinistic conscience, thoroughly honed in the days of my youth, had never lost its sharpness. Only take off the sacking in which it was ordinarily wrapped and like the scythe in the toolshed at home it was ready to cut to the bone. And that night the sacking was off, all right. To what depths I had sunk in a matter of a few weeks! Until I had left England I had tried to live up to a high moral code. Thou shalt not lie in words or with loose women or indeed with any woman at all until thou hast married her in a church. Thou shalt not drink anything stronger than communion wine except at Christmas when thy mother maketh thee apple wine according to her great-grandmother's recipe. Thou shalt not gamble or swear or break a promise or sit in the presence of a standing lady. Thou shalt honour thy father and thy mother and thy elder brother and his moll, also God and culture ... By and large I had been able to toe the line for twenty years.

But now ...! I hadn't opened a poet for weeks. I had started to consort with publicans and sinners, and of course there was the highest precedent for so doing, but in my case it was not because, like George Fox, I could see 'that of God which is in every man,' but because I had discovered that that of the Devil which was in a good many men was in me too ... One girl in Korat had been only fifteen. And the fact that she'd extracted two hundred tics out of my shirt pocket with her toes (after I'd told her not to bother to lay the shirt out so tidily at the foot of the bed) while I was engrossed in other matters (and imagined she was too) made no difference. My crime had been the greater. Mine was a crime against a child. Therefore against all mankind. Therefore against God ...

And what was going to be the end of it all? I had put a ring in my own snout: was I to be led around by it for the rest of my days? I had a stupid outlook on life, different from other men's—but instead of making me happier than they were it made me even more frustrated. And so there was never anything but bitterness. Sheila had been wondrous for a time, then that was that. Vilai had been taken as an antidote, and now I'd become an addict—but she was faithless. All her talk about if I'd marry her tomorrow she'd drop everyone else—if I'd take her to Chiengmai she'd forget the other two thousand—but she was now a dancing-girl and she must smile at and be nice to the other men—so go home darling and go to sleep and later maybe I will knock at your door—'Oh, hell,' I groaned, leaping out of the chair ...

I was still ordering beers in the small hours and the boys were out of sorts with me too.

That was Saturday and the next day I was due to leave with Windmill for Chiengmai. I had a busy morning at the office getting everything squared up before my departure and afterwards lunched with Windmill at the Sports Club. It was around four when he dropped me at the hotel. (It was his weekend to have the Riley. He was the only Thai on the staff that ever did get it.)

We'd had quite a few drinks and I was feeling cheerier than at any time since about midnight Thursday—at which hour I hadn't yet lost hope that she'd come that night. But I was cheery now for the opposite reason—because I'd convinced myself I'd never see her again. And in daylight, and after a few beers, and knowing I'd be getting out of Bangkok on the morrow anyway, that prospect seemed easily supportable. Her word wasn't to be trusted. And she had jilted me, after robbing me of almost every penny I possessed. Good riddance then, I thought. For a few more nights I'd yearn, no doubt almost unbearably, for her body, but that yearning could be side-stepped, and probably would be in Chiengmai.

I even sang under the shower. I sang 'I wonder who's kissing her now.' The theme wasn't uncomfortably poignant, not in mid-afternoon. I sang *con bravado*. In all probability nobody was kissing her just at that moment ...

While I was towelling myself Arun came in. He was the boy I'd sent to the Bolero the previous Saturday with the note. He was grinning all over his handsome face. 'Dis morning dat woman from Bolero come. De fat one. She say last night she come look for dis hotel, cannot find. She say tonight she go see *khon* at Silapakọrn Theatre, after dat she come here see you—'

I couldn't believe it. I didn't want to believe it. Even on normal weeknights she'd been unable to pass up 'business' in favour of 'love.' It seemed unlikely therefore that she'd throw away a Saturday—usually the most lucrative night—to visit the theatre and me ... At that moment I was not expecting ever to see her again. For pride would prevent me from going to the Bolero to fetch her—like a wife hauling her husband home from the local. And by the time I returned from the North I'd be cured, by the grace of God, of my infatuation, for what the eye doesn't see ...

From five till six I slept and ten minutes later she came. I recognized her feet, red-nailed, in flashy white sandals, under the half-door with an incredible upheaval in my bowels. It was like the instant after a terrific flash of lightning in one of these tropical storms, when you're getting yourself all keyed up for the thunder clap in five seconds but it comes instantly and shatteringly; you knew there would be thunder, but you never guessed it would come to promptly, so overpoweringly, as this ...

She was in a pretty green frock which she immediately took off. She had on a petticoat for the first time, and I didn't like that much; it was too occidental: it carried me right back to *Weldon's Fashions,* of which my mother had stacks and stacks. She wrapped herself in a towel and thus accoutred called for *oliang yen,* giving the boy a gratuitous thrill.

She wanted three hundred at first, later asked for five, and this was the madness, I gave it to her. Why? I could hardly explain it myself. It had taken me three days to earn that much. She got it in two hours. Her excuse for asking for more was that I was going away for a while. 'You not like usser man. You not giff me money just for slip wiss you. You giff me money 'cause you luff me. And soon I must pay for room—sick hundred—and if you not giff, maybe I not haff, then I must go wiss very bad low man—' It was the right line to take with me.

She told me something about her life but I don't know how much of it was true—certainly this version didn't tally altogether with some later ones. She said for instance that she came from Songkhla in the South, but in all later reports her birthplace was Korat. The same number of husbands figured in the story—three—but this time there was a gap of several years between numbers one and two, whereas in later editions number two was the elder brother of number one and she'd joined his household pretty soon after number one's body had been reduced to ashes. I forget what number two's shortcomings were in this first account (number one never had any) but the trouble with number three was that he was a drunk.

'You've never had any more husbands since?'

'No. Not want Thai man. Not good.'

'You could marry a *farang.'*

'Huh. What *farang* want marry wiss Siamese dancing-girl?'

My kiss was intended to show her there was one. She accepted it calmly.

'You see all the girls take notice to you when you come in Bolero last night?' she asked.

'Yes. They did seem to goggle a bit.'

'They always take notice to my man. If I go wiss man more than one time they know he must be good.'

'I wish to hell you could leave that hole.'

'How I do then? Can not liff on nussing.'

'Live with me. I'd give you everything I earn.'

'How mutss that? Four t'ou-zand every munss? Five t'ou-zand? I can make ten t'ou-zand by my-self. And just for my-self.'

'Money isn't everything—'

'Besides, I not work, what I do? Slip all day? Then I get fat. No good, I sink. Not want get fat. Not pewty.'

'You really mean to tell me you'd rather live this hellish life you lead now than be decent with me, just because you're afraid of getting a bit tubby?'

She answered, 'Maybe I marry wiss you one day. But not now. Now many men want me. Can haff good time, make mutss money—'

'And finally, when you're old and poxed and ugly and nobody else'll look at you, I can have you for my very own?'

She laughed. 'Now you angly again. I neffer know boy angly all the time like you. I not like. You must be good to me, darling, 'cause I tell you more than I tell usser man. You know how unhappy my story, you must be sorry to me.'

I took that rebuke to heart. I could never forget Udom. But it seemed as though she herself sometimes did. And I would resent that. I mistook her courage for callousness.

That afternoon we achieved wonderful accord. She babbled away as Lena used to do after a bottle of stout. She had been to the matinée at the theatre—Arun had got mixed up between 'afternoon' and 'evening'—and the classical dance drama had been 'pewty, pewty, darling; sometime I want us go see togesser; oh very very pewty. And they dance—' She wasn't able to find words to express the beauty of the dancing, but she reproduced some of it with stately arms. 'It all fighting, like *Iverhoe*—'

'You went to see that movie?'

'Yes, I go one day. It good movie, I sink. You haff see?'

'Yes, in England. I liked it too. In fact I was just going to see it again last Saturday when—' I stopped.

She said, 'I going then, too. But we go *ron-piya-ban* instead ... That last movie Udom see, Wretch. I sink he must like very mutss. Horses, fighting. All the time he want to be cowboy when he big. Sometimes I sink very good you run over him wiss car—'

'What! Me?'

She corrected her English. 'I mean, good sing he die. If he big—he man—I sink he bad man, he cowboy, very bad. I not want that for my son. I bad myself, I Number One Bad Girl in Bangkok, but I sink bad

Mama, neffer mind, she always must want good for her son. When he big, I want he Number One Good Man in Bangkok, but maybe—'

'Don't think about it, darling.'

'Wretch, you good boy to me. I like very mutss. I sink no one good more batter than you. Sometime I sink you like the God. I sink I want you go wiss me to country, see my Mama. I sink, if Udom had liff, I want he like you in *every*sing—'

No woman had ever talked to me like that before. My mother had always laughed at my 'cack-handedness' and called me a 'dreamy Daniel.' Sheila had only said, 'If you tried you could do something worthwhile. You've got the brains and the personality. But all you do is ride round and round dirt-tracks and write poetry that nobody will ever read.' Even Lena, who'd never missed a meeting I rode at in London, and who'd saved me from trouble with the police when I'd tried to kill myself in her back bedroom, had been disappointed in me, I knew: and her vast delight over some trivial success—a poem in the local weekly or a raise of five bob—had discomforted more than silence would have done; the very over-emphasis of the praise had underlined how rare were the occasions for any praise at all ... Yet some men must have the adulation of the women they love and be convinced they deserve it ... Vilai could make my heart swell with pride.

'I tell you secret,' she said. 'Vilai not my truce name. Every dancing-girl must haff two name—her truce name and usser one. My truce name—Jamnien.'

'Jamnien? That's a lovely name.'

'My truce name, darling. And you only man in Bangkok know.'

Too soon she said she'd have to go. We dressed and I took her out the back way because coming in by the front door she'd recognized a fellow worker in the foyer and it had upset her: 'This hotel haff girls?' she'd asked, and she'd sounded so indignant I'd had to laugh. Going down the stairs she said, 'Don't forget what I tell you, Wretch. You want I go to Chiengmai wiss you next time, must giff me money before. I sink ten day before, so can make dress for day. Now I night-girl. I not come out when birds sing. Not haff any dress for day. If I go Chiengmai wiss you, must haff t'ree for here—blue—' touching skirt-region—'four or five for here'—touching bosom. 'Not more. I sink four hundred tic enough.

You giff me, darling?'

'You aren't exactly stark naked at this moment, and you say you earn ten thousand a month—'

'What you mean? You not giff?'

'I'll give you, sweetheart, I want you to look the smartest you've ever looked when we go on our honeymoon—'

'What mean moneymoon?'

'Never mind.'

We said goodbye with clinging hands. 'Goodbye, Wretch. Take care you-self.' She brushed her eyes and staggered almost onto the flowerbed as she turned away.

'Vilai! Vilai! Don't go!'

'I must. I very late for Bolero—'

'God blast that place to all eternity.' I almost shouted. The sky was red with sunset. I wished it had been the reflection of that building going up in flames.

That night there was a bit of a breeze and it was from the wrong quarter. Every now and again I could hear the music from the Bolero wafted across the house-tops. I went to bed early but I couldn't sleep. I thought of her dancing, dancing, sick as she was, broken-hearted as she must be. How in the name of Heaven could she actually prefer this fearful life she led to life with me as my mistress or my wife?

I still couldn't bring myself to believe that she was 'bad,' in the sense that Jezebel was bad to my father, and all actresses, especially Hollywood ones, to my mother. At every visit she paid me she gave fresh evidence of virtues which I had been taught were possessed by the 'good' alone. For instance, she was courageous and independent and forthright and realist as I would have liked to be myself but was not; she faced up to life with a clear eye; she seemed indomitable. The worst I could say of her was that she was rather a gold-digger. But how serious a sin was that? What could you expect of any woman deprived of legal support in a society like this—or indeed in any society? Probably her education was insufficient anyway to enable her to secure what we call a decent job. So she'd become a dance-hostess. And that's a job in which the basic rate of pay is low and the labourer has to make up on incidentals. It's a job too at which the worker can make a respectable income only while she's young ... Life is telescoped for a woman, I told myself. All her red-letter days come at the start; she can't look forward to increasing honours in old age, as men do; she makes her mark early or never. No wonder women often seem feverish, greedy, and unreasonable to men, for whom the sands run out at only half the speed ...

'Yes,' I said to myself. 'Vilai's got guts. Even that shocking business a week ago hasn't got her down. She's facing up to the worst calamity in her life much more bravely than I faced up to mine three years ago. She's going to come out on top of this tragedy, triumphant. And I pray God that I may help her, so that her hour of triumph will be mine, too.'

Nine

Windmill and I spent two weeks in Chiengmai. They should have been most enjoyable—a foretaste of the delights to come when Vilai would be my companion. For Chiengmai turned out to be an enchanting place. Here was no featureless, steamy-hot plain such as that which surrounds Bangkok; no jungle like that I had seen in the Northeast, as parched and stunted as the people who inhabited it. Chiengmai, I found, was a clean prosperous city set amidst green fertile fields. The horizon was a ring of wild blue mountains, the nearest and highest of which, Doi Sutep, cast its shadow clear across the city at sunset. From morning to night the sky was an ineffable clear sparkling blue in which pearly cloud formations, astounding in their scale and variety and grandeur, majestically deployed themselves, being subtly and silently re-moulded and re-grouped almost minute by minute. I never tired of watching that enormous stealthy drama in the sky. Yet there was much to admire at ground-level too: numerous temples blazing like jewels in their settings of palms and bo-trees; daily religious parades, with a long wooden drum shaped like a vase carried on a pole in front, girls in traditional garb, one shoulder bare, holding flower-brimmed silver urns against their breasts, troops of older women under sunshades brilliant with painted flowers and birds, and then the cart, burdened with flowers and trees made of paper money, towed by the laughing men; shops full of fantastic silverware, lacquer-work, red and black pottery, handwoven fabrics, and the like; the processions of bullock-carts, each with its own gay geometrical design in front and carved elephants at the rear, drawn creakingly through the streets by pairs of sleepy, amber-sided beasts; the Meping rippling idly between its far-flung, willowy banks ... Several times we went into the surrounding countryside and it was like making trips to fairyland. Baby mountains covered with deliriously jungly jungle. Brown streams flowing blandly through the forest or breaking white over hidden rocks. Flowers as big as birds and birds like flying flowers. Once I saw elephants. There were three of them, bright yellow from a mudbath. They stood chest-high in the undergrowth, with a semi-circle of trees behind them, and above and beyond the tree-tops, a wavy line of mountains. They watched our car go by with those kindly, tolerant smiles which give their species such charming expressions. And the sunlight drowning us all in gold and greens and blues. And every leaf a mirror flashing back the light ...

It is incredible that I could have been disconsolate in such surroundings. Windmill was enjoying himself tremendously. Commercially the trip was a success too. And there were numerous outings, for our Northern clients proved no less hospitable than their counterparts in other regions. (We went amongst other places to the temple high up on Doi Sutep, to a waterfall at its foot, to an agricultural school where (to my untutored eye —Andy might not have agreed)—the fields seemed less well-cultivated than the surrounding farms, and to some hot springs near the Burma border.) Eagerly I took in all the details of these places, but not because I was getting any pleasure out of them then. I had only one thought in my head—that soon I would be bringing Vilai to see them. I wanted to be an efficient guide when the time came.

Vilai ... She was like an unseen presence throughout those two weeks. Never was she out of my thoughts for more than a few consecutive minutes. For hours on end, as we were travelling to Lamphang or Fang or Tha Chom Pu, I'd be gazing out of the window of the bus or train or car, as the case might be, blind to the blur of brilliant foliage riding by, living only in fantasies in which my feats of single-handed valour and endurance redounded always to the glory of her name. Sometimes I would come out of my dreams with a jerk and blush at their futility, at the sheer impossibility of them. I would try to fix my thoughts on worthier subjects—or just try to use my eyes and absorb as much as I could of the passing pageant of hill and jungle—but it was hopeless; in a few moments I would be back in dreamland again. This made me tedious company for Windmill, and one day he remarked on it.

'What wrong with you these days? All the time you—moping—like you love-sick.'

'Perhaps I am.'

'What?' Of all admissions it was the one most likely to catch a Thailander's interest. 'You have a girl?'

'Sure I have a girl' (What a relief it was to let the secret out at last—to share my pride and joy—even with—)

'What she like? She Siamese?'

'Yes, sir.'

'Is she beautiful?'

'Of course. All Siamese girls are beautiful.'

'How old she?'

'Twenty ... seven, I believe.' Stupid to tell the truth. 'My age.'

'Tcha! She too old. Too old for young boy like you, too old for any man. Old girl never any good. Must have young. Only young girl fresh, eager ... Where you meet her?'

'In Bangkok.'

'She prostitute?'

'No—never!'

'What is she then? How you meet her?'

'She's a dancing-girl. The number one dancing-girl at the Bolero.'

'The Bolero—tcha! You not want fall in love with that sort girl. She just want your money. What her name?'

'Oh, never mind.'

He wasn't offended. After a while he said, 'Dancing-girl, prostitute, all the same. All bad. You must not trust. You must just poke once, or twice if very good, then on to the next ...'

I sighed. I'd heard the argument before. It was the doctrine of Somboon and Frost. They also condemned all prostitutes out of hand as bad, advising me to have only my fun with them, then leave them to their badness. To me that was an outrageous proposition. There was not much of the conventional Christian in me but, for some reason that seemed almost instinctive, I had an indestructible belief in the essential goodness of human beings, especially the female sort; and an impulse to 'save' those who according to my judgment had temporarily strayed from the right path would flare up in me quite as fiercely as in a missionary, though of course fewer people seemed 'lost' to me than to a missionary. And since I'd discovered the Siamese brothel this impulse had been continuously burning in me. The Korat Venus—I *knew* she was a good girl—just unfortunate, that's all. How could I have been so attracted by her if she'd been—*evil*? All she'd needed, I'd been convinced, was to be shown the way out of the hell she'd got into and she'd take it. Of course our ideas of the way out had differed somewhat. Mine had all included myself in a highly romantic role; whereas she had based her hope of redemption on a Singer. (That is the generic name for sewing machines in the Far East, and what she meant was that if only I'd give her a couple of thousand tics she could set up as a dressmaker.) These recollections, coming back to me then, made me slightly uncomfortable; just how far had I committed myself, discussing them with the girl in pre-Vilai days? Hadn't I more or less promised ...?

Windmill was saying, 'You better come for walk with me tonight. I find new place. Very charming girls. All young—no hair. There's one—her name is Yupin—I think maybe she is only fifteen, and she *cho-ker-li* only three month. She like angel—out of this world—and only fifty tic. If you like I fix for her to come to hotel tonight.' He saw my boredom and tried one more throw. 'Her bubs—' He whistled his admiration. 'Just like she have two pomelo in her shirt—'

I listened with disdain. I wasn't to be tempted. Vilai was still too real.

I thought then, there in Chiengmai, that the one thing needed to make me happy was to return to Bangkok, which meant to Vilai. But the reunion gave me quite as much pain as joy ...

The train reached Bangkok at eight in the morning. I went to the hotel for bath and breakfast, then strolled through the streets to the office. Many stalls along the New Road where our office was were selling cards that were festive with robins, holly, snow-scapes, tinsel bells, sleighs—all most anomalous, since even a learned man like Windmill was puzzled about the difference between snow and ice. With a shock I realized that it was only a few days to Christmas. The temperature was about ninety in the shade—my shirt was glued to my shoulder-blades—and I was quite unable to work up the proper feeling. However, when I found a few relatively restrained cards with coloured photographs of Thai architecture I bought them. Reaching the office I directed them to the old folks at home, to Lena, Slither, the Samjohns, Frost and Drummond, Windmill and the office girls. When I'd remembered everyone worthy of remembrance there was still one card left over. I wrestled with myself for a long time, at last scribbled on it, 'To Andy and Shee. From R.' I hesitated about sending it, but when Verchai came to empty my OUT tray I threw it in along with the rest. After all, it was the season of goodwill. And the perfidy that had blighted my life for three long years seemed less heinous now, since it had driven me into Vilai's arms ...

My reception at the office had been nothing like our previous triumph—I'd just made a routine reappearance and in five minutes was addressing the cards. I tried to make this disappointment—for such it was—the keynote of the day. Even returning to the hotel in the Riley at four I still refused to let myself hope. But—blessed are the poor in spirit. Arun, meeting me in the lobby, was one joyous grin. 'De fat lady come!' he announced. 'I give key like you say. She in your room, way-it for you.'

I went up the stairs three at a time.

Before going to Chiengmai I'd told her the date we expected to be back but I'd never dared to hope she'd remember it. All the time up North I'd been talking to myself like a Dutch uncle: 'Don't forget, my lad, you're only one pebble on a very shingly beach. Can't expect to catch that eye twice ...' But I saw now that my caution had been unnecessary. All the time I was up North I could have basked in the certainty that the moment I got back to Bangkok she'd come to me. This was no one-sided affair as the Sheila one had been: Vilai returned my own feelings. The most sought-after woman in Bangkok—a woman who could pick and choose between generals and filmstars (she'd slept with them all in her time)—had selected me for her lover. It was a personal triumph—the biggest of my life ... And she seemed to share my joy too, at least that first afternoon; but of course she wasn't so demonstrative as I was.

She stayed until long after she ought to have gone to get ready for 'work'. I think the time passed as quickly for her as for me. We arranged the financial side of our proposed trip to Chiengmai to her great advantage. She questioned me closely about my travels, especially about the number of girls I'd had. She flatly refused to believe I'd been celibate. 'No man can go two week wissout slip wiss girl,' she said: 'imposs-bull.' But she was broad-minded on the subject. 'I not mind you slip wiss usser girl. You must, when you go country so long. But be careful. Mind you not sick. You sick, cannot slip wiss me ...' She returned to the subject more than once. 'Must watss your step upcountry. Not want giff girl too mutss money. Every girl want you money, I sink, 'cause you *farang*, she sink you must haff plenty money. But you must kip you money for *me*. Country girl very dirty, maybe she haff huss-band too. You not want luff her: you luff *me*. You must just pass her, one time, then quick quick forget ...' It was the Somboon-Frost-Windmill doctrine again. But this was no time for controversy. I let her lecture me as long as she liked, happy just to hear her voice, though of course she was wasting her breath; I had dedicated myself to her; she need fear no rivals.

She'd unpacked my bag for me before I came back and while putting my clothes away had noticed their bachelor state. 'Tomollow I bling—you know, somesing make good,' she promised, making the motions of sewing, and she kept her word. When I returned from work next afternoon there she was, stretched on my bed, in brassiere and navy-blue slacks, with my torn clothes all around her and needle and cotton and scissors to hand. She finished the needlework while I had a shower and subsequently almost frightened me by the violence of her love-making. Up to that point everything was perfect but then the question of money came up and with it the question of did we trust and love each other. The answer was of course no, not entirely. I had given her three hundred tics the day before on the understanding that it was to cover two visits. Now she said it wasn't enough. I accused her of breaking her word and she accused me of trying to welsh on her.

'Of course you not giff me money yesterday for today! You sink t'ree hunderd enough for two day? Huh: I White Leopard. I very high girl. I neffer slip wiss man for less than two hunderd—'

'OK. Here's another hundred. That makes four for two days.'

'So! Now you try to make me look low. Next sing you want me slip wiss you for nussing. Before you go Chiengmai you make me very high, pay me four, five hunderd. But now you haff usser girl in Chiengmai, I sink, you like her more zan me—'

'She's wonderful. She's very small and dainty—'

'There you are! Before you say you no haff Chiengmai girl—'

'And she costs me only twenty tics per game. And she's much

younger and—and *eagerer*—than you are. And I like her far, far better than I like you—'

'Huh. She cat. I leopard—'

'She loves me and she wants to marry me.'

'Tee-hee! You belief that? What Siamese girl want to marry wiss *farang*? She just want money from you.'

And so on. In the scrimmaging I dropped my watch and broke the glass. She stopped quarrelling at once. 'You know where you can buy new?'

'No.'

'I take. I bring back next time I come see you.'

So she wasn't so mad at me that she intended to drop me ... 'You'll have to hurry up,' I said. 'Straight after Christmas I'm off to the Northeast again.'

'Oh, Wretch. All the time you go away. Why you not stay in Bangkok? I not want you go country all the time, giff you money to *cats*. I want you stay here, wiss me.'

'So I can give all my money to you, eh?'

'Yes.' She never made any bones about it. 'Why *you* want? You no haff house, no haff wife, no haff nussing. But I must pay for many sing. You no giff me money, what I do?'

'What you did before you met me. What you do now. Lie with any man that'll slip you a hundred tics—'

'Not hunderd, darling. I Leopard. I—'

'Don't tell me lies. I know Bangkok as well as anyone. Any Bolero girl will sleep with a man for a hundred—'

'Usser girl, maybe. But not Vilai—'

'—whether he's poxed, or scrofulous, or stinking, or depraved—'

'Stop, stop, Wretch. You not want say any more. Only say bad sing. Hurt me. Hurt you-salf ...'

So it went on. There was anything but the serene domesticity I longed for in our relationship. Together, we were always in a fury of love or violently quarrelling. Apart—well, of course, I don't know how much *she* thought about *me*. I can only speak for myself. Alone, I was always racked with longing for her or marching up and down my room calling on Heaven to expunge her from my life—depending on how we'd parted last time. I could never take a middle line and just like her. It was always the extreme of love or hatred with me.

Actually we didn't see much of each other for some time. I got thoroughly involved in Christmas festivities. There were cocktail parties all over and the Samjohns invited me to spend the day with them. They were really extremely nice to me. Mrs. S. gave me the latest Hemingway. There was fresh turkey and plum pudding out of a tin. Drinks were unlimited. In the afternoon we called on neighbours of theirs for yet more drinks. I should have enjoyed myself. But my last session with Vilai had been stormy. She'd flatly refused to see me during the holidays. 'It big day for American; I must dress up, show myself around.' The fact that I was having the day off and could have spent several hours with her made no difference. 'I not want you come wiss me. You good boy. I not want you go Champagne Bucket, all those places; they not nice for you. Better I come hotel, see you Saturday ...' I hated being kept hidden as if I were a guilty secret. I'd cut up rough and, I feared, offended her unforgivably. So I was desperate and miserable ... When Saturday afternoon came, and she with it, I was overcome with remorse because of my doubts of her and with gratitude and affection. Every time she turned up again it was like a miracle: I could never convince myself, when she was absent, that she'd ever return to me ...

The next day, Sunday, she came too; and this was the first occasion she let me see that all was not well with her. I think I sensed it the moment she flounced in. She was in gaudy red slacks and an off-the-shoulder yellow blouse that almost shouted 'Here's a harlot' to the startled eye, but she had on scarcely any make-up and her hair was wildly dishevelled. As usual I attempted to kiss her but she eeled out of my arms and ripped off her clothes. She'd ordered a coffee for herself and the boy brought it while she was doing herself up in a towel.

As she brooded over her coffee I was horrified by the alteration in her appearance. It was not just that the skin of her face looked so much coarser than usual, the eye-sockets puffy, the lines from nose to mouth more marked, but her whole expression had changed. Her eyes were wells of pain, almost black, and her mouth was pushed forward in grim twisted lines of discontent. I knelt in front of her and tried to encircle her in my arms as my habit was but she snarled 'Not want,' swerved her knees in my way and sucked at her coffee savagely.

'What's the matter with you, darling?'

'Nussing matter.'

'Yes there is.' I made another attempt to get my arms round her and this time she didn't repulse me, though she sighed impatiently. 'You're in some sort of trouble. Tell me about it. I might be able to help you.'

'I not want halp. Haff very strong heart. Can look after mysalf.'

'All right, if you want to be independent.' I got up, offended, and went and lay on the bed. I was still full of sentimental notions about people in love, and one of them was that the female, when properly constituted, instinctively sobbed out her troubles on the staunch male shirt-front. And the fact that Vilai never would do this seemed to me to be just one more proof that she didn't regard me as her man. I was failing with her just as I'd failed with Sheila before her.

After a gloomy minute she came and stretched out beside me. I rolled towards her but she shook me off. 'No, slip now.' She turned her back on me. And then I realized she was crying.

I think if snow had started falling out of the Bangkok sky I couldn't have been more surprised.

For while, like most introspective people, I never fail to magnify my own woes, I very easily underrate other people's. And because, since that first week, Vilai had never mentioned Udom again—because, every time I'd seen her since, she'd seemed as gay or tigerish, as buoyant, self-assured, money-mad and libidinous as before—I'd comfortably assumed that she'd forgotten the tragedy or at least taken it in her stride. I'd even found arguments to justify her apparent heartlessness. It was wrong to call it that, I'd told myself: Siamese mothers don't dote on their offspring any less than others do; it was simply that her religion meant more to her than it does to most women. She fully believed that life was hell and death heaven; that Udom was now translated to a state of total nescience and therefore of complete happiness; that he had received his reward for his virtue—utter extinction—while she must remain on earth to suffer, through his death and her aloneness, for her sins. So I had come to admire her for her self-control, and when this broke down I felt I had been personally let down by her.

Yet at the same time I was relieved to see her weeping because according to my understanding this was how a woman ought naturally to behave in the circumstances. I tried to get her to turn over and do her crying in my arms but she kept her back resolutely towards me. After a few minutes she got up abruptly. 'Must bass. Not haff bass today. Smell bad. I not go home since yesterday night.'

'Why, where've you been?'

'I come from sip.'

'Sip?'

'Yes, darling. Big American sip. At Klong Toey.'

'Ship? You mean you've been down to the docks? But what for?'

'I often go sip, darling. Haff fun. Make good money.'

'But damn and blast it, don't you make enough money at the Bolero? And out of me?'

'I not go Bolero for t'ree, four day,' she said indifferently, going into the bathroom and tweaking the towel off.

I lay across the bed on my belly glaring at her. I was seething with rage at yet another insult. She knew she could come to me for money at any time, but she preferred to earn it by being promiscuous in the most degrading ways ... She didn't use the shower: she threw water over herself with the dipper. She looked superb standing there, moving so gracefully, her skin golden against the blinding snow of the sunlit tiled walls.

'You sink pewty?' she asked, seeing the admiration in my eyes (for I couldn't hide it). 'Last night American say very pewty. He say my face not so good, but my ass number one ass in the world. He say any girl haff face good like my ass, she must be most pewty girl ever liff—Miss Uni-worse.'

She laughed gaily. I groaned aloud. I was shaking. At last I managed to grate, 'And how much did *he* give you? Fifty tics? Or fifty-five?'

'Oh, mutss more than that. He very good boy. Like me very mutss.'

'I hope to God I never meet him. I'd kill him.'

'Why you say that? He good to me, darling. If you luff me you must like anyone who good to me.'

I leapt off the bed and started pulling on my clothes. Coming out of the bathroom, dabbing herself with the towel, she sighed. 'Now you want fight again. What for this time, for God sake?'

I was in the mood to explain. 'I'll tell you, you strumpet, and then you can go, for good. I'm a decent chap, see? I'm not the whoring, drunken, blasphemous, hell-bent sort you're used to. But for some reason I've fallen in love with you. I'm crazy about you, Vilai, crazy. And I've tried to do the right thing by you. Your life is bad—you admit that yourself. All right—I offered to take you out of it. Oh, I know I'm no great shakes compared with your other—friends. I don't earn much, I'm not very cheerful company, I probably don't make love as well as they do. But which of them would give you every bloody penny he has in the world, the same as I've done? Which of them would offer to marry you? And that's what I'm doing now, Vilai—again—for the last time. I *want* to marry you, darling. I want to take you out of your present hell. I can give you enough to clothe and feed you and you can live with me here in this hotel. And you can get tight every damn' night if it makes you any happier. But at least give up your old life while the going's good. Now you're still the number one girl at the Bolero, you're like a queen there, almost every man that sees you wants you. But how much longer can it last? Soon you'll begin to show signs of cracking up. You'll begin to lose your looks. Men won't want you so much. They'll only be willing to pay a few tics for your favours. You'll have to sell your jewels. You'll have to take more and more men—any man that'll give you a little money—whether they're sick or not. One day you'll get sick yourself ... Can't you see it, Vilai? You must have seen it happen to dozens of girls at the Bolero.' I threw myself on my knees beside the bed, on which she was lying, and clasped her hand. 'Vilai, grab your chance while it's here. Marry me—and live happy ever after.' The last words were said jocularly—I was self-conscious about having been so earnest and eloquent.

She didn't make any answer at all but just lay with her hand inert in mine and in the end I realized there wasn't going to be any answer. With a sigh I got up and lay down on my back behind her.

After about ten minutes I knew by the regularity of her breathing that she'd gone to sleep.

She slept for two hours without moving. At first I lay there admiring the lines and planes that had called forth such high praise the night before. But during the second hour I began to grow restive. The impudence of this tart! Coming to see me and then spending the whole afternoon in sleep. Ignoring my ultimatum, my declaration of love, my proposal of marriage! How much more could she slight and hurt me? Instead of lying still as a stone, as up till then, I began to move around when I wanted to, and in the end more than necessary. At last I disturbed her. She awoke with a violent start, lay rigid for a moment, then rolled on her back and looked at me.

'Wretch, what the time now?'

'Never mind the time.' Throwing an arm across her.

'No, no.' She tried to struggle free. 'What the time? Must go four o'clock.'

'Four? You always stay till seven. That gives you plenty of time to get ready for the Bolero.'

She clicked her tongue impatiently. 'I *ask* you I not go Bolero.'

'Why not? You lost your job?'

She said, 'No, oh, no,' but there was so much surprised vehemence in the denial that I was sure it was false. I stopped wrestling with her and got up and looked at her watch—(she'd taken all her jewellery off when she bathed). 'It's nearly five.' I walked back to the bed.

'Goddam!' She leapt off the other side and ran to the towel rack on which she'd draped her clothes. She began rapidly putting them on.

'Are you going without—?' I was choking with rage.

'Half no time, darling. I late now. You let me slip too long—'

'Who is it? That damned Yank?'

'Oh, Wretch! Why you worry so mutss to him? He nussink to me.'

'Yet you'd rather go to him than stay with me.'

'Of course, darling. He only here two, t'ree day. But you here all the time. Can see you any time you want.'

She'd got herself dressed and gone to the mirror and was pulling out hairclips. 'He like me too mutss, darling. Pay very well. Must get he money while he here.'

'You haven't forgotten of course but I'm going to Ubol tomorrow?'

'Tomollow?' It was clear she had forgotten. 'I sink you say *wan-ti yip-kao*—'

'That's right. Tomorrow's the twenty-ninth.'

'Goddam.' She was combing her hair with long fierce strokes. Then she parted it, and began picking up hairclips, opening them with her teeth, and shoving them home above her ears. 'How long you go country this time?'

'Three weeks at least.'

'Goddam, goddam.' She dropped her comb in her bag and started forcing her bracelets over her hands. 'What time you go tomollow?'

'After lunch. We're going by jeep this time, not train.'

'You here in morning?'

'No, I must go to the office.' I knew the sensible thing would have been to leave it at that. But I was too weak. 'I *could* come back, of course. About twelve. For an hour.'

Ready except for her shoes she came and sat on the edge of the bed beside me. When she bent to force her feet into the shoes the yellow blouse slipped off one shoulder. I put my arm round her with a groan. She suffered the embrace for a full minute, kneading my thigh with her knuckles. But as soon as I tried to get a better purchase on her she broke away. She stood up, sliding a hand inside her blouse to straighten her brassiere. 'You giff me money today?'

'Certainly not. Get it off Uncle Sam.'

'I come tomollow at twelve, how mutss you giff me?'

'Hell, Vilai, you're a moneymaniac. Don't you ever think about anything else at all?'

'How mutss you giff me?'

'I'll give you nothing. It's time you gave *me* something.'

'But soon I must pay for room. And you go away for t'ree, four week—'

The worried look on that changed tragic face broke my heart. And my body was yearning for hers which was poised sturdy yet somehow forlorn before me. I pulled her between my knees and encircled her hips with my arms. Very lightly she clasped my head to herself. I knew I was being managed. But I was powerless to control my desires.

'How mutss you giff me if I come tomollow?'

'How much d'you want? I'll give you half perhaps.'

She stated her requirements with great exactitude. 'I want one t'ou-zand four hunderd. Four hunderd for make dress for go Chiengmai. One t'ou-zand 'cause I not see you so long ... Not very mutss money for me, darling. Must pay four hunderd for clo'es, sick hunderd for room—'

'Your room's three hundred.'

'Yes, but must pay two time if you go country for t'ree week.' I began to get rough with her again and she pulled herself away. I let her go, sitting on the edge of the bed with my arms dangling.

'Vilai, why did you lose your job?'

'Oh—I ask you tomollow. Must go now.' She gave her hair a final toss, peering into the mirror, and picked up her handbag. I accompanied her to the stairs. She went down very cautiously, mincingly, sideways, as her habit was. At the bottom she stopped to wave and throw me the usual dazzling smile. But that was the trouble. Today it wasn't dazzling. It was a deathly grin that failed to mask the tragedy behind it.

Of course when I got back from the hotel during the lunch-hour the next day there she was and of course I gave her the money. I don't think she'd expected the whole fourteen hundred but that didn't prevent her from asking for an extra hundred to make it a round figure. 'Then I can haff fife hunderd for my-self.' An extra hundred seemed hardly worth squabbling about so I handed it over. I didn't tell her that that morning I'd had to borrow a thousand from Frost, giving unexpected Christmas presents as my excuse. Or that Frost had been most sceptical about this excuse, saying, 'I hope to God I'm not loaning you this so you can just chuck it away on a lot of whores upcountry. I'm short myself, and giving you this'll just about break me. I want it back early in the New Year—you understand?—or I'll be sunk ...'

She returned my watch, mended. We ate a large meal and shared a bottle of beer. All the time she was picking titbits out of the dishes and placing them invitingly on my plate. I tried to find out why she'd been fired from the Bolero, but she was evasive. 'I ask you before, when d'unk I fighting girl'.

I clicked my tongue. 'Oh, Vilai, all the time you make life harder for yourself. Why d'you have to get drunk? It's dangerous for a girl in your line. When you're drunk you don't fully realize what's going on. One of these days some rotter'll get you tight and do you serious harm—'

'What mean ham?'

'Make you sick. Or hurt you. Maybe even kill you—'

'Huh. What I care that? I not care how I die, when I die. I sink haff man kill me I very happy. I sink when he—peep!'—she mimed firing a revolver—'I say, "sank you, sank you."'

'Vilai, don't be so self-centred. Maybe *you* don't care what happens to you. But what about those who love you?'

'Who? Who you sink luff Vilai now?'

'Your mother. Me. Perhaps somc other silly ass you've never told me about—'

She laughed. She was transformed from the preceding day—and not just because she was made-up—her spirits had revived, and she was bewitching in her laughter. 'I sink my Mama very happy haff me die now,' she argued. 'Now I still Number One Bad Girl in Bangkok. I sink my Mama not want me number one t'ou-zand and one. I sink I want to dancing for t'ree, four more year. Then I not pewty, man not want, I lost my shob. Batter I die before—'

'But you've lost your job already.'

'Neffer mind. Now can get new. Every man know White Leopard. Every man want her to dancing. I sink every boy go Bolero now, he ask manager, 'Goddam, where White Leopard tonight? Why I want come Bolero if no haff White Leopard? I must go where haff White Leopard, 'cause she number one dancing-girl in Bangkok—'

I shook my head helplessly.

When I'd packed and paid my bills I took her to the Chalerm Krung cinema in the jeep. She showed no emotion whatever when we drove over the spot where Udom had been knocked down. At the cinema she climbed clumsily out of the jeep crying 'Wait, wait,' ran round to my side and standing on the kerb, looking down her flat straight nose at me, pressed my hand. 'You not go Ubol alone?'

'No. One other bloke.'

'You haff gun?'

'Of course not. Why?'

'Oh, Wretch, be careful, be careful. Many Thai men cow boy—'

'Don't worry about *me,* sweetheart. *You* look after yourself, that's the main thing. You're the one that leads the dangerous life.'

'Goodbye.' She gave my hand a last squeeze and turned away. As

I moved off I noticed a tall weather-beaten foreigner emerge from the theatre foyer on to the steps. He *could* have been an American. For one hideous moment—but I scotched that idea promptly. If I drove away believing that she'd let me drive her to an assignation with some other man I'd be dead by my own hand in a few days ... Besides, neither of them had appeared to recognize the other. And I could still feel the pressure of her hand on mine. She had touched me and spoken to me with genuine affection, with genuine concern for my welfare ... I was a stupid, low-minded bastard always to be thinking the worst of her, I told myself severely. Half the pain I suffered in life was in fact of my own making and it was time I pulled myself together ...

It had been my own idea that future trips to the Northeast should be made by jeep, except during the rainy season. The office had been sceptical—'These roads', Samjohn had said—'are not like English roads and garages don't exist', and Windmill frankly alarmed, but when we reached Lopburi I heard him say proudly to the hotelkeeper 'We've made it from Bangkok in five hours.'

Windmill went off on his own after dinner and I settled down my room with a book. But scarcely had I started to read when a girl came to the door. She was quite a good-looking girl in a scarlet blouse and black sarong. She looked at me briefly, then went. A few seconds later the boy came in to ask if I wanted her. And as a matter of fact I did but out of loyalty to Vilai and sheer weariness I declined. I had a second bath in the huge tiled tub—it was the first I'd seen since leaving England—and then I leaned on the verandah rail enjoying the night air ... After thirty minutes I saw what I'd been half-expecting to see. Two *samlors* arrived with a handsomely got-up tart in the front one and Windmill in the other. She went into the hotel as if she had no connection with him but I saw him pay both *samlor* boys. A few moments later I heard her follow him into the next room and the bolt was shot home. At intervals I could hear their voices, soft, friendly and intimate.

This little episode filled me with envy and self-pity. Sure, I was tired out, I'd already had one girl today, I was yearning to return to my Puritan ideals. But at the same time I was lonely and miserable—in love myself, but knowing myself unloved. In fact, what was Vilai probably doing that very moment? Getting tonight's load on? Already in bed with some sweating, tattooed Barnacle Bill? Floating face downwards in the estuary of the Chao Phaya with her skull split open? I went to the door to see if the girl in the red blouse was still around, but the passage was empty. I swore and bolted myself in. There wasn't a millionth of a chance that Vilai was thinking about me at that moment. I hurled myself into the suffocating mound of feathers. 'Never mind. Tomorrow we'll make Korat. Maybe I'll make Ratom too—she was always pretty easy before—'

I tried to console myself with visions of what might be but even as I recalled the enchantments of Ratom's flesh I hated myself—

Perfidy, that's what it was—

The word brought me bolt upright under the net, aghast. So I was no better than Andy. I was as treacherous as my stinking treacherous elder brother—and his moll. I couldn't trust myself any more than I'd ever trust them again. I was ready to betray even Vilai. In spite of all my protestations, which she had always scoffed at—in spite of my vows which I'd thoroughly believed in myself—

Instead of sleeping better than in Bangkok, as I'd hoped to do, I slept that night a good deal worse.

Ten

This insomnia of mine continued throughout the six weeks of the trip. No matter how thoroughly I drugged myself with alcohol before going to bed, time after time I'd awake in the small hours to my spectres. I could never forget the drunk I'd seen her deliberately select for her bedfellow that first night at the Bolero. Sometimes I would get on my knees (self-consciously, even in the darkness and solitude) and pray to God to protect her. But prayer gave me no comfort, because I knew God couldn't help her. She was bent on self-destruction. Then the visions would begin. I got so that I began to dread night, or at least going to bed ...

During the daytime things were nothing like as bad, especially during the first half of the trip. There was a sense of emancipation in escaping from Bangkok and the emotional and financial strain. Our days were pretty full too, what with the attempts to sell everything from sewing machines to mouse-traps, from Scotch whisky to hair-oil, with the ceremonial Eastern meals and the hardly less ceremonial bottle-parties. Most important of all, there was the driving. It was chiefly owing to this that, for the first time since I'd retired from the speedways, I was happy at my work. I'd enjoyed my previous trips in Thailand, but carted around in trains and buses I'd always felt rather like a tourist. Now I was relying on my own abilities to go places, and this knowledge gave a wonderful zest not only to the places but also to the hot bumpy dusty miles between them.

It wasn't all plain sailing. There were anxious moments, especially fording streams which had washed their bridges away during the previous rainy season. We were always having punctures from the nails which had worked loose in the bridges that remained. We got stuck in deep mud between Korat and Pimai. We got stuck in deep sand somewhere near Muangphol.

But these were minor nuisances, less hard to put up with than saddle-sores and dysentery and malaria would have been in days gone by. If we had been called on to suffer still more I would still have thought the bargain was worth it, for during those six weeks that jeep carried us right into the hot green heart of Thailand ... Lopburi at dawn, and the ancient towers blooming for the day like giant fir-cones ... The ruins at Pimai: acres of broken blocks of red stone tumbled amongst the weeds. Wat Podeng, where the Buddha has left another of his numerous footprints, this one larger than most; it was half full of water, owing to a leak in the roof. Weavers at Pakchongthai, women for the most part, blouse-less and supple-armed, producing gorgeous cloth from looms that were little more than a few bamboo poles set up under their houses ... All these things we saw the first week, together with endless miles of flower-filled forest interspersed with stretches of paddyfield, ponds choked with water hyacinth and lotus-flowers, elephants working at the lumber-camps, water buffaloes heaving themselves contentedly over in their stinking wallows, egrets stalking in the fields, vultures squabbling over the corpse of a dog ... And when we reached Ubol it was Boat-race Day: the broad river was dotted with sampans; the air was a-shiver with drums; people were doing the *ramwong* in boats, singing and dancing in boats, drinking in boats, falling out of boats; and every few minutes there'd be another race, the long lean craft, each with thirty men toiling at the paddles, streaking downstream like garish centipedes, fireworks booming from their sterns and flowers streaming from their bows ...

Then one evening, in a remote town called Mukdahan we met a fellow traveller, an Englishman peddling patent medicines. He was even younger than I was, only twenty-four: a pale, freckled, copper-haired, cynical type, wider through the hips than he should have been at that age, and with fingernails bitten down to nothing. His name was Keeling. We sat up for hours over a Vietnamese brew called Jonque d'or, which was as rough as the drawing of the wheat-sheaf on the label. Keeling had left Bangkok less than a week before, but he was already pining to get back. He loathed everything in the Northeast—the dirty hotels, the hard beds, the trains which went too slow, the buses which went too fast, the heat, the dust, the peppery food, and the people. When he heard about our exploits he thought we were demented. Only one aspect of them held any interest for him. 'Do you ever see any big game?'

'Yes, plenty. We've seen barking deer, gibbons by the dozen, snakes of course, a lizard as big as a crocodile, a young bear, Himalayan, I think—it was black with a creamy-white bib—and once, near Dejudom, one of the greater cats—'

'What d'you mean by that? A tiger?'

'No, it wasn't a tiger. No stripes. We didn't get a very long look at it. We came round this bend and there it was, bang in the middle of the road, about a hundred yards ahead. It gave us one look, then it just—*sailed* into the jungle—you never saw such a leap. It was breathtaking. I only wish I knew what animal it really was. My guess is a panther or—or a leopard—'

'Leopard!' He laughed sourly. 'No leopards upcountry in Siam, so far as I know. You have to go to the capital to find *them.*'

My heart was beating painfully. 'You mean—those two girls at the Bolero?'

'I mean those old bags.' There was utter disdain in his voice and I looked at him with hatred. 'I saw the White one only my last night in Bangkok,' he was saying. 'Leastways, it was hardly night any longer; it was about five o'clock in the morning by then. She was in a hell of a bloody state. Drunk and staggering, crying, clonking people right and left—'

'Where—was this?'

'Outside the Champagne Bucket. I never saw such a mess. Ruddy drunken virago—'

'What happened to her, do you know?'

'How the hell should I? You don't think I went up and offered her my arm, do you? I like my dames a little less well reamed out than she is.' He poured himself more poison. 'She's a real hard case, if ever there was one.'

'Some people say she has her good points.'

'Yes, and how right they are!' He shouted with laughter. 'I know a couple of good points she's got myself ... But I bet they're the only two good points she *has* got.' His amusement smouldered on for a minute, then he asked, 'Is she a friend of yours? You look as if you wanted to blub.'

I pulled myself together. 'Hell, no. Leopards are too big game for me. I prefer cats.'

I waited for the cock crow, but it didn't come. At least, not until six hours later. I was still awake even then, and completely distraught.

After that evening I'd had to face the truth: all my hopes and dreams were nonsense. There could never be a reformed, domesticated Vilai living with me in a bungalow with bougainvillaea round the door: the dream was too futile to be indulged in any more.

From that moment my thoughts had been in a complete hubbub. Half of me wanted to dash straight back to Bangkok but the other half had only sneered. 'Why? What d'you think you could do? You've tried before and she wouldn't let you. A man of any spirit ...' and so on.

Still the other half of me wouldn't be quelled. 'All right, I'm in love with a whore. She needs me too. I'm probably the only genuine friend she has in the world. Her life is hideous with sorrows and suffering. She tries to make it bearable through licentiousness.' It was when I had reached this point in her defence once that I stumbled on that phrase. 'But her licence is only—pathetic licence. It's not like most licentious people's—pernicious.' I remember I'd added a wry comment to myself. 'And I hope this isn't just poetic fallacy ...'

This battle, between commonsense and lust, had been going on incessantly since that night in Mukdahan. My work had suffered. My temper had gone to pieces. I'd hardly slept in three weeks. And I'd taken to drinking more and more ...

The trip dragged wearily on. Nakorn Panom, where the mountains of Vietnam, seen across the mighty Mekong River, look as if they had been copied off a Chinese scroll ... Sakol Nakorn, on the banks of a large rippling lake ... Udorn, all dust and bustle ... Loey, a Laotian centre at the end of a vile road ... Khon Kaen, where I bought some bamboo pipes and tried in vain to learn one of the speedy, wheedling, syncopated local melodies ... Eventually we came to Korat again, our last stop before Bangkok.

We had dinner with Boswell and Prosit, and as we left the restaurant the latter hailed a *samlor*. I protested: 'It's only a few yards to the hotel. I can walk …'

'Hotel?' He looked amazed. 'Not go hotel. Go see your friend.'

'What friend?'

He puzzled that out for a minute, then burst out with his cackling laugh and caught me in the ribs with his elbow. 'She luff very much,' he lisped. 'Many time ask how long you come Korat.'

'You mean—Ratom? Asked about me?'

'Your friend.' He sketched her torso with lithe hands. 'She luff very much. She say many time.'

The *samlor* was even then swerving round the statue of Surat-nari. I should have bawled *'lew kwah'*—go right—for the hotel. I said nothing. We went straight ahead, straight towards Chakri Road.

Ratom wasn't on hand. Prosit, apparently expecting to find in me the easy adaptability of his own race, tried to get me interested in a buxom type who was alleged to be new to the game but of unparalleled virtuosity; but her obvious distaste for the proposed union, coupled with my distaste for her particular brand of beauty, put me in timely mind of my vows. I made a fresh effort to escape, but Gold Teeth told me she'd ordered mekong and savouries, and while we were waiting for it to arrive she encouraged a girl in a white blouse and a neat blue skirt to sit on my lap. The costume, which is worn by office-girls in Bangkok, gave an air of respectability to the proceedings, and moreover the female flesh spoke through her silks and my drills to my male flesh with unexpected force. The girl was very small, with dainty features, and a very pleasant scent in her hair. I didn't want to go ahead. But it was weeks since I'd touched a girl. And what was the use of being faithful to Vilai week in and week out? She didn't expect it—she'd told me that herself …

So soon I found myself ascending by Jacob's ladder to a temporal *ersatz* heaven. And many are the mansions in Heaven, but it was to Ratom's usual room she led me. The girl went to fetch the implements of her trade. Gold Teeth strolled in and sat down on the bed beside me. I fumbled her a bit by way of flattery and she reacted like a ticklish virgin from the same motive. While she was straightening her hair again I asked her how Ratom was.

'She's all right. She told me to give you this if you came.'

She pulled a photograph out of the top of her slip. I was quite startled by it: I'd forgotten how handsome Ratom was. 'Beats Miss Thailand hollow,' I exclaimed.

She turned it over, and written on the back in English letters that looked queerly like Thai script were the words, 'To Raj, with loving from the derest lady Ratm.'

I was rather moved. 'Ratom's a first-class girl.'

'Yes. Why don't you take her away with you? She is tired of this life. She's had seven years—two with me. We've never quarrelled once. If she could better herself, I'd let her go—'

'But I have no house. All the time I travel, staying in hotels—'

'Never mind about that. She often stays in hotels too. She likes you, and I know you like her. She would go with you everywhere, give you a good time, and she wouldn't want too much money, not like Bangkok girls—'

Had Windmill been talking to her?

Before I could say any more my girl returned. Gold Teeth gave me a smile and left us. But there was no joy in betraying Vilai. We had a most perfunctory session. No dalliance. No endearments. No words at all. And all the time I imagined I could hear Ratom's derisive chuckles behind the mosquito net ...

But of course, I overpaid the girl—I always overpaid them. She didn't say thanks but she leaned against me gratefully for a moment. Stowing the extra note in her skirt-top she said, 'I need money badly. I am not a prostitute. I am a graduate nurse. But the hospital wages are very low, and I must pay two hundred tics every month for my new bicycle. So I spend my spare time here—'

Four days later we returned to Bangkok. I dropped Windmill at his house and drove straight to the hotel. It was about five o'clock—and who should be at the gate, just turning from the Indian doorkeeper with a disappointed look, but my only true love? Her face lit up, and so I'm sure did mine. But she was 'sick' again—'I always sick when you come Bangkok, darling; I not know why.' Before long we fell out seriously over the usual subject—money. She said the Chiengmai trip had been put off so long she'd used up the original advance and she needed another, since she was behind with her rent, and also she fancied a durian fruit, and if I gave the boy a hundred tics he could bring one straight away, and she'd eat it before she left. I told her heatedly she only wanted my money and not me, so damn' well clear out, and she said yes of course she only needed my money, for she could have the other thing forty times a day if she wanted, and what did I amount to, I was only a low-grade worker in a very insignificant concern, but she was very high pipple, she was like Hitler and Tlueman and Ivanhower. At the height of the engagement there was a knock at the door and thinking it was only the boy and glad of any interruption I threw it open. There stood Mrs. Samjohn, with a smile rapidly evaporating from her desiccated face.

No wonder either. Vilai had on nothing but a towel and her earrings and I was in my underpants.

I slammed the door in her face and threw on a shirt, shorts and sandals. She was just getting into the Riley when I caught up with her. I noticed that she was genuinely flushed under the heavily powdered artificial flush she always wore. The wrinkles round her mouth were set as if carved in rock.

'I'm sorry about just now,' I babbled, wondering if even that was being too specific. 'I thought it was the boy—'

'Never mind, never mind.' She seemed as apologetic as I—as if I'd caught her eavesdropping. 'Mr. Samjohn said you were expected home today. I happened to be passing. I thought if you weren't too tired after your journey you might like to come to the House for a bite to eat—'

'I would indeed.'

'But you aren't dressed and—' She looked at her watch, and I knew her problem was, not how long it would take me to change my attire, but how long it would take me to get rid of my company.

'But you needn't wait for me, you know. I have the jeep here, so I can get out to the House under my own steam—'

I saw that this solution to the problem only increased her grimness. She'd been hoping it would prove insoluble. But she was very well-bred. She said, 'In that case I'll be going and we'll expect you at—say—seven? Seven-fifteen?' She sounded about as effusive as a dead cod looks.

I returned to my room, torn between a desire to laugh and vexation.

Vilai had dressed. 'Who she?'

'That's my boss's wife, darling.'

'Why she come here hotel? She come before?'

'Yes, once or twice.'

'Oh. Reely. She come before, see you.' Suddenly she flared. 'Why she do that? She in luff wiss you?'

'Don't be such a twerp, Vilai. She'd old enough to be my grandmother.'

'Old make no differnunt. Old girl haff mutss money can haff nice young man if she want ... You be careful, Wretch. You haff 'nusser girl, very bad luck for you.'

'Why, what would you do to me?'

'Maybe I not do nussink. But anyone do bad to me, very soon he die, I sink. 'Cause I good girl. The God like me very mutss. Anyone not good me, like I good them, he kill.'

'Bunk. If the God liked you, he'd find a new job for you. Has He done that?'

'No. No shob yet. Doctor say must wait maybe one more munss.'

'Doctor? What's he got to do with it ... Vilai, you aren't—really sick—are you?'

'You know I sick. I ask you.'

'Vilai, Vilai!' Another milestone on the road to hell! 'How long have you had it?'

She was very cool. 'Today make t'ree day. Tomollow OK.'

I realized that we'd been misunderstanding each other but I continued suffering from shock.

She went on, 'I go see mutss, mutss doctor. All say same. Must wait one more munss, then will get shob, good more batter than Bolero—'

So by 'doctor' she meant fortune-teller. Exasperated I cried, 'But aren't you making any effort to get a new job now? Are you just waiting for it to fall into your lap—?'

She said, 'I try many place. But the girls all jealous me. They not want me go their place. They ask manager, he giff Vilai shob their place, they must all go 'way. 'Cause they know if manager giff me shob their place, man not want go wiss them any more, only want go wiss Vilai.' She laughed happily.

'And so now you're just walking the streets.'

'Neffer.' She was hurt and indignant. 'I Leopard. I neffer haff to walk street in my life. I just *stand*, one hundred men must want. Old man wiss no here'—(touching her head)—'young boy not haff pass girl yet—'

I gave that subject up too. You never realize how many pitfalls there are in the English language until you start trying to make a Siamese understand it. I tried another line. 'I met another Englishman upcountry who knows you. He said he saw you one night outside the Champagne Bucket—'

'Who he? What he name?'

'His name's Keeling.'

'Killing? I not know that boy. Why you spick him about me? I not want you spick usser man about me. Not nice for me.'

'What he said about you wasn't nice for me, either. He said you were sozzled and crying and hitting people—'

'Ah, he lie to you. Must not trust pipple everysing they say, darling. Many pipple not good. I hate very mutss. All time they jealous me, 'cause I very high girl, I not low like them ... Why you do?' (I was putting on long trousers.) 'You go out now?'

'Yep.'

'Where you go?'

'I'm going out to dinner with Mrs. Samjohn.'

'Who he?'

'Mrs. S.—the woman who was here just now. My boss's wife.'

She was perturbed. 'Why you want go her house? She haff huss-band?'

'Of course she has. I keep telling you he's my boss.' Perhaps that term wasn't known to her. 'He's manager where I work, darling. It's he that pays me my money.'

'Yes, she haff very mutss money, I sink. I see her. She haff gold here, here, here.' She touched her fingers, wrists, neck and ears. 'Too many pipple haff plenty money, plenty gold. Only Vilai neffer haff enough. All the time Vilai work, work, work—like she slav', I sink, but she neffer make any money ...' I refused to rise to this fly. 'You giff me money today, darling?'—wheedlingly.

'I've told you already, I've got none on me.'

'I look your wallet?'

'You still don't trust me even now, do you?'

'I trust, darling, but I just want look see.'

Knowing there was nothing in it, I threw it on the bed. She pounced on it like a real leopard on its prey. But a quick search showed that there was no notes. She was just on the point of closing it when she came on Ratom's portrait, which I'd forgotten. That really caused a sensation. She tore it out and devoured it with her eyes. 'Who this girl?'

'Which?' I glanced over my shoulder with nonchalance. 'Oh her. She's a friend of mine. Upcountry.'

'Why she giff you pickser?'

'Why does any girl give a chap her picture? Because she likes me, I expect.'

'Why she like you? You giff her money?' She turned the snap over and saw the inscription. 'What all this?'

I took the photograph away from her and screwed up my eyes over the writing. 'It says, "To my darling Reg, with all my love, from his one true sweetheart."'

She was outraged. But with an effort she controlled her fury. She said gravely, 'I ask you before, Wretch—you must be careful. Country-girl very bad girl. She only want your money—'

'And what the hell else do *you* want? If I told you I was never going to give you another ruddy penny as long as I live would you ever come to see me again? I'll answer for you, sweetheart: NO. You're utterly incapable of loving anyone but yourself. But this lady'—I looked tenderly at Ratom again before I returned her to the wallet—'she really loves me. I think if I asked her she'd go to the ends of the world with me—'

'She tell you that? You not want trust, darling. Many girl haff very sweet mouse but not spick truce. All the time very hard here.' She touched her heart. 'I not like that sort girl, darling. My mouse not sweet, but spick only truce. I say I come see you, I effer break my plomiss?'

'Yes, once.'

'No, neffer.' I opened the door while she put the finishing touches to her hair. 'I want you giff me pickser that girl.'

'What for? She gave it to *me*.'

'She no good for you, darling. She want hurt you—break your heart.

I take pickser to temple, I show the God, I ask him this girl very bad, I want he kill—'

'Bah! What's she matter to you? She's only a tabby cat, you're the mighty Leopard—'

She wouldn't let me take her anywhere in the jeep. 'I go *samlor.*' Outside in the yard she clung to my arm. Her face was worried. 'Don't forget what I ask you, Wretch. Country girl wiss sweet mouse no good for you. You want usser girl beside me, must take that old girl come to hotel just now to see you. She haff many ring, I sink plenty money. And I sink maybe she like you very mutss, 'cause she old and ugly, but you strong and very good look. I sink she giff you anysing you ask, you silly if you not take—'

'And hand over to you?' I was bitterly ashamed to be involved in such a conversation. I felt soiled all over, as if I'd fallen into a cesspool. It was a feeling I quite often got when talking to Vilai. Suddenly this woman who to me was so bewitching would speak 'truce words'—would reveal with brazen honesty the true nature of her mind. And it was always a bitter shock to me, that revelation, when it came. For I was all the time romantically dreaming of lifting her up to my level through the power of my love, but at such moments I realized how foolish the dream was: she had already pulled *me* down a long way and there was still further to go ...

The *samlor* came and she got into it. She said something to the *samlor*-man but nothing more to me. The *samlor*-man sneaked his foot over the crossbar and swerved away with bulging calves. I shouted 'Saturday' after her but she gave no sign that she had heard. I watched them pass through the gate and then re-entered the hotel. *'Ah, krab-ma-lao'*—so you've come back—said the boy Arun with a delighted grin, meeting me in the lobby. I found it difficult to make a suitably jaunty reply. Yes, *krab-ma-lao* ... Back to the same degrading infatuation that I couldn't escape even when I went away ...

Eleven

Dinner at the Samjohns went off a lot better than I'd expected it would. Mrs. S. apparently hadn't described the tableau to her husband—yet. That she hadn't forgotten it though was clear from her silence during the meal, and as soon as the coffee had been poured, she left us.

I slept, as much as I did sleep, in a fool's paradise that night; but next morning the storms broke. Two of them in swift succession. Frost was furious that I hadn't repaid his thousand, and though I told him I could do it that day he remained unmollified: 'You promised to let me have it back quickly ...' I felt flushed for ten minutes after he's finished dressing me down because I knew I deserved it. Then Samjohn called me into his office. Ostensibly it was about the trip we'd just finished but he came on to another subject at the end. 'This is not easy to talk about, Joyce. You're not a child—you're of an age to look after yourself—and of course you *could* do at home. But here—well, let's put it this way—you're still a bit of a child as far as the East is concerned. Don't think I'm a prude—in my day I was quite the gay dog too— but, well, you don't want to *throw yourself in the gutter,* Joyce. Have a good time by all means but—don't make yourself conspicuous. Broderick Peers has a great reputation in Thailand and we don't want anyone to spoil it ... In future, if you get into financial difficulties, come to *me.* I won't talk, for the sake of the firm's name ... But my real meaning is, don't get into financial difficulties in the first place. Your salary is small—at least the part that's paid out here is—and that's for a sound reason. It gives you enough to have a good time on, but not enough to have *too* good a time on ... Don't take me amiss, Joyce. You have the makings of a valuable man. Compared with most of the young hopefuls England exports nowadays—well, anyway, I'd be sorry to see you go—a competent man—just because of indiscretions ...'

I started to say something but he put his hand up. 'Don't forget what I've said. And now I want you to bung off down to Petchburi just as quick as you can in the jeep—'

'Today?' I was dismayed: Vilai was coming at five.

'Right now. It's important. One of the clerks will go with you—Windmill doesn't seem to have come in this morning, for some reason. I'll get the clerk in and tell you what you've got to do—'

I drove off fuming. Going to the hotel first I told Arun to make my excuses to Vilai and tell her I'd be back by eight without fail ... It was exactly eight when I got back to the hotel, after about three hundred kilometres, mostly smooth. She wasn't there, but a durian on the table and spilt powder on the dressing-table testified that she had been. I wondered how long she'd waited. Arun had gone out, so I couldn't enquire: I never mentioned Vilai to the other boys. I ate and bathed and threw myself on the bed. I wondered if she'd come again that night. There'd be no sleep until she did, and then very little, I thought to myself wearily ...

She didn't come, and I had less than two hours, and when I got up a pain in my back which had started on the way home from Korat a couple of days before was suddenly acute. I could neither stand up nor sit down without sweating. I waited till nine that morning to see if she'd come, then cleared off to work. Samjohn was so pleased with the results of my labours at Petchburi that I thought it would be safe to ask him for three days extra off at the weekend, when there was to be a three-day national holiday which our office observed. He told me he'd let me know. At lunch I returned to the hotel to see if she was there and also to rub myself with one of the liniments the firm dealt in. She wasn't there, but had been: half the durian was gone and a pair of pearl eardrops were placed conspicuously on the bed. Cheered, I returned to my boring reports. I asked Verchai to book a compartment for us on the train, but owing to the holidays they were all taken, and this dashed my spirits again, as during the lunch-hour Mr. S. had sent me a memo granting me the three extra days. 'Why don't you fly?' Verchai asked. 'Go train take twenty-four hour. Go plane, I think four hour only ...' Arun had told me she'd come at five, and by five I was bathed and ready, but it was six-thirty before she burst in, with a whirl of wide green skirts. Apparently she'd met an old friend the night before: sex unspecified, but not in any doubt.

To my amazement she presented me with a gold ring, thus becoming the first female outside the family circle who'd ever gone beyond a tie or handkerchiefs. It would fit only my little finger, and she was annoyed at that: 'I want you have here,' she pouted, touching the third finger of my left hand. I perceived that a change had come over her during my six weeks' absence ... She was good company during that whirlwind stay. She said she didn't mind flying to Chiengmai but it must be soon, soon. I think she'd told all her friends that she was being taken to Chiengmai and she'd rather have gone all the way by wheel-barrow than not go at all. 'If cannot go, must haff gold chain for here'—touching throat—'not two baht—any girl haff two baht—I want five baht, darling: you can do?' (The ring was one baht, or Thai ounce.) She gobbled durian and blamed my back on that girl upcountry—'I want *kill*—she no good for you,' and then galloped off—'can not stop long tonight, 'cause I not know you here or not here, so I tell *samlor*-boy wait me.' And she never once mentioned money. Nor did I. She said she might return that night; if not, then definitely on the following one. Just as she was leaving Somboon appeared. 'That *she*?' He spoke with as much awe as if he were in Rider Haggard's Africa. But later his true sentiments came out.

'She very old. Not beautiful at all ...' I was tremendously proud of my ring, and Somboon liked it too. He was surprised I'd been able to buy anything so good in Korat.

She didn't come that night, and the next day I discovered why. In the small hours she'd been going home from wherever she'd been 'working' to change into daytime clothes so that she could spend the whole day with me at the hotel, but the *samlor* had hit the kerb and overturned, spilling her into the road. Her left leg was blue with bruises, she had a swollen wrist and a grazed hand, and, what vexed her most of all, she'd cut her head open, and had had to have some hair removed from around the wound. The bald patch, yellow with iodine, was easily hidden, but she was dreadfully conscious of it. Naturally, she had little desire to go to Chiengmai in these circumstances, but meanwhile I'd bought tickets for Mr. R. and Mrs. V. Joyce on the Monday morning plane.

Now began one of the most momentous weeks of my life. For all the time we were in Chiengmai it was just like being married, with good times and squabbles: I'd never imagined such a life. But as usual, love, of which people tend to think such nice things, brought out the worst in me: I turned nasty with Vilai as I had done three years before with Sheila, and years before that with girls like Annette and Dilys, the first dim female idols of my adolescence. Yet I didn't fall out of love; in fact, just the opposite. My love grew and grew, and when the moneymoon finished and we were parted again I found that the mere sight of a girl who looked the least bit like her would give me a painful lurch of the heart, while, driving, I could think of no one else. This was probably what annoyed Vilai most in Chiengmai: an infatuated person is always a pain in the neck to anyone who is uninfatuated with him.

She was to spend the Sunday night with me; and when I returned from dinner with the Samjohns she was awaiting me in the lobby, excited and happy. She'd bought some very queer odds and ends of food in banana leaves. With burning mouths we climbed onto the bed together and tried to sleep. We were like two kids who knew they'd be going to the seaside tomorrow ...

Too soon it was four o'clock and she was up to make her usual complicated preparations for being eyed by the world. I bathed and dressed and lay on the bed to watch. But I couldn't be wholly obsessed by the contemplation of beauty. Duen had been ordered to call for us at five, but he was notoriously unreliable on early morning calls, and if he didn't come how long could we safely wait for him? In the end, at five-twenty, I called two *samlors* and we sped through the darkness to the air-office. It was a good thing we did so. Duen reached the airfield only a minute before we were conducted to the plane. In the meantime we'd gone to Don Muang by company, bus. He went on his knees to me, almost, to sign his trip-book, to make it look as though he'd not missed his appointment. Almost as superstitious as Vilai, I feared that if I didn't—if I got the man into trouble at the very outset of the trip—I'd invite reprisals from heaven and the moneymoon would be ruined. I signed.

Vilai, like myself usually on the brink of a journey, was suffering from a nervous stomach, but she gave no indication of it to casual observers. Dressed in immaculate white sharkskin slacks, with a green woollen jacket over her blouse, and a gold bell tinkling at her wrist, she was a sight for jaded eyes, especially as excitement had laid a wash of colour under the Chinese white of creams and powders. She was easily the smartest woman at the airport that morning, and I was proud to be her escort.

At last we took off. Our seat was one of the front ones, with a good view. As the earth fell away Vilai's tenseness fell away too. Clouds and paddyfields were of no interest to her and after ten minutes she shut her eyes. But she didn't sleep—every so often she'd open her eyes and smile at me. She ate a lot of breakfast though it was poor grub. She kept her safety belt fastened round her all the time. It was hot in the plane, which never gets time enough to make any height between landings, and she took off her jacket and tied a scarf round her cascading hair at the base of her skull. 'Where I hurt show?'—'No, my pet.'—'Vilai want go pee-pee.' I indicated the *suam*. 'You want I go alone?'—'Yes. The hostess'll help you.' She looked at me hard a minute, then undid her belt and went. She came back delighted with herself.

Of course there was nobody to meet us at Chiengmai airfield, and I had quite a job to prevent a suave Thai gentleman who apparently knew Vilai from mixing her baggage with his and bearing her off to town in his car. In the end we reached the air office by company bus, and went from there to the hotel by *samlor.* I was glad to find we'd been put in the room I'd had before. Vilai approved of it too, with the snowy linen, and the pink curtains blowing, and the roses on the table, and the two netted beds, and the grass and flowerbeds outside. In fact she was already in love with Chiengmai which was so clean and pretty and quiet and cool compared with Bangkok. She constantly exclaimed, 'Oh, this is pewty, pewty, Wretch. I like too mutss.'

I hired a car for the afternoon and took her to eat at one of my favourite shops. She reckoned to eat only one meal a day, at noon, having a notion that such a regimen kept her slim. But her appetite at this one meal was stupefying. That first day she had two bowls of rice-noodle soup, followed by two plates of rice with cold pigs' liver, fish in paprika soup, beef fried in oyster oil, and four coffees ('no merk'—milk was a hard word for her to pronounce) and to the astonishment of the staff she ate half a jamjar of green chilli with all this. 'In Chiengmai chilli not hot,' she explained to me, sucking in her breath to cool her tongue. 'I hot girl,' must haff hot food too.'

When she was satisfied I took her up to the temple on Doi Sutep. She was entranced by the beauty of the country. At the foot of the mountain we stopped to drink coconut milk. There was a parrot she coveted. (Everywhere we went she saw something she wanted me to buy or beg or steal for her.) The parrot, a bedraggled green specimen, sat on the edge of a basket lifting out red chillis with his mauve monkey paw and cracking them open with his mauve bill. He opened pod after pod, apparently convinced he'd finally find something edible in one of them. I said that he seemed like a very stupid parrot, not worth buying. 'Steal him, then.' When I only laughed, she mourned, 'You not like my son. Anysing I want, he giff me. He not care how he get.'

Mention of Udom momentarily depressed us, but the long twisting climb to the temple revived our spirits again. The road was a picture, now tunnelling through green caverns of foliage, now baking in the glare that poured yellow off the exposed flanks of rocks, and she was as responsive to its beauty as I was. When we reached the small waterfall near the top she was rapturous in her delight. I stopped the car and we scrambled over the rocks. 'Can I d'ink?' she cried. We did. She scooped up handfuls of sand. 'Gold,' she murmured ecstatically. 'I love gold.' But for once she didn't mention necklaces. The water spurted out of the cliff, causing the crowded leaves to drip dankly all round us.

From where the road ends a huge flight of steps goes up to the temple. At their foot she bought flowers and sticks of incense and gold leaf. 'Giff the girl twenty tics, darling.' The long climb up the steps, every one of which has a plaque on it commemorating the people whose subscriptions paid for it, was painful to her because of her leg. This was now swollen and blue from ankle to knee. Already I had noticed her piety: she had saluted every *wat* we passed in the car: 'I am pray God to giff me everysing I want,' she said. She seemed to be unimpressed by the seven-tongued serpents whose tails stretched right up the mighty flight of stairs, forming the banisters, or in the goddess of irrigation whose hose, made out of her pigtail, was that day not functioning. But at the top of the flight where the temple gates are guarded by two fearsome gods of Chinese ancestry she performed the first ceremony. Having first bowed her head before one deity, she lighted a little shock-headed candle with a match, then lighted three sticks of incense from the candle. She placed the incense in a stone urn containing soil and many other sticks, some still smoking; the candle she glued to the god's knee. Then she placed a rose in his lap and pressed a square of gold leaf to the hem of his gown, which was already well-encrusted. Then, careless of her knee, she knelt and prayed in the pretty Thai style, silently, head bowed, palms joined with the tips of her fingers to the tip of her nose, for perhaps five minutes. I stood beside her, wishing I could pray too.

In the temple courtyard when we came to the huge bronze bell with its inscriptions in five different forms of writing and its Zodiacal signs she asked me to strike it for her. 'Why don't you do it yourself?'—'Can not. I woman. Must not tutss.'—'And I'm a Christian, probably I shouldn't touch it either.'—'Never mind you Clisschan, you man, can tutss ...' I swung the huge wooden clapper and a stern glooming note roared out over the plain. Vilai used the rarest word in her vocabulary. 'Sank you. Now the God hear what Vilai ask.'

'Why don't you go into the temple to pray?' I asked her.

'Not want take sooze off.'

'You don't have to. There's no raised wall round this *wat.* Last time I was here we all went in with our boots on.'

She wouldn't believe until I showed her that the foreman of the builders who were repairing the place was wearing solid western-style clodhoppers. Then she went in.

Inside she found just what she was looking for—a Buddha who could tell her fortune. She made long obeisance to him first, using up the residue of her flowers and incense and gold-leaf and candles. She didn't touch the statue herself—the foreman did. As a woman she couldn't. But she was one of those lucky women who can get men to do anything they want. The foreman seemed to be worshipping her as sincerely as she was worshipping the Buddha.

The first method of fortune-telling I didn't understand. The foreman handed her a long wooden rule. Squatting with outstretched arms she held one end in the inch-long nails of her left hand and strained herself to reach as far along the rule as she could with the other. At the point she reached the foreman made a mark with a piece of yellow chalk he took from the altar. She made several more attempts to overreach this mark but failed. All the time she was chatting to the foreman. The only thing she said to me was, 'My hand very long. Lucky.'

The second instrument was more comprehensible—the wheel of fortune. After prayers she spun it and it stopped at six. The paper out of drawer number six cost ten satang. It was bursting with good luck. She translated it as we dawdled down the four hundred and twenty steps. 'Everysing, everysing, good. I want marry, now can do. That good too.' It was the first time she'd mentioned the subject for months, and the last time she was to do so, except in a rage. I think that afternoon she could even contemplate the possibility without cynicism. Everything seemed joyous and hopeful in that sunlight, to both of us.

We returned to the hotel. We bathed and made love a bit, and then she dozed while I had a hearty European dinner on the verandah. When I returned to our room I was surprised to find her in one of her Bolero gowns and elaborately making herself up. 'Where the hell d'you think you're going?' (I was peeved because I'd expected to lock the world out of that room for the rest of the night.)—'I want go dancing.'—'What, in Chiengmai? This is the backwoods, darling. They only have dances here on New Year's Eve.'—'Make no differnunt. I go. You not want go, can stay here.' We had had a slight altercation just before my dinner, about money needless to say; I'd cashed the cheque for three thousand I'd given her (one thousand more than the bargain struck) before we'd gone up Doi Sutep, but already she had started demanding two thousand more. This spat had made us both bitter, this and our weariness. However, we *samlor*'d downtown and she promptly found out that what I'd said had been only too true: the town was already asleep; even the Chainarong Hotel was shut. She'd seen both movies in town and decided the only thing to do was to eat some Thai food. I led her into a place I knew was good. There happened to be three girls sitting at one of the tables. 'Why you bling me this place?'—'Because the grub's good, sweetheart.'—'Huh.'—I omitted to pull her chair out for her, not from spite so much as from my habitual awkwardness; it was a long time since I'd last squired a lady around, and anyway she gave me no indication of the chair she was going to choose. We sat in grim silence. Later she accused me of ogling the three girls. She didn't eat after all. She had the foods packaged in banana leaves and refused to let me carry them for her. We *samlor*'d back to the hotel wordlessly. Then she broke out. I had treated her without respect. I had been rude to her in front of low girls. I had tried to make her look small. I didn't love her truly in spite of all I said. I was mean. I wouldn't give her a necklace, or a radio, or a diamond ring. And so on. I put a pillow over my face and cried for mercy. She couldn't help laughing but she continued the quarrel. She went to the window and leaned out, still fulminating. I gave her a playful pat on the behind. 'Goddam, now you hit me ...' I went to my bed and dropped the net. The manager came to the door to find out what all the fuss was about and she went out on the verandah to him. I don't suppose she told him what we were scrapping about but she was talking to him for hours and together they finished the foods she'd bought. Then she got into her own bed. After an hour, being thirsty, I got up to drink water. I knew she was awake, for every time I'd turned over in bed I'd heard the gold bell tinkle in hers, as if she was signalling that she was awake too. Accidentally I knocked a tumbler over and I put on my torch to clear up the mess. 'What you do?'—'Mopping up water. I just knocked a glass over. D'you want a drink?'—'Yes.'—I passed one through the mosquito net and our fingers touched and lingered together. After that I think we both slept. We were both dead beat.

Relations were still strained next morning. I asked her if she wanted breakfast. She said no. I ate alone on the verandah and then took her in a cup of coffee. She said she didn't want that either but when it had got quite cold she gulped it off. I took this as a sign that I was forgiven and plucked up enough courage to stay in the room while she dressed.

Finally she pronounced herself fit to be seen by the world. The powders, the creams, the perfumes, the mascara, the lipstick, the rouge, the hairclips had all been applied; drops had gone into the eyes; the lashes had been curled with a fearsome instrument; the sarong had gone up and down and on and off thirty or forty times, and at last been replaced by a pink brassiere, panties embroidered with flowers, a tight pink sweater and a billowing skirt. She had bought new sandals in Bangkok but they were so fashionable they nearly crippled her, so now she wore plain white ones. She tidied up carefully after herself. She permitted one brief caress.

'Now we go eat? I haff pain, I so hungry.'

Most of the restaurants were shut because of the holidays, but we toured the town buying little bits of tastiness in banana leaves and took them all to an Islamic place that was open. I recall raw pickled pork, four different sorts of curry provided by Islam, the odd assortment of tree-leaves the Thai call salad, salt fish that really stank, glutinous rice, beer, sour mango, and unrecognizable things. We both intensely enjoyed this repast and all bygones were bygones. I'd hired the car again and the forty kilometres of rough road to Me Fack greatly aided digestion. It was a dull day with clouds lying drugged on the mountains. She liked hills and forest but disliked open-country with paddyfields but no trees; most of all she liked to look at houses and next to them at farms. A small house, even if only made of matting, if clean and set in a grove of bamboo or tall trees, with flowers and vegetables growing around it and dogs sleeping and children playing, and a background of forest or distant mountain, was enough to send her into ecstasies. At least it was for the first two or three days. After that the gleam of a green peppermint, the strain of 'Hold that Tiger,' the fumes of whisky breathed by some drunken white man into her ear, the old familiar sensations of a steel-strong lust blundering blindly, irresistibly, into the very core of her being, began to regain their old attractions for her. ''Cause I that sort of girl. You know where you meet me first ...'

She wasn't greatly captivated by Me Fack, and without sun it wasn't anything special.

But on the way back we stopped to watch the clouds rising off Doi Sutep and on the other side of the road, across a reedy swamp, a rainbow was glowing faintly under a muddle of grey and gold mist. Suddenly she caught my hand. 'Wretch,' she said, 'I sink I neffer happy before more batter than today.'

This was Eden all right, with the paradisical setting, the insatiable Eve, the doting Adam; all that was missing was the Serpent, and he appeared that evening. His name was Dan Birkfield. He was an American—a fact patent in his clothes, his figure, his walk, and his speech. He had an overfed look that had not congested his face, but made him a little too puffy at jowl and waist. Vilai had already sighted him from the verandah as he slouched moodily around the rosebeds and since to her the American male was synonymous with easy money she'd promptly begun to evince a professional interest in him. Even to me, the man's obvious forlornness in this foreign land was somehow appealing ... Once again Vilai had declined dinner and I ate in solitary state, but after her bath she joined me for a soft drink. At this point Dan emerged from his room, the one opposite ours, where he'd been writing as it seemed to me ever since we'd arrived in Chiengmai, and wandered aimlessly down the verandah and back again. Just like the Leopards amongst the chairs at the Bolero ... 'What's the trouble, chum?' I asked him as he was about to re-enter his room. 'No trouble. Just bored.'—'Sit down and have a drink then.' So I started it. I'd felt lonely so many times myself. I sympathized with him.

Besides being inordinately large, as I've said, he was very fair, with a crew-cut and mild blue eyes that, peering from behind thick lenses, gave him a wondering, child-like look; and this impression was enhanced by a soft baby-mouth and chin. He turned out to be curiously evasive when questioned about himself—but he was equally slow and hesitant in his reply on impersonal matters. He said he'd been trained to paint but he'd found his art was out of touch with the masses and he was now touring the Orient to see if he could find more satisfaction in humanitarian work. He'd been in Thailand only two-three weeks. He didn't drink, smoke or swear, and at twenty-six was unmarried and unengaged. From the first Vilai, giving him the glad eye from behind a Veronica Lake hairdo she'd contrived for the evening, set out to undo the poor chap. He sat cuddling his fat breasts in his bare arms—he was shirtless, white and hairless—and eyeing her with bulging pale blue irises through the frameless pebbles. Once, when she left us for a minute, I said:

'Have you ever been to the Bolero?'

'No, but I've passed it.'

'Why didn't you go in?'

'I was with friends. They wanted to go some place else.'

'You oughtn't to miss it. It's educational.'

'Yeah. My friends told me that. They said there was some whore there. Wonderful to watch her work.'

'Did they tell you her name?'

'Yeah. I guess they did. But I forget. Wait a minute, though—wasn't it the White somep'n—'

'The White Leopard?'

'Yeah, yeah. I guess that's right Is she as hot as they say?'

'Well, you ought to know, chum. She's working on you *now.*'

His eyes bulged more than ever. He was breathless with excitement. 'Is—*that*—the White Leopard?'

'That's her all right.'

'Gee—*whizz.*'

Then Vilai returned with the gold bell tinkling. He looked at her as a rabbit might at a snake. After a few more minutes he got up, saying, awkwardly, 'Well, I guess you two wanna push off.' He pushed off himself. Vilai led the way to our room.

'He like me very mutss,' she said. 'He not say, but I know. But he no good for Vilai. Young man neffer haff any money. First time he giff me maybe two hundred. Nex' time he sink maybe he nice boy, I want he, he can haff for nussink. That no good.'

'He knows all about you,' I said, and repeated our conversation.

'What he frand mean?' she exclaimed indignantly. 'I at Bolero, I neffer work to get man. *Now* I not work. No need. Too many man want me always ... I not like he frand say that.'

We slept in our separate beds. 'I tired,' she said. To tell the truth I was tired out too. And I felt I could look to the dawn with every confidence.

We were still almost lyrically happy the next day, which was Wednesday. Making love, breakfasting, bathing, and the long process of Vilai's donning her armour took us from six until eleven-thirty. For a long time while I breakfasted she lay on the bed with a small mirror before her removing hair from her armpits with tweezers. Somehow she got onto the story of her life. It was the same one she'd told me before, substantially, but considerably amplified. Not much additional information about the three husbands. But she gave birth to and killed off an additional child, a daughter. The fullest details related to her adventures after the failure of marriage number three. She'd lived in Bangkok before, respectably, with husband number two, until the Japs came. Then she'd gone back to the country. Now the Japs had gone, husband number three was no good, one day she couldn't stand it any more. She dumped Udom on her mother and cleared off to the capital. 'I haff frand there—her name Jamnien—'

'What, same name as you?'

'What, you mean, darling?'

'You told me your real name was Jamnien.'

'No, no, darling. When you sink I tell you that? I neffer tell you my real name, not in my life.'

'I must have misunderstood. Go on.'

I don't know how much truth there was in it all. There was a long story about how it was Jamnien who had introduced her to a Madame in Bangkok.

'And so you became a prostitute.'

'Yes, but only two weeks. I not like *cho-ke-li,* darling. Make mutss money, but not good for me. Every night must haff sick, seven men. Any man want me, I must haff. Maybe he d'unk, or bad heart—neffer mind, if he want, if he pay money. I must let him pass me. I make very mutss money that time, darling, but all the time hurt here.' (Touching heart.) 'All time want to get away, go home my Mama.'

'And how did you get out of it?'

'You know Black Leopard? She very very bad girl, I hate very mutss. But then she my frand. She not work in that house, but sometime she take man there. She see I very great pewty, more than she I sink, and she spick wiss me many time. She say, "Why you work this house? That lady chit you. She giff you fifty tic every time. She say she only kip fifty tic for her-self. But you not hunderd-tic girl. This not hunderd-tic house. Every man come here must pay two hunderd-fifty, t'ree hunderd ... Why you not come my house, liff wiss me there, work wiss me? I truly giff you half what man pay. And I titch you dance. I bling you to work at Bolero. Then you can pick good boy. Not haff to slip wiss any old sing that will pay."

'I believe truce, tarling. I belief everysing she say. I go her house, liff many munss. She titch me dance. I like her very mutss ... But I tell you she very bad. Pipple call her Black Leopard 'cause she black here' (touching her arm) 'but I call her Black Leopard 'cause she black here' (touching heart). 'I find she just like that usser girl from Korat. She giff me eighty tic, say she only kip twenty for her-self, I no longer t'ree hunderd-tic girl. But I find out man must pay her t'ree hunderd tic to slip wiss me—she chit me, darling ...'

'And so the feud began.'

'What food? I not want yet, darling. Too early ... Sometime I glad I not dancing-girl at Bolero now, 'cause every time I look Black Leopard face I haff head-aitch. That night I lose shob, she very bad to me, darling. She want fight wiss me, she say I steal her man. Huh, what I want to steal *her* man? Can haff many man all the time, good more batter than she can haff. She try hit me. I say, "Not here. Now we make money. When finiss, if I haff no man, I go Pramane Ground, I kill you." Very bad, darling: I sink just she, me, go fight, I kill her, that I go Champagne Bucket by my-salf. But goddam, mutss mutss pipple come to see, usser girl, *samlor*-boy, very low. I say, "Come on, fight." But she only want to fight wiss mouse. I not want that sort of fight. I wants to kill. I pull her out of *samlor.* We fight very bad. Maybe you not know how girl fight—you good boy, you neffer see. They not just hit, like man. Bite wiss teece, kick wiss foot, use claws. I fight very good. I pull her clo'es off, blood run out her nose, I hurt her very mutss. But then policeman come. Stop us. Take away. Keep us lock up all night. Next day we must pay hunderd tic. She pay hunderd, I pay hunderd. Policeman say, "No more fight, or real trouble for you two."'

'And then the manager sacked you?'

'Yes, 'cause nex' night Black Leopard cannot work, 'cause then she Black-eye Leopard.' She laughed, but was immediately serious again. 'You not know how bad that girl to me, darling. Many time she try to kill me. Giff cowboy maybe five hunderd tic. But he not kill. He come to me, say, "Black Leopard giff me money to kill you. But why I do that? I like you good more batter than she." Her hussband cowboy too. Very ritss—oh, so ritss I cannot say. She try to make him kill me too. But he like me very mutss. Want to slip. I ask him, "How I can slip wiss you? You want to make trouble more for me" I not like him. Will not slip.

'Sometime I wiss you cowboy, darling. Then you kill Black Leopard, 'cause you luff me ...'

That day we gorged at a shop overlooking the river. She liked both the food and the setting. 'I sink you no good for me, Wretch. Come Chiengmai, I eat and slip too mutss. Get fat. Get black. When I go back Bangkok, I sink man not want to dance wiss me any more. He say, "Vilai, you too fat, too black. Go 'way, honey. Now there *two* Black Leopard in Bangkok ..."'

We went to Lamphoon. Again the day was overcast. But the fifteen-mile-long avenue of magnificent soaring trees, smothered in mustard-coloured blossoms as they were, would have been stirring in any fight. I made detours to the Square Pagoda and the Reclining Buddha, but Vilai, having got the promise of another two thousand as soon as the banks re-opened, had nothing further to pray for. We spent an hour in the silk-weaving factory. Vilai, in a vivid red blouse and the shiny white slacks, made all the local beauties look drab. She bought cheap cloth as presents for her maids and a length, not so cheap, for herself. Of course, I paid ... Going back to the city, she seemed to have trouble with her conscience. 'That *pha* you giff me, it too dear, darling. I not want. Batter you spent your money on somesing I want very mutss. Now I no haff shob, maybe I want you buy many sings for me soon ...'

Our next stop was at Silver Village. Here after two solid hours of chatter in various shops she bought a huge beaten silver bowl, and a silver stand for it, and a silver ladle, for doling out charity food to the priests. The total cost was twelve hundred tics but as I automatically reached for my wallet she stopped me. 'No, this I buy wiss my own money. It for the God.'

'Your money's my money, anyway.'

'No, after you giff me, it mine. Is what I earn.'

'If I'd known you were going to chuck it away like this—'

'I want some *irom*' (painted sunshades) 'too. One for my maid, one for cookee, one for me. You can pay for those ...'

We took all the booty back to the hotel. Dan was on the verandah, making a watercolour. He looked as if he'd been waiting for us. He kept his sketchbook at such an angle that I couldn't see what he'd been doing, but Vilai went right round to his side of the table and leaned over his shoulder, the red blouse, as I instantly noted, actually touching his ear. She looked, smiling, at his work for about ten seconds before she spoke, and I could see he was in suspense, ready to stand or fall in her sight on the effect this daub had on her. I don't suppose she had any idea how important he thought her criticism. At last she said, 'Humph. Very pewty. You clever boy, I sink.' He actually flushed with pleasure, but at the same time he threw an embarrassed glance at me.

'Thought you'd given up art,' I said.

'Oh, I still sketch a bit.'

'Why you not make pickser of me?' Vilai asked, moving away from him and making for the door of our room.

'Gosh, if I could ...' He swung round with such eagerness that a cup full of paintwater crashed to the floor. He made an inarticulate exclamation and seemed to forget Vilai immediately, staring down at the mess in horror. Vilai laughed.

We had some orangeades with him, and invited him to go with us to Huei Keo—'you can make pickser while I swim'—but he seemed anxious to be left behind, and returned to his work as soon as we left. He still hadn't let me see what he was doing. 'When it's finished,' he said evasively ...

Huei Keo is the prettiest place in all Chiengmai. The water descends several hundred feet in a series of falls with deep clear pools between them. Bare sheer cliffs hem it in on one side, a steep forested slope on the other. I drove the car in as far as it would go and we scrambled up to the nearest deep pool. Because it was late we had the place to ourselves. Whilst I clambered further up exploring for a deeper pool Vilai, standing on a rock in midstream, undressed. Forty yards away and maybe fifty feet higher I turned round to look. Stark naked she tossed her hair and waved her green costume, her body a lovely contained form, shapely and tan amongst the greys and greens of rock and leaf and the flashes of white foam. Here, I felt, was the ecstasy which has only two notes of sadness in it, the knowledge that it cannot last, and that this particular rapture can never be repeated.

She sat on a rock and washed her clothes, soaping and rubbing and beating and twisting them in the thorough Eastern manner that removes all the dirt and pretty soon most of the fabric too. Then she took off all her jewellery except for the tinkling golden bell to which she had become so attached (because I liked it?) that it seemed to have become permanently attached to her, and dived and swam and wriggled about, stopping every minute to let water out of her ears and to rest her knee, which was still black and blue. Then she would laugh and dive again and splash again and come up laughing and spitting. I lay on various rocks and watched. I'd never wished I could swim before, never felt a bore because I couldn't ...

In the end we knew we must go. She stood on a rock and I handed her a towel and she dropped her suit to her loins and began drying herself carefully. Soon she was dressed and had put on the ring with the thirty-seven diamonds, and the other ring with its huge translucent yellow stone, and the watch with its bracelet of golden hearts, and a thin necklace with a small heart-shaped gold pendant, and pearls in her ears. Then with many backward glances we walked down to the car. We knew we'd never go back again.

Back in the hotel we bathed, and I dined on the verandah and she dozed until Dan came to talk. Then she appeared and she liked the look of the fish and had some and then she liked the smell of the coffee and had some of that too, and then she knocked some coffee all over her slacks but showed no signs of annoyance—just as when I'd knocked the beer over her skirts at the Bolero. We'd decided to go to see *City Lights*. She had no enthusiasm for Mr. Chaplin, a silly man and not hansum, but she agreed to go as a concession—a gesture of gratitude, all the more valuable as coming from such a (usually) self-centred person. We took pity on Dan and invited him to accompany us. He was pathetically pleased: the watercolour had turned out 'a mess' and he'd torn it up. She only took about ten minutes to get ready. I forget what she wore but I know it was pretty. She had put big gold loops in her ears instead of the usual stones. But there was nothing flashy about her appearance although every woman eyed her critically, plainly recognizing a lady from the big city. The men eyed her too of course—to the last male eye, as always.

We were too early for the show so we went, to Dan's consternation, to a coffee-shop. He was eventually persuaded to drink an orange-crush, swarming with germs though it undoubtedly was. The germs had caught up with me (or perhaps it was all the chilli I'd been eating) and I had to leave them together for ten minutes. The trend of their conversation could be judged from the remarks Vilai made when we went to bed.

'What Dan mean when he say he "look me up", when he go Bangkok?'

'He meant he'd call at your house to see you.'

'I sink so too. He like me very mutss. He ask me he want to make luff wiss me, but he good boy, will not do 'cause now I here wiss you.'

'Good God. Don't mind me. Go ahead. He's good for five hundred any day.'

'I sink not. I sink he very poor. He say he twenty-sick, he neffer haff slip wiss girl. If he haff plenty money like you say, he must slip wiss differnunt girl every night.'

'I know more about men than you do, darling, in spite of all your experience, and I'm telling you that guy is rolling in the stuff—yet when he tells you he's never had a woman it's God's truth. You want to land him if you can.'

'Pah. I care nussink for him. He tell me lie. Vilai neffer trust any man.'

'I know, dear. You're daft. You think all men are like those you make your living off. You don't recognize good ones when you see 'em. You'll never learn, it seems ...'

That was my honest opinion at that time—that she had two exceedingly good upright young men dancing attendance on her. Dan's infatuation was now almost painfully obvious. During dinner he'd told me a bit more about himself. It was all mixed up with *The Moon and Sixpence*. He'd convinced himself that he had nothing to say to the world in his painting. Yet he was yearning to martyr himself in some romantic way. He was currently considering devoting the rest of his life to work among the lepers. He'd been to give them a look over in half a dozen countries in Africa and Asia. He liked the Siamese type best, but he was fearful that it might be less on their account than on account of the fact that theirs was the most agreeable country to live in. He'd learned, too (and it was a sad disillusionment), that lepers could easily be taught to inject each other, and furthermore that far from being highly contagious, leprosy was quite a difficult disease for a healthy man to contract—in fact, no particular heroism was demanded of the worker among them these days. But masochism was inextricably mixed up with his idealism; although he was as Protestant as they come, he had to mortify his flesh as vigorously as any monk. The non-drinking, non-swearing, and nonsmoking were all part, too, of his burning desire to crucify himself on the most splintery cross he could find. And then things like Vilai happened to him ... Over my fish and soup, before Vilai had joined us, I'd waxed quite eloquent with him. I'd said that he'd started off just as I'd started off years before, observing the tablets of an outmoded Law and damaging my brain and body and spirit thereby, imposing on myself abnegations which were advocated by all my mentors and strengthened by my personal timidity, but false. 'Such self-denial never gets a man anywhere unless he's got religion and can turn himself into a monk,' I'd said. 'Like Crashaw and his "sweetly-killing dart." It was a bloody sword going into the chest of an under-teenage girl, that's what that "sweetly-killing dart" was. A few good nights out with something like that'—I'd jerked my head in the direction of our room—'would have turned poor old Crashaw into a master-poet, instead of a trunkful of conceits. But you're no poet; you're trying to sublimate your glandular urges in good works, which is even more futile than poetry. Good works won't unbind you, chum. You need a female chest with bubs on it, and half a bottle of *mekong* inside you—'

'You mean you're happy?' he'd asked, in a tone which suggested he was damn' sure I wasn't; and then Vilai had appeared and we'd dropped the discussion, temporarily ...

All Chiengmai seemed to have gone to see Chaplin, but at last the torrent of colours and eyes and mouths stopped pouring down the stairs, and she and Dan and I went up them. There was a long Thai propaganda film first. Photos of Korean atrocities were hardly a suitable apéritif for comedy. But it is amazing how quickly horror can be erased from the memory, especially if you have a magician waving the wand, instead of a bumbling psychiatrist ... I'd never seen *City Lights* before. I revelled in it. Dan, who *had* seen it before, revelled in it. Vilai, between us, with one hand in mine, and, as I suspected but couldn't quite make out in the darkness, her other in Dan's, revelled in it too, much to her surprise. As fast as we translated the English captions to her she translated the Thai ones to us. The beauty of the blind girl moved her, Charlie's hapless efforts to raise funds broke her heart, and time after time she squeezed my hand and cried, 'Oh, I like this movie too, too mutss.' Only at one point did her nationality assert itself: when Charlie called on the girl when her grandma was out. 'Now he slip wiss her?'—'No, no, of course not. He loves her with a pure flame.'—'Of course he slip wiss her. Her Mama go out. He giff her money and she ride in his car. She *must* let him slip wiss her.'—'No, sweetheart, no.'

Back in the hotel she said, 'Not want you slip wiss me tonight. I tired. Tomollow night slip all night togesser.'

'That's a promise,' I said.

I was supposed to wake her at five-thirty next morning so that I could go to the station to book our seats for the return journey while she got ready to go to market; but at six it was she who woke me. I spent an hour kicking my heels in the station-master's office before he showed up. Grudgingly he granted us berths fifteen and sixteen—next door to the toilet, which I knew Vilai would be angry about, for that department really stinks on Thai trains. I hurried back through the morning mists. She was just about ready to go out. She peered through Dan's verandah window as we passed. 'Lacy boy. He still slip.' I wished she wouldn't show so much interest in him. But she was off to the market with *me*.

It was six years, she alleged, since she'd last gone to early morning market. She made up for lost time. She first bought a glass jar to put one of the more obscene-looking messes in, and then a big hamper which she gradually filled and I carried. She darted from stall to stall, bargaining and laughing and happy. A Thai market is certainly one of the sights of this world. In few places are so many varieties of meat, fruit, fish, vegetable, and amalgams thereof, brought together in joyous juxtaposition. In few countries do such gay, handsome, brightly-clad people do the buying and selling. The smells also are intoxicating in number and variety. I was intoxicated with Vilai too. I enjoyed myself as much as she did. Everybody stared at us, the tall fair foreigner and his Thai wife with her expensive tastes in jewellery and her very Thai tastes in grub. We were there for more than an hour. I had seldom seen her so animated, except professionally.

The truth was that she was feeling and looking a lot better than when we'd come to Chiengmai. Much of the strain had gone out of her face. She seemed younger and happier. Her knee was still bothering her, also her wrist and scalp; and her legs were stiff from so much walking.

But her spirit was not disabled by these injuries. Back in the hotel she gave herself to me with an abandon that took my breath away. There was something desperate about her passion, as if she sensed the end was at hand, that we'd reached the peak of experience together and from now on must slide downhill, and finally lose each other ... There was something of the same painful urgency in my own emotions too ...

We breakfasted in the room, she lying on the bed. 'Now you go bank?'

'Yes.'

'How long you go?'

'I don't know. Got to find a bank that'll cash my cheque. I may be two hours, may be only twenty minutes. I can't say.' I kissed her—on the lips, a salute she usually refused. 'What will you do while I'm gone, darling?'

'I slip.'

I was gone longer than I expected. When I got downtown the banks still weren't open. Then I had to find one that would cash my cheque. I wandered about, worrying. More than once—that infernal jealousy of mine—I thought of dashing back to the hotel to see if I'd catch her with Dan. Of course, I disdained to do so, but the suspicion, an ignoble one I felt, was in my mind. It was a relief when my business was finished. I drew four thousand—two thousand for her, two thousand for the hotel, fares, and my own tiny expenses. The bank manager accepted a Broderick Peers card with respect. Of course the cheque would bounce, but by that time I'd be back in Bangkok with another payday behind me. Surely I'd be able to attribute everything to a mistake ...

I tore back to the hotel. She was lying as I'd left her, covered with a sarong, dopey-eyed. Dan's room was shut up. 'The expense of spirit in a waste of shame.' That was said of lust, but it applied even more to jealousy, I thought. Lust at any rate pays some dividends to the non-spiritual but jealousy is just a drain on any man's strength, it is entirely evil, it does no good either to the one that is jealous or to the object of jealousy. I put the two thousand into her hand.

I lay on my own bed until she got over her drowsiness. That day she wore an off-the-shoulder dress with a tight waist and a full skirt: it suited her to perfection. The design was complex but could be resolved at last into green discs as big as oranges on a white background with a barbaric script in black scribbled all all over. Of all her dresses this was the one I liked the most. She seemed amused to hear this.

We went to the riverside café again, but she had been sampling delicacies bought at the market and was less hungry than usual. She then went to buy a shampoo powder, and became interested in a set of silk panties, seven pairs, one for each day of the week. She ordered them. 'Giff the girl the money, darling.'—'Not me. I've given you the last penny I'm giving you in Chiengmai. You're nothing but a damn' mercenary bitch.'—'But you tell me they nice, darling. Don't you want to giff me pless-ent?'—'No.'—She laughed and cancelled the order, bought only the shampoo.

I took her to a hairdresser's recommended by the chemist and left her there. Went to the station and bought our tickets. Called in at the hotel for a beer and had three while I was about it. Returned to the hairdresser's to pick her up. She was still perfectly happy but I wasn't. I'd brooded too long over the beers. Nobody, I was damn' sure, had ever taken her any further than Hua Hin for a weekend. Nobody else had ever, in spite of her boasts, paid her five thousand eight hundred in one week, plus hotel, food, fares, and incidental purchases. At least, nobody as poor as I was. Yet there were no limits to her greed, it seemed. Nor would there have been any limits to my generosity, I thought, if she'd once acted satisfied—if she'd once shown love (as opposed to mere lust). But I was convinced she was indifferent to me. The first quarrel we'd had had really been the end. For what I was seeking was blessed accord with one woman. I was not just seeking carnal delights intermingled with strife ...

Nevertheless wandering along the roads to Doi Suket and Sang-kon-peng, looking at houses and farms—stopping at wayside shops to eat noodles or drink iced coffee—we were in holiday mood. When we got back to the hotel she borrowed a push-bike from one of the boys, changed her frock for a blouse and scarlet slacks, and went for a ride around the flowerbeds and out to the station and back. She returned with her face glowing: 'I not do since I luttun girl. Giff boy ten tic, darling, 'cause he let me do wiss he—' A gesture sketched the bike.

Dan appeared at his door as soon as he heard the gold bell tinkling on her wrist and the rest of the evening passed in talk. She curdled our blood with tales of the American she liked best—'I sink maybe I luff him littun bit'—and before she'd told us half, Dan and I were ready to murder the man. He sounded such a bastard, and she so naive. It was he who'd taught her to drink whisky, 'and now I not want peppermint any more: it too slow. When I d'ink whisky, very quick I d'unk, I happy; 'cause you know dancing-girl must be very unhappy sometimes. She know she neffer can haff what she haff if she good girl ...'

Dan and I both gave her lots of good advice and lurid warnings, especially about the demoralizing influence of unprincipled Americans (Dan got very worked up on this point) and I described how the demon whisky creeps up on a girl and one morning she wakes to find that overnight she's turned into an old harridan. But she was supremely confident. 'Whisky neffer bad for Vilai. Well, only one time.' She turned round and showed Dan the back of her head, parting her hair. 'You see? You see where I hurt?' She caught hold of his hand and placed it on her scalp. 'You can feel?'

I exclaimed, 'What d'you mean? I thought your *samlor*—' She barely noticed the interruption—all evening she'd been showing more interest in Dan than in me—she only said, 'Why you sink *samlor*? Dick—that my frand—he come my house, I get d'unk. I go pee-pee—fall down stair ...' She showed Dan her wrist and tried to show him her knee but the slacks wouldn't pull up far enough. I sat sulking; lied to again. Dick ...

There was one other fragment of conversation that disturbed me. Dan was making sure what time our train left in the morning. 'Why you ask?' Vilai asked. 'You want go Bangkok wiss me?'

'No, no.' He flushed slightly. 'I was just thinking, if I got up early, maybe I could finish—'

She made an almost imperceptible movement and he stopped.

Jealousy sharpened my wits. 'What, have you been painting her portrait—while I was out this morning?' I asked Dan.

She said, 'I sink you cannot get up early. You very lacy boy. I sink when train go tomollow, you still slip. Every day Wretch, I, go out, I look you window, I see you on you bad. Like you d'ad ...' She looked at her watch. 'And tonight you stay up very late. I sink tomollow you not get up at all, you slip all day ...'

She'd chattered on so long, I couldn't put my question to Dan again, without making it quite clear that I suspected she'd kept me in the dark about something.

At midnight the party broke up. She lingered at our door for a private farewell with Dan. Coming into our room she said, 'He do this to me,' making the gesture of blowing a kiss.

'He's loopy about you.'

'I know. But no use. Not haff money.'

'Then why do you encourage him?'

She didn't hear. Got into bed. I got in with her.

'No. Not here. Slip your own bed.'

'Last night you said—'

'But I tired. Later maybe. Now—oh, go away.'

Then it happened. The sudden frantic uncontrollable rage. I poured out obscenities. I hurled myself around the room. She lay on her bed, rigid with fear. I tucked in her net. I put out the light. Then I threw myself on my own bed, sobbing and twitching and swearing. The fit passed off in a few minutes, and I just lay sobbing, occasionally shuddering violently. She lay very still, frightened out of her wits. She fell asleep and snored a little and scared herself awake again. She listened a long time. And I stifled my weeping. It was all spoiled now. Even for five days I couldn't live with a woman. I remembered the fear in Annette's eyes, and, years later, Sheila crying and crying like a beaten child ...

At last I fell asleep. Soon after, as it seemed, I was awakened: Vilai had switched the light on and was going to the bathroom. Coming back she switched the light off and got into my bed, not hers. I turned my back on her without a word. With her, too, I had failed.

Next morning I got up first. She joined me on the verandah while I was finishing my bacon and eggs. She watched me silently out of the corner of her eyes for several minutes. At last, realizing I was at fault, I began, 'I'm sorry about—

'What matter wiss you last night?' she pounced. 'You d'unk? I fright very mutss. I fray you kill me.'

'I'd never kill you, Vilai. Myself more like. I never get angry with the girl. Only with myself.'

'But why you—?'

'I don't know. Every time I love a girl too much this happens. That's why I'm not married.'

'Ah, I not want talk marry. All the time you tell lie. No man want to marry wiss dancing-girl.'

'Only me.'

'You cracy. We fight now, when we not marry. If we marry we fight fight all the time. Too mutss trouble.'

'We might fight some of the time, but the rest of the time we'd make up for it.'

'I not want man who fight wiss me.'

'Of course not. I know I'm not good enough for you, darling. This discussion is purely academic.' I got up.

'Where you go?'

'Don't you want me to fetch the raw pork you ordered? You told 'em to have it ready by eight this morning.'

'You go alone?'

'Darm-chai khun.' (It's up to you.) 'I've got no car this morning, but we fit into a *samlor* quite snugly, you and I.'

'No. I stay here. Pack my sings.'

'OK. That'll give Dan a chance to finish the portrait too. I'll be gone about an hour.'

She gave me a sharp look and went into our room. I followed to put my shoes on. She was taking things out of drawers. As I started to go, she caught my arm. She looked up into my eyes with the blackest pain in hers. 'Wretch, you come back?'

'Of course I'll come back. I'm only going for the *mu-som.*'

She still clung to me, searching my face, and suddenly her eyes filled with tears. She dashed my arm away and turned back to the chest of drawers. I dithered a moment, daunted by a woman's tears as always. But then I steeled my heart. No sense in starting all over again, yet. A few tears might soften her up. We'd have plenty of time to work things out in the train.

I was gone about forty-five minutes. When I got back our door was shut. I thumped on it for a few minutes, first thinking she might be dozing, then getting slightly exasperated. Just as I was preparing to give the door a real bang, the boy who was cleaning up in Dan's room came out. '*Bai-lao*,' he said, in the laconic Thai style.

'Gone! Gone where? *Bai-nai*?'

He shrugged. '*Mai-ru*.'

'You don't know? Did she leave any message? Er—*bok arai-na*?'

'*Bok hen khun satani*.'

'Oh, she'll meet me at the station.' I can't express the relief I felt. 'OK. Open the door. *Burt ba-daw*.'

He produced a key and opened up. The emptiness of the room hit me like a smack in the face. Nothing lying about anywhere, everything shut up and dusted off. My bag was standing, ready strapped up, in the corner, but hers had gone. 'So she took her things!' The boy shrugged again. He was grinning slightly.

I paid the bills, and the boy carried the bag and the hamper of *mu-som* down to a waiting *samlor*. As we passed Dan's door. I asked, '*farang yu mai yu hong*?'—is the foreigner in his room?

'*Bai-lao*' said the boy again. I didn't know whether he meant gone out on business or gone for good. But I imagined he'd gone to the station with Vilai ...

They weren't on the platform. They weren't in our compartment. Neither was her luggage.

I had more than an hour to wait before the train would leave. I paced up and down the platform. I could only imagine now that they'd gone to the market—Vilai had said she'd wished she'd bought a few other delicacies—or to complete her portrait against some really delectable background. I only hoped they wouldn't become so absorbed in whatever they were doing that they missed the train ...

After half an hour I began to get badly worried. I wanted to go and search for them—but which way should I turn? I hadn't the faintest idea where they were—or even whether they were together ...

At nine-seventeen the brass bell on the platform was tolled three times. 'All aboard.' Three more minutes to go.

I got on the train in a sort of dream. I shut the door on myself for some reason. I leaned right out of the window, staring towards the entrance. There was hardly anybody in that direction, only the station-master, in superb uniform, standing by his bell. His hand reached out and it clanged again, once, twice, three times. There was the shriek of a whistle up ahead, a green flag waved. Suddenly I had the sensation that I was swooning. The train was on the move, that was all; Chiengmai was beginning to slip away; the moneymoon was over.

Ten minutes later, after the ticket-collector had been told the sad news—my wife had been taken ill, and had had to stay behind at the McCormick Hospital—I threw my gold ring out of the window. It hit a bathing water buffalo and bounced off his back into his wallow.

Twelve

When I got to the office the following Monday I found an airmail letter marked 'Personal' awaiting me. It was from Chiengmai, and addressed in a spidery, wayward sort of hand. Turning to the signature first, I found it was from Dan. Its contents astonished me.

Dear Joyce,

You make a great point of parading your intellectual honesty, so you will appreciate it if I talk straight to you.

I think you are the most despicable man I ever met.

It is not merely that you revel in your own depravity, but you constantly try to corrupt others as well. I shall not soon forget how you constantly enticed me to drink, ridiculed my ideals, and, on one occasion, suggested in the most shameless manner that I should sleep with your mistress.

But all that is superfluous. The unforgivable part is your treatment of Miss V. The very first night you were in Chiengmai, before we had met, you had a drunken quarrel with her in your room; during which I heard her cry out that you had struck her. I was just on the point of intervening when the manager did so; otherwise I would have dealt with you then and there.

Last night you again assaulted her shortly after I left you. It is true that on this occasion I did not hear her cry out—I only heard your drunken shouts—but this morning, after you had left the hotel, she awakened me, in obvious agitation, and told me the whole story. She also showed me her bruises, which spoke for themselves.

She tried to defend you by pretending her wounds were received in other circumstances, but I knew she was lying out of fear of you. I advised her to leave you, and it is on my advice that she has done so. I wanted to wait at the hotel until you returned, to punch your head, but she was terrified of seeing you again. I consequently conducted her to another hotel, and at her request stood guard until we were sure you had left Chiengmai.

I cannot state too plainly my belief that Miss V. is a very fine character who has been temporarily led astray by evil-doers such as yourself. I am anxious that she should have a chance to redeem herself, and in fact I am helping her to start a new life. I write this letter as a warning to you—KEEP OFF. If I find you have been molesting her again, I shall have no hesitation in giving you the thrashing you already deserve.

In conclusion, I would like to give you a bit of advice. Pull up before it is too late! You seem to have had a respectable upbringing and I am sure there is still some good in you. That you will take this advice in the spirit in which it is given, forego your present evil ways and strive to be a power for good in the world, is the earnest prayer of

Your sincere friend
D. Birkfield
c/o US Consulate (approx. 2 more wks.)
Chiengmai

Vilai re-appeared at my hotel the next Saturday afternoon.

'What, broke again already?' I sneered.

She ignored that. 'Can I haff ice-coffee? I cannot stay long.'

'Dan waiting?'

She ignored that too.

I bawled to the boy to bring iced-coffee and another beer.

'Why you want beer more?' she asked. 'You d'unk now. I not like you d'ink beer so mutss. You good boy. I not want you go bad like all the usser men.'

'Why hast thou appeared unto me, Saint Vilai? To preach?'

'I not unnerstand p'each.' Arun shuffled in with the drinks. His face broke into an ear-to-ear grin and as soon as he'd set down the tray he saluted her Thai style, which pleased her. 'He good boy, I sink,' she said when he'd gone. 'He haff good manner.'

I got up to shut the door but she stopped me. 'Not want. You d'unk again. I fright very mutss.'

'How did Dan turn out?' I asked, leaving the door ajar and coming back to my chair. 'Rich, like I said? Or penniless, like *you* said?'

She looked at me steadily. 'I not want you spick bad about Dan. He very good boy. Before I sink you number one good boy in the uni-worse, but now I sink maybe Dan good more batter than you.'

'Of course he is. He's more recent.' I grabbed her knee. 'Has he given you five thousand eight hundred this week, like I gave you last week? Tell me that.'

She sighed, 'Oh Wretch, only sing you sink about your money'—and I laughed until the tears came into my eyes.

She finished her coffee and got up to powder her nose at my mirror. As she worked at it, she talked. 'Wretch, I leaf you in Chiengmai 'cause all the time you d'unk and I fright you very mutss. I sink no good you, me, make luff any more—only make you mad, and one day maybe you hurt me. But I still want you for my frand. Not want to finiss wiss you angly me, darling, that no good. Now Vilai not haff good life. No haff shob. No haff son to help me. And now polissman very bad. This week must go to polissman house, get—oh, what you call? wiss pickser—'

'Identity card?'

'Yes, yes, ident cart. I sink maybe the polissman make too mutss trouble to me. Girl no haff shob, polissman always very bad to she. Want money *mark mark*—'

'Sure, sure.'

'And now, you know, bad girl can not liff in Bangkok any more. Poliss go she house, and she not haff huss-band, not haff shob, they take her away. Before I at Bolero, I dancing-girl, haff shob, OK. But now, not safe for me come hotel any more, darling. If polissman come this room now, find me here—' She turned to me helplessly. 'Why everyone want to make so mutss trouble for girl who bad?' she asked. 'I not understand.'

'It's the end for you, kid. You'll either have to marry Dan or jump in the river—'

'I neffer marry wiss Dan.' She slumped onto the bed, returning her compact to her handbag. 'Dan good too mutss, darling. Only sing he sink, how can he halp pipple who sick. I fray if he marry wiss girl like

Vilai, his Mama very unhappy. He ask me she old now—fifty-t'ree and sick all the time. I sink if he marry me, she die—'

'And I'm not in the market any more.'

She said, 'Vilai neffer marry again. But you, me, long time good frand, Wretch. Maybe you want finiss now—you not want me any more—but I still sink you best frand I effer haff—'

'Better than Dan?'

'Ah, you not understand. He *too* good. He not know how bad I. And I not want he know—'

'You in love with him?'

She was silent.

I repeated the question.

'What mean luff?' she said in the end. 'All the time pipple talk luff, luff, luff, but I sink no pipple know what luff is. It just—talk.' She draped her handbag from her shoulder, a sign that she was about to leave. 'Wretch, I know you not like me like before. I not good to you. But I want to ask you one sing. If I in very big trouble—you help me, darling? I not ask for littun trouble, I plomiss. But if big?' She put her hand on my arm and gazed into my eyes. 'I sink you not say no, 'cause before you luff me very mutss.'

'But you've just said love is all talk,' I snapped. Then I softened slightly—because after all she was still Vilai—the girl I'd tried to make my wife. 'OK, Saint Vilai, I never want to see you again. You've dragged me though hell, but you gave me glimpses of heaven too, and I won't forget them either. If you're ever really in the soup, I'll help. But you'll have to convince me you're really up against it. If you try any of your tricks, I'll spit in your face, Vilai—I'm telling you now ...'

The summons came two months later. Once again Windmill and I were in the Northeast. That day we'd travelled, separately, from Khon Kaen to Korat. Windmill, not fancying subjecting his plump person to the potholes and water-splashes between Muang-phol and Dalarttsai, had taken the train, while I'd done the two hundred kilometres by jeep alone. We nearly always split up like this now, if Windmill could find alternative transport to the jeep; and the arrangement suited us both fine.

Going to our usual Korat hotel, I found that Windmill had already checked in, but his room was locked on the outside, signifying he was out. I had a beer and a cold splash, put on clean clothes and went in search of food.

Night had fallen and the town centre was a blaze of lights. I walked to Ahan-tou, Windmill's favourite foodshop, but again he wasn't in evidence. I sat at one of the small round-topped marble tables and ordered One-Eye to produce horse piss eggs, Chinese sausage garnished with sugar and spices, and boiled duck; also beer, of course. I expected to enjoy my meal none the less because I would be eating it alone. I was now quite used to being solitary.

However, before One-Eye had produced anything more than a bowl and a pair of chopsticks, I heard my name mispronounced and looked up to find myself confronted with one of Broderick Peers' biggest customers. He was a stout round-jowled Chinese with a pock-marked face and a loud, rough voice; he was accompanied by three or four other men, all slighter and tamer, whom he proceeded to introduce. He wouldn't hear of my eating alone and I had to shift to a larger table. Then the evening began to develop along familiar lines. These led through too many rich dishes and too many *pecks* of mekong to another café at the end of Chakri Road where we all swallowed raw eggs to get our strength up. I was tired out and an hour before had believed I would be faithful to the memory of Vilai for the rest of my life, but this was business, and besides I was quite enjoying myself. I always felt a bit above par after completing a difficult journey singlehanded; and moreover mekong has aphrodisiacal properties, especially when mixed with beer. So when we finally turned into the pitch-black tunnel through which Boswell and all that gang had first ushered me so many eons ago, I was not bringing up the rear of the procession, I was pretty drunk, and I was craving to see Ratom, whom I hadn't seen for months.

'Oh, Letchee, you come back, Letchee, Letchee, you come back!' Ratom cried, throwing herself into my arms; and I could detect nothing spurious in her joy. She dragged me to her room, sat me on the bed, pulled out my shirt at the waist, and gave me a Siamese kiss. This consists of a strong ecstatic sniff and a simultaneous backward toss of the head and it leaves the recipient with a fine sense of being adored. I replied with a

European kiss and my fidelity to Vilai, which I had preserved intact since Chiengmai, crumbled into powder—scented powder—there and then.

I'd been with her for about an hour, I suppose, and she'd brought me drinking water in a handsome silver bowl with sweet-scented white petals floating in it, and I'd helped her to choose the lottery ticket she would buy in the morning by shaking numbered sticks out of a bamboo container, and I'd greatly overpaid her, stuffing a hundred-tic note into her chemise, and she'd just brought up the months-old subject of Singers again, when there came a knock at the door, and Windmill's voice called, 'Hey, Reggie, you dead? Or you going to stay with that girl all night?'

'Why, Windmill! Don't tell me you've reached Korat at last!'

Out in the corridor he gave me a scolding. 'Why you so long with that girl? Mr. Chu tired of waiting. You must not be so unconsiderate, he important customer.' He handed me the telegram then. 'Prosit give me this. I think for you.'

It was too dark to read it in the corridor, and in the inner sanctuary I got involved in apologies and badinage for several minutes. Then Chu and the two friends that remained with him got up to go, but Windmill was waiting for Prosit, who was up the ladder, and I told them that Broderick Peers men always stuck together, so I'd say goodnight and see them in the morning. Windmill shook his head at me and to make amends for my lack of courtesy accompanied them to the door.

Ratom was sitting on my knee when he came back. 'You should have gone with them for one more drink,' he said. 'They wait for you long time ... Have you read your telegram yet?'

'No. I'd forgotten it.' I took it out of my shirt pocket and unfolded it (they don't bother to put telegrams in envelopes in Thailand). It was in Siamese: a solid line of squarish characters with wild free loops and hooks above and below odd ones here and there. 'It's in double Dutch,' I said, handing it to Windmill. Already I was feeling slightly apprehensive. The firm always communicated with me in English. To only one other person had I ever given our Korat address ...

'Who's it from? What does it say?' I asked nervously.

'I think not for you.'

I took it back. 'It might be. Who does it say it's from?'

'It not signed.'

That made me practically certain. 'I think I know. I gave her—I mean him—I mean I only gave Prosit's address to one person. Is it addressed to me?'

'It not clear—'

'But what does it say here?'—pointing at the first letters.

'The spelling hope-less. It say 'Lecher Joy' or something like that—'

'That's me! Of course that's me! You must have realized that means me, just as Prosit did! What—what does the rest say?'

'It from that Bolero girl?'

'Never mind who it's from. Tell me what it says.'

'The Siamese is very bad—uneducated—'

Ratom took the form from my hand and scrutinized it. Then, 'I think this must be important, Letchee,' she said in Siamese. 'It says, "Return Bangkok immediately. Serious trouble. Relying on you. Don't forget your promise."' She handed the form back to me. 'Who speaks to you in that way, Letchee? Have you a wife in Bangkok?'

I'd lifted her out of my lap while she was still talking and stood up.

'Where you go?'

Windmill was looking troubled and annoyed.

'I'm going to Bangkok.'

'What—now? But you have work to do, here, Buriram, Pimai, Sraburi—'

'You can do all that, by train, except for Pimai. And you can go by bus to Pimai. I'll take the jeep—'

'But you've been driving all day—'

'And I'm going to drive all night.'

'Look, Reggie, you can't do this. Samjohn will be mad like hell—'

'I'll phone him tomorrow, when I reach Bangkok. Tell him I'm taking leave—'

'You can't do it.' Windmill had never before spoken to me so emphatically and I looked at him in surprise. 'Now listen,' he went on, 'Two, three month ago Mr. Samjohn tell me he very browned up with you. He say you like naughty little boy, and I must look after you like *amah*. He tell me he rely on me to keep you out of—what the word he use?—miss-chife, that's it. He tell me I responsible for you. You do something wrong, I must get in hot water too—hot like boiling, he said.

Most important thing, he said, I must see you not get in hot water with woman. Especially White Leopard—'

'What? He knows about her?'

'Everybody know about her. Frost—he see you with her, isn't that right? Somboon see her at your hotel. Mrs. Samjohn see her in your room—'

I felt myself flushing with shame and fury. 'Don't tell me a respectable female like Mrs. S. is familiar with Bolero girls.'

'Why not? Sometimes Mrs. S. go to nightclub with her husband—and who go to nightclub in Bangkok and not know White Leopard? That beech go everwhere after dark—everyone must know—'

'So Mrs. S. recognized her!' There was something maddening about that; the subject of my passion was not anonymous; the Samjohns could prattle about her over their toast and marmalade.

And they'd kept their knowledge to themselves; I'd never guessed how much they knew, how deep they were ...

'To hell with Samjohn and his old woman too! I've got urgent business in Bangkok and it's nothing to do with Leopards. I finished with them two months ago. A friend of mine is in a jam—a man.'

'And you go Bangkok you in jam too. And I in hot water. But never mind. Now I've told you what Mr. Samjohn say. If you still want to go Bangkok, that your business. I wash my hands of it.'

'And that's all right with me. Wash your hands in the hot water ... I'm going to the hotel now for the jeep and my duds. You coming?'

'No, I wait Prosit.'

'Right-ho, then. So long.'

I marched out—out through the stinking corridor and the outer dungeon where a couple of *samlor*-men in straw hats and shorts were experimentally pinching a couple of squealing girls—out into the street, going at the double, though Ratom came running after me to the door crying 'Letchee, Letchee, wait a minute, why don't you say goodbye'—beginning to sprint, even, when I got out of Chakri Road, because Vilai had not forgotten she could rely on me, Vilai in some sort of trouble had called to me for help ... and suddenly life had point again, suddenly there was something important and urgent for me to do ...

The first hour of the run was almost pleasant. I like driving at night, especially along deserted roads. I like the splotches of ink that are shadows on your path of gold; the way the silver trees slowly catch light and approach and then vanish at the corner of your eyes; the veils of grey-blue smoke, never noticed by day, that lie in perfumed swathes across the road; and the way the road itself, unmade beyond the end of the headlights' beam, rapidly lengthens and develops, like a ray of light from the sun unreeling across black space.

But after a while I discovered something which I hadn't anticipated. Either because of my hard driving that day or my hard drinking that night or both, I was all in. It seemed that every scrap of energy I had was required to keep my eyelids from dropping. I repeatedly missed the ramps of bridges and got into some bad slides in the loose gravel on the crown of the road. I craved sleep. I considered returning to Korat, but it would have looked too damn' silly, dashing off like that for a few miles and then succumbing to exhaustion. I also considered curling up in the back seat for a couple of hours but the thought of Vilai spurred me on. Disaster can happen in a split second; one moment's delay on my part might seal her doom ...

So I kept my right foot down ... Since nightfall the lightning had been continuous, though distant. Out here in the night it was quite plain that the storm was ahead of me and that sooner or later I'd be in it. That knowledge filled my dulled brain with further anxieties, for a tropical storm can destroy a dirt road in a few minutes; doped as I was, I might easily run into a wash-out and break my neck ...

And then there was all the muddle and uneasiness in my mind. All my life these sensations had accompanied me, and tonight a new climax had been reached. For ever since I'd flung out of the House of Joy I'd realized what a crack-brained expedition this was. Who but an utter idiot would rush through the tropic night to rescue such a tart as Vilai? If she was in trouble it was entirely her own fault. Long ago I'd offered her the means of escape from all dangers; whatever nameless horror threatened her she'd now have been safe from. And meanwhile I was rushing to my own ruin. Samjohn had warned me plainly enough—Windmill had underlined that warning. In Galahading off to avert Vilai's doom I was only sealing my own; I would be sent home in disgrace, and after that

Vilai would be denied my help forever ...

And how could I be sure that this cry for help was genuine? Possibly she just needed a few tics to square a policeman or buy herself a new necklace. If only she hadn't said, 'Don't forget your promise.' Those were the words that had sent me headlong into the night. For I was proud that, out of the hundreds of men she knew, I, Reggie Joyce, this weakling, was the one she relied on. No matter if it was because I was the most easily fooled of them all. Whatever the grounds of her faith, she *did* have faith in *me*. I would never betray that trust. Never confirm her in her cynicism —'all men are false; Wretch, even Wretch, let me down in the end—'

Suddenly the world turned to chalk in the brightest flash of lightning yet. It was so bright it jerked my thoughts outward from myself.

Every other second the night was annihilating itself in these violent blazes of white light. The rumble of thunder was almost continuous above the high whine of the transmission and the roar of the tyres on the rough gravel. Branches around and above threshed madly in the wind which sometimes smote the jeep like an almighty fist, almost knocking it off the road. Torn-off palm leaves sprawled in front of the wheels, bleached by the headlights to look like the fossil ribs of giant mastodons ...

I realized that I'd reached the mountains, so-called. They hardly deserve the name. They are about like the South Downs, say, but instead of being grassy are smothered with forest. A good road snakes over them, easily graded, with not more than a dozen hairpin bends ...

I looked at my instruments. The temperature was a bit lower than usual—running by night, I supposed. The generator was charging and the oil pressure was normal. Only the fuel gauge gave me a bit of a shock. Although I'd filled up at Korat, the tank was already more than half empty. A leak? No, the engine was running fine. I realized I'd been driving full speed—wasting fuel.

And then the storm really hit. For a few moments there'd been an ominous under-rumble that was neither the thunder nor the wheels. I'd heard it before once or twice and I knew what it was—a solid wall of rain smashing its way towards me over the cowering trees. Suddenly the windscreen was blinded out and the shirt on my left shoulder was soused and icy. I lifted my foot from the accelerator pedal—that was a reflex action—leaned forwards to set the windscreen wipers going, sideways to shut the open air-vent. But the wipers were useless—not only because of the deluge cascading down the glass but in a moment the glass had misted over inside and I could see nothing. I jerked my foot towards the brake pedal but in the same moment I knew I was heading off the road and still going fast. I wrenched at the steering wheel but the offside road-wheels were already over the edge; the wrench only increased the jeep's tendency to topple and over it went with a horrifying lurch. Somebody screamed—and I know it can only have been me. A flash showed me I was upside down and still rolling. There was a shattering crash in the pitch darkness, then another brilliant flash that seemed more inside my head than outside of it, then a second heavy jarring crash. Then silence, or something very like it ...

I lay half-stunned for a few seconds—I don't think it was longer than that. I was upside down, with the twisted wheel jammed against my ribs and that horrible singing in the head with which a lot of speedway crashes had made me familiar. Yet my first reaction was one of elation: 'I've done it again—and again I haven't killed myself—quite. I'm the luckiest son of a bitch ...'

Then I remembered Vilai, and panic seized me.

As soon as I tried to move I found out I was hurt. Seemingly the same ribs that had been stove in that last time when I piled up on the speedway had taken another heavy blow. Every movement made me sweat with agony as I wriggled out from under the wheel and got myself right way up; and the rain, coming down in suffocating force and bitingly cold, added to my misery. And I couldn't see the road. The lightning fit up the slope of soil and mashed bushes down which I had rolled—already it was like a waterfall, and my hands sunk inches deep into the treacherous, slithering mud—but squatting there I couldn't see how far I'd fallen ...

'Vilai, Vilai!' I croaked, grabbing at her name to prevent myself from spinning off into a faint.

Somehow, hanging on to the upturned front wheels, I pulled myself onto my feet and clung there, reeling, waiting for a flash to show me just how bad things were.

As if to mock my anxiety, the lightning held off for a whole minute.

Then a single flash revealed everything.

The jeep had been stopped from rolling any further by the upright trunk of a tree. It was lying about twenty feet below the road on a slope which went down, covered with scrub out of which more straight trunks soared, for apparently quite a distance. There were no trees between the jeep and the road and the first person who came along by daylight would be bound to sight the wreck.

But even as I put my situation into this optimistic light I realized that I was over-simplifying it. There were two very important considerations which immediately occurred to me. The first was, how soon would help arrive? I might have to hang on here till the middle of tomorrow afternoon. And the second was, supposing help arrived, and we got the jeep back on the road again, would it be possible to put it back in running order? Supposing something disastrous had happened to the steering or one of the axles—or even that the battery was wrecked beyond repair? There were a hundred things that could happen to a jeep in a crash like this—things that would immobilize it. I might struggle for hours to get it back on the road, and then still find it unserviceable ... and myself as far away from Vilai as ever ...

Thus I rationalized my position. But I only did any thinking while I was hanging onto that front wheel, convincing myself I could stand. As soon as I was sure of that, my usual emotionalism swept all my thoughts away. If I could stand I could walk—and I just hadn't the patience to sit and wait, hoping for help to come. I'd got to act for myself. I'd got to do something violent. Maybe I'd only injure myself more—put myself further from Vilai instead of nearer—make a bad mess worse. But I'd got to do something. Only if I was on the move, struggling towards her, could I feel quite sure that I was doing my best for Vilai.

'Get going, get going,' I muttered to myself.

And all at once I let go of the wheel and began to struggle from bush to bush up the wall of sliding mud to the road. Though the climb was short it was terribly hard and I barely managed it. The rain had eased off quite a bit, but it was still falling torrentially by English standards; and ice-cold rain, if you've nothing to protect you from it but a shirt, seems to flog your body with steel rods; you can't believe that mere falling drops of water can tire and demoralize a man so fast. And besides the rain there were those ribs; I didn't know whether they were broken or not—most probably not—but all one side of my chest was aching cruelly. Once when I was about halfway up to the road, I slipped and all my weight came on my right arm and the jolt of pain was so bad—as if someone had swung at me with a crowbar—that I let go of my hold and slithered down smack into the jeep again. I had to lie there for a minute, and during that minute I wept like a child who's been spanked. But then I started crawling upwards again, this time with more care.

And so finally I dragged myself over the edge of the road. I lay there for a short while, almost swooning with pain and retching to get my breath, but I guessed that the worst was over, and just lying there, inert, with that comforting thought in my head, did wonders for me. I told myself, 'What you're suffering from mainly is shock. If you just hold on to yourself you'll soon be all right. There's nothing wrong with your legs, and if you're careful what you do with your arms you can avoid hurting your chest too badly. As for this bloody rain—it can't go on like this for ever. Soon—in another minute or so—you'll be able to get up and start walking towards Bangkok ...'

And so I did. I dragged myself to my feet and started to stagger along the road through that cold hard rain and the inky darkness which was only relieved now at lengthy intervals by fading, distant flares. Soon the sky began to lighten and there was less danger of my stumbling over the edge of the road or twisting my ankle in one of the deep gulleys the deluge had carved in the gravel. Twice I was able to cut off considerable stretches of road by scrambling and glissading down the sodden hillsides between hairpins.

And at the foot of the last pitch I had a real stroke of luck; I came to a lumber camp where a timber-trailer was just being readied to go to the nearest railway station. That was a hundred kilometres further on my way, just this side of Lopburi. The crew easily believed my tale of a crash in the storm, accepted as my reason for wanting to go immediately to Lopburi that I had friends there who would help me to recover the jeep, offered me a lift, and then, with typical Siamese courtesy, found me a check waist-cloth and a tin dipper so that I could have a bath first. When

I'd got most of the mud off myself and some of the dried blood out of my hair (for I found I'd cut my head open too) they had a glass of hot water ready for me to drink. Hot water is not a favourite beverage of mine but at that juncture it seemed as stimulating as rum. In the cab I slept fitfully.

My luck held when we reached the railway. Only ten minutes after I'd said goodbye to the timber-trailer crew a slow train snuffled in from Pitsanaluke. It dawdled along to Banphagi junction, where I caught the express from Korat—the very train I could have caught that morning in Korat if I hadn't dashed off on my mad nocturnal drive. At four o'clock in the afternoon I jumped down on to the platform at Hualalomphong Station—only twenty minutes by *samlor* from Vilai's house.

Going there in the *samlor* I was so worried and anxious I couldn't sit still. I hadn't been to Vilai's house since that night when I'd first made her acquaintance. She'd always been very insistent that there was no need for me to do so—'you want see me I come your hotel, darling'—nor had I ever felt any desire to argue, being fearful of what I might be confronted with if I did. But these were exceptional circumstances. She was in trouble; I couldn't afford the time to go to the hotel and send her a note and wait for her to come; I knew I just wouldn't have the courage or patience to stay in a hotel room until she showed up. I was racked with suspense and this once I must disobey orders and go and brave her in her den ...

Because I had been in such a preoccupied state that first night I now had only the vaguest idea where her place was and what it looked like. I could recall a deserted alley and a corrugated iron door. When the *samlor*-boy turned into a narrow passage choked with stalls and pedestrians and the overwhelming cacophony of competing radios I thought he must have misunderstood me and brought me to the wrong place. I shouted the address to him again and he pulled up, nodding his straw-hatted head. I thought he was nodding acknowledgment of my words, but then I realized he was actually indicating a direction. On my left, behind a travelling dried-squid stall complete with charcoal fire and mangle for making the hard flesh harder still, was a twisted, rusted, groggy door with a lewd drawing chalked on it. I looked at it in amazement. I had a recollection of metal glistening like silver in the reflection of distant lights that night. Could this really be Vilai's home? I glanced incredulously at the *samlor*-boy, but he only laughed and nodded again and made a disgusting sign with his fingers.

For a second I was tempted to do what I knew I ought to have done in the first place—go to my hotel and direct operations from there. But only for one cowardly moment. Then I got out of the *samlor* on shaky legs.

As soon as I knocked on the rust a sort of hush came over the street. Half a dozen ragged little boys appeared from nowhere and stood around me in a semi-circle, gaping. The *samlor*-boy, folding my bill into the top of his shorts, said something to the remarkably ugly old Chinese who was squatting behind the dried-squid stall. The old man cackled. The open shop-fronts behind me seemed suddenly banked with staring eyes. I felt a flush come up from my shoulders in a wave to the top of my head and I knocked again, loudly, conscious of making myself ridiculous yet once more.

Nobody answered the knock and I turned half despairingly. At that one of the small boys squirmed in front of me, rattled the door violently and bawled. From somewhere within came a grumpy female response and all the boys laughed at me—it was really so simple.

The grumpy voice sounded again, from just inside the door. Not catching a word I didn't reply, but the half-dozen boys said almost with one voice, '*Farang maliao*.' There was the sound of a latch made from a piece of wire and the door opened inwards about one inch. I got a long narrow view of black hair, a very brown face, a dirty slip; was held by a surly eye. 'What do you want?' the half-mouth asked in Siamese.

'I want to see Miss Vilai.'

'She's not in.'

'Tell her it's Reggie Joyce.'

'She's—Wretcher?' The name seemed to impress her. 'Do you live in a hotel in Bhalangpoo?'

'Yes, yes. Miss Vilai knows me well. Please let me in.'

The door opened and I passed through. I heard all the boys laugh out loud and scamper away, shouting out my shame to the whole convulsed street.

I waited awkwardly just inside, half afraid that Vilai's furious eyes were already on me. The house stood on stilts, so close to the gate I was almost under it. In the darkness under the floor was the usual clutter of jars and broken boxes and bottles and other rubbish. Water was dripping through the floor from an upstairs bathroom and creeping through black and green slime to a smelly puddle over a stopped-up drain. Behind the drain a half-grown mongrel who was black with mud halfway up his skinny ribs stood whuffing halfheartedly at me, ready to flee at a flick of my eyelids. The smell of the eternal puddle was almost overpowering.

The old woman finished latching the door and turned and looked me up and down critically. I could see she was wondering what on earth her Mem saw in me.

'Is Miss Vilai in?'

'Wait here.' She kicked off her sandals and shuffled up a ladder past the bathroom door. Watching her ascend, I marvelled at what monstrosities women, once presumably reasonably fair to look upon, can sometimes turn into. Corpses still able to move ...

Standing at the foot of the ladder, I heard her go down a passage, tap at a door, and mutter 'Mem.' So Vilai was in ... Then the old woman began in the exasperating Siamese manner to alternately tap and mutter, tap and mutter, never raising her voice above the conversational tone or giving the door a solid bang—and prepared to go on like that forever, it seemed. Often I'd heard boys in hotels thus ineffectually working away at a door for an hour or more—it has something to do with the fact that the soul goes roaming while the body sleeps, and if the body wakes too suddenly it may do so before the soul has had time to return to it and then the soul can't find its home and becomes a wandering ghost and a public nuisance. I made a move towards the ladder and the mongrel retreated about five yards and went into a paroxysm of accelerating yaps that finally merged into one long-drawn hysterical howl. Only somebody who'd been drugged could have slept through the racket he made and Vilai wasn't that. Her voice sounded angry—the way it always sounded when she was awakened—and I felt a rush of jumbled emotions—at any rate she was alive—and quite unchanged ...

The dog had made so much commotion that I hadn't been able to hear what was going on upstairs.

Then the old woman appeared again at the top of the ladder. She paused there to gather up her sarong in the spidery monkey fingers of one hand and holding it between her knees began to descend.

Before she was halfway down Vilai arrived. She shot to the top of the ladder and jerked to a stop. She was still tucking her sarong in on her chest. It was a plain black sarong such as country women wear. She had nothing else on, not even sandals. Her hair was what Sheila would have called 'a sight'. Her face wasn't made up—or rather it only showed a few traces of make-up left over from last time ...

'Why you come to my house?' she grated. 'I *ask* you many time, I not want you come my house.'

It was the reception I'd half-expected, and that made me twice as resentful about it. It was like dropping potassium permanganate into water and instantly what was colourless is purple. All my pent-up anxiety and fear for her, all my unwilling love, all my guilty sense of imbecility and besottedness, all were transmuted at a stroke into rage. I could feel my features wrenched into epileptic disorder. I could hear myself screaming: 'You bitch, you low-down bitch! You sent for me, didn't you? You implored me to come at once! God damn it, I nearly killed myself to reach you—I nearly killed myself—'

She came racing down the steps and hurled herself upon me. Her face was a picture of concern. She threw an arm around my waist and tried to draw me under the house. 'Wretch, Wretch,' she said earnestly, in a low voice, 'you not want make so mutss noise. Usser pipple sink you d'unk—I not like that. This my house; every pipple here know I very good girl—'

I started laughing then. That concern for me (as I'd thought it was at first) and the feel of her arm about my body, had put 'paid' to my rage. But immediately it had appeared that what I had thought was concern for me was actually concern for herself—and it was really too funny—

She placed a box for me and I slumped down on to it, half-laughing and half-crying like a hysterical girl.

She stood in front of me, gripping her biceps with opposing hands and shifting her weight uncomfortably from one leg to the other. The old woman was there too, discussing me critically with her Mem. A third woman now arrived from behind all the rubbish, a very fat one with a crimson bodice that she was struggling to fasten as she approached. '*Ami mai-di*?'—what's the matter with him?—she asked, and Vilai's answer was as clear as a bell: '*Mao.*'

'I'm not drunk,' I said sulkily.

'Then why all your clo' dirty like you fall down on road?'

'I had an accident. In the jeep.'

'You haff accident, why you not go hotel, haff bass, before you come see me? I not like man come here see me wiss cloze all dirty. Pipple sink I very low dirty girl, haff dirty man come see—'

'Oh, shut up about my clothes!' I'd got over my hysteria and was turning angry again. 'If you didn't want me to come straight here to see you, why did you send me this ruddy telegram?'—and I whipped it out of my pocket, though it was by now illegible and in shreds. 'From the way this telegram was translated to me, I reckoned you were already tied to the stake and the rotten English had their torches to the faggots. But you don't look even singed to me. In fact you don't look any worse than you normally do when you aren't made up—'

'What matter wiss you? All the time you spick too mutss, too fast: I not unnerstand—'

I got up off the box. 'What's the trouble, Vilai? Why did you send me this telegram? Is it a hoax, or is there really something wrong?'

She said, a little uncertainly, as I thought—'I haff trouble, yes. Bad, bad trouble.'

'Then what is it? Give me the facts. I might be able to help—'

'Not want spick this place. Maybe bad pipples hear what I ask you. That not good.'

'Then let's go to your room.'

'What?' She gestured vaguely upwards and when I nodded, shook her head emphatically. 'No, no, not want you go—'

She was so emphatic my suspicions were aroused. 'Why not? Somebody else there already? Don't tell me I have a rival!'

Her eyes blazed. 'I sink you very bad boy, Wretch. All the time you only sink bad sing about Vilai. All the time you spick luff luff luff, but you not ac' luff. If you not luff me, why you must come to my house like this?'

I seized her wrist. 'Listen, sweetness. I've come through hell and high water to help you. I've cooked my goose as far as my firm is concerned and in fact my whole bloody life is in ruins. In other words, *I'm* in real trouble, Vilai, and if you aren't—if you've just been playing with me—'

She gave a weary sigh and muttered what I thought was probably a curse. Then she said, 'You hurt me too mutss when you angly to me like this. All the time you not trust Vilai. All the time you must try to hurt me 'cause you angly to me. You not good to me any more like before. But neffer mind. Vilai haff very strong heart, she not fray nussink ... This time you can come my house, but I not want you come here again, you unnerstand what I spick, Wretch?'

She led the way upstairs. There was nobody in her room. She moved around clearing things up. There was a lot of empty soda water bottles scattered about and she'd spilt face-powder all down the front of the dressing-table. I pulled the door shut behind us and sat down in the deckchair. Behind a curtain I noticed dresses—innumerable dresses, hanging from a whole army of clothes-hangers. I didn't remember having seen them on my previous visit. There was an expensive-looking radio, too.

'Not many signs of poverty here,' I remarked.

'Please you not spick me like that. I want you spick me why you come here today, then quick-quick go.'

I didn't know how to begin. I said, 'Look, darling—'

'Oh, God. You just want spick like fool, eh? You come my house in dirty cloze to make luff to me—'

'No. I came here in dirty clothes because you asked me to. What's behind that telegram, Vilai?'

She sat down with her back to me on a stool in front of the triple-mirrored dressing-table. She opened a drawer and turned over a lot of underclothes, selected one soiled item, then bundled it in her hand and began wiping up the face-powder with it. Her jewellery jingled musically as she moved tins, pots, vials, bottles, tubes, cartons—all the staggering mass of paraphernalia that faced her. I thought she wasn't going to answer me but suddenly she dropped the duster and swung round. 'Wretch, how mutss money you haff? I mean altogesser—in bank and—'

'So that's it! Just the routine stick-up! I might have known.' I got up and started tramping the room. 'If only you could have an *un*-financial worry just once in a while, Vilai, people might take your financial ones more seriously.' I sat down on the bed. 'Anyway you're out of luck this time—I'm broke.'

'Why you sit on my bed wiss your—'

'Sorry.' I almost laughed—only a woman, I thought, could worry about a man sitting on her bed in dirty trousers when she was in desperate trouble. I crossed to the deckchair again, took out my wallet and inspected its contents. 'I've got about two hundred and that's all—'

'So! Now you start spick lie to me, like usser men—'

'How dare you say that?'

'When you come back Chiengmai you still haff littun money. And since then you haff t'ree, four pay-day—'

'And no *you* ... Is that what you mean?'

'I sink you bad boy, now, Wretch. Before, I ask you giff me money, you neffer say "No haff"—you giff me. And if you no haff, you ask your frand bollow you, and giff me everysing I want. But now you spick lie to me, ask me you not haff money. That not truce word, Wretch—how can you spend so mutss up-country?' She turned to her mirrors and thrust her chin towards the middle one. 'I want ten t'ou-zand today, darling. I must haff. You cannot giff, I neffer want see you again. Can not.'

She spoke in such flat matter-of-fact tones that she might have been asking me to squeeze a blackhead out of her chin, instead of demanding five hundred dollars—two hundred quid—or else ...

I got up and stood behind her. She continued to give her chin the sort of rapt attention an astronomer accords the heavens. I was tempted to grab her shoulders and wrench her round. Instead I burst out: 'Suppose you tell me what you need this—fortune—for?'

'I neffer spick you that. Can not.'

'And I know very well why you can't, too. I've been rooked by you too many times already. You aren't in trouble at all. It's all a yarn. You think I've got money now, and you're just trying to—'

My voice trailed off, because she was crying.

Whenever she did that she put me in a quandary. Cynicism about woman flourishes in vicarages and I'd known since childhood that all women except a few outstandingly good ones like your own mother can cry to order and often do when they want to gain a point. On the other hand all women good and bad can be made to weep real tears too—tears of distress that well out of their eyes involuntarily. And the problem for a man is to distinguish between the genuine article and the false. Which was worse, to be made a fool of or to act ungenerously? There wasn't any doubt in my mind: if I let her down I'd have to live with the memory for the rest of my life. I was going to help her—but I'd be gruff with her to save face ...

'For God's sake stop that sniffling. What in hell have you got to blubber about? You sent for me and here I damn' well am. You know quite well I'll do anything, *anything*, you ask, to help you.

'What can you do? You spick me you not haff ten t'ou—'

'I can do plenty. At least I can do something besides continually ramming my hand into my hip-pocket. I can use my brains, for a start.' I brushed against her experimentally but she jerked away with a scornful exclamation, still weeping. So I said, 'Look around you, Vilai. This room's crammed with money. There's a radio for one thing that's worth a lot more than sixpence. There's clothes—stacks of them. And somewhere there's all your jewels—'

She spoke with a sort of incredulous fury. 'What you mean? You want I sell my gold?'

'Of course. Why not? You're rich, Vilai. If you really want to raise ten thousand—'

'Ugh!' I'd seldom heard so much disgust in a voice before. 'Once I sink Wretch good—I sink no man in world good more batter than he. I sink he say he luff me, he spick truce. But now I know Wretch *mai dee—mai dee mark*. He bad, like usser man. He spick me sell my sings—'

'And why in blazes not, if it'll keep you out of trouble?'

'Sick, seffen, eight year I work work work. No pipple giff me nussing. I dancing-girl, everysing I haff I get my-self—'

'I know, I know. Nobody could call you lazy, whatever else they might say ... But surely this is why you've worked so hard, Vilai? So you'd have money for a rainy day—'

'Wretch.' Her voice was peremptory. 'You giff me ten t'ou-zand—you haff in pocket now?'

'No.'

'You can get for me, giff me tomollow?'

'No.'

'Why you no can get?'

I sighed. 'Because I'm a poor man. Use your crumpet, Vilai. Where do you think a chap like me—'

'You could sell jip.'

'What!'

'Sell *jip,* darling. Many pipple want jip. Cowboy too—I sink cowboy giff mutss money for jip, then he look like soldier or plissman, can fright pipple very mutss, make them giff he money—'

'My jeep happens to be upside down on a mountain two hundred kilos from here. Also it's not my jeep. It's the firm's—'

'What matter that? They not know what you do. You sell, giff me ten t'ou-zand, maybe twenty—'

'You're incorrigible, Vilai. Don't you realize that if I did what you say I'd be finished? I'd be bundled off back home in disgrace. I'd never be here to help you in the next crisis—'

'I not want you halp me nusser time. I want you halp me *now.* When you go back America, I halp my-self.'

'England, darling. God damn it, I've been crazy about you for months—I'm calmly discussing going into crime for your sake— and you still can't get my nationality straight ...'

I was so exasperated with her I wheeled away towards a corner. She went to the bed and lay down. After a moment I mastered my feelings and seated myself beside her. She'd stopped crying but there was still a glitter of tears amongst her lashes. I couldn't help noticing that her face was pinched and drawn as I'd only seen it once before, that day just after she'd lost her job. The skin in the eye-sockets seemed swollen and brown, as if it had been bruised and then treated with iodine. The lines from nose to mouth were carved deeper than before ... She seemed to me very pitiable, and infinitely more appealing in this moment of defeat than when she was full of confidence and fight ... When she turned and looked at me at last her eyes were beseeching.

'Wretch, you very good boy, I know. Sometime you make me angly to you, then I spick you bad like usser man, but I not spick truce, darling.

All the time I know you number one good frand for me—'

'Yeah? And what about—?'

'Sometime I mad because you so good. I sink if you bad more worse—if you cowboy—batter for me. If you so bad you not care what you do, you get money tonight—'

'But I've just told you—'

'I not mean sell jip. Batter way.'

'Then spill the beans, sister. My morals seem to be getting more and more flexible. Maybe the crime won't seem so heinous to me now as it would have done a few—'

'Wretch, where that old girl liff?'

'What old girl?'

'The one that like you. The one that come your hotel see you, ask you go her home slip wiss her—'

'You mean Mrs. Samjohn? I didn't go home to sleep with her, darling. How many more times have I got to tell you she just wanted me to go to dinner—'

'I ask you where she liff.'

'Bankapi. Why?'

'She haff—gold—very mutss—here, here, here.' She touched herself in the usual places. 'I sink she haff mutss mutss money. And she like you too, 'cause she old and ugly, you nice young—'

'Are you suggesting I touch my boss's wife for ten thousand? Let me tell you—'

'What is tutss? I not unnerstand. But I know that old girl like you. I see her face when she look me, look you. I sink you go her house, she very happy to let you in. Then you spick her nice, she ask you go her bad room—'

'And then I hit her over the head and rip off her jewels. Is that what you're suggesting?'

'I sink no need hit her head, darling. Can giff her somesing make her slip—'

'Christ, you've really got it all worked out, haven't you!' I stood up and walked across the room to get away from her. 'If only you used your brains for something else—' Then I asked the question which had been uppermost in my mind all along. 'Where's Dan? Why can't you ask him to do your dirty work for you?'

'Dan? I not see him long time. He go to souse part of country.'

'South? What for?'

'Oh, I not know. He sink pipple sick there, more than Chiengmai ... Wretch.' She spoke rather sharply, and I turned round to look at her. She was sitting cross-legged on the bed, Thai-style. She had a gun in her hand—I suppose it must have been hidden under the pillow. She wasn't pointing it at me—it just lay on her palm, as if she were weighing it. She raised her eyes from the gun to me. 'Wretch, I not haff ten t'ou-zand by twelve o'c'ock tomollow—' She turned the muzzle towards herself and pressed it deep into her left breast.

'Ah—Cleopatra, now, eh? With a tin asp.' It was a cheap, stagey gambit. It only irritated me. 'You're a good Buddhist,' I pointed out, coldly. 'You can't take life. You can't kill yourself.'

She said, 'If I s'oot wiss gun, I not kill my-salf. The gun kill me ...'

Suddenly she started to laugh. I thought she was off her head and when she saw my expression she laughed even more. She threw the gun away and rolled over on her side and held a pillow to her face, laughing into it with her smooth brown shoulders shaking.

'What in hell is the joke?'

It was a minute before she could answer, then she said, 'I sink somesing very joking, darling, but it not good joking, it very bad joking for me. I sink I Number One Bad Girl in Bangkok—I still that—and I know mutss mutss bad pipples—oh, I sink maybe one t'ou-zand more—but now I want cowboy do somesing, I not know one cowboy who do for me. Only Wretch want to do what I ask him, but he not cowboy, he haff too good heart; he not know how to do ...'

At about eight-thirty that night I asked one of the hotel-boys to call a *samlor* to take me to the Chalerm Krung cinema. I gave this boy a hefty tip in the hope that it would fix my destination in his mind, and so help me to establish an alibi if necessary later on. At the cinema I bought a ticket for the nine o'clock show: I thus threw away fifteen tics in case the *samlor*-boy was watching what I did. The current show still had twenty minutes to run, so there was nothing odd in my wandering off for an iced coffee. I wandered and wandered until I was in the comparatively dark and unfrequented square where the Giant Swing, on which the loyalty of the royal courtiers used to be tested (if they fell off it proved they'd had treachery in their hearts), reared up like a ghostly guillotine against the black, star-studded sky. Here I took another *samlor* as far as the National Stadium. Then I walked Bankapi-wards until I was overtaken by an almost empty tram. On that I went as far as the highly respectable crossing where the British Embassy stands. From there I decided it would be wisest to walk. Foreigners inhabit Bankapi by the thousands, and the sight of one walking is not all that unusual, for sometimes their cars break down. I had about a mile to go before I reached the house—main road choked with cars all in a hurry, and practically free of pedestrians. I calculated I would reach the house about nine-thirty, anonymous and unobserved.

Vilai didn't know I was acting on her plan. Shortly after she'd had that fit of laughing, there' come a pounding on the gate and she'd jumped up and rushed to the window. I thought she'd turned pale; certainly she'd looked scared and worried. I'd tried to squint down obliquely through the curtain myself but she'd turned on me in a rage. 'What you do? You want every pipple see you in my house?' Then she'd thrown on a blouse and gone out, first shouting questions and instructions at the old woman from the landing, then, after the gate had opened, going downstairs to join in a lengthy and apparently urgent conversation with some men who'd come in. I'd tried to open the door and get a glimpse of them but of course I was locked in. My first impulse had been to burst the lock, but I'd calmed down, helped myself to some mekong I found behind the bed, and turned over the pages of a movie magazine. Soon the men's voices had quietened down and moved away; it seemed, whoever the visitors were, they'd been conducted to a backroom; and shortly afterwards Vilai had come upstairs and released me. She'd been very curt. 'Go, quick quick go. Not want usser man see you. I spick you many many time before, I not want you come my house, but you neffer do what I ask—'

'Who are those guys anyway?'

'Goddam, Wretch, go—*go*!' She'd given me a hearty push in my damaged ribs, not knowing they were damaged, of course.

So I'd gone to the usual hotel and told them I'd broken down just outside Bangkok—hence my filthy clothes—and left the jeep at a garage to be repaired. Then I'd tried to sleep, but it was impossible. The pain in my side was intense and my mind nearly unhinged.

Even at that stage I'd known what I was going to do. I'd known that all the mentors of my youth no longer counted for anything: Vilai called the tune ...

And so here I was walking like a common thief towards the house I proposed to burgle. But I knew I was worse than a common thief, for I was going to steal from people who had befriended me.

I couldn't understand my own motives. It seemed to me that all my life I had been swimming aimlessly this way and that in an ocean without any horizon, unable to see any object to strike out for, conscious only of my aloneness, and of the immeasurable cold expectant depths beneath me. More than once my strength had given out, and I'd gone under; and now I was going down again, perhaps for the last time.

Why did I keep walking towards the House when there was nothing to stop me from turning tail, returning to the hotel and the right side of the law? Vilai was not relying on me to carry the thing through. She'd said I couldn't do it—I wasn't the type. She's probably dismissed me from her thoughts altogether—was searching for help in other quarters, or had given up all hope of succour, and was placidly awaiting whatever was coming to her.

And what could that be? If only she'd told me! Perhaps I could have laughed the whole thing off. But there was just a possibility that she was truly threatened by something ghastly. In my saner moments I adjudged that pretty unlikely too, yet I have always been able to imagine unspeakable horrors more vividly than the odds against their happening, and that night my mind teemed with tragic possibilities ... And suppose I *didn't* get her the money, and shortly afterwards I heard that something dreadful had happened to her, something that could have been averted if only I'd done my bit? That would be the end of my sanity: I couldn't fail *her* too ... Oh, she was worthless if you looked at her from the angle of your father's pulpit or your mother's kitchen, she was worthless for that matter if you looked at her critically from under this lamp-post on the Paknam Road—for what had she ever given you but the pangs of jealousy and unrequited love? Yet she was the very core of your being, and must be guarded with all your powers; whatever harm befell her would fall a thousand-fold on yourself ...

I suppose it didn't take more than ten minutes to walk that mile, but it seemed like an hour. When at last I turned into the lane where the House was I was gasping, as if I had actually been walking full speed for an hour.

I hadn't the faintest idea how I was going to do the job. I didn't even know whether the Samjohns were in or out. Only one thing I was decided on: I must succeed. I'd got to get Mrs. Samjohn's baubles. I'd got to see Vilai's face light up as I poured them into her lap. Whatever happened after that was beside the point. Nothing mattered except to make Vilai safe—and perhaps fleetingly grateful ...

The House was the third on the right. Long before I reached it I could see it. A long unilluminated fence stretched between us. Above this the House floated like a cloud lit up from within. Every window seemed to be ablaze and I regretted that the one thing that is really cheap in Bangkok is electric power. I felt like a cat caught in a car's headlight beams: you know how the cat is paralysed ...

Approaching the gate I walked slower and slower. Each of the tall brick gate-posts was surmounted by a globe which tonight was lighted. Together they threw a soft yellow glow for several yards around.

I crossed to the far side of the lane and stood staring through the open gateway at the House. The fact that the gate was open and those lamps left on meant that somebody was out in the car. But who? It might be the Samjohns, but it might just as likely be Frost or Drummond.

After staring through the gateway for a short time I realized I'd have to go in nearer to the House to find out. There were too many banana palms and mango trees between the House and me, and the ornate trellis-work over the front porch, with the tangled arcs of the bougainvillaea sprays drooping from it, practically blotted out the lighted ground-floor windows of the Samjohns' quarters.

I made sure that there was no one to see me in the lane, then I bent down and quickly unlaced my shoes. I took them off and walked as naturally as I could across the lane to the gate. Under the lighted globes I paused and peered at one gate-post as though I were a stranger trying to ascertain the number of the House. I was still afraid someone might be watching me. Then I walked through the gate onto the granite chips which bit into my stockinged feet painfully. I dropped my shoes behind the gate-post as I passed by it. I was relieved to find that I could walk quite silently on the drive in my stockinged feet.

I never considered how I was going to explain away my shoeless state if I was surprised. I never considered being surprised by Frost or the others at all. It was not in my plan to be surprised.

Just where the light was least satisfactory, from the watchman's point of view, there was a small tree about six yards from the drive. Without altering my pace or crouching suspiciously or anything like that I turned off the drive and crossed to this tree. I stood behind it, visible perhaps from the lane, but quite invisible, I was sure, from the House or the servants' quarters.

I parted the branches and looked at things carefully. As I had expected, the view from this tree was much better.

I could now see clearly into the Samjohns' sitting-room. There was the Old Man all right, peaceful in an armchair, reading. The light from a standard lamp poured down over his white hair and one pink cheek. He had on heavy-rimmed glasses which he never wore at the office and the usual cigar was smoking idly in his mouth. As I watched, he removed it, and lifted a glass. He held the glass at his mouth while he turned a page, then tossed off the drink and resumed smoking. He even settled himself a little deeper in his chair; he was obviously very much at his ease and relaxed.

I couldn't see any signs of his wife. She might be in a chair that was invisible to me, or on the other hand it might be she that had gone out in the car. I couldn't be sure.

Then I turned to the Frost-Drummond half of the House. There were lights on in all the rooms, upstairs and down. The French windows of their sitting-room were open but the ceiling fan wasn't working. I was pretty sure it would have been if the room had been occupied. Perhaps they were out too—or perhaps they were upstairs. Drummond had a habit of retiring early and reading under his mosquito net. Frost, a more gregarious character, was much more likely to be out than in bed.

I was entirely satisfied with this situation. It never occurred to me that a burglar generally makes a more thorough reconnaisance of a building before he enters it. Nor did I realize that, after making wholly inadequate observations, I'd jumped to some very hasty conclusions. The coast was clear: all I'd got to do, I thought, was walk straight in ... And this I did.

Now that I was inside the House and unobserved I believed that the hard part of the job was done. I began to feel a little stir of excitement for the first time—not because I was aware of any danger—I never felt more at ease on that point in my life—but because I could see triumph in my grasp—I could visualize Vilai's delight to come. Partly I'd agreed with her up till then—I wasn't the cowboy type, it would be just like me to make a mess of this job as of most of the others I'd undertaken—but now I was feeling a lot more confident. Everything was turning out to be so easy. Nothing could go wrong, surely, now I'd come so far ...

I walked past the open door of Samjohn's sitting-room with the quiet unhurried tread of a servant going upstairs on some household errand. I don't think he was conscious of anyone passing at all. He was facing the window, not the door, and he was entirely absorbed in his whisky, his smoke, and his book. I looked into the other sitting-room, opposite Samjohn's, on the right, as I passed, but without stopping: it was as I had anticipated, empty.

I walked up the thickly-carpeted stairs. There was one tread that creaked and I tried to remember which it was, though I didn't think it mattered much. I avoided the tread which I thought was the noisy one but it was actually the one two steps higher up. Or maybe another tread had started to creak since I was last on those stairs. It made rather a loud noise, but I wasn't bothered. Probably my ears had exaggerated the sound anyway. I kept going.

When I reached the landing I found myself quite breathless. I had to pause a minute with my hand resting on the top of the bookcase. No doubt the injuries and exertions and the lack of sleep during the last forty hours were taking their toll of my strength. Not to speak of the emotional tension I was under. I was momentarily scared I might faint.

With an effort I got control of myself again. It would be absolute farce if I cracked up at this point.

I bent and opened the sliding glass panels of the bookcase. Ever since I'd set out from the hotel I'd been obsessed with the importance of arranging alibis. I seldom read crime fiction, but this one point seemed to have been made in all the examples of the genre that had come my way: if your alibi's no good, you've had it. So I'd determined to select two books and leave them on top of the bookcase when I went into the bedroom. Then, if I was interrupted, I could say I'd come to the House for some books to read—there they are, over there on the bookcase—I didn't want to disturb anyone because it was so late—I took my shoes off because they were muddy after walking up the lane—I though I heard a suspicious noise in the bedroom and I just peeped in to investigate—and so on. The tale seemed to me perfectly plausible as I made it up ...

This is why I took time off in the middle of my burglarizing to study literature. It wasn't easy to choose the right books. Two whole shelves in the case were devoted to crime and the Wild West and as I'd never shown any interest in them before it might look suspicious if I did so now. All the rest of the books were on the bottom shelf, and there weren't enough of them to fill it. Moreover, some of them I'd read already, and Mrs. Samjohn, who always took great interest in my literary predilections, might happen to remember which. Then there were books like *Adam Bede* and *East Lynne* which nobody ever reads—you just let people assume you've already had a go at them and have benefited greatly thereby. What was left was a duck-shooter's reminiscences, a first-aid manual, a system of statistics, a study of Chinese porcelains, three Ethel M. Dell's and a very ancient volume of *Punch*. I chose porcelain and ducks.

I placed these books conspicuously on top of the bookcase and looked around me. The stairs were empty. All the bedroom doors were shut—Frost's and Drummond's on the right, Samjohn's ahead—except for Mrs. Samjohn's on my left. Hers was wide open (except for the screen-door)—inviting me to enter.

I walked across the landing and pushed the screen-door gently. I noticed it squeaked, but what matter? Everybody on the premises was absorbed in his own affairs. I could make as much noise as I liked, and whoever was in the house would assume it was somebody else whom he knew to be in the house moving around as usual ...

The screen-door squeaked wide on the end of my finger. I lifted my foot to go in—and stopped aghast. My heart came up into my throat and started to swell there like a frightened toad. I felt the bones in my legs liquify. Mrs. Samjohn was there. Sitting in front of her mirror, in a very decollete pink nightdress, combing her hair. With her back to me, as it happened, but still there ...

For some stupid reason it had never occurred to me that Mrs. Samjohn could be upstairs. I'd imagined that Frost or Drummond might be—had been prepared all the time I'd been on the landing for one or the other to emerge from his bedroom. But I'd somehow got it fixed in my mind that, since she wasn't in the sitting-room with her husband, Mrs. Samjohn was out visiting somewhere. The shock of finding that she wasn't almost paralysed me for a moment.

But only for a moment. Then suddenly I saw red. Dear God, I wasn't going to let an old frump like her interfere with my plans. I'd come this far for Vilai's sake: now nothing could turn me back ...

In my first dismay at seeing that woman in her room I'd let the door shut but I now thrust it violently open again and took a long stride—

'Joyce.' The word came from behind me, to the left—from the stairs. The voice was Samjohn's—not raised, but with a sharp imperative note in it that pulled me up short as if he'd thrown a lasso round my neck. 'Joyce,' he said again, even more sharply: 'just exactly what's your game, young man?'

He was standing on the stairs—cut off from the waist down by the edge of the landing so that he looked like some old time windjammer's figurehead—but standing upright, not slanting forwards, and modernly whiskerless. He still had on those heavy black-rimmed glasses and their lenses were pools of reflected light that completely obscured his eyes. He watched me for a second or two, then came on up the rest of the stairs. One of them creaked loudly under his foot. He was carrying a decanter, and for one wild hopeful minute I thought he had just caught me by accident on his way to bed—that he was taking the decanter with him for a nightcap before he turned in. But the next intant I realized from the way that he was carrying it that it was a weapon—the first that had come to his hand.

‘Well?’ he said, stopping a few feet away from me. I could see his eyes now, very wide and wary; but his voice sounded more puzzled than angry, and I noticed that the arm that held the decanter was slowly relaxing. ‘I asked you what you’re doing here.’

I remembered my alibi. ‘I came to borrow some books, sir.’

He didn’t answer, but abruptly walked past me and opened the screen-door to his wife’s room. ‘Sorry to trouble you, dear, but have you any books in here?’ he called in to his wife.

‘Books?’ She sounded most surprised. ‘Why, no. Only the Agatha Christie I’m going to read in bed.’

He let the door shut again and turned to me, his bushy white eyebrows clamped down over the black-rimmed glasses. ‘Just why were you barging into Mrs. Samjohn’s bedroom, Joyce?’

‘I—I thought I heard someone in there, sir.’

‘Very likely, too. Mrs. Samjohn happens to be getting ready for bed.’

‘I mean, I thought it was a burglar, sir.’

‘You mean you mistook Mrs. Samjohn for a burglar?’

‘No, no—’

‘But surely you recognized Mrs. Samjohn sitting at her dressing-table—the *first* time you opened the door?’

So he’d been watching me for some time. I hadn’t the faintest idea how to answer him—my mind had gone numb.

But just at this moment Mrs. Samjohn came out of her room. She’d thrown a frivolously lacy dressing-gown over her shoulders. ‘Whatever’s going on?’ she asked her husband, and then catching sight of me, ‘Why, Mr. Joyce!’ She pulled a handful of lace over the yawning neck of the nightgown. ‘What a surprise to see you back so soon! I thought you were still in the Northeast. And you look so ill—really, dear,’ turning to her husband, ‘Mr. Joyce looks as if he’d just seen a ghost.’

‘He has,’ said Samjohn drily. ‘Joyce seems to be suffering from a whole lot of hallucinations, in fact. But don’t you worry about him, dearest. You go to bed and read yourself to sleep. *I’ll* deal with this young man downstairs.’

I’m not going to give a verbatim report of that interview. Samjohn made me sit down, settled himself in his own favourite chair, painstakingly prepared a cigar for the burning, and then, talking out of the midst of a cloud like certain ancient deities, launched into the subject of my defects. After twenty minutes, having brushed aside any small protests I tried to make, he lighted another cigar and began his summing up. 'It all mounts up to this, Joyce,' he said. 'You've been acting in a very peculiar manner indeed. First of all you seem to think you can chuck your job and come gallivanting up to town whenever it suits you. If you did that in the Army you'd be court-martialled for deserting your post—you might even be shot for it. Well, business isn't run like the Army—which is probably a pity in some ways, but damn' lucky for irresponsible people like yourself. The fact remains that you just walked out on Windmill without any consideration for the firm, or Windmill, at all. You say you did so for 'personal reasons,' but you decline to say what those reasons were. Now, frankly Joyce, as I've already told you, I can't conceive of a young single man in good health like yourself having *any* personal reasons strong enough to warrant his walking out on his job. I may be wrong about this, but I think if your personal reasons were really adequate—or if they were completely honourable—you'd have no hesitation whatever in telling me what they were.' He paused a moment, giving me one last chance to make a clean breast of it all, but I remained obstinately silent. So he continued:

'Right-ho. You drop everything and come rushing up to Bangkok. In the firm's jeep, as it happens. And in your haste to get here you apparently drive down the face of a precipice. You blame this mishap on a storm. Well, I'll give you the benefit of the doubt there—there *was* a storm last night—a remarkably bad one. But the points that puzzle me are these. Why can't you tell me how badly damaged the jeep is? If it's only upside down, as you say, couldn't it have been turned right way up again sometime today? Why did you just leave it there upside down? And why haven't you done a single thing about recovering it yet?' He took his cigar out of his mouth and squinted at the wet end.

He tried an experimental puff and resumed smoking. 'Well, where have we got to? You've ditched Windmill and you've ditched our jeep and some time this afternoon you arrive in Bangkok. You check in at your hotel and after all this violent rush to get here you hit the sack—

according to your story. You make no attempt to phone me that you've come home ahead of schedule or that you've smashed up the jeep. You certainly don't feel it necessary for you to come out to Bangkapi and tell me these things to my face. However, after a nice sleep you wake up and find you've got nothing to read. It's fairly late in the evening by now but you feel you've got to do something about *that.* So you make the journey from Bhalangpoo to Bankapi—to this House. I presume you entered by the front door. If you *did* enter by the front door, Joyce, you *must* have seen me sitting reading in this chair. Now remember, *I'm* the senior representative of Broderick Peers in the Far East, and *you're* a very junior member of that concern. Doesn't it strike you as extremely odd conduct on your part not to come in and make some sort of explanation to me—I mean, considering all the circumstances?'

'I've already told you, sir. I didn't want to disturb you at this time of night.'

'Yes, I recall your saying that. I'm grateful for your consideration, Joyce, but at the same time I feel if you'd had a fitting sense of the seriousness of the trouble you're in ... But we'll skip that. You preferred to slink by behind my back like a thief in the night—by the way, where *are* your shoes—?'

'Outside, sir.'

'—but the stairs gave you away. We call that creaking one our burglar alarm. The servants never, or hardly ever, come into the House after dinner and I hadn't heard Frost and Drummond come back in the car. So you see, Joyce, *you* thought you heard a burglar in Mrs. Samjohn's bedroom and I thought I heard one on the stairs—'

'I'm sorry—' I began but he put his hand up.

'I accept your explanation that you came to borrow some books,' he said. 'After all, I saw the great care with which you selected them. By the way, you've left them upstairs. You'll have to collect them before you go.'

I said 'Yes, sir, thank you,' perfunctorily.

'Well, I don't want to rub it in any more,' he went on. 'I don't understand why you had to take two peeks at my wife before you were able to distinguish her from a burglar. Maybe your eyesight is defective, or maybe there's something wrong with your mind. All I know is this—and it must be pretty obvious to you, too, by now, Joyce. You're finished as far as Broderick Peers is concerned. I warned you pretty sternly once before. We have to have men in Siam we can rely on. Men that aren't likely to bring disgrace on the firm, or for that matter on Britain. Men with some slight sense of responsibility. You have your merits, of course, Joyce: you'd be a monster if you hadn't. But—well, to put it in a nutshell, you've been a big disappointment to us. I'll review your case again in the morning, at the office, and if you have anything further to say for yourself you can say it then. But, from the way it looks now, we can't afford to employ you any longer in Thailand. In fact, young man, you can look forward to repatriation within a very few days ...'

He made me go upstairs and fetch the books I'd picked out, then he came out with me to see where I'd left my shoes. When he saw them just inside the gate he gave me a very funny look indeed. 'Good gracious, Joyce. You really *were* anxious not to disturb us. But run along now. And be sure to be at the office tomorrow morning at nine. You understand? That's an order.'

I knew it wasn't any use going to Vilai's place immediately. I'd got to give her time to get back from whatever nightclub she'd gone to with whatever man she'd happened to pick up. To kill time I walked all the way back to the hotel. The boy Arun was in the lobby. He gave me a big friendly smile and about a minute after I'd reached my room he appeared with a bottle of beer. I hadn't ordered it and I didn't want it but I realized what a kind gesture it was: for months he'd never known a time when I *didn't* want a drink. I motioned him to set it down on the table.

I locked the door behind him. Then I poured all the beer down the lavatory pan. I did this solemnly, as if performing a symbolic act. For I was through with all that, and with a good many other aspects of my past life too.

I lay on the bed though I knew I couldn't sleep. I tried to read a bit but the duck-shooter seemed to glory in killing the very birds he claimed to love and there was blood all over his book, and as for the porcelain, how could I pay attention to anything so fragile and dainty and completely alien? Constantly the words and illustrations whitened away and a vision of Mrs. Samjohn's body as it might have been, flat on its back on the floor, floated up before my eyes ...

For Samjohn had been justified in all his strictures, but he'd been completely off the point. He'd complained about my irresponsibility, my lack of loyalty to the firm, my impulsiveness—but these were mere peccadilloes, failings that almost any young man in his twenties is capable of. He didn't know that I'd entered his home intent on burglary. He didn't know that I'd turned into a criminal, and that night, but for his lucky intervention, I might have ...

Yet such was indeed the case. When I'd found that Mrs. Samjohn was in her room—an ugly old bitch who by her mere presence was going to thwart my plans—suddenly I'd been blinded by pent-up fury, I'd felt my fists clench and my teeth had grated together; I'd burst the door open again and that first long stride I'd taken had been a stride towards murder ...

'*Joyce!*'

For a moment I hadn't been able to get him in focus, but as he came clear, like the top-half of a broken accusatory statue, a huge horror had begun in my bowels and swiftly enveloped my whole being. It was as if, after staggering about in a drunken daze for years, I'd barged into a solid full-length mirror and with that one blow knocked myself sober. Suddenly I'd seen myself from the outside, instead of from my usual interior viewpoint: seen myself as I must look to others—to normal, sane, decent citizens like Samjohn himself, for instance, and—good God, what had I come to?

Once, a few years before, I'd tried to kill *myself*. Brokenhearted over Sheila, frustrated by my blind-alley job, out of sorts with all the world in which I could make no mark, and conscience-stricken over Lanky, I'd lain on my bed in Lena's backroom, methodically crunching up tablets and washing them down with lemonade ... Three days later I'd come round—still in Lena's back bedroom. I'd found myself black with bruises, and tied to the bed. Lena had always refused to say how she'd managed me in my maniacal fury, and I don't remember anything about it. All she'd said was, 'God has been good to us, Mr. Joyce. He made me drink too much tea at supper time and I woke up and heard you moaning. It was a miracle really, and I think He's saved you for a definite purpose. I think you've been saved to do something really worthwhile in the world ...'

I'd hoped so too at first. But then—back to the old bacon-counter. And now this ...

God, how easy it was to kill other people! For years I'd been tortured by remorse over Lanky's death. Time after time a grisly doubt had come into my mind: perhaps if only I'd laid my bike down an instant faster Lanky needn't have died. But I'd been too intent on getting another first: seeing a chance to drive through on the inside I'd refused to throw that chance away I'd thrown away another man's life instead ...

But this was different. Lanky's death, when all was said, and done, had only partially been my fault. (In fact the coroner had exonerated me entirely.) It had been just the luck of a hard game, that's all.

But Mrs. Samjohn hadn't been pitting herself against me in any sort of rivalry. She was just a rather silly old woman who had happened to get in my way. Yet I'd lost control of myself—I'd let something incredibly violent and amoral deep down inside myself take charge—I'd deliberately started into that room with intent to kill ...

My eyes filled with tears. I'd lowered myself a long way into the mire. Then my hands had slipped and suddenly I was submerged in it.

But again I'd been saved. I who had been prevented from self-murder by the weakness of my landlady's bladder—by an extra cup of tea—had now been saved from the murder of someone else by an imperfect piece of joinery. A stair had creaked and brought Samjohn to the rescue ...

I knew what my parents and Lena would say. They had no doubt that the universe was run by a Deity who was almighty in power yet loved and respected every creature it contained, even the repulsive ones. They believed that, having set the universe to run like a machine, He was yet prepared to throw a spanner in the works at any moment in answer to a prayer. 'Nay,' my father would say, 'He doesn't always wait for the prayer even.'

It wasn't true. But if only you could believe it! ... People who did believe it were obviously happier, more serene, more humane, than people that didn't. And they fitted into the scheme of things more comfortably too. They never attempted to kill either themselves or their neighbours ...

Up till that night I'd always rather despised my father. Not only for his benevolent metaphysics, which didn't fit the facts of life in my opinion, but because of his whole outlook. What a footling way to spend your days! Slaving over sermons which nobody ever really listened to. Puttering in the garden. Sipping tea with old ladies. His greatest problem in life was to keep his pipe going, it had seemed.

Yet how fundamentally decent, how wholesome, the man was! He might be rather hedged away from the world behind the *Daily Telegraph* and his garden wall and the pulpit rail and the blue smoke idling upwards from his mouth; but he'd never hurt anyone in his life, he saw the good in every living soul and strove to draw it out—he'd even seen good in Sheila when my mother, and I, couldn't. He would see some good in Vilai, too, if he ever met her, I was sure.

I could never live like him, of course. But I *could* move a lot nearer to him, and I realized that in that direction lay real happiness on earth.

I wanted to re-model my life at once. I would have to begin of course with a few renunciations. Well, the last bottle of beer had gone down the glory-hole. That was renunciation number one.

I was going to have to renounce the East, too. Actually there wasn't much choice about that. I could of course defy Samjohn— find myself a new job and stay on in Bangkok in spite of him. But what would be the point of doing that? Three hours ago my idea would have been to stay because of Vilai—in case she needed me. But now I was renouncing Vilai too.

When I thought of Vilai I couldn't prevent some bitterness from creeping into my mind. I was far from blaming her for everything that had happened. Long before I'd met her I'd set out on the path which had finally ended this evening at the door of Mrs. Samjohn's bedroom. But Vilai had helped me along in the last stages. Before I'd met her I'd been taking the route that almost any beaten-up, self-pitying man is liable to take if he has money enough. I'd found a means of forgetting, for most of the time, the crushing memories of defeat. My drinking, the cheap and easy conquests in the stews, the daily atmosphere of feasting and good-humour, had wrapped me in an almost perpetual cocoon of animal well-being. Swiftly, cheerfully, I had been turning into another no-good—but a harmless sort of no-good, the sort that is little trouble to anyone but himself, and a positive angel to brewers and pimps ...

Then Vilai. I knew it would be unjust to say she'd deliberately made me fall in love with her. For that I was wholly to blame. But when in my re-discovered longing and loneliness I'd done just that—fallen in love with a tart—she'd taken quick advantage of the fact. She'd battened on me like a leech. Today, working on my emotions, she'd incited me to theft and violence. I had simply acted like a marionette while she pulled the strings, or like a man she'd hypnotized. And there had very nearly been a ghastly tragedy ...

I'd intended to stay in the hotel until two in the morning but by half-past twelve I couldn't stick it any more. I'd got to go and have it out with Vilai. Inform her that I had failed her—thank God! Inform her that I was casting her off forever, that henceforth she would be on her own, that I had my own soul to save and (since that was the way she wanted it) to hell with hers ...

I went downstairs and told Arun that it was too hot, I couldn't sleep, I was going out for a breath of fresh air. He grinned and wagged his finger at me and put his arms around an imaginary girl. I grinned back—that would explain a lengthy absence. Outside I caught a *motor-samlor* and had the driver take me to a famous nightspot on the New Road. From there I walked to Vilai's house.

There was a light in her window but that was nothing to go by. I had to keep pounding on the door for five minutes before anyone came. As soon as the latch was lifted I put my shoulder against the door and shoved—I had no intention of being refused admittance. I thought it would be the old woman letting me in but it was a complete stranger. A blowsy type with an elaborate perm and heavy make-up. She was holding a gaudy kimono around herself with calculated negligence. When she saw me she let it slip even further awry.

'Why, darling,' she said. 'I not ex-pact you.'

'Is Vilai in?'

Her smile vanished. 'You mean White Lappard? No, she out.'

'When will she come back?'

'How I know that? She very bad girl. Roam all the time. Roam at night, roam in day too.' Her face covered itself with a smile that was meant to be seductive and she turned sideways to me so that I could see her curves. 'Why you worry about that old Lappard?' she said. 'She very low class, fight all the time, want too much money. Men not like her any more—'

'She's here, I know, and I'm going to see her.' I crossed to the foot of the stairs. The woman closed the door behind me, saying as she did so, 'I think I not see you before. You very handsome man. You come my room, darling? I not like White Lappard. I Python. I give you very good time—'

But I was already pounding up the stairs and she screamed after me, 'Hey, where you go? I tell you White Lappard—'

I burst into the room. At first sight it looked normal but then I saw it wasn't. The stool in front of the dressing-table was overturned. Some of the scent-bottles were knocked over. The mosquito-net, which was down, had been torn from its moorings at one corner, and the bedclothes were half on the floor. The radio was still standing under the window, turned on but relaying static only. All the dresses had gone from behind the curtain ...

'What I told you?' the Python said, coming in behind me. 'The White Lappard—'

'What's happened? Where's she gone? I've got to see her—'

'I think you never see White Lappard again,' the Python said slowly. 'I think you have sense, you forget White Lappard, forget altogether. I think it time for you to get a new girl, darling ...'

The next few days were sheer agony. I had gone to Vilai's house planning to dispense with her but I was now distraught with concern about her fate. I moved to a new hotel so that Samjohn wouldn't be able to find me. Every day I went to that lane to see if she'd come back. The first two mornings the Python answered the door but she would tell me nothing. She just made fun of my concern for Vilai and tried to get me to transfer my interest to herself. On the third morning she refused to open the door. 'Go 'way,' she shrilled from inside: 'I sick and tire' of you come every day. If you not go quick, I call policeman come ...'

Every night I made a round of the night-haunts. The Hoi Tien Lao, Chez Eve, La Roulette, Salathai, the Champagne Bucket—I even took in the Bolero one night, though I knew it was the forlornest hope of all. And every day I lunched at the Singsong Lounge—that place where I'd been with Dick the day her son was killed. Each day I'd stay there for hours, drinking and drinking until the swingdoors swam before my eyes—for I'd renounced my renouncement of alcohol the minute I'd lost her. But although a good many Bolero girls came in, including once the Black Leopard, I never saw Vilai.

The nights were absolute hell. Yet really I don't know when it was worst—tossing on my bed in the small hours, tormented by hideous visions, or walking restlessly through the burning streets by day. In the visions I would see Vilai floating face-downwards in the river with the back of her skull a bloody pulp—Vilai being beaten up by *naklengs,* the sort of bandits who will kill anyone for a few tics—Vilai imprisoned in some unspeakable dive at Koh Sichang in the mouth of the Chao Phya river. There was no foundation for any of these dreams except an overturned stool in her room a few nights before, yet to me they were as real as established facts. They made it impossible for me to sleep, and with the first light each day I'd be out of the hotel, peering into every shop, pushing my way through congested markets and crooked alleys, swivelling to catch the faces in every passing bus, tramping, tramping until I could hardly stand. And all the while, of course, at the back of my mind, sapping my resolution, was the knowledge that this was madness, and madness without any method to it. Scouring the streets like this I could light on her by luck only. I could pass within a few feet of her, straining after some other woman whose hair or figure or walk was almost the same, and simply not see her ...

On the third day, Saturday, I engaged a room at my old hotel and waited for her to turn up as she had done regularly before on the Saturday afternoons when I was in town. She didn't come, and at seven in the evening I left.

On Sunday night at nine I phoned to Arun to find out if by any chance she'd appeared that day. She hadn't.

That hotel idea had been my last hope. I was sure that, if she'd still been in need of help, still in Bangkok, and still at liberty to come to me, she would have sought me out there. But she hadn't done so, and that meant one of three things. She could be dead, or she could be in captivity (either legal or otherwise), or she'd decided that I couldn't help her any more. Whichever way it was, the affair was over.

That night I came to terms with this fact. There were two paths open to me. I could still stay around, hunting for her, without a job, without money, without proper papers, dodging the police, combing the alleys of Bangkok and the tiniest hamlets in the forests, driven on by despair, refusing to give in, not because I had any hope left but because if I gave in I would be finished. But that way lay madness and the utter waste of a life. Vilai just wasn't worth it. I loved her but I knew that much. In fact I knew that much because I loved her ...

Or I could go home. At times I flinched at the thought. Everyone knew I'd come out on a three-year contract; seeing me home so soon they'd know I'd failed again. No doubt my mother would shut herself up in her room again to weep over another mess, while my father, locked out from her, would wander about the house, constantly knocking out his empty pipe and putting it back empty into his mouth again. Andy would be all 'I-told-you-so's'—the younger brother too was returning defeated from abroad; he'd shore up his ego on it—'*nobody* can make good abroad now ...' And what would be the reactions of Sheila and Lena and Slither and the rather obnoxious Denny? They'd all shake their heads over me, I was sure: even Lena and Slither.

But success in business wasn't everything. And success in life hadn't much to do with just holding down a job. In fact success in life had nothing whatever to do with your paid occupation. It consisted more of winning battles over yourself, private battles that nobody else had any inkling of ...

And that night I'd won such a battle. For all my inclination had been to throw myself away for Vilai's sake. But I'd decided to do the hard thing for once—go home and start a new life. It was a sensible decision rather than an emotional one. And it was the first such decision I'd ever made in my life. It showed I was growing up ...

The next morning, Monday, I went to the office. Ignoring the chatter of girls and typewriters on the left I pushed open the half-doors on the right. Samjohn was dictating to Verchai. He didn't even start when he saw me. He just went on with his dictating, leaving me standing awkwardly by the door. When the letter was finished he told Verchai to go and type it—'and bring it back the minute it's done so I can sign it,' he called after her. Then he crushed the stump of his cigar into a full ashtray. 'Now, Joyce. About time you showed up, young man. We've booked you B.O.A.C. You fly tomorrow night at nine. And meanwhile ...'

They kept my nose to the grindstone that day, for besides all the formalities with passport and air-tickets I had a lot of routine work to clear up in the office. It was pretty late when I got back to the hotel and I was tired out. I ordered a stuffed omelette flavoured with curry and a bottle of Green Spot and toyed with them without enthusiasm. Then I lay down on the bed and tried to read the book on porcelains. It was pretty dull, and I'd almost bored myself to sleep when I suddenly remembered my mail. Verchai had given it to me in the morning but I just hadn't had time to read it. I got up and got the letters out of my shirt pocket.

There were four altogether—three from England and one with a Thai postage stamp on it. I recognized the spidery, wayward handwriting on the latter at once—Dan's. What in hell had he got to write about? I put his letter aside and glanced at Lena's, my mother's, and Slither's, first.

They gave me an uncanny feeling that I was already back at home although I was still half the world away. Nothing in those lives seemed to have been violently altered; all three people were still jogging placidly along, absorbed in the same old interests which had absorbed them a year ago. Lena devoted two pages to her cats and the movies. As for Slither, he was in mourning over the first match of the season: 'Gripes, they wiped the floor with us, 45-27.'

And then there was my mother's parish chronicle. She'd had the usual winter anxieties over my father's chest. The last two Sundays one of the diapason pipes of the organ had begun to syphon halfway through Father's sermon; Mr. Butt the organist said he couldn't understand it, but she herself didn't trust that Crookshank boy who was blowing these days, no knowing what he got up to in the organloft; he was supposed to come out for the sermon but often he didn't ... So it went on for three pages. The real news was left to the last. 'I suppose you must have heard by now that Andy and Sheila have separated,' she wrote in a calm postscript. (Who in hell did she think would have told me?) 'Sheila became more impossible than ever after she had her miscarriage, I believe. I never could understand what you two boys saw in that young lady. I always thought she was an uppish young madam. Well now she is a typist in London and Andy has had to hire a land girl. He does not say much about it, but I think on the whole he is happier these days ...'

It was all too far off to mean much. I picked up the letter from Dan. 'And what have you got to say for yourself, Daniel?' I muttered to myself. I expected another lecture. But it turned out to be the newsiest missive of the lot.

Dear Joyce,
I have been thinking about the last letter I wrote to you and I want to ask your forgiveness. I wrote it under the stress of strong emotion and as I recall it I was much ruder than I had any right to be. Please forgive me if you can. I shall be glad to see you if ever you come to my part of Siam.

I am now in the deep South of this country, in a small amphur *near Songkhla where I expect to spend the rest of my life. I am hoping to start a leprosarium here—in fact, I have already started in a small way. I have land and syringes and a case of Chaulmoogra oil and even three lepers! The main thing now is to get some land cleared so that I can put up a few preliminary buildings and start growing vegetables. I also plan to plant rubber. My aim is to make a self-supporting community of about 250 people in 3–5 years.*

My father has staked me with a very substantial sum and I'm trying to get various UN agencies interested in my project. Meanwhile I'm ready to accept contributions from any source including individuals. (NB. This is a hint. I'm a shameless beggar!)

For the first month I was down here entirely on my own, but for the last two days I have had a companion. You will never guess who it is, so I will tell you—our mutual friend Miss V.!!! Yes, the other day I was just sitting on a log, burning the tails of some leeches in an effort to make them withdraw their heads from my ankles, when I looked up—and there she was! From the start of course she has always shown a keen interest in my project, and in fact the last time I was in Bangkok she promised to donate ten thousand ticals to the cause. But it appears that a partner in some business deal failed her and she couldn't produce the money. But she produced herself—and I think she is going to be infinitely more helpful to me than baht 10,000!

I wanted to stop and consider what I'd already read, but I had to go racing on.

... As you doubtless know, Miss V. has been deeply dissatisfied with her life in Bangkok ever since the death of her son. I have often suggested to her that she might be able to find consolation for her loss in devotion to the welfare of the poor or sick on some such project as mine. I never specifically suggested my *project, as it is so very tentative at present. But now she has arrived here she seems to be delighted with my place. She wants to stay here and act as my interpreter and perhaps business manager, she says. We haven't arranged anything definite yet—I have told her she needs at least a month here to see how she likes the work—and* me! *Anyway, at present she's living in the hut I had just finished building for myself. (The three lepers have built me a new one of leaves.) She won't go anywhere near the lepers yet—she is dreadfully afraid of catching leprosy and being disfigured—but she has cooked me some wonderful meals. (I have been living on bananas and coconuts, mostly.) Tonight she has gone to Hadyai. I'm sure you have heard of that place—it's the very gay town where all the rubber men go to throw away their money whenever they make any—but it also happens to be an excellent shopping centre. It is just over 30 miles away and she has gone in by bus. I expect her back tomorrow morning with all sorts of things to make her hut a bit more comfortable. She is also going to look into the possibility of buying a Landrover or some such vehicle: as she points out (and I agree), we should be independent of the buses, which run very infrequently and break down every 5 or 6 miles. I can't tell you, Joyce, what a tremendous fillip the arrival of this lady, and her obvious confidence in my project, has given to me. I didn't realize it before, but now she has gone to Hadyai tonight I do—I was lonely and frightened here when I was on my own. But I cannot write any more as it is now 10 p.m. and I have to be up at dawn to get on with the construction work. If ever you need any exercise, come down here and we will put you on to felling trees or grubbing up roots! (I enclose map of how to get here from Hadyai junction.) I myself will be delighted to see you at any time, and so no doubt will Miss V., who was speaking very generously about you only last night.*

In haste, but with all best wishes.

Dan

'She's fooling him.

'She's cottoned on to it at last—the silly bastard really *has* dough and she's gone down there to batten on to a good thing. Like those damn' leeches that get inside his socks. But he'll never singe *her* behind in an effort to make *her* let go. He'll enjoy having her feed on him.

'*He's* a silly sucker. *She's* an unscrupulous bitch. And *I'm* a goddamned idiot.

'God damn it, I've been driving myself distracted, believing she'd come to some ghastly end. Fool, idiot, crackpot! A woman like her never comes to a violent end. She knows too damn' well how to look after herself. She always leaves the sinking ship just as a raft floats by.

'*She's* sitting pretty. But *I'm* sunk.'

... Suddenly I began to laugh. All the time I'd been reading Dan's letter a great wave of relief had been welling up inside me, and now it broke and swept all my bitterness away. I laughed and laughed, almost happily. Vilai was off my hands. There was no need to worry about her any more. She'd done better for herself than ever I could have done for her with all my striving. She was secure—at least until she got the urge to move on again.

For of course she'd never stick it out for the rest of her life, living in a hut in the forest, surrounded by lepers, and thirty miles from the nearest dance-hall. Even if Dan provided a car, as no doubt he would.

Once, before she'd ever met Dan, describing the only sort of man she could possibly love, she'd described *him*. A man who respected her for what she was, a man who wasn't forever importuning her to leap into the nearest bed with him ...

But no, I refused to believe that Dan was her man. That twerp! One day in the not too distant future he'd wake up to find her hut empty. No doubt he'd worry himself sick about her fate then, just as I'd worried myself sick about it during the last week. But that would be his grief, not mine. This night she was safe. For the next few weeks, while the memory of her was still sore, I could console myself with that thought. 'She's safe. There's no need to worry about her right now. Maybe she's even profiting from her life in the jungle with Dan—not merely as his business manager.'

Meanwhile, gradually the poignancy of the memory of her would decrease. New scenes, new interests, new experiences, would pile up in the forefront of my mind. Steadily they'd push her backwards into the shadows. Of course, I'd never entirely forget her, any more than I'd entirely forgotten Sheila. Once in a while I'd jerk up in my bed in dismay: 'But what on earth happened to her in the end?' It would be a passing shock, though. I'd fall back on my pillows again. 'For that matter, what happened to Lena? To the girls in Denny's car? To Ratom? To the air hostess at Karachi?'

At six the next evening all the Thais on the office staff—the three girls, Somboon, and Windmill, who has returned from the Northeast only that afternoon—entertain me at a farewell feast. They invite Frost too. They ask me where I'd like to go, and I choose a place as far as possible away from any of Vilai's old haunts—the Happy Bar just outside Lumphini Park. We sit on the terrace enjoying the little gusts of cool air that come off the lotus-filled canal. The food is first-class—raw pork with toasted peanuts, my favourite horse piss eggs, beef cooked in oyster oil, a tongue-skinning prawn salad, frogs' legs, and chicken fried with mint, garlic and chilli—and as I haven't eaten a square meal for many days I pitch in with relish. Not much is said about the reasons for my departure, but what is said is good for me to hear. Windmill is spokesman. 'The firm too stric',' he declares. 'Every man must fall in love sometime. And when he in love he like mad. But never mind. He soon recover. No man can stay in love more than a few weeks. Before you meet that girl, you work very good. And I think in about one month more, you can work very good again. Mr. Samjohn should give you holiday one month—that plenty. But he silly to send you home.' He chewed a lump of raw pork. 'I think one thing very important about you—all the Thai people like you—'

'—Especially Verchai,' shouts Somboon, already a little drunk.

Emphatic protest from Verchai, whom all present know to be an intense admirer of Frost. Cheers and hearty endorsement from all the rest of us, including Frost.

'Well, I don't want to make a speech,' Windmill goes on, but as this is the phrase with which he always *does* begin one, he is hooted down and two more bottles of beer are ordered.

They all go to the airfield to see me off. Frost drives the Riley, with Windmill and Somboon in front, and the three girls and me in the rear. At the airport we have more drinks and sweetmeats. Verchai, as the office's leading lady, presents me with a very handsome fountain pen. 'We want to give you lighter and cigarette case,' she says, 'but you no smoke. So we give you this. You like?' I only nod in reply. I am still feeling weak and emotional—disgracefully close to tears ...

We leave the formalities to the last minute and arrive at the barrier only just in time. I shake hands with the men and cheered on by them kiss Verchai and the taller of the other two girls—but the third shyly eludes me and gives me a Thai salute instead. Then I shake hands with Windmill and Somboon again and turn away, a lump in my throat. Frost strikes up 'For heez' and the whole damn' posse of them join in 'a jolly good fell-low ...' Now my eyes are stinging. I swing back and give Windmill a belt on his fat paunch, make another playful feint at the shy girl. And then, to the relief of the ticket-inspector, I stumble past him ...

The last time I was here I was on my way to Chiengmai with Vilai, for our moneymoon ...

I walk with the rest of the damned across the sward to our tumbril that is glinting silver in the moonlight. The refined accents of the air hostess make my own language sound foreign after months of hearing it mangled in less precious ways. She leads me to my seat and I strap myself in like a baby in his pram. The door slams shut; the red light comes on; the plane begins to tremble slightly as one after another the engineers are started up. And then we begin to trundle through blackness to the end of the runway. There they will rev up each engine in turn, then all four engines in concert. And the next time the engines roar, it will be for the take-off. We'll hurtle across the field, lift, dip, lift with more assurance, and then go rumbling up into the utter blackness between the invisible earth and the pinpoint stars ...